Angélique and the Ghosts

Previously published by
Sergeanne Golon in Pan Books

Angélique Book 1
The Temptation of Angélique Books 1 and 2
Angélique and the Demon
Angélique in Revolt

Sergeanne Golon

Angélique
and the Ghosts

translated from the French
by Marguerite Barnett

Pan Books in association with
Heinemann

First published 1976 by Editions de Trévise
under the title *Angélique et le Complot des Ombres*
© Opera Mundi, Paris 1976

First published in Great Britain 1977 by William Heinemann Ltd
This edition published 1979 by Pan Books Ltd,
Cavaye Place, London SW10 9PG
in association with William Heinemann Ltd
Translation © William Heinemann Ltd 1977
ISBN 0 330 25538 X
Printed and bound in Great Britain by
Richard Clay (The Chaucer Press) Ltd, Bungay, Suffolk

PART ONE

A Nightmare

CHAPTER 1

ANGÉLIQUE AWOKE in the dead of night. The gentle rocking of the ship as it rode at anchor was the only sign of life of which she was conscious. A pale glimmer of moonlight shining in through the poop windows threw into relief the shapes of a few of the elegant pieces that furnished the state-room of the *Gouldsboro* and glinted on the gold and marble of choice curios.

The moonlight extended only as far as the edge of the alcove, to the foot of the immense oriental divan in which Angélique lay curled up.

What had woken her was a need for love, an almost painfully acute longing, coupled with a sense of anxiety, even dread, that something terrible was going to happen, that some menace hung over her. She tried to recall the dream that had aroused these intense emotions – fear and desire – that had wrested her from her slumbers. Had she dreamt that Joffrey was taking her in his arms, or had she dreamt that someone was trying to kill him? She could remember nothing.

What persisted was the voluptuous sensation that possessed her from the pit of her stomach to the tips of her breasts, and to the very roots of her hair.

And fear too.

She was alone, but that was not unusual. Beside her the bed still bore the imprint of the body of the man who had rested there for a few hours. But it was a frequent occurrence for Joffrey de Peyrac to leave her sleeping when he got up in the night to go the rounds of the vessel.

Angélique gave a sudden start. For the first time since they had begun the voyage up the St Lawrence River, what had so far been only a passing thought came home to her with the force of full realization : *they were in the King of France's territory.*

3

Her husband, a man once condemned to death, and she, an outcast with a price on her head, had entered the very kingdom from which they had once been banished.

They were, of course, entering in force. They had a fleet of five vessels. But the power wielded by Louis XIV, albeit from afar, was surely greater than theirs. His arm stretched out to these remote regions.

Many an enemy awaited them here, enemies whose actions were governed by him. The Sovereign's authority was the arbiter of life and death even here.

Since the time when she had hazarded her destiny, back in the forests of Poitou, by rising against the King of France, never had Angélique felt so strongly that she was trapped, was hemmed in. It had cost them superhuman efforts to get away from France, to find freedom in America, and here they were yielding recklessly to the temptation to go to Quebec, to re-establish links with the Old World, with their homeland.

What madness! How could she ever have allowed Joffrey de Peyrac to do such a thing? How was it that she had not seen clearly from the moment he had said: 'Let's go to Quebec!' that it was a crazy idea, that there could be no possible remission for them, and that wherever the all-powerful King ruled, there lay, and always would lie, danger? By what illusion had they allowed themselves to be ensnared? What nostalgia had they succumbed to? Why had they suddenly persuaded themselves that fraternity of birth would be sufficient to overcome all obstacles and that time had softened the rigour of the King's Justice? And now they were once again in his power.

The darkness accentuated these violent feelings and gave Angélique the impression she was having a bad dream. She felt as if she had really returned to France and was living again in her chateau in Poitou at the time, which was, after all, not so very remote, a mere six years back, when she had been so utterly alone, abandoned by everyone, and when she used to waken in the night, tormented by desire for a man to love her, by longing for her lost love and by dread of all the dangers that lurked about her.

She began to tremble all over, unable to shake off the

feeling that it had all happened once before, a sense of irre-trievable disaster.

She got up, groping at the furniture in an attempt to re-establish contact with reality. There was the porphyry globe, and the astrolabe. But they did nothing to reassure her.

She saw herself as a prisoner of the stateroom, of these motionless objects, of the glass screen formed by the poop windows, divided into silver squares by the relentless moonlight, that seemed to her like prison bars through which one could never pass.

Behind lay life.

She herself was dead.

And the King was on the watch for her, too. The great screen of trees that covered her impregnable province where she had set rebellion upon its tempestuous course no longer afforded protection. Nothing was impregnable to the King. Flee as she might, the King could always reach her and vent the fullness of his spite upon her. She had rushed headlong into the trap, and now it was all over and she was dead.

As for Joffrey, he had vanished. Where was he? Where was he? He was on the other side of the world, where the sun shone in place of the moon, where life glittered, not death. Never again would he come to her, his strongly-built body naked and avid with desire. She was condemned to re-main a prisoner of this ghost-ship, of these Stygian shores, forever tormented by the memory of terrestrial delights, of his embraces, his frenzied kisses, gone beyond reach. She was in Hell ...

Her sensation of loss made her cry out in pain and her courage almost failed her. Not a second time! Not a second time! she begged.

Overwhelmed by inexorable despair, she hearkened to the cruel night and heard something like the sound of footsteps. Her sense of reality returned to her with this faint but regu-lar sound, a living sound, and she said to herself: 'But we are in Canada!' and once again touched the porphyry globe, no longer with the feeling of being in a cheerless dream world, but in order to convince herself of its reality.

'We are on board the *Gouldsboro*!' she repeated to herself.

5

She said *we* in order to conjure into being again an entity, the painful recollection of which sprang fresh to her memory. First and foremost, there was Joffrey de Peyrac, doubtless up on the poop-deck, scanning the calm night, this remote and wild region of the New World. And all around him were his men, his ships, his fleet lying at anchor beneath the cliffs of Sainte-Croix-de-Mercy. Now the name had come back to her: Sainte-Croix-de-Mercy.

It was a fiord, a sheltered retreat, away from the turbulent waters of the river still roughened by the swell of the sea. Their St Lawrence pilot had said: 'This is Sainte-Croix-de-Mercy. We can anchor here for the night.'

The name and the point of the coast were perfectly clearcut and yet they continued to have, in Angélique's mind, a sinister, quasimythological significance, as if the pilot with the woollen cap had suddenly been transfigured into a ferryman on the Styx. Death reigned over the place. It was the gates of Hades ...

Without giving a thought to what she was doing, she dressed herself.

She had taken care not to light the candle that stood, erect and white in its silver candlestick beside her bed. She feared lest, if she made the light shine abruptly forth, the horrible certainty might be confirmed, that she was dead and that he had disappeared.

She threw a cloak over her shoulders and opened the door. Outside, the heavy-scented night air caught her by the throat and she recognized the familiar smell of the ship: a smell of salt, of well-scrubbed decks, of rope and of sailcloth, along with an indefinable aroma of smoke, of food grilled over braziers, and of the dishes sailors are wont to cook up whenever they get a chance, according to the customs of their native places. And heaven only knew how many varied recipes were to be found among this band of men recruited from every corner of the globe.

Angélique leant against the door. Her composure was returning. She breathed in deeply and the pounding of her heart began to die down. Joffrey was near. In a few moments she would be with him again. All she had to do was to take a few paces, climb a flight of polished wooden steps on her left and she would catch sight of him: there he would be, standing up as tall and straight as a *condottiere*, against the sky. She would see his powerful shoulders beneath his doublet, his slender waist that hid such burning passion, his legs tight moulded in luxurious riding-boots. He would not notice her presence at first, for he would be absorbed. It was in the solitude of the night watches that he drew up his plans, that he tied the threads of his innumerable projects and ventures.

She would go up to him and he would say:

'Aren't you asleep, my love?'

And she would reply:

'I wanted to see you, to be near you, to be sure you were there, my darling. I had a nightmare. I was so frightened!'

And he would laugh. She would glow with the warmth of his glance.

She had learned that she alone had the power to kindle that joyful expression in those fine manly eyes, at times so haughty, so piercing, on occasion so implacable, eyes that could grow so gentle, transformed with tenderness when they lighted upon her. She alone could lay her hands on him and make him tremble with weakness, the weakness of the male, the only one he allowed himself, he, the master of so many destinies, the weakness that brought him to her knees. With a single glance she could overcome this haughty nobleman, this man of war, toughened by so many a bloody combat. And with a smile she knew that she was binding up his hidden wounds, that his moments of abandon atoned for the inordinate humiliation and injustice he had had to suffer. And that he was not lying when he told her that, thanks to her, he was the happiest of men. The sure knowledge of her power over this redoubtable seducer of women, who had granted to her, and her alone, the dangerous privilege of making him jealous, the awareness of the bond that had grown so strong between them, completed Angélique's solace and heightened her craving for love. Only a few steps more and she would be beside him.

She would timidly clasp his warm hand whose strength, beauty and delicate scent of tobacco she loved, and would kiss his fingers one by one, as a man loves to kiss a woman's fingers, and he would caress her cheek and murmur, 'You foolish darling!'

7

CHAPTER 2

He was not there.

Angélique saw no one but the Scandinavian Erickson, puffing away at his long-stemmed pipe as he kept watch with the rock-like steadfastness so characteristic of him. He was second to none when it came to carrying out orders, understanding everything without requiring it to be spelt out to him, a wizard of the sea, a redoubtable, flinty character who guided his craft with scarcely a word uttered, a veritable watch-dog, whose jaws closed tight on anything entrusted to his care.

Angélique scrutinized him closely until she was quite sure that it was he and not Joffrey. In a flash, the poop-deck once again became the fateful arena in which her destiny was being played out. And once again the forest beyond the glistening water seemed like a black screen, anonymous and inhuman. She stepped forward and spoke:

'Good evening, Mr Erickson. Do you happen to know where Monsieur de Peyrac is?'

As she moved towards him, she could see through the poop-rail that the shore was nearer than she had thought and lit up by a fire burning on the bank.

'Has he gone ashore, by any chance?'

Erickson got up and stood before her on his bandy legs, raising the plumed felt hat with which he had adorned his head since he had been made captain of the *Gouldsboro* on its voyage to Europe during the winter, a promotion that had been greeted with universal satisfaction, for the authority this little stump of a man wielded over his crew was unquestioned.

'Yes, he has Madame! Monsieur de Peyrac was rowed ashore about an hour ago.'

'Did he take an escort?' Angélique heard herself asking in a toneless voice.

'He only took Yann le Couennec, his equerry, with him.'

'Yann ...'

She again glanced towards the dark shore. The dense Canadian forestland stretched out endlessly, the refuge of bears and Redskins. To what end had he gone ashore that night, and gone off into the forest, leaving behind on the narrow bank of the river, among the half-submerged tree-roots, two watchmen and a dinghy to await his return?

She went back to Erickson, searching his pale, impenetrable eyes.

'Did he tell you where he was going?'

Erickson shook his head. He seemed to hesitate, then, taking his pipe from his mouth, he murmured:

'Someone brought him a message.'

'Who? An Indian?'

'I don't know. But His Lordship seemed to know what it was all about. I only saw him read the message, then I heard him give orders for a dinghy to be lowered with just two oarsmen. He told me to take over the watch because he was going ashore and that he would be back in an hour or two!'

Angélique suddenly felt utterly sobered. All sensation had left her, both stirrings of desire and tremblings of fear equally. She had become clear-headed and cold. This was it! This was precisely what she had been warned about in her sleep. Danger. They had entered the territory of the King of France, albeit uninhabited territory, the trap.

She said to the Norwegian, 'I see!' and walked slowly away. She went down to her cabin.

Then all of a sudden she began to act very quickly.

She struck a light, lit the lamps and rummaged in a drawer for her pistol, her bag of priming charges and her powder-horn, swiftly loaded her pistol and slipped it into her belt.

Once again she went up on deck, scanning everything about her. What was she looking for in the depths of this sharp-smelling night, redolent of brine and burnt-off undergrowth?

One of the crew went by, yawning as he donned his jerkin. After losing at a last game of dice, he was on his way back to his hammock. She recognized him as Jacques Vignot, the carpenter of Wapassou. It was like a revelation: suddenly she knew what she must do.

'Jacques,' she said, 'go and fetch Kouassi-Bâ and Enrico Enzi. Tell them to arm themselves and meet me at the top of the gangway.'

She went up again to the poop-deck and saw the boatswain's mate who had just taken over the watch.

'Erickson is waiting for you below, Madame,' he told her.

Erickson already had a boat lowered.

'I thought that you too would wish to go ashore, Madame. So would you allow me to accompany you? I fear Monsieur de Peyrac would be angry if I did not do so.'

She realized that he too was anxious and had seized upon this pretext, taking advantage of Angélique's initiative, to find a way round orders about which he was far from happy. He too was sometimes given a rough time by his master, and his devotion to him occasioned him much distress. For Joffrey de Peyrac's spirit of independence and his love of risk did not always make due allowance for the agonies endured by those devoted to him.

'Mr Erickson, I think that you and I understand one another,' said Angélique with a smile of gratitude.

At Angélique's request, Erickson summoned the St Lawrence pilot whom they had taken on since Gaspé. Angélique wished to be informed about this deserted region near a headland, where the fleet had anchored that night.

'What is this place, Sainte-Croix-de-Mercy?'

'It's ... well, it's nothing really.'

'But surely, there must be something at Sainte-Croix-de-Mercy? An Indian encampment? ... A trading-post? ... A hamlet? ...'

'No, there's nothing,' the man repeated.

'Well,' she asked herself, 'whatever business could Joffrey de Peyrac have in a place where there was *nothing*?'

'Well ... there is that, up there.'

'What?'

The man pointed towards the top of the cliff.

'A little old ruined Capuchin hospice, where the Redskins sometimes store their furs during the trading season.'

Who could have made an assignation with Joffrey in that godforsaken spot?

The men she had sent for joined them: Kouassi-Bâ the Negro, Enrico from Malta and the carpenter Vignot.

They all climbed down into the longboat and soon reached the shore. Erickson left the two oarsmen with the sentries watching over the fire, asking the latter in which direction Monsieur de Peyrac and his equerry had set off. They pointed to the starting-point of a track.

CHAPTER 3

THEY BEGAN to climb at once. They had extinguished the lantern. Only an occasional beam of moonlight finding its way through the trees lighted the precipitous path that led to the top of the cliff.

This stealing through the woods made Angélique lose all sense of time and place. Once again she became the woman she had been in Poitou when she had set out upon her devil-may-care adventure, her revolt against the King of France. Thus had she prowled through the woods, her followers like a pack of wolves at her heels, fearsome bands of men fired by hate and resentment: Huguenots and Catholics, villagers and squireens, all dogging her footsteps to deal death and destruction. Silent and as dark as the night from which they sprang, tumbling down cliffs, dropping from the trees on to the King's cavalry on the sunken roads, for over two years they had managed to hold in check the 'jackbooted missionaries' who were ravaging the province, and had driven back even the King of France's regiments sent in to quell them.[1]

And so it was that as she climbed up the path, driven on in a kind of trance that prevented her from feeling either the fatigue of the ascent, or the scratches of brambles and branches that tore at her as she went by, she found her mind filled with memories and sensations as if a former self had taken possession of her body ...

[1] See *Angélique in Revolt*.

11

But this time she was fighting to defend, to save the man she loved.

The clearing which they reached was small and narrow, sloping sharply down to the edge of the cliff, with one spur projecting over the dark waters of the St Lawrence. Gaspé was still not far away, with its high, vertical walls riddled with crevices in which thousands of birds nested. The ocean extended into this salt-laden estuary; they could hear the sound of waves breaking and a keen wind chilled the perspiration of their brows.

As she examined her surroundings, Angélique could make out nothing more than the blanched grassy slope of the clearing that stopped short at the edge of the abyss, but someone nudged her to attract her attention. Vignot gestured, pointing out something to her higher up the slope on their right, where she could make out a faint glimmer and the shape of a log cabin. The shadow of the forest, at the edge of which this hut had been built, hid its main lines, and all that revealed its presence, set back as it was, was the intermittent, scarcely detectable, glow of what was probably a candle or a fire burning inside the cabin.

The group of men halted and remained standing at the edge of the forest. Angélique turned to Kouassi-Bâ and gestured to him. Drawing the hood of his surcoat over his white hair in order to make himself still more perfectly invisible in the dark with his black face, he slipped away along the edge of the clearing until he reached the hut.

They guessed he had drawn close to it and was looking in through the window. Then suddenly, there he was again, whispering that this was indeed the source of the light. There was a fire burning inside the cabin, but he had been unable to see inside clearly as the window-panes were made of opaque fish-skin. But he had overheard a murmur of voices, as of two men talking, and was prepared to swear that one of them was Count Peyrac.

So he was there! Who was he with?

Angélique relaxed somewhat, feeling relieved at the thought that he was nearby and still alive.

Someone had summoned Count Peyrac, who had gone to the agreed meeting-place without bothering to take a bigger guard to protect him in case of need. He had merely taken

Yann Le Couennec with him, rather than his Spanish Guards, which showed that he knew with whom he was dealing and that he had probably even been expecting this encounter. He did not always tell her everything that was going on. She had come to know him and was aware that he planned his expeditions well in advance; he had a network of informants and intelligence agents everywhere.

And what about this trip to Quebec! Who only knew how long he had been thinking about that? She would not have been astonished to learn that he was dealing with an envoy from the Governor of New France, Monsieur de Frontenac, who was on their side, but who, knowing the hostility and fear which his people felt towards the Peyracs, was obliged to act with the utmost secrecy.

And yet, although reassured, she was still unable to bring herself to make a move.

For some obscure reason, there seemed to her to be something sinister about the place, and the fear she felt, although she allowed no hint of it to become apparent, seemed nevertheless to communicate itself to her companions and to make them all extremely serious. They too made no move; they too felt uneasy. As she looked at them in the dim light that filtered through the leaves, she could see their fixed, stern, watchful expressions. Once again one of them touched her arm and pointed to something. Someone was moving on the far side of the clearing. They held their breath, and saw Yann Le Couennec come out into the open and stroll nonchalantly round the clearing. The young equerry made his way down to the edge of the cliff, looked down into the darkness of the abyss, seemed to listen to the breaking of the waves over the rocks below, then walked back up towards the hut. Half-way up the slope, he stopped and lit his pipe. Then he gave a yawn. He seemed to be finding it a long night. The circumstances clearly did not call for his keeping a very close watch.

Angélique was reluctant to let their presence be known to Yann, for, being himself so obviously unapprehensive, he would find it difficult to understand why they were there, as indeed might Joffrey.

But that was of little importance. Shortly before, Angélique had seen in a flash the other side of this expedition to

13

Quebec into which Count Peyrac, along with part of his contingent and of his fleet had thrown themselves, not lightly, but – no doubt because they were all Frenchmen by birth and were on their way to meet other Frenchmen – it was as if some of the obstacles that awaited them had been wiped from their consciousness. It was as if they had *forgotten* the cruel fate that had banished them once and for all from their motherland.

And even Yann himself, who had once killed one of the lord of Helgoat's gamekeepers who had hanged his father for poaching a hare, even Yann, so true and merry a companion, was forgetting that on French soil a hemp rope still awaited him.

Instead of forging boldly ahead, they must be doubly wily and cautious, realizing that here no one would protect them from the laws and the opprobrium cast upon them that made them gallows-birds in the eyes of their compatriots. For each and every one was a marked man on more than one score.

It was their strength, their daring and their vigilance alone that would enable them to emerge triumphant and unscathed from an over-bold, though necessary venture, as the salamander passes through a blazing fire.

The great thing was not to delude themselves.

Even in these still uninhabited regions along the banks of the great northern river, they should bear in mind that every contact with the local people, be they Indians, peasants, fishermen, friars or officials of the King, could spell death.

She had reached this point in her musings when, glancing up across the clearing, she thought she was having a dream that was the continuation of her train of thought.

Swift and silent as two birds of prey, a couple of men sprang out of the wood opposite, made a dash for Yann and threw themselves upon him. There followed a brief struggle in which the Breton, who had been taken by surprise and struck on the nape of the neck, quickly succumbed. He was knocked unconscious, and lay motionless on the ground.

A rough voice broke the silence of the night.

'No need to tie him up. We'll just tie a stone round his neck and chuck him in the river. That'll be one of them dealt with, at any rate!'

It was one of Yann's assailants who had spoken. But in the murk, and the patches of darkness and light cast by the moon, blurred from time to time by swathes of mist, the attack had taken place so swiftly that its unseen witnesses, standing at the edge of the forest, had scarcely realized what was happening.

It was only when they saw the equerry's inert body being dragged towards the edge of the cliff that they reacted. Angélique rushed forward and the men leapt after her as swift and silent as the unknown attackers had done a few moments earlier. By general agreement they did their best to avoid any noise or shouting, in order not to alert the men's accomplices who were, no doubt, inside the hut with Count Peyrac.

Erickson's ancient rapier, wielded by his redoubtable hand, cleft the skull of the first assailant almost in two, and he fell all of a heap to the ground, like a tree felled by the axe.

The other man turned round. A mighty blow full in the face thrust the cry he was about to utter back into his mouth. Kouassi-Bâ's black, gnarled arm circled his neck with the strength of a boa constrictor crushing its prey, then, with a violent backward wrench, broke the man's neck.

A life of constant struggle and danger had made most of Peyrac's men, especially his oldest companions, into formidable killers.

Two corpses lay on the rough grass beside the unconscious Yann.

Angélique made signs to drag them off to one side, for she wished to examine them and try to find out who could have sent them: whether they were sailors who had deserted their ships, trappers or servants of some lord or other, at all events they were certainly thugs. She had no doubt that they had been sent not only to get rid of Yann, but to attack and kill Peyrac when he left the hut to which he had been lured.

The scene seemed unreal against the background of still almost virgin forestland, loud with the rushing of waters and the cries of wild creatures. But Angélique's forebodings had been justified. This was the beginning of the war to be waged against them.

Meanwhile, disturbed by the furtive comings and goings

and by human violence, the birds that had been asleep in the clefts of the cliff face, flew off squawking furiously. White wings could be seen wheeling in the black of the night, then some returned and settled, chattering, in the clearing itself.

Noticing movement inside the log cabin, Angélique and her accomplices hurriedly withdrew into the shadow of the trees, dragging the bodies with them.

Prepared for anything, they glued their eyes on the hut door, which they heard creak.

'What was all that noise?'

'Nothing, just birds,' came the sound of Joffrey de Peyrac's voice, as his tall silhouette stooped to cross the threshold, then straightened up again. He took a few more steps forward.

He stood out very clearly in the moonlight. They guessed he was looking about him. He must have sensed something amiss from certain imperceptible signs.

'Yann!' he called.

The faithful equerry did not appear, and made no reply, which was hardly surprising.

At that moment the other occupant of the hut came out behind the count.

As far as they could tell at that distance, he was a man of mature years, slightly stooped, loosely built with an off-handed, disillusioned manner. He did not look dangerous.

Just as Peyrac had done, he looked towards the clearing, at the birds, pecking and fussing:

'Someone has been here,' came Peyrac's voice, 'or else it was Yann. But in that case where is he? ...'

The husky tones of the voice that was so dear to her made Angélique's heart flutter. Joffrey was not even wearing his mask. By the palid light of the moon she recognized his loved face whose scars, that stood out as hard shadows, lent it heightened character, a formidable face but one that could also bring reassurance to those who were aware of his deep kindness, his intelligence, his vast store of knowledge and his multiple talents.

Angélique's heart throbbed wildly with love. He was alive. She had arrived in time. The apparent indifference the two men displayed had no effect upon her, for she knew for

16

certain that danger still lurked. And possibly Peyrac himself was beginning to suspect as much, for she sensed that he was on his guard.

Angélique's hand gripped the butt of her pistol which was ready cocked.

Her eyes never left the nobleman who remained slightly behind Peyrac, near the door, but who also cast questioning glances about him.

'He must be wondering what has happened to his henchmen,' she thought. 'I wager he's thinking they're taking their time about leaping out at Joffrey and striking him down from behind, as planned. He's not the man to perform that kind of task himself.'

At that very instant, as if to belie her words, she saw the man rush upon Peyrac with uplifted sword.

She gave a shout, firing at the same time.

Count Peyrac had leapt to one side and was already standing on guard, sword in hand. But the shot stopped the wretch in his traces.

He staggered. A second shot rang out and he sprawled full length, looking incredibly long and thin, like a snake on the moonlight-whitened ground. Peyrac looked up and saw Angélique standing erect at the edge of the wood, her hand, untrembling, still clutching the gun from which there rose a thin wisp of smoke.

She looked as stately as a warlike apparition.

'Good shooting, Madame!'

Those were the first words that Peyrac uttered as she went towards him, her feet seeming to glide over the ground in a manner that made her look even more ghost-like. The moonlight accentuated the pallor of her face, and she looked almost translucent with her fair hair like a halo round her head and her silvery sealskin cloak thrown over her shoulders. The only hard, substantial thing about her was her gun which she continued to brandish, its wood and steel glistening and looking singularly out of place in that frail, slender hand.

But the strength of that frail wrist was revealed in the way she held the gun for, heavy and cumbersome as it was, it did not waver, as she gripped it, ready to kill again, and her eyes, still on the look-out, darted warily back and forth in a manner unknown to Peyrac, as if she had been in the habit of piercing the shades of night and the heavy darkness of the woods.

She went up to him and stood beside him, still on the alert, and he felt as if he were seeing the picture of a guardian angel, which every human being is supposed to have watching over him, become a living reality.

'They tried to kill you,' she murmured.

'Yes, there's no doubt about that. And had it not been for you, I would have been dead by now.'

Angélique shuddered. If she had not stepped in, he would have died.

And she would once again have known the unspeakable nightmare of separation from him, of losing him for ever.

'We must get away from here,' she said. 'Why, oh why did you ever do such a reckless, unwise thing?'

He misunderstood what it was she was referring to.

'I admit I was at fault. The fellow represented himself to me as an envoy from Monsieur de Frontenac. I never would have suspected him of such treachery. It has taught me a lesson. In future I shall be doubly cautious. Had it not been for you, my love ... But where is Yann?'

Yann was just coming round. The men gathered round Count Peyrac and gave him a brief account of the attack on his equerry, which proved that men had been positioned there expressly to murder them.

Peyrac knelt down beside the dead man and turned the body over. The first bullet had struck him full in the chest, while the other had entered his back as he fell. He was well and truly dead, no doubt about that, and his sagging face with its gaping mouth bore traces of astonishment in its expression.

'The Marquis de Varange,' said Peyrac. 'The Governor of New France sent him to me with a message in which he bade me more or less welcome. Knowing how little his policy towards me is liked, but wanting to pursue it to its ultimate conclusion, he advised me to maintain the strictest secrecy concerning the interview. He wants Quebec to be faced with a *fait accompli*, and that I can understand. I admit that I followed his instructions and told no one about this first meeting. I began to regret it as soon as I found myself face to face with Varange. He immediately aroused my suspicions, though I found it impossible to say why.'

There was a crackling in the undergrowth from the path that led up from the shore, then a voice called out: 'What's going on?'

Alarmed by the sound of shooting, two sentries left to watch the fire and the dinghys had set out to look for them.

'Deal with all this, Erickson,' Peyrac said hurriedly. 'This business must not get about.'

The captain of the *Gouldsboro* ran towards his men.

'All is well, m'lads. Back to your post . . .'

Then he came back to the others and they held counsel. There were three bodies, one of which was that of a well-known colonial official, the right-hand man of the Governor of New France. But the isolated spot chosen to perpetrate this dastardly attack on Count Peyrac would itself make it all the easier to obliterate all traces of the events that had occurred.

'The forest is huge and the river is deep,' said Peyrac. 'And you chaps can keep a secret. It won't be the first, either, my friends.'

He cast a sharp glance at the men who had accompanied Angélique. They would be as silent as the grave. Their memories were more discreet than a dungeon. Anything that had to be forgotten was well and truly forgotten. Even on the rack they would never have remembered a thing.

Joffrey de Peyrac's arm slipped round Angélique's waist, and with a squeeze he brought her back to earth from the half dream-state she had been in, with her finger still on the trigger.

'And how, Madame, did you come to find out what was going on, that you were able to get here at so opportune a moment?'

'It was a foreboding I had, nothing more, but it was so strong! It was an impulse, the fear of knowing how ill-protected you were for any encounter in this country which is bound to be full of traps for us. I found it impossible to sit and wait in such a state of anxiety, so I asked these men to accompany me. But I can assure you that no one else is aware of anything.'

'Had it not been for Madame la Comtesse you would have

19

been in a pretty pickle, my Lord,' said Erickson.

'Pickled in the St Lawrence!' jested Peyrac, pulling a wry face.

Angélique began to tremble and beneath the palm of his hand the Count felt the shuddering of the woman's body that had a little while before remained impassive, as if cast in steel and which was now quivering with womanly weakness.

Angélique's imagination offered her a horrifying vision. Joffrey assassinated, his body hurled with a stone round its neck from the top of the cliff. Once again he had come within an ace of being taken by surprise and killed by treachery.

Joffrey was right. This crime had been intended to be perpetrated in complete mystery – and no one would ever have known anything about it – and now what had occurred must be cloaked in the same anonymity. All traces must disappear.

For they were heading for Quebec burdened with an already formidable reputation and could certainly not afford to add to it the responsibility for the death of the Marquis de Varange. That would be judged a hostile act rather than one of self-defence. People would cry murder, and slaughter.

'I don't know what this idiot had in mind,' Peyrac went on after a moment's reflection. 'But I'm virtually certain he was not acting under orders from Frontenac. That's out of the question. That he should, on the contrary, have disregarded the assurance of a warm welcome repeatedly given me by the Governor, seems more likely. Quebec is split down the middle over us. Frontenac's only error was to have picked the wrong messenger. Did he even pick him, I wonder?'

When he had knelt down beside the dead man, he had, in searching through his pockets, taken out various papers and objects, which, after examining them to discover whether they contained anything that could throw light on to the instigators of the plot, he put them back where they had come from.

'No traces! There's nothing in our possession that could lead anyone to think that we had ever encountered these men. I'm leaving Frontenac's letter in Monsieur de Varange's pocket, so it will look as if it was never handed to me. And they will vanish just as they had planned to make us vanish.'

He sent Erickson to inspect the log cabin lest any trace of their meeting remain.

Then he whisked Angélique away and they began the climb down to the shore while Kouassi-Bâ, Vignot and Enzi stayed behind to clean the place up.

Half-way down the path, in the shadow of the trees, Joffrey de Peyrac halted and took Angélique in his arms, clasping her passionately to him.

'You saved my life, my love. Thank you a thousand times.'

The piercing cries of the sea-birds, disturbed yet again and now wheeling about in the darkness, reached their ears as they rose up all around the cape. All trace had now vanished of what, in that soot-black night of the St Lawrence wilderness, seemed to have been but a nightmare.

The *Gouldsboro* was the refuge where death could no longer reach them. She wanted to go to earth there with him, for there alone would she be certain that she had saved him.

When the longboat pulled out strongly for the motionless ship, whose three fine poop-deck lanterns shaped like torches, their glasswork red and gold, were reflected in the still waters of the night, she was still trembling. She clung to Peyrac's arm while he glanced down at her from time to time, but said nothing.

He realized that after the tension of the past few hours, she was badly shaken. So was he, in fact, though less on account of the danger that had hung over him than because of this miraculous intervention. From every point of view it had been a surprise, a shock: she had materialized there, so efficient, so indomitable, indeed so pugnacious, ready to do anything to save him. And she had saved his life. He was more fully aware how much she loved him, of the place he occupied in this woman's heart, and after seeing her standing there astonishingly at the edge of the wood, with her arm stretched out, implacable, raising her gun to shoot without flinching the man who threatened his life, he found he had discovered a further mysterious, strange side to her character. Struck by this revelation, he held her very preciously close to him, with a feeling of wonderment stronger than all his other emotions. He told himself that he would always remember this incredible night as if it had been a festive one. He had been within a hair's breadth of death, but it had not been for the first time. What had been new was the delectable feeling of happiness, the euphoria of being alive and owing it to the woman he loved; the fact that she had, at the most unexpected moment, given him the gift of life and a dazzling proof of her love: that was what counted, that was what set a star against this Canadian night.

Angélique, however, huddling against him, was not finding it as easy to get over the stress she had been through. The sharp pain of the anguish that had awakened her, like a cry that tore her from her own body, had left her feeling profoundly distressed. Indeed, she felt positively ill.

Once she found herself alone with him in the cabin on the *Gouldsboro*, that splendid stateroom, their own private domain that had witnessed so many a scene of love and passion between them, her nerves gave way and she broke into a string of vehement reproaches.

'Why did you do it? What rashness! ... You might at least have warned me, have kept me informed. I would have sensed the danger beforehand ... I know about these things, I have faced up to the King of France. I know just what treachery his men are capable of ... I led the Poitou Uprising. But you don't trust me. I don't count. I'm only a woman whom you look down on, whom you don't know, and whom you don't even want to know.'

'My darling,' he murmured, 'calm yourself. Are you going first to save my life, then create a domestic scene?'

'The two are not incompatible.'

Then she threw herself into his arms, almost fainting as she clasped him.

'Oh my darling! My darling! I thought I was reliving the nightmare I used to have over and over again, when I was all alone, far from you. I was running towards you through a forest, I knew you were in danger, but I always got there too late. It's dreadful!'

'This time you did not arrive too late.'

He kissed her and stroked her soft hair where it fell against his shoulder.

Suddenly she threw her head back and looked straight at him.

'Let's go back, Joffrey! Let's go back to Gouldsboro. Don't let's go on any further. I have just realized what a crazy thing we are doing. We are entering the Kingdom, and even though we are far away in America, we are placing ourselves in the power of the King, and his Church, the King I fought against, the Church that condemned you to death. We have managed to escape from them and regain our freedom and here we are putting ourselves back into their hands again. It's crazy.'

'We are returning with ships and gold, with treaties and the blessing of lapsed time.'

'I don't feel safe.'

'And are you, my warrior girl, the one to throw in your hand after the very first tussle? That was nothing: just a skirmish. We have proved that our alliance is strong enough to win the day.'

He clasped her very tight in order to communicate his strength and his faith to her, but she was not reassured.

'Do we really have to go to Quebec?' she asked in a voice in which he could hear the ring of unreasoning anxiety. 'I thought it was all straightforward: we were returning to our own people as friends. Then suddenly I saw the other side of the picture. They were lying in wait for us, luring us towards them the better to catch us to bring us down at last.'

'Now calm down! Things are indeed not simple, but neither are they as serious as that. We have reliable, faithful friends in the stronghold.'

'And implacable enemies, too, as we have seen!'

She shook her head and repeated:

'Do we really have to go to Quebec?'

He did not reply immediately.

'Yes, I think we do,' he said at last in a firm voice. 'It's a risk we must take, a hurdle we have to clear. But it is only by coming face to face with our enemies that we can triumph over the hostility that has built up against us. And if we do triumph, we shall obtain the peace essential to our survival and that of our children, our servants and our friends, and without that the freedom we have gained would be nothing but a snare and a delusion. For the rest of our lives we would remain hunted creatures.'

He had taken her face in his hands and was looking into her eyes, those eyes with the emerald lights, in which he could see the reflection of some unfathomable distress, the distress of the lovely Marquise de Plessis-Bellière, when she had stood alone with her feeble forces against the King of France, she, an unknown woman, leader of the Poitou Revolt, whose image he had glimpsed at the edge of the wood.

'Don't be afraid, my love,' he murmured, 'don't be afraid! This time, I shall be there. There are two of us, we are together.'

He was succeeding in wresting her free from her haunting obsession, in bolstering her confidence in the future and in their destiny. Bit by bit she began to feel reassured and to see the lucky chance that had led her to his rescue as an omen of good fortune rather than of defeat.

Joy began to replace fear. The rapture of certainty, of the dream of having found him again at last come true, went to her head and made her giddy with happiness. Once again a warm glow suffused her body, upon which Joffrey's hand was resting. She blinked to signify her assent, her joyous submission.

'So be it! So we shall go to Quebec, my dear lord and master. But in that case, promise me ... promise ...'

'What?'

'I don't know! ... That you'll never die, that you'll always care for me ... that nothing will ever be able to separate us, no matter what happens ... no matter what ...'

'I promise.'

He was laughing.

Their lips met. Forgetting everything else they gave themselves up to the love that united them, more firmly with every day that passed, the love that was already a victory.

PART TWO

The Journey Up River

CHAPTER 4

'Ah!' SIGHED the little Marquis de Ville d'Avray, sniffing the damp, brackish air from the river. 'How I do adore this atmosphere of love!'

Carlon, the Provincial Intendant, looked at him, completely baffled.

They were standing on the deck of a ship on a cold November evening, and the fact that the leaden sky had lifted along the horizon to allow a glimmer of golden light to filter through did not warrant such a lyrical outburst. The water was a greeny-blue, choppy, almost suspiciously devoid of life. Beneath their woodland pelt which autumn had tinted with hues of dawn and of fire, the Laurentide mountains hid hostile natives, the long-haired Montagnais Indians with their pierced noses and lacerated ears, of Algonquian race, as uncouth and fierce as wild boars.

Every now and then a flight of birds would wheel across the sky, their mournful cries echoing in their wake.

Where was love in all this?

'Do you not feel the rapture, Carlon, the love?' the Marquis went on, puffing out his chest beneath his furry otter-skin cape. 'Ah, love! What a blessed clime this is, the only one where a human being can truly blossom and disport himself like a fish in the water. How pleasant to steep oneself in it, to regenerate oneself. Rarely have I felt its presence all about me with such intensity.'

'But . . . love of *what*? . . .' asked Carlon a trifle uneasily.

The Marquis of Ville d'Avray was an eccentric, granted. But there were moments when one feared for his sanity . . .

Under the other's cold, suspicious scrutiny the Marquis waxed still more lyrical.

'But just plain Love, of course! Love with all its delights, its swoonings, its voluptuous contests, its exquisite moments of tenderness, its moments of anticipation charged with mystery, its intoxicating surrenders, its tiffs, its fears, immediately calmed, its painful, corrosive rancours which a smile melts away as the sun melts the snow, its hopes and its certainties, all that thrilling fire which is constantly renewed by the pulsations of the heart and the flesh, enriched by every detail and every moment of wonder life has to offer, that causes one to live in another world where there are just two people, *just two*, ready to die if need be there and then, for every minute, every hour, every day is the threshold of an almost paradisial bliss whose wonders one can never cease to tell, and whose intensity one can never again surpass ...'

'I think you must be raving,' said Carlon, 'either that or you're drunk ...'

He cast a suspicious glance at the light collation that awaited them close by on a low table. Wine cups, crystal goblets and silverware glistened in the setting sun, but the decanters of wine and liquers showed no sign of having been broached...

'Yes, I have been drinking,' Ville d'Avray admitted. 'I have become intoxicated with the divine elixir of which I speak – Love. It gleams so subtly, is almost impalpable yet so very intense, so vast, so burning that the feeling swirls about me like an exquisite bouquet which I cannot but be sensible of, which I cannot but relish ... What do you expect, you see, I am such a sensitive soul ...'

'Bouquet,' Carlon repeated, 'Yes, there's a bouquet all right, but there's nothing heavenly about it. It's a strange thing that although we are well inland, the smell of the tides is still pervasive here.'

'Who's talking about tides?' wailed the Marquis. 'You are so dreadfully prosy. Here I am doing my utmost to touch some chord within you, and all in vain.'

He turned away, disappointed, and helped himself to a sweetmeat from one of the crystal dishes. This tit-bit appeared to restore his good spirits and he livened up again.

'Now, look! Even in this sweetmeat I see an emblem of Love. Can one not interpret this as the master-stroke of a love-stricken heart that has found means to bring such delicacies to these remote and desolate shores, so that, in spite of the inclemency of the place, the beloved paragon should not suffer its rigours? Is this not love indeed, to spread at the feet of the beloved all the riches of the earth, never ceasing to captivate her mind and heart by this enchanting enterprise? Are not these the marks of a climate of passion and tenderness to which no one – not even you – can remain indifferent? No, not even *you* . . .'

He poked a finger at Carlon's chest, and gave it a series of little jabs.

'You're raving,' Carlon repeated, 'and you're hurting me . . .'

But Monsieur de Ville d'Avray, the Governor of Acadia, was well away.

He seized the fellow by the lapels – Carlon being a good head taller than he.

'Come now, you are not going to tell me that you are insensible to all this? However puny the miserable carcass of the Civil Servant of the King that you are may be, you are not going to make me believe that beneath that pale cold-fish skin of yours a heart does not beat, a male organ does not throb?'

Carlon wrenched himself free, absolutely appalled.

'Governor, I am accustomed to your unseemly remarks, but this is the limit. Let me say once and for all that I comprehend nothing of your ravings. It is cold, night is falling, we are sailing towards Quebec where endless complications await us, and suddenly you declare that you feel steeped in an atmosphere of love! . . . Love of *what*, I asked you.'

'But why should it be Love of *something*?' replied the Marquis, stamping with irritation. 'You might at least ask love of *whom*? . . . Well, there, look, blind that you are! . . . Look and see who is coming towards us . . .'

With a triumphant, theatrical gesture, he waved his hand in the direction of a group that had just appeared on the gallery overlooking the poop-deck. Silhouetted against the light, these people, whose feathered hats stood out black against the golden sky, were hard to distinguish one from another, but it was possible to make out that one of them was a woman.

'Now then, can you see *her*,' the Marquis went on, all a-tremble. 'Can you see the one and only *she*? A woman adorned with every grace nature can bestow, with every charm of utter femininity, whose merest glance dazzles,

29

whose every utterance, falling from those wonderful lips, leaves one for ever ravished, whose gentleness beguiles, whose violence bowls you over, with whom one never knows whether she is appealing to your strength to protect her charming weakness, or rousing your weakness the better to reveal her hidden, invincible strength, by making you want to cuddle up to that warm bosom as one would to a mother's bosom, a woman who leaves one for ever uncertain whether it is her quality of openness that is so seductive, or whether on the contrary it is her more formidable side. But one thing is certain, and that is that it is impossible for any male creature, or indeed for any creature at all, to be indifferent to her charms. A property, an irresistible charm that is, to my mind, the most important and most subtle quality of any woman, of *woman* in her very essence . . .'

He had to pause to get his breath back.

Carlon said nothing, although a glimmer of interest flickered in his eyes.

At that moment Angélique, the Countess of Peyrac, escorted by her husband and the officers of the Count's fleet, captains, mates and leading seamen, all superbly decked out, began to descend the polished wooden stairway leading to the first deck. Even at this distance the radiance of the woman's face was striking, and it was impossible to tell whether the glow that emanated from it was a reflection of the setting sun, heightening the colour of her warm complexion, or whether its source was the smile full of charm and gaiety that parted her lips as she listened to the remarks of her companions, remarks which the two men were unable to hear, being still at too great a distance, but which seemed to be exceedingly lively and bantering.

She was wearing a broad-brimmed white felt hat at a somewhat jaunty angle, which looked like a pale halo about her head. Her white satin coat lined with white fur was partially open, revealing a bodice with a three-tiered collar of Malines lace worn over a pink faille dress, the skirt of which, in the prevailing fashion, was drawn up at one point over the folds of a garnet-red velvet underskirt with two rows of silver braiding along the hem.

With one hand she had gathered the folds of her skirt, to enable her to negotiate the steps more easily, while the other was tucked into a white fur muff suspended round her neck by a silver cord.

So graceful were Angélique de Peyrac's movements that Ville d'Avray murmured:

'Is she not worthy to descend the great staircase at Versailles at the side of the King himself? ...'

'They say she's done just that ...' Carlon muttered.

'What? Come down the great staircase of Versailles? Beside the King?'

Carlon made no reply but merely gave a knowing sniff. Ville d'Avray seized hold of him again.

'So you know something about her, do you? Tell me everything! Ah, so you don't want to say anything, but I'll make you tell it all one day ...'

Standing out darkly against the bright sky, the furtive silhouette of a small animal appeared at the ship's rail, and in a few lithe bounds joined the assembled company, alighting on the deck in front of Angélique where, after carefully scrutinizing her, it stalked solemnly in front of her, its tail held high.

'The cat!' exclaimed Ville d'Avray, gleefully. 'Note that even animals act as escorts to Countess Peyrac and love to submit to her yoke. Oh, if only you had seen her at Gouldsboro with the bear!'

'What bear?' Carlon said with a start.

'A huge, furry creature, horribly fierce, and there she was, kneeling in front of it, stroking it and talking softly to it.'

'But that's a very disturbing piece of news! You never told me that Madame de Peyrac possessed such powers.'

'It was an unforgettable sight.'

'It could be due to magic.'

'Of course it isn't! It's just her personal charm ... Can't you see how exciting this all is?'

'Yes and no. I'm thinking of the fact that we are in the hands of a man who was once a filibuster, and that we have every reason to regard ourselves as his prisoners. That's no reason to put out the flags.'

'But it's not like that at all! How apt you are to look on the dark side of things! We are merely Monsieur de Peyrac's guests and he is a gentleman of adventure, a Gascon by birth, and furthermore the richest man in North America.

After coming to our assistance when we were making our tour of inspection in Acadia, he has been so kind as to bring us back on his ship to Quebec, where he himself is going to pay his respects to the Governor of New France, Monsieur de Frontenac.'

'And what about you? How about the way you always see life through rose-tinted spectacles?' said Carlon ironically.

'I am a happy man. That's the way I am. I look on the bright side of things, and what could be more pleasant for a man of my sensitivity than to find myself aboard this vessel, in pleasant company, yours included – yes! yes! make no protest – and free to engage in conversation with the most delectable woman in the world. I am bringing back a ship Monsieur de Peyrac gave me as a gift to replace my own *Asmodée* which was sunk by bandits. Look how pretty she is, lying at anchor over there! I haven't yet decided what I am going to call her ... I'm bringing back merchandise: a considerable number of furs, many flasks of Jamaican rum ... a tiled stove ... shush! ... a beauty! Monsieur de Peyrac had it brought over from France for me. Just look.'

' "Look ... look!" That's all you ever say; you are exhausting me ... Well, I'm looking and what I see is a situation that is becoming more and more dubious and complicated, and the prospect, as I told you, of endless difficulties, precisely because Monsieur and Madame de Peyrac are people out of the ordinary run, who epitomize, as you yourself testify, Love and its pleasures. Well, we can look forward to a fine rumpus in Quebec! Is that a prospect to rejoice in? For a start, there will be an exchange of gun-fire, I'll stake my life on that, and then, if we manage to survive that, it will be you and I, whom events have forced to come to terms with them, that will be saddled with the blame, the disgrace, and why not, while we're at it, excommunication? You know that the Bishop, Monsignor Laval, and the Jesuits don't regard questions of sorcery and free-thinking as laughing matters, and I don't see them welcoming these particular visitors with a smile.'

'How you do run on, my dear feller? You're exaggerating! Of course there will be incidents and a fair amount of weeping and gnashing of teeth. But of course I adore all that, I must confess ...'

'Yes, of course! We know you. On that score, I would agree with Madame de Peyrac when she says that nothing delights you more than to turn an entire city topsy-turvy.'

'Did she say that? How right she is! Isn't she delightful?'

'But in any case, there's no point in arguing with you, since you are in love.'

'No I'm not in love ... or at least, only a little ... You know, you haven't understood a single thing ... You depress me ... I shan't discuss things with you any more.'

The Marquis of Ville d'Avray turned away, sulkily.

When Angélique de Peyrac and her escort reached the two men, they found them equally gloomy.

After a further day's sailing, the fleet had once again dropped anchor in a deserted bay along the northern shore of the St Lawrence. As was their custom, the captains of the other vessels had come on board the *Gouldsboro* for a meal to discuss the day's events and plan the following day's run.

'We shall soon reach Tadoussac.'

'The first French outpost!'

'Let us hope they won't give us too unfriendly a welcome!'

'But why should they? It's only a small, isolated township with little by way of defence. We shall arrive in full force. And furthermore, our intentions are peaceful.'

The fleet was in fact in splendid fit. Anchored in the lee of a cape that protected it from any surprise attack, it consisted of three ships of 200 to 350 tons, which, while not being of large dimensions, nevertheless carried around sixty cannon between them. A couple of small Dutch-built yachts, highly manoeuvrable and lively, sailed on their flanks to act as guard-dogs and scouts. These were designed to carry two cannon each in the 'tween-decks, and two culverins fore and aft, capable of causing a great deal of damage when skilfully aimed.

One of the yachts was called *Le Rochelais* and the other *Mont-Désert*. Cantor, Angélique's and Count Peyrac's

33

younger son, commanded the *Rochelais*; for he was already, in spite of his sixteen years, an officer with a thorough knowledge of the sea. He had undergone his early training in the Mediterranean where, from the age of ten, he had sailed with his father, and then the Caribbean.

Vanneau, erstwhile boatswain to the pirate Gold Beard, was captain of the *Mont-Désert*. Count Peyrac had picked him rather than some of his longer-standing companions, on account of his excellent reputation, since he had never been convicted of any crime in France, and because he was a Catholic.

This matter of religion had obliged them to select the crews and appoint the higher-ranking officers with the utmost care. It was out of the question to bring any French members of the Reformed Church into New France, for they would have risked immediate arrest, and probably the gallows, as they were considered traitors. It was equally delicate a matter to bring in any foreigners. But, as Count Peyrac was visiting Quebec as a private individual, on an independent footing, beneath his own flag, his crew, regardless of its composition, would benefit from whatever welcome he himself was given.

Nevertheless, even from this restricted field, there had to be a process of elimination. The command of the *Gouldsboro* had remained in the hands of the Norwegian Erickson, a taciturn, prudent man who knew how to keep out of the public eye. Joffrey de Peyrac retained the four Spaniards who formed his personal guard, men who for a long time had been accustomed to ensure his safety and who would have been at a loss if deprived of this particular task.

Nor did they run any risk of attracting comment. They kept themselves to themselves and would no more have thought of mixing with the French Canadian population than they did of hob-nobbing with Peyrac's sailors or settlers.

The captains of the two other ships were Count d'Urville and Monsieur de Barssempuy, both gentlemen from good French families who would not appear out of place in Quebec high society, provided no one enquired too closely into their reasons for leaving France to sail the seven seas.

As she approached the two men, Angélique immediately

34

noticed Ville d'Avray's downcast countenance and the stiff, sullen expression worn by Carlon. Oh, dear! The two of them had been quarrelling again ... While still at some distance from them she had seen the Marquis gesticulate, then turn away, stamping his foot.

Poor Marquis, so keen to maintain that 'life is wonderful!' Angélique was never unmoved by the unhappiness of others.

Ville d'Avray felt consoled at finding himself an object of interest to those eyes, as perspicacious as they were beautiful. He liked people to pay attention to him, to show concern about his moods. Angélique sent him into raptures by coming over to where he stood.

'What is wrong, my good friend?' she asked. 'It would seem that all is not well.'

'Yes indeed, well may you say so. That creatures like that feller should exist and that one should be obliged to associate with them is proof, in spite of what the theologians tell us, that purgatory begins here on earth.'

'Are you referring to Monsieur Carlon?'

'Who else?'

'Sit down beside me and tell me all about it.'

He flopped down next to her on a seat strewn with cushions.

As Angélique listened attentively to his plaints, she looked about her.

It was a fine evening. After two days' torrential rain, it was a pleasure to breathe the pure air.

After the halt at Sainte-Croix-de-Mercy, the journey had begun again, or rather continued, without the merest whisper of the tragic incident in which some of them had been involved that night.

There were moments when Angélique wondered whether she had not dreamed it all. The most concrete result of the whole hidden drama was a subtle change in her relationship with her husband. It seemed to her that he looked at her with a new expression of admiration and curiosity in his eyes, and that she inspired greater confidence in him, and more firmly based respect.

He was more ready to bring her in on his plans, and he sought her advice more often. There were many matters to settle or consider before they eventually dropped anchor beneath the walls of Quebec, the King's fief in New France.

But for the moment, that objective still seemed a long way off. It felt almost as if they were being on another planet, especially when to the tang of the icy air, mingling with the sea-smell rising from the river, and the smell of the vast forestlands encompassing them, was added the unexpected, luxurious savour of sweetmeats and pastries, or the exotic aroma of coffee in its copper ewer, of chocolate, or of the tea which the newly-appointed major-domo, Monsieur Tissot, insisted on the assembled company tasting, saying that it was all the rage in Paris.

He had been taken on by Erickson while on his last voyage to Europe, on the recommendation of an associate of Count Peyrac's in Rouen. He seemed to know his job and was more than a mere cook. At that moment he was standing, warmly wrapped up but looking solemn, as he supervised a small kettle that stood poised over the edge of the glowing coals in one of the braziers.

'He's the most narrow-minded man I know,' Ville d'Avray continued, sampling the stuffed pistaccios.

'Are you still talking about the Provincial Intendant of New France?'

'Yes, of course.'

'I do not share your opinion in this matter, Marquis. Monsieur Carlon may be moody, but he is a man of considerable culture and an interesting talker. My husband takes great pleasure in conversing with him, especially on commercial matters, about which he seems very knowledgeable.'

'And what about me? What about me?' Ville d'Avray protested. 'Am I not also knowledgeable about commerce?'

'Yes, indeed.'

'And am I not a man of culture?'

'Of course you are ... you are one of the most cultured men I know ... and one of the most charming.'

'You are enchanting,' the Marquis murmured, kissing her hand devotedly. 'How greatly I am looking forward to having you more to myself ... Wait and see,' he went on, taking up his favourite refrain once again, 'Wait and see how cosy we shall be in my little drawing-room in Quebec, sitting in front of my tiled stove, while the stormy winds rage outside. I shall prepare you a cup of the China tea that Father de Maubeuge gives me an occasional sealed packet of – he has it sent direct from over there ... You will settle in my best chair – a Boulle, very comfortable, that I had copied by a craftsman whose name I will let you have ... and the cushions are covered in Lyons silk brocade ... You'll see ... You'll settle down in it and tell me everything, everything about your life.'

It was obvious that the most difficult thing about this Quebec business would probably not be getting themselves made welcome, but managing to get through the winter at very close quarters with the over-curious Marquis without his ending up knowing everything there was to know about her and her past, right down to the minutest details of her existence.

This was something that it was now certain that she would be unable to escape ...

But they would see. They were still not in Quebec.

And in spite of Joffrey's optimistic view – he had refused to regard the attempt on his life as part of a concerted plan, still less as having originated from the Governor, Frontenac – it still remained true that powerful enemies awaited their arrival, and it was by no means clear that these men would not finally triumph.

'Who was the Marquis de Varange?' she asked Ville d' Avray without thinking.

He gave a start.

'Varange? You've heard of him, have you?'

'Well ...'

'And why did you ask who he *was*? He's not dead as far as I know.'

Angélique bit her tongue. She could have kicked herself. Since she had entered French waters, she seemed to have been totally out of step with the situation. She thought of herself as being at home, in France, whereas the exact opposite was the case. She lied brazenly to cover up her blunder.

'Someone mentioned him to me, I forget who. Oh, yes, it was possibly Ambroisine de Maudribourg, over on the East coast. I think she said he had been called back to France.'

'That's impossible. I've never heard that!' exclaimed Ville d'Avray indignantly.

He reflected for a moment.

'Actually, it would have been quite plausible if our dear duchess had had epistolary or other connections with him; it would have been rather like her. A handsome old bore, who got himself transferred to the colonial service after some scandal about morals. He's got some minor job as paymaster in Quebec, but I don't see anything of him ... That strumpet really did seem to know everyone here without ever having set foot in the place. What a termagant! I shall be doubly cautious in my dealing with Varange in the future ...'

In order to change the subject, Angélique signalled to Kouassi-Bâ.

'Yes, I'd love something to drink,' said Ville d'Avray. 'I've been talking a lot, and most of it quite pointlessly to that narrow-minded feller, Carlon. Yes, I was telling him marvellous things about you, that I shall tell you one day, things that should have stirred his passions, opened his eyes; but he just met me with that stone wall of logic that never wants to see beyond appearances.'

The tall Negro Kouassi-Bâ stooped before them, holding a copper tray with little cups of scalding hot Turkish coffee.

Kouassi-Bâ was the very soul of fidelity, the one person who had remained with them for the whole of their lives. What tales he could have told about the past lives of Count and Countess Peyrac, tales that Ville d'Avray would have dearly loved to hear! ... From the time when, as a slave in Toulouse, he had seen Angélique, the bride in the golden dress, driving up in a coach, until this twilight evening on the St Lawrence when yet again he could bow before her, he had been an integral part of their lives. In order that he could accompany them to Quebec, Count Peyrac had brought him back from Wapassou on the Upper Kennebec where he was working in the mine.

That evening, to serve the noble assembly, Kouassi-Bâ again donned his gilt-bedizened livery, which had, however, been warmly quilted to protect him from the cold. He was wearing white stockings with gold clocks and very high-heeled buckled shoes. His hoary head sported a plumed scarlet silk turban, that served to keep him warm while setting off the striking features of his black face. Two large, solid gold earrings, from which hung a pearl on the end of a tiny gold chain, adorned his ears: a recent gift from Count Peyrac to his faithful servant.

Ville d'Avray eyed the tall Negro enviously, registering the aristocratic grace and deftness of his movements.

'He'll be the talk of the town in Quebec, that Moor of yours ... Why ever didn't I think of getting one myself ...'

He clicked his tongue in annoyance. One lost all sense of fashion in that godforsaken town of Quebec ... His friend the Duchess of Pontarville, who lived in the Saint-Germain district of Paris, had two young page-boys from the Sudan. She would willingly let him have one of them if he asked her, but by now it was too late to send a courier over to Europe, the matter would have to wait until the following spring.

Monsieur de Vauvenart turned to Peyrac:

'Why, Monsieur de Peyrac, did you leave it so late to begin to sail up river? The season is a mild one but we might well have run into ice.'

'Better ice than ships!'

Carlon, overhearing this remark, glanced resentfully at him.

'You appear to be well-informed about the problems New France has to face. You are right in thinking that by the end of October all ships have sailed for Europe and you run little risk of finding yourself face to face with any sizeable vessel that could do battle with you. New France has no fleet of its own and that is a matter of dispute between me and Monsieur Colbert. But what if Quebec closes its doors to you? Will you be able to return the way you came, or won't you find yourselves trapped by your own calculations?'

'But why do you imagine Quebec will close its doors to him?' Ville d'Avray retorted sharply, determined that no one should spoil his evening for him. 'I'd like to see it happen. The people of my circle will be on the quayside to give us a right rousing welcome ... That's how it will be. Here, have another of these delicious pastries ...'

So excited was he that Angélique feared for the cup of

coffee she was holding, but the Marquis's keenness to stand up for them and to assure them that all would be well delighted her.

She managed to avoid having coffee spilled down her dress. The little copper bowl fitted firmly into a porcelain support which made it possible to hold it between three fingers without burning oneself. She took several sips.

The journey up river gave them a breathing-space. The fact that everything was going so quietly as to be somewhat disturbing did not suffice to make one forget that, since Anticosti Island, they had been sailing up the St Lawrence, a French river, deep in the heart of Canada. For those who were prepared to look the facts in the face, it was as in her dream of the other night, they were advancing through *enemy territory*. But in spite of everything they were among friends.

Meanwhile the river remained deserted. All that they ever glimpsed was the occasional flotilla of Indian canoes vanishing rapidly through the swathes of rain in the direction of the river banks, or a fishing boat manned by isolated settlers engaged in farming the land around some out-of-the-way hamlet, who were not anxious to show any excessive curiosity about the intentions of this foreign fleet making full sail for Quebec under an unfamiliar flag.

Since the early days of November Cape Gaspé with its plume of screeching birds had faded from sight, and they had sailed past islands that were the haunt of seals, and later of ducks and teal. They had tacked back and forth to avoid the harsh, sudden squalls frequent upon this great river, whose waters remain salty as far as a hundred leagues inland.

The remarkably clear weather they had enjoyed while crossing the Gulf and sailing north off the coast of Acadia had broken once they passed Cape Gaspé. The ships were now shrouded in a virtually impenetrable atmosphere and sometimes lost sight of one another, being obliged to resort to their foghorns in order to re-establish contact. Then, through the mists, a dawn-like glow emerged and spread to the farthest horizon as the pink tints of the vast forestlands came into view, their foliage ablaze with the glorious hues of autumn.

It was less cold on the river than it had been during the

crossing of the Gulf, and it was more agreeable to go out on deck.

In addition to the ships' captains – Roland d'Urville, Erickson, Vanneau, Cantor and Barssempuy, who had come on board the *Gouldsboro* for the daily briefing – there were also the French royal officials Joffrey de Peyrac had taken on board in the Bay of Fundy and on the East Coast of Acadia, following attacks by the English and incidents that had deprived them of their own vessels.[1] There were also Monsieur de Vauvenart, Grand-Bois and Grand-Rivière, local lords from Acadia who had seized the opportunity to leave their distant fiefs in order to come and pay their respects to Monsieur de Frontenac, the Governor appointed by the King of France, whose more or less obedient subjects, like it or not, they remained.

'You have cast a gloom over her,' said Ville d'Avray to the Provincial Intendant. 'Look what you have done ...'

'I'm most terribly sorry, Madame,' Carlon declared solemnly.

'... With your uncalled-for comments ...'

'Not at all; Monsieur Carlon has every right to make the odd pessimistic remark,' Angélique retorted defensively.

Joffrey de Peyrac had been represented to the French citizens of Canada as an alley of the English, who had settled in the Upper Kennebec region for the sole purpose of keeping the settlers of French Canada and Acadia at bay. In the eyes of others, he was as unscrupulous and dangerous a pirate as Morgan. So many things had been said about him that he was not wrong in thinking that only a frank explanation, delivered face to face, could ever put men's minds at rest. Hence his daring plan to go to Quebec and make himself known.

And now the presence on board his ship of the Provincial Intendant, whom chance had led there, still further complicated the situation.

'I can understand what is worrying you, Monsieur Carlon,' Angélique went on, 'and why you sometimes quarrel with Monsieur de Ville d'Avray, who does not like to look on the darker side of life.'

[1] See *Angélique and the Demon*.

'This Carlon feller is appallingly jaundiced. He's for ever worrying about what is going to happen when we get to Quebec.'

'We are all worried about that,' she retorted.

'Except him, I'll wager ...'

Ville d'Avray motioned towards Count Peyrac with his chin; the latter did indeed appear not to have been affected by Carlon's remarks.

Angélique shook her head.

'He! ... He's always delighted in braving the storms.'

Joffrey continued his conversation with Monsieur de Vauvenart and the surveyor Fallières about the appearance of the ice and the state of the St Lawrence in winter. He had put down his coffee cup and Kouassi-Bâ, holding a burning coal in a pair of tongs with one hand, passed him a small stick of tightly-rolled tobacco leaves with the other. That was how the Count liked to smoke. He lit the roll of tobacco on the glowing coal and puffed a number of blue, redolent wreaths of smoke into the air with obvious pleasure.

'Just like in Toulouse,' thought Angélique.

And the vision comforted her. Everything seemed to be pointing towards a rebirth, a regeneration.

And thus it was that she passed from moments of exaltation when every obstacle appeared trifling, to an oppressive apprehensiveness, born of past experience, of which she had never managed entirely to rid herself. Then she would look at Joffrey.

He seemed so calm, so sure of himself, that in the end one came to share his confidence.

Just looking at him gave her strength, convinced her that all was well, that there was nothing to fear.

His attention was caught by her gaze, and the Count's own dark eyes turned towards hers; through the wispy smoke-cloud she caught the glint of tenderness that lit them. He gave an imperceptible nod to show her that she had nothing to fear. Once again he was assuring her that they must go on. What had she to fear now, since she was with him? A year ago, at the same season, they had both been plunging into the forests of the New World; exposed to unknown and terrible dangers, together they had braved the hostility of the Canadians, the vengeance of the Iroquois, the deadly grip of winter, and famine, while today here they were in force, on board well-armed, comfortable ships stacked with mechandise, and with the support of a wide variety of North American allies and establishments conforming to Count Peyrac's policies to protect their rear. Was not all this something not far short of a miracle? Did it not appear to be due to some extent to magical arts? Where he was concerned, things never seemed to turn out exactly as one had predicted or as others had imagined they would. He had remained a magnificent duellist, an expert in the art of unnexpected thrust and parry.

During the course of that year they should have perished a hundred times over.

Their defeat had been proclaimed, nay, even their death; they had been thought for ever vanquished.

And here they were advancing proudly on Quebec.

CHAPTER 5

THE CONVERSATION was cut short by the sound of children's shouts and laughter, and the noise of running footsteps on the deck.

Angélique saw her young daughter Honorine spring into view, followed by her small friend Chérubin. The pair were chasing the cat that was displaying an almost human sense of fun by scampering out of reach as soon as they caught up with it, leaping from the top of a pile of rope on to the ship's rail, then from there up into the lifeboat that was secured in the middle of the deck, where it crouched down, ready to leap out like a jack-in-the-box, just as the children, after clambering painfully up, thought they were on the point of catching it. They shouted with mirth, puffing and blowing, whirling hither and thither.

'You'll be the death of us,' Honorine shouted to the cat.

Chérubin was a chubby little lad, not so tall as the irrepressible young lady, although they were both aged four.

43

The boy's somewhat delicate position as the Marquis de Ville d'Avray's natural son had caused him little loss of sleep to date. He was first and foremost the son of Marcelline-la-Belle, celebrated as one of the great pioneering women from the furthermost reaches of the Bay of Fundy in the south, a colourful Acadian with a heart as big as a barn and with enough courage for one of the King's regiments, as well as being without her equal when it came to the rapid opening of shellfish.

She had only allowed Chérubin, the last of a long lineage of varied episodic paternity, to set off on this journey because Angélique had undertaken to care for him and because her eldest daughter, Yolande, who was twenty, was going with them too. The fact that his father, the Marquis, wanted to have him educated as if he were a prince, did not make much impression on Marcelline. All right! The lad could go to Quebec for the winter with the folk from the *Gouldsboro*, then there would be time to see what was what.

At that very moment big Yolande made her appearance in the wake of the two children, and so did Adhémar-the-Soldier and Niels Abbial, the Swedish boy who had been picked up as a waif on the New York wharves and cared for by the Jesuit priest Louis Paul de Vernon. So all this little company, including the cat, were on their way to Quebec. In the lives of these humble folk, assembled under the protective mantle of Angélique and Joffrey de Peyrac, this journey was of major significance.

For the first time ever, Yolande would see the bustle of a real city with a cathedral, churches and a chateau, whereas she had hitherto known only trading posts, wooden forts, and humble missionary chapels on the fringes of the sea and the untamed forest.

For his part, Adhémar risked being hanged as a deserter.

As for Chérubin ... Ville d'Avray tried to guess, as he watched him, how the worthy city of Quebec would probably react to him. The Marquis was not for avowing him openly – there were enough scandals to cope with as it was. He was relying on the resemblance between himself and the boy, which he considered striking, to open the eyes of his fellow-citizens to the truth, little by little over a period of time. For the moment, he eyed his offspring fondly and made plans. One day, Chérubin would be a page at the King's Court. The bore was that that would entail the Marquis's returning to France. But there was no hurry.

Taking it all in all, for many persons on the ship 'life was good' . . . and the voyage delightful.

The cat noticed Angélique and went to her immediately. She felt that the little creature was particularly attached to her. At the beginning of the summer at Gouldsboro, she had taken it in as a pitiful stray kitten and they had been through some strange adventures together.

Seeing the cat bounce up to Angélique, Honorine also came rushing over and put her arm jealously around her mother's neck.

She eyed the cat grudgingly as it installed itself on Angélique's knees.

'You're the one he likes best anyway,' she said sadly.

Since they had all been together again, she had made a point of addressing her parents in formal style, perhaps to show that she was no longer a baby, or perhaps to let it be known that she rather resented having been left alone for a time at Wapassou.

'Do you really think so? I think he has more fun with you than with me, but he remembers that I looked after him. He's a grateful cat, almost human.'

Angélique told her how the kitten had been injured, but didn't say by whom. That was why she had left him in the care of the Berne children, she explained. She was delighted that they had thought to bring him back to her now that he was well again, for she had been missing him. And a cat is always useful on a ship, just like in a house.

Honorine listened to what Angélique was saying while keeping an eye on her rival, who was also watching her through half-closed eyes. She rubbed her cheek against Angélique's caressingly, and Angélique gave her an affectionate kiss. She looked at the wilful little face cuddling up against her and proudly stroked Honorine's copper-coloured hair. Her daughter was beautiful, and there was something of the princess in her bearing. She had a long, proud, strong neck, and her skin was not freckled, as might have been expected, but delicately golden like Angélique's. In her rounded oval face, with its well-shaped features, her small

45

dark eyes were the only feature that would have seemed unattractive if their fearless, earnest expression had not impressed those on whom she fixed her cool, shrewdly watchful gaze. She was quite a character.

'Will you be welcome at Quebec too?' Angélique wondered to herself. 'And yet you are French, born in the heart of Poitou, and delivered by a real-life woodland sorceress, Mélusine.'

She shook her head to dispel an incredible memory, but not such a very remote one, after all. And yet how much had happened since then and what a change there had been!

'Don't you like that biscuit?' asked Honorine, who was watching her interestedly.

Angélique became aware that she had without thinking taken a sugar biscuit from the tray held out to her, and that she was holding it dubiously after having bitten off a mouthful, and, doubtless by force of habit, she had, while pursuing her thoughts gone on apparently attending to the conversation between her neighbours.

The cat was waiting for its share, and so was Honorine.

All was quiet on the ship. Night was beginning to spread its dark wings. Faces and lace cravats stood out as light patches against the indistinct silhouettes. The red glow of the coals in the braziers grew more intense.

One of the wheelhouse men came up and his shadow merged with Peyrac's as he joined him.

Only the sound of his voice could be distinguished, announcing quietly: 'A ship is following us.'

CHAPTER 6

AT CHALEUR BAY they had picked up a St Lawrence pilot, whom family and other business had brought to the east coast of Acadia, and who wanted to return to Canada while making a little bit of money on the side. He offered to put

46

his knowledge of the St Lawrence, its currents and hazards from one island to another, at the disposal of the passing vessels, and several Acadians who were on board having vouched for his trustworthiness and qualifications, Joffrey de Peyrac had given the pilot a considerable sum in order to make doubly sure of his unwavering devotion. Esprit Ganemont – for such was his name – was now determined to ensure that the fleet committed to his care arrived safely at Quebec.

It was he who had given Peyrac the quietly spoken warning: 'A ship is following us.'

Angélique heard what he said and immediately stood up holding Honorine and Chérubin to her in an instinctively protective gesture. Seeing her rise, her guests did likewise out of politeness, but they had not heard and their eyes turned towards Peyrac.

He had received the news calmly.

Since everybody was standing, he also got up, at the same time raising his cigar to his lips.

In any event it was now dark, the sailors were hanging lanterns on the rails, and a damp chill was rising from the river. The moment had come to break up.

He inhaled a last puff of blue smoke slowly and with obvious pleasure, then put what remained of the stick of glowing tobacco in a small silver vessel containing a little water.

'What's going on?' asked Ville d'Avray.

The Count repeated the information: 'A ship is following us.'

Instinctively all heads turned to gaze into the impenetrable darkness downstream.

'You mean to say a ship is coming up the St Lawrence behind us?' exclaimed d'Urville.

Then with a shrug, 'At this time of the year? It's out of the question,' he went on, 'It would be madness!'

'Perhaps it's a warship despatched by the King to Quebec's assistance,' said someone.

Peyrac smiled.

'What danger is Quebec in? And how could anyone have known in time over in France that I intended to go to Quebec in the autumn?'

'Sometimes thoughts travel faster than ships and can influence minds at a distance.'

The Count shook his head.

'I don't see any room for calculations of that sort. The King of France is not the sort of man to manage his kingdom by mumbo-jumbery or to be influenced by it.

'In any case, as you pointed out a moment ago, I think the King would have seen to it that the ship arrived at Quebec before the ice ... and us.'

'You don't believe in witchcraft, Monsieur de Peyrac?'

'I didn't say that.'

Peyrac leaned forward to try to make out who was speaking. Perhaps it was Fallières or one of the Acadian noblemen, Vauvenart or Saint-Aubin. Erickson had come up.

'Have you any instructions for me, my Lord, with regard to the reported vessel?' he asked.

'Not for the moment. We are at anchor, and the best thing we can do is to stay here until dawn ... Which is doubtless what the unknown ship will also do since it can't sail on in the darkness.'

The St Lawrence pilot confirmed that the ship in question had indeed hove to early in the afternoon a little to the lee of Pointe aux Rats on the north shore.

'That's a long way off,' said Carlon thoughtfully, wrapping himself up tightly in his coat, the collar of which came right up to his nose. 'How did you get word of them?'

'From the group of men I have had acting for me on shore since Gaspé; they cover our rear by following along on the south shore of the river. They sent an Indian runner with the message.'

'Perhaps it's a ship from Acadia,' suggested Angélique.

'I don't think so, because we would have had wind of its movements when we were at Tidnish. Apart from our own ships that we left there – and they were given their sailing orders before we parted from them, either to stay on the east coast or to return to Gouldsboro – and apart from the *Sans-Peur*, the privateer Van Ereck's ship, which sailed for the Caribbean, I find it difficult to imagine any Acadians venturing into the St Lawrence in this season. Don't you agree, Monsieur de Vauvenart; you yourself preferred to come on board my ship rather than put your cutter at risk?'

'Of course!' said Vauvenart with a shrug.

Little did he care. He was going to Quebec to try to obtain a tax exemption and to visit a lady whom he had it in mind to take to wife. Living as he did in the depths of the forest, he was not well-informed about the matters at issue between the Lord of Gouldsboro and New France, and he did not see why he should not take advantage of the opportunity of a well-found ship being in the neighbourhood in order to make the journey to the capital as comfortably as possible.

'An English vessel, perhaps?'

It was a possibility to be considered, but Peyrac shook his head.

'No, not that either. Apart from our cheeky friend, Phips, who has, I think, had quite enough to cope with for this year and is bound to have returned to Boston without looking for more trouble, I can't imagine any Englishman from New England venturing alone into the French net at a time of the year when he runs the risk of being trapped in the ice and captured. No, for my part, I am inclined to think she's a merchant ship that sailed on the late side from Le Havre or Nantes and was held up by unfavourable winds. It probably took them four months to make the crossing instead of one, that's all there is to it.'

As he spoke, the Count had taken several steps forward. Suddenly he found himself at Angélique's side and she sensed his presence rather than saw him, for it was very dark, but her entire being recognized his, and the fragrance of tobacco and violets that clung to his clothes, and she felt his arm go round her shoulders, drawing her close to him, just as she continued to hold the two children tightly to her.

'What do you intend to do?' asked Carlon.

'I've told you – wait, wait for dawn and for the other ship to come up with us.'

'And what then?'

'Then ... it all depends on his attitude. If he attacks me, we will fight. Otherwise ... in any case, I will speak to him to find out where he comes from, what persons he has aboard, and what booty we may find in his hold.'

'That's pirate's talk!' cried the Intendant, spluttering with indignation.

'I am a pirate, Monsieur,' replied Joffrey de Peyrac

49

dangerously quietly, 'at least that's what people say.'

Angélique could imagine the smile upon his lips in the darkness.

'And I'm a sorcerer too,' he went on, 'a sorcerer who was burned alive on the Place de Grève, in Paris, seventeen years ago.'

There was a deadly hush. Then Ville d'Avray affected to treat the matter as a joke.

'Yet you're still very much alive,' he laughed boisterously.

'Being a sorcerer, I managed to get myself out of the predicament ... But let's be serious, gentlemen. The King of France – a gramercy to him – suspended the sentence. The Count de Peyrac de Morens d'Irristru, Lord of Toulouse, was only burned in effigy, but that doesn't change the fact that he disappeared for good. Today he is making his comeback.'

This time the silence was prolonged. What they had just heard put all thoughts of the reported vessel out of their minds.

'And ... and the King granted you a free pardon?' enquired the Intendant finally.

'Yes and no ... it slipped his mind rather. But that's one more reason why I am now making my way to his fief. I want to remember myself to him. It's high time. I've done a great deal of knocking about the world as a result of that sentence.'

Sailors appeared holding strips of burning tinder at this point and they halted to light lanterns supported on wrought copper brackets, and suddenly the whole scene grew bright, and faces came into view wearing various expressions. Ville d'Avray was gloating. Things were warming up, things were getting interesting. Carlon was white in the face. The hornet's nest he had blundered into was even more unhealthy than he had thought. Peyrac's old companions, Erickson, and d'Urville, showed no surprise, merely puzzlement that he should choose to make such sudden revelations. They could expect anything from their chief, and they were used to his ways. He never acted haphazardly, but always in accordance with a plan worked out in advance and with a specific objective.

The newer men to serve under his command, such as

Barssempuy or Vanneau, were also largely unconcerned. They were all gentlemen adventurers who had followed their various destinies and knew that all of them concealed some dark secret, which was theirs alone, and that it was entirely up to them whether they revealed it or kept it until their deaths.

That evening, the leader of the Gouldsboro fleet had chosen to speak. That was his business.

Angélique was surprised and disconcerted. She had shuddered on hearing her husband come out so forthrightly with such a terrible statement.

At a time when she was conscious of the weight of the King of France's disfavour bearing heavily upon them, however far off he might be in person, here was Joffrey suddenly exclaiming: 'Here I am, Your Majesty! Here is the Lord of Toulouse restored to life, whom you allowed to be condemned in years gone by in an attempt to drag down his proud spirit that was an affront to your own ...'

Was not such a provocation madness?

The Intendant Carlon echoed her thoughts: 'You must be out of your mind! Such an admission! In our presence! The King of France is vested with immense power and you set it at defiance.'

'In what respect? What did I say that His Majesty does not already know? Although I refuse to believe that he could have foreseen that I would go to Quebec this winter, I am quite certain that he is well informed about us from the reports sent to him about my establishment in Maine. The fact is that for the three years since I landed in North America I have not concealed my true name: Count Peyrac de Morens d'Irristru. I have given him time to remember his vassal who was condemned and banished in years gone by and perhaps to take another view of him. Today I also am vested with a certain power. Years have passed. The King is at the height of his glory. He may take a more favourable view of the existing situation.'

'All the same, what audacity!' repeated Carlon.

'I do not think that he would be displeased.'

'You are a gambler.'

'And are you not, Monsieur the Intendant, a trifle hypocritical? Have you not heard these matters referred to? Are not the Quebec authorities already in possession of the facts? They are bound to have been mentioned in the report which must have reached Monsieur de Frontenac. I repeat that since I have been in the New World, I have never attempted to hide either my true name or my titles, and it would have been a simple matter to obtain all particulars concerning me by reference to Paris. I know that Father d'Orgeval saw to it that this was done.'

The Intendant shrugged his shoulders and gave a windy sigh.

'Of course, rumours have been circulating, but, as far as I'm concerned, I admit that I have not needed them. People used to say at one time that ... your wife was the She-Demon of Acadia, which I considered ridiculous. I regarded the tittle-tattle about you, alleging you had been condemned as a sorcerer, as the wild imaginings of the populace. It comes as a jolt to hear such things confirmed out of your own mouth.'

'You have never had occasion to read the report yourself, Monsieur the Intendant?'

'No, Sir! Our governor, Monsieur de Frontenac, kept it secret. I don't even know whether he transmitted it to Monseigneur Laval. In any case, not to the Jesuits.'

'Now that really is splendid!' exclaimed Peyrac happily. 'I expected no less from a man born in the same part of the country as myself, and I regard what you tell me as a good omen for the coming campaign. Gentlemen, there is no need for you to work yourselves up into a frenzy. I am going to Quebec to dispel misunderstandings. I do not know how many years remain to me on this earth, but, however many or few they may be, I want to spend them in the full light of day, in peace with my fellows, and my compatriots, each one working for the good of all and, above all, for the good of the country in which we are trying to establish ourselves. Do we not agree about that, Gentlemen?'

'Indeed, indeed,' said Ville d'Avray, expressing warm approval; 'pirate or sorcerer or both, as far as I'm concerned, only one thing matters, I must admit: you are the richest man in America, and it is obvious that it can only be to our advantage to reach an understanding with you. Is that not so, my dear Intendant? One more little drink to the success of our enterprises, whatever they may be. This wine is excellent. It would be a little sweet to drink with meat, but it goes very well with pastry. It's a Spanish wine, isn't it, my dear Count-Sorcerer?'

'Yes it is. Van Ereck brought me some back from New Mexico. I had suggested that he should try to find me a few barrels of French wine, Burgundy or Claret, but ... the opportunity did not occur. I have only two barrels of French in the hold, brought from Gouldsboro, and I'm keeping them for Monsieur de Frontenac. I know he often gives banquets, and that he complains that he misses French wine. He is a connoisseur.'

'We're all connoisseurs. It's a French failing and being on board your ship is not likely to cure us of it. So let us drink! Come along, Carlon, smile, life is good! ...'

Kouassi-Bâ went the rounds filling the goblets once again.

CHAPTER 7

HONORINE WAS comfortably installed in her bed between her cat and her treasure box. In the spacious, well ventilated 'tween-decks, where the La Rochelle Protestants had travelled on their journey to America, room had been found to give the two children and Marcelline's daughter a little privacy. With good mattresses, cushions and furs they were as well provided for as princes. Curtains that could be pulled up during the day separated them from the quarters in which the King's Girls had been installed under Delphine du Rosoy's custody. The three chaplains who had come aboard at Tidnish – the two attached respectively to Monsieur de Vauvenart and the Chevalier de Grand-Rivière, both being Recollect Fathers, and Monsieur Quentin, who was an Oratorian – were lodged at the other end. Naturally, Adhémar had found a dossing place in the vicinity, which amounts to saying that he had dumped down in a dark corner of the battery the miserable swag that he had been humping around with him ever since he had set out on the Upper Kennebec campaign, via Port Royal and Boston, where he had been held prisoner by the English, until the latter, feeling quite unable to cope with this peculiar specimen of French soldiery, had sent him packing back to regions more congenial to such an extravagant personage.

For the moment he was learning to play Chérubin's reed pipe, while watching Yolande out of the corner of his eye vigorously brushing her hair, of which she had indeed a great deal, that she tucked up during the day under a stout white cloth bonnet.

From the King's Girls, kneeling on the floor, came a pious mumble as they finished saying their rosary. They blessed themselves, got up and began to prepare their rough beds for the night.

Honorine was sorting over her treasures: sea-shells, pebbles, dried flowers, a golden rattle given to her when she was a baby, a ring that Joffrey had given her on the day they set foot on the shore of America, etc.

'I'll show them to people when I'm in Quebec, but only to those who are nice to me,' she said to herself.

It was obvious that Intendant Carlon's pessimistic observations had set her little mind running although she had not appeared to be listening. She was laying her plans.

'I'll till the others.'

Angélique repressed a smile. It was a long time since Honorine had used such extreme language. The voyage to Quebec, the French atmosphere which subtly and bit by bit was coming to predominate, must have brought back memories of her early childhood when she was at La Rochelle and had vaguely sensed the inexplicable dangers surrounding her. In those days, when the feeling came upon her, she would take a stick and set upon the person who was making her feel anxious – 'I'll till you . . .' On one occasion she had wanted to 'till' a man by the name of Baumier, a Catholic official who had come to stir up trouble for the Bernes, who were Protestants, under their own roof. While she was putting her treasures away carefully in their little coffer, Angélique stroked her chubby cheek with her finger, and Honorine shook her head crossly. There were times when displays of affection disturbed her in her occupations.

'I used to have a treasure box too,' Angélique told her.
'Did you?'

Honorine appeared interested. She had put her box down beside her and was slipping under the blankets, getting ready for sleep.

'And what was there in it?'

'I don't remember very clearly any more ... There was ... a pen, yes, a goose quill that had belonged to a poet in Paris who wrote songs, and there was a knife, an Egyptian dagger ...'

'I haven't got a knife,' said Honorine, suddenly opening her eyes again. 'I must have one. Monsieur d'Arreboust promised me one ... Where is your coffer?'

'I don't know any more.'

Honorine's eyelids were falling. She made one more effort and asked 'And ... where is the poet? ...'

Angélique was about to leave the 'tween-decks after having kissed her sleeping daughter and Chérubin too.

Yolande said softly to her; 'Madame, would you like me to serve you in your apartment? I will help you to fasten your dresses. My mother said that I was to serve you in every possible way, and it seems to me that you do not call sufficiently upon my help.'

'You've enough to do with these two little mischiefs.'

'There's nothing to it. I'm used to children and work. I'm just twiddling my thumbs on this boat. Now you wouldn't be fearing, would you, that I don't know how to look after fine ladies' falderals? They're fussy perhaps, that's true, but I'd not be long in getting used to it. I was always a dab one with my hands though I may not look that smart.'

'Whoever said that?' Angélique protested with a laugh.

She was fond of the good-hearted creature, who was powerfully built and rather lubberly, but who was capable of the most whole-hearted and effective devotion, as she had recently proved.

'I know that you are a daughter worthy of Marcelline-la-Belle, isn't that so, Adhémar?'

'Now that's a fact,' the soldier agreed enthusiastically. 'She can do anything, that girl, just like her mother.'

'Not opening shells, I can't,' protested Yolande, blushing

modestly. 'No, that I can't! I still can't open 'em up as quick as her.'

'No one will ever equal her skill.'

'I do miss her, and that's a fact,' confessed Yolande, 'but there's no helping that. She'd never have had any peace of mind if she'd let you set out alone for Quebec, Madame, you and Chérubin, if I hadn't gone with you.'

'She's a wonderful friend.'

Angélique was touched to be linked with Chérubin among big Marcelline's preoccupations.

'I miss her too. But we'll all see one another again at French Bay next spring and be able to feel we've done good work in Canada. Don't worry about my clothes, Yolande. I'd rather you stayed and looked after the children than became a chambermaid.'

'Suppose you were to take one of my girls,' suggested Delphine du Rosoy; 'Henriette, for example. She gives herself airs, but that's just it, it's because she was in service with a great lady and she's very capable in such matters. It was she who always used to help Madame de Maudribourg with her things.'

'Oh, no! No!' exclaimed Angélique, hastily declining the offer.

'Well, what about me?' suggested Delphine shyly. 'I'm accustomed to that kind of duty, and I would make a point, Madame, of serving you to the best of my ability.'

'No! No!' repeated Angélique.

The mere mention of Madame de Maudribourg had been enough to give her the shudders.

'You are both very kind, but for the moment I will manage very well on my own. Later on at Quebec we'll see. Yolande, undo me just a little there down the back, at the top. Afterwards, I'll cope.'

The man who had accompanied her with the lantern was Enrico Enzi, the Maltese. He guided her across the cluttered deck for the darkness was quite dense.

'I used to have a treasure box too,' Angélique recalled once again as she followed him absentmindedly. 'Where did I leave it? Or have I lost it?'

She tried to remember the objects that she had put in it. They were relics of the events that had marked the various stages of her life in the Kingdom of France and especially the time in the Court of Miracles in the slums of Paris. There was the pen of the Starveling Poet, the pamphleteer who had been one of her lovers and who had died on the gallows, and the dagger of Rodogne the Egyptian, a long blade of the type used by hired assassins, with which she had killed the Great Coesre ...

She drew her cloak tight about her. An unexpected drizzle had begun to fall. It was more like a mist, through which the moon cast fitful metallic glimmers.

Angélique caught sight of Joffrey on the poop-deck and her heart swelled within her. He was standing out as a darker shadow against the pewter-grey of the night. Because of the mist, he seemed even bigger and stranger than usual. It was as if he were on the lookout for what might be coming from downstream. Was he worried about the ship that had been reported? Did he foresee a battle in the offing?

'Do you think the ship which is following us means trouble?' she asked Enrico. 'What do the rumours say?'

The Maltese shook his head.

'Nothing at all ... Monsieur thinks that the vessel must be one that was held up by damage and unfavourable currents. There's nothing to do but wait. In any case, she's alone and we are in force.'

He made a sweeping gesture to indicate the other ships invisible in the darkness, but whose presence was revealed by the sound of voices calling to one another and by the glow of riding lights or flashes of lanterns piercing the murk.

'Monseigneur has doubled the watch and advised commanding officers to remain on the alert throughout the night and not to hand over till dawn. Some men have also gone ashore and are watching the bank.'

After negotiating the two staircases leading to the third bridge, Enrico and Angélique stopped at the carved, panelled door of the great cabin.

Two carved ebony statues representing Moors with white agate eyes, and supporting gilded wrought-iron candelabra, flanked the door. The area was brightly lighted by the two lamps of thick opaque Venetian glass, behind which the flames of several wax candles licked upwards, sheltered from the wind. The candles were capable of burning for a long time and gave a very bright light.

'Madame the Countess can rest without fear,' added Enrico with a bow. 'It's not the first time that we've been put on the alert on account of a suspicious vessel. We're quite acustomed on shipboard to keeping watch and looking after ourselves.'

Angélique thanked him with a smile.

'It must be a pleasure for you to be at sea again, I should imagine, Enrico. You prefer that to living in a hole in the ground in the forest at Wapassou.'

The Maltese replied promptly with typical Mediterranean gallantry:

'Wherever I am, I am happy if I can find myself in the company of Monseigneur Rescator and yourself, Madame the Countess.'

'You're too clever at turning compliments, Enrico. You are going to cause us a lot of bother at Quebec with the local girls ...'

Enrico Enzi gave a merry laugh and went off with his lantern very happily.

Angélique was about to enter her apartment when she felt herself observed, and looking up instinctively, could just make out Joffrey leaning over the balustrade of the poop-deck. As it passed between two clouds, the moon made a sort of halo around him, but she could not distinguish his features.

'I heard you laughing, Madame; with whom were you talking so gallantly?'

'Enrico, your Maltese; he was reassuring me.'

'And why did you need to be reassured, little lady?'

'That ship ...'

'It's a vessel in distress. It will not concern itself with us. It's as much as it can do to keep afloat.'

He added after a silence.

'On the contrary, when the time comes I will concern myself with it.'

She gave no answer but stood looking up towards him, her hand holding together her cloak against the cold. He had frightened her that evening when he had openly stated: 'I am a sorcerer and was at one time burned in the Place de Grève.'

She would have preferred that all that should remain hidden. She feared the light falling on that obscure part of their life and the time when, hounded by all, she had taken refuge in the Paris underworld, having no choice but to depend for survival upon the protection of the bandits of the Court of Miracles. He had disappeared, banished, presumed dead and loaded with ignominy. When she thought back to that time, memories came flooding back vividly. The air of the St Lawrence river became heavy with the smell of the executioner's pyre, a reminder that the distant King who had condemned Count Peyrac had also set his seal on these wild regions. They were going to encounter his supreme might and Joffrey had that evening revealed that he had made up his mind after so many years to confront him face to face. Would not the forthcoming struggle be decisive?

The man's beloved voice came to her again a trifle muffled but rich in affectionate overtones and as gentle as a caress.

'You'll catch cold, darling. Do go in quickly and get warm. I'll be with you shortly.'

In the poop stateroom of the *Gouldsboro*, a brazier on a solidly-made wrought-iron tripod gave out a cosy warmth. At the far end an alcove whose brocade curtains had been raised displayed the luxuriously soft bed with its lace sheets turned down over silks and furs.

The room was comfortable and equipped with all sorts of beautiful objects. The large poop windows admitted a diffuse glow from the riding-lights outside. The soft brightness sparkled upon the bronze and gold of the furniture and the costly bindings of the books that stood in rows in a rose-wood case.

Whenever Angélique took refuge here she invariably felt a sensation of well-being and security.

She threw her cloak over the back of a chair, went into the alcove and began to undress. But almost immediately she despaired of her task. Good-hearted Yolande and Delphine were right. In order to cope with her new, luxurious attire she would either have to have chambermaids to help her to get it off or be as supple as a snake to reach the innumerable hooks and catches and as patient as an ant to pull out the incredible number of pins without forgetting a single one. Tired as she was this evening she jibbed at the undertaking. She sat down on the edge of the bed and slipped her garters down her Lyons silk stockings. She knew why she was reluctant to ask the assistance of the helpful young ladies. Nonetheless she would have to resign herself to it. Did one ever see a great lady tending to her own toilet without the assistance of at least one servant? In the Gay-Savoir days she had had Margot and later, when she had become Madame du Plessis-Bellières and was attending the King's Court, she had had, in addition to Javotte – who had married David Chaillou, the chocolate-maker – a whole host of maids who wasted a lot of her time with their chattering and their foolishness, but whose presence was absolutely indispensable if she wanted to be decked out adequately to dazzle her rivals beneath the chandeliers of Versailles. At Quebec it would not be possible to do otherwise. She would have to keep up her rank. What a pity she had not been able to bring Elvire or Madame Jonas! With them she had never felt in any danger of indiscretions. But they belonged to the Reformed Religion, and for them too – regarded as gallows birds, criminals fit only for the galleys, dear good souls! – the air of New France was too unhealthy.

Angélique wriggled and succeeded in bursting open a few hooks and eyes down her back. She then set about pulling all the pins out of her bodice sewn over with pearls, pulled down her stays of satin-covered ivory and succeeded in freeing her bust and arms. With a sigh she gave way to the customary reaction of all society women once freed of their encumbrances and massaged herself to enjoy the sensation of relief. She would have to get used to wearing corsets again. That would not be much of a bother. She would have been quite glad to enjoy wearing complicated clothes again were it not for the complication of being unable to dispense with outside assistance. Earlier that evening Joffrey had helped her to get dressed. But she could not call upon his assistance constantly though he went about his task very capably. She would have to find someone, and that would involve facing up to one more ordeal: the fear of openly exposing what could not be wiped away. She slid her hand over her naked, smooth warm shoulder, and felt with her finger a little lower down on the shoulder blade the mark of shame, the fleur-de-lys that the King's executioner had in years gone by branded upon it with a red-hot iron.

The brand was still there. What a pity! She would never again be able to wear very low-cut dresses like those she had appeared in at Versailles, exposing her shoulders and her back as far as the shadowy hollow that gave a hint of what lay below in the curve of her hips and the wide sweep of her ample skirts. And how the King had gazed after her! ...

In thus returning to the old life that she had thought gone for ever, the difficulties were becoming apparent one after the other. Had Joffrey taken full stock of all that the journey to Quebec involved and realized that it was tantamount to a return to France, their forbidden homeland?

CHAPTER 8

At the end of it all lay Quebec.

Quebec, pinned to the heart of the American continent like a hidden, dazzling pearl.

During its brief history, Quebec had been several times conquered, lost and regained. And for whom? And for what?

Quebec had no meaning.

There it was, buried in the darkness of the American forestlands, and for more than seven months of the year cut off by ice from the rest of the world.

At this point of her musings, Angélique suddenly realized that she would not give up going to Quebec for anything in the world.

Come what may, they would cope with everything, whether cannonballs or the hostility of the populace, but they would land at Quebec and she would spend the winter there. She felt an overwhelming desire to do so. 'That, only that,' she implored in a whisper, making a childlike prayer. To spend the winter in a real French town, that was warm and full of life. She would go to the ball, or to processions.

She would have neighbours and friends whom she would invite in to take coffee and chocolate and, naturally, there would be evenings by the stove with Ville d'Avray – that was a long-standing engagement. She would send Honorine to the nuns to learn to read. She herself would find time to peruse the new books which had come from France. For years now she had been out of touch with what witty and intelligent society people talk about. She would go and buy pretty trifles in well-stocked stalls or shops with a fashionable clientele. There would be skating parties on the frozen St Lawrence, Christmas celebrations in the cathedral with a long sermon by the Bishop, the Twelfth Night banquet at the Governor's, and Carnaval with the most delightfully scandalous carryings-on under cover of masks and fancy dress. Ville d'Avray had promised to keep her informed of all the current amorous intrigues.

Quite carried away by these visions, Angélique came close at times to saying goodbye to Wapassou in her own mind. She had had enough of the wilderness, of fear and of death lurking behind trees.

A year before, Joffrey had said to her as he clasped her to him in the port at Katarunk, which had fallen into the hands of the Canadians: 'If we ever come through our perils alive, I guarantee that we will be stronger one day than the lot of them . . .'

And it had so come about. They had survived, and they were stronger than the lot of them. Barely a year had passed and they had an abundance of gold and silver, numerous trading posts established along the rivers, mines in the heart of the mountains, busy ports open to the wealth of the Atlantic, alliances with the leading Indian tribes, and just recently Joffrey de Peyrac had extended his influence to the east coast of Acadia by acquiring the entire territory that had belonged to old Nicolas Parys with its fisheries and its shingle beaches rich with the 'green gold' of cod.

But she could not help shuddering when she thought back to all they had been through. What he had said had come true. They had survived. But they ought by rights to have died on a hundred occasions – at the hands of the Canadians, of the Iroquois and in the harshness of the ensuing winter. The Katarunk fort had been burnt down leaving them without resources in a remote and desolate region.

There had been sickness, the earth sickness[1] famine, and, if Outakké's Iroquois had not appeared miraculously towards the end of the winter period, bringing beans from their remote province of the Five Nations, they would have starved. There were only provisions for two days at Fort Wapassou by that time.

The giddy sensation of hunger came back to her as she thought of those days, together with the memory of Honorine huddled drowsily against her, pallid and frail, her gums swollen, when the death that had overtaken so many other pioneers in the pitiless wastes of the New World was advancing upon them.

No, she would never be able to go through that again, at least without having had a taste of an easier life.

She told herself that she no longer had the strength to cope with the lot of a pauper living among the poor, as she had experienced it in the Upper Kennebec.

She could no longer bear to spoil her hands lighting fires, to break her nails hanging pots on the hook over the open fire, and her back carrying bundles of wood to feed, tend and keep a few frail though precious beings alive in the depths of the hostile woodlands.

She needed to live and dance, to be reborn, to be her old self once more, Angélique, Grand Lady of France, Countess Peyrac, favourite of the King, and to assert her title as the Lady of the Silver Lake, her new legendary role.

Above all she must grapple with the lurking shadows from the past, which swirled around her like phantoms, like trailing mists that parted to reveal forgotten faces ... 'Angélique! ... Angélique! ... Where are you? What has become of you ... you whom we have never been able to forget? ...' And there were other vague shadows, upon which it was difficult to put names, that she would have to detect with unerring hand, people who had drawn together to give vent to the turbulent emotions and passions that are aroused by what is strange, by beauty, by what is different, by what is not understood. Quebec seemed to have been singled out as their place of abode, which explained her conflicting

[1] See *The Countess Angélique*.

emotions about the town, sometimes feeling drawn to it and looking forward to the festivities and pleasures in prospect, at others thinking it wiser to abandon the journey because of the risks involved, both those which she clearly perceived and those she vaguely guessed at. But did she still have a choice? Destiny was driving her and her companions ever on and closing the jaws of a vast land behind them.

Since Gaspé they had been advancing upon the town along the river as wide as the sea which led towards it. They had tacked back and forth, beating up the wind, borne on by swirling ocean waves, while fog shrouded the horizon. But, however far off the shores might be, and hidden from their gaze, it was impossible not to wonder whether the St Lawrence Estuary, upon which the five vessels of Count Peyrac's fleet had entered with all sails spread, might not in fact be a trap laid to ensnare them.

The far northern autumn was like a cruel-hearted jailor, marshalling his ice, his snows and his storms to prevent them from turning back. They had to keep on sailing up the river, deep into the silence of a mysterious region, into a wilderness of water and remote wooded heights rising in dark festoons against the clouds. Then, finally, when they felt themselves lost in the midst of unexplored regions in the heart of the dark, untamed endless mass, they would come upon a *town* ... a town of white stones and silver-shingled roofs, a town loud with the peal of bells, bustling, aggressive, sovereign – French Quebec.

It was a surprise jewel, a miracle without a reason, a kind of island, a little Paris, a corner of Versailles, talkative, intolerant, elegant, pious, cock-sure, devoted to prayer and the arts, to luxury and war, to mysticism, adultery, repentance, political intrigue and dashing adventure. It was an island in the ocean, an oasis in the desert, a flower of civilization in the heart of primitive barbarism, a refuge and succour against the untamed, treacherous elements that seemed bent upon working the death of man: cold, starvation, hostile savages.

It was indeed as Father de Vernon, to whom she had made confession in the summer, had said: 'Go to Quebec. That's the penance I'm giving you. Go to Quebec! Have the courage to confront the town without fear or shame. After all, perhaps some good will come of it for the land of America.'

Now he was dead, murdered. In memory of him, she felt more than ever compelled to carry out the penance that he had imposed upon her. Go to Quebec!

And what did the fleur-de-lys branded upon her shoulder matter? 'Life was good ...'

That winter she would go to the ball, would play cards and would enjoy midnight suppers and, when the sun was bright, she would go for walks with Honorine on the ramparts and gaze out at the wild Laurentide mountains in the distance.

—CHAPTER 9

ON COMING in he sensed that she was asleep. There were traces of her now familiar feminine scent in the half darkness. Seeing her garments strewn here and there he smiled. What had become of the puritanical, stand-offish little Huguenot woman from La Rochelle, dressed as a servant, whom the Rescator, sailing to America, had brought to his luxurious cabin that long-ago day to attempt to tame her? What, indeed, had become of the woman pioneer who throughout that long, terrible winter in the Upper Kennebec had remained at his side, assisting him with never-failing courage? He picked up a scrap of lace, a bodice whose silk still retained the shape of her full curves. After being a nameless servant, then the helpmate of an explorer of the New World, here at last was his Angélique turning into Madame de Peyrac, Countess of Toulouse, once again.

'May God so will it!' he murmured to himself, casting an ardent glance in the direction of the alcove where the sheen of her hair was faintly visible.

She was asleep. He walked across to the mahogany bureau and picked up a venetian-glass night-lamp, which he lighted. Then, treading softly, he drew near her. Standing at the bedside he gazed down at her.

She was sleeping deeply and peacefully as she usually did when she had undergone violent emotion or been through an ordeal which had drawn for a time upon her entire strength. He had noticed that that was how it was with her. Usually she was a light sleeper as women are whose hearts remain on the alert and whom a trifle disturbs and makes start up or turn over, ready to respond to a child's cry or a suspicious noise.

But when the hardest part was over, and she could feel that everything was well, that her loved ones were out of danger and no longer needed her for the time being, she would curl up in a corner and go to sleep as if she were sinking into a swoon. He had often studied her in this strange repose of hers that was made deeply seductive by the gracefulness of her yielding feminine figure and the beauty of her face enclosing an inner world of absence. Where was she at this moment? Buried deep down, more inaccessible than ever. She wandered alone on shores that were hers alone ... She had disappeared, withdrawn into the inviolable sanctuary of the soul that every person carries within them, to which, Joffrey told himself, he would never be able to find access.

At such moments, the love he felt for her was akin to pain.

Once again, during the summer, he had almost lost her, and once again he had rediscovered her as a changed person.

He would never forget the moment when he had seen her racing along the beach, laughing and crying, her arms outstretched. He would never forget the expression on her face when she had thrown herself against him, clasping him wildly to her, stammering out inarticulate words of love that had faded from her memory. From such depths of the heart did they come, where she had held them hidden, buried, for long years! She had cried them aloud at that moment, ready to die if necessary, but not away from him ... Not away from him! And he had understood in a flash what he meant to her and with what love she loved him, with what love she had always loved him, in spite of fifteen years' separation. That outburst of feeling on her part had filled the void that had tormented him when he had imagined her indifferent to his memory.

And after that? How could one convey the impression of a

convalescence and a renewal? Now that the squalid business of the She-Demon had been settled, that the region had been pacified and preparations made for their departure, they were together again, just the two of them alone. He was intrigued by her, sensing the presence of a new being behind her calm smiles, her sensible words. She had still been holding herself back.

But once they had left those accursed shores, once they had set sail for Quebec, the exhilaration of victory had transformed her. She bubbled over with gaiety, delighting everyone around her. With their French shipboard companions she was all witticisms, amusing anecdotes and peals of laughter. Far from giving the impression of sailing on a warlike mission, Peyrac's fleet seemed as if it had set out on some romantic embassy to seal abiding alliances by some princely match-making. It was she who set the tone, to the point where even the crew had begun to show greater joviality and good humour. She could twist them round her little finger ...

Cut off from the land, they sailed on, free, sure of themselves. The sky and the sea were pearly and the islands in the gulf glistened like so many jewels.

Angélique was full of laughter, amused by everything that Ville d'Avray said, every slightest incident, and she busied herself with a myriad plans. It was as if she had forgotten the rest of her life.

Meanwhile he was busy discovering the woman she had been at the French Court, the fashionable, intrepid Angélique, the one who had belonged to 'the others'.

'She will do wonders in Quebec ...'

He felt an irresistible impulse to delve into her past, to discover more about the hidden life of this woman, her true nature, all the things he had up till then brushed violently aside, as if unwilling ever to know the full extent to which she had been false to him.

But by now his bitterness had lost some of its virulence and the painful imagined scenes some of their hold over him. A barrier had fallen and that, so it seemed, was the doing of the She-Demon. From now on what mattered to him was the fact that she was there, alive, that she loved him passionately, and that he could go to her whenever he wanted to and take her in his arms.

The rest mattered little. Indeed, there were moments when he felt he wanted to share some of the secrets of her life with her in order to draw closer to her.

'My wife!'

Joffrey de Peyrac lowered the lamp a little to examine the bright band that circled one of the fingers of her trailing hand.

He knelt down and kissed her fingers one by one.

How sound asleep she was! He almost became alarmed. On such occasions he felt himself overcome by unreasoning dread.

He put the night-light down on a small table beside the bed and drew still closer to her, scanning her impassive face for some sign of life, some breath upon her lips. Then he told himself not to be a fool. He who had so often gazed upon the hideous, frozen face of death, or its premonitory signs, what did he think he was doing anxiously searching for such signs on that lovely, radiant, sleeping face? She was resting, recruiting her strength.

'Who sustained her when I was not there?' he asked himself. 'What men were they?'

He saw in his mind's eye those softly-glowing lips touched by the lips of strangers, seeking sensual delight in them while at the same time communicating to this responsive woman the strength of the passion that intoxicates and restores. And far from being distressed at the thought, he accepted the fact that, fortunately, there had been men to bring succour to her, to take in their arms at those critical moments, to save her from despair. She was so fragile at times. And yet she had broken formidable adversaries: Moulay-Ismaël, Louis XIV ...

What weapon had she used to smite to the heart of the cruel Sultan and the intolerant monarch?

He realized that he no longer felt jealous – or scarcely so. He longed to know the secrets of her heart, as he did those of her body.

Since he had slipped that ring on her finger, it seemed to him that he had asserted his rights over those invisible, nameless rivals from the past, and he had ceased to hate them.

Was this not all very childish? Was it not better to admit that the ordeal they had been through had, by excising all their wounds and sweeping away all their doubts, purified their hearts?

What was this unknown past of Angélique, images from which no doubt stirred again behind those closed eyelids? He did not know everything. Scraps of the story came back to him. But since the Colin Paturel affair she had been reticent whenever he had tried to steer the conversation into confiding channels.

It was his fault too, for he had behaved appalling harshly towards her. His anger, which had been a cloak for the terrible pain he felt at the injustices of life, had been yet another blow struck against her.

'My little darling!'

He bent down passionately over her sleeping form and, yielding to an irresistible impulse, laid his mouth upon her half-opened lips.

He reproached himself for disturbing her slumbers but his impatience to see her open her eyes and recognize him, to catch the glint of delight as she saw him standing there, proved stronger than his scruples.

'What will be the first word she utters? What will she say?'

Angélique stirred and he murmured:

'Sleep! Sleep! my love.'

But she opened her eyes and, seeing him so close to her, a bright happy light came into those emerald orbs, still clouded with sleep.

'You were smiling in your sleep; what were you dreaming about?'

'I was on the beach, in your arms.'

'What beach?' he asked with a touch of irony. 'We've known so many beaches ...'

She laughed, threw her arms round his neck, and pressed her face up against his, seeking the contact of his cheek against her warm smooth cheek.

'I wonder ...,' he said.

'What?'

'On which shore you were most beautiful, most moving, most glamorous? I don't know ... I see you everywhere, in the wind and the sun, in the blasts of the gales at La Rochelle, or running towards me the other day ... I can't make up my mind on which beach you were most beautiful.'

'What does it matter? I wasn't concerned about that when I ran towards you.'

She had raced, flown ... She had no longer felt the ground beneath her feet, possessed by the wild desire to reach him, to press his living form to her ... even if he were to thrust her away.

But he had not thrust her away. He had opened his arms and hugged her to him with all his might.

That moment at Tidnish amid the noise and tumult of battle continued to be a light between them that had changed many things. It was a miracle, a gift from Heaven, blessing their constancy among the hazards that had been strewn in their path to lay them low. The evil spirits must not be alerted. Through their eyes, through the rituals of love they were communicating to one another that unspeakable, novel feeling.

She had become conscious of his kindness: a forthright, genuine, practical kindness unimpaired by any hint of weakness. His only weakness was to love her too much. He had told her so. She blamed herself for having allowed herself to be overawed during their first year together again by his handsome looks, his cutting sharpness of speech, his strength, his domination over others and his onward moving destiny that nothing seemed capable of holding back.

In actual truth he was not a man whom it was easy to know intuitively, for, while he wished to be understood, he did not much mind if he was misunderstood.

His strength derived partly from the fact that few persons and few things were capable of making him suffer.

A strange man that one could have hated for not being cast in the common mould! He had seen his works, his palaces and his wealth vanish, but it had not proved possible to strike at him by such means, for he derived his joys and his sorrows from less obvious values.

'What are you thinking about?'
'About you.'
Bending over her, he was smoothing her golden eyebrows

with one finger as if delighting in softly tracing over their gentle curve. He kissed her fingertips and drew the lace sheets up over her bare shoulders. But she pushed them back, sat up, raised her arms and pulled her lawn nightdress deftly off over her head.

'Kiss me! Kiss me!'

'Foolish girl!' he laughed. 'It's cold!'

'Warm me up!'

Her naked arms encircled his neck and drew him to her. She was seeking refuge in him with all her might, with all her weakness. 'Oh, you!' she thought rapturously, 'a man who loves me!'

He saw coming and going on her lovely face the dazzle of the fleeting smile that betokens ecstacy and the sudden desperate, almost painful expression that often accompanies love's strongest thrills.

'A man who loves me and wants me there. A man who needs the warmth of my body just as I need his heat. He frightens and reassures me. He eludes me, and yet I know that he will always be there for me, that he can't run away any more. What bliss!'

She held his rough head passionately against her breast and laughed a little wildly, and he embraced her, impatient to respond to the womanly desire that burned in her, to satisfy the hunger for loving that she dared avow to him without shame. Ever since Acadia, she had stopped being frightened to reveal herself as a voluptuous and coquettish woman. 'Was she like this in the arms of her lovers?' he wondered.

No doubt ... Perhaps ... He imagined Madame du Plessis-Bellière, the queen of Versailles ... and who else, in the arms of what other men had she laughed thus, unfeignedly and without restraint? Colin's? The King's? At such moments he had to admit to himself that he knew nothing about her, or very little. With which of them had she ventured to do such daring, such clever things, with which of them had she studied the subtle art that is learned only from a number of masters, each contributing his particular tastes and fantasies? What men had taken this intoxicating Venus in their arms, had thus laid their heads upon her breast, had set their seal upon her? But she had set

71

her seal upon them even more ...

That was his revenge.

That and making her forget them in the fever of pleasure. To him she was ever new. By some enchantment what they ventured upon together had the exciting savour of initiation.

She was propped up on her pillows, naked and beautiful, her hair spread around her like a veil. With one hand he drew it aside and exposed her snowy shoulders the better to caress them and her breasts upon which he delighted to set his greedy lips. They glided down her marble goddess-like body, pale and tinged with gold, with shadowy hollows full of sweetness.

She was moaning, distraught, unrecognizable in her abandon, yielding up to his kisses her throbbing, desirable femininity in an unreserved surrender in which he saw that she no longer feared him and welcomed him to these sports of love as an equal partner.

Today he had become less her master than the lover that pleases, seduces and to whom nothing more is owed than the pleasure of a single night, generously given and fairly shared, and that feeling gave their relations a hint of the illicit and the licentious.

He was delighted by her frenzy and surrender, and they came down to earth again, exhausted and delighted, in a mood of friendly complicity that had the enormous advantage of thrusting into the background all cares other than that of enjoying pleasure to satiety and then savouring in one another's arms the sense of well-being in weariness and of coming down to earth again to the accompaniment of simple whispered words.

'Was it good?'

'It was marvellous!'

'You're not afraid of me any more?'

'Oh, yes I am!'

'That must be why you are trying to beguile me away from myself and captivate me by your witchcraft.'

She laughed and he told her once again, smothering her with passionate kisses, that he was wild about her, that he had been made very happy by her, that no woman had ever given him so much pleasure as she, and he teased her, telling her that he understood why all the men were jealous of him and, wanted to kill him, for he possessed in her a treasure without its like.

Between them everything seemed free, shining and delightful.

'Oh! if only we could always stay on a ship, sailing along, the sea before us ...' sighed Angélique.

'Never fear, good things await us on land too.'

'I don't know, I have dreams ... but it's as if the further we go the further the dream moves out of my reach and becomes inaccessible. Everything that separates me from it arises, I discover, from facts that I had forgotten, people as they are. I know them too well.'

'But you do not know yourself well. You will only have to appear ...'

He pressed the point: 'You see yourself in the past, but you are unaware of your present strength.'

'I have no strength but in you,' she said cuddling up to him.

It was pleasurable to exaggerate her dependence so as to be cherished the more. He was not taken in by her wiles, but he kissed her.

'We'll talk about it again. I've seen you with the pistol in your hand. For the moment we're still a long way from Quebec and are free upon the river. We'll put in at Tadoussac and rest from our travels. I bet we meet up there with friends, or friends to be, with whom we'll begin to form alliances. I have high hopes of Tadoussac.'

'Unless we're received with muskets and mortars ...'

'No, it's only a trading post, a farm and a chapel, a pocket-sized town inhabited by colonists and Indians, who trade, pray, make a living out of their flocks, or by watering ships and who have little opportunity to enjoy themselves. We'll give them the chance. Banquets and dances on the riverside, what do you say to that?'

'Looked at in that light, the conquest of New France sounds quite delightful.'

They fell silent. The ship rocked them. Outside the fog carried the echo of various noises, voices or calls, scattered throughout the darkness, revealing the presence of the men on watch. But still everything was peaceful.

Angélique had closed her eyes.

Did she fall asleep? She saw herself rushing through the flames of an executioner's pyre to reach him, over in France, a tall silhouette bound to the stake, black against the gold of the flames whose roaring and heat kept her from him – the sorcerer, the man accursed who was burned in the Place de Grève.

The vision lasted only a second and she woke up, thinking she had uttered a cry.

He was sleeping at her side, miraculously present, strong and serene.

Without waking him, she laid her hand on his smooth, warm wrist and felt the life throbbing under her fingers.

The dream she had just had was superimposed on the sensations she had felt when she had leapt over the Basques' fire on Monegan Island on Midsummer's Night.

The iron hand of the harpooner Hernani d'Astiguerras had made her bound, indeed fly, through the flames and land safely on the far side of the blaze.

'You are spared now, Madame,' the Great Basque had told her. 'The Devil will have no power against you for the coming year.'

He had stooped down and planted a smacking kiss on her lips.

CHAPTER 10

THE SHIP that was following them came into view towards the middle of the following day. It emerged from a greenish mist that hung over the river, damping down the brilliant colours of the forestlands and blurring the pale line of the horizon.

Peyrac's fleet, drawn up in a half circle from one point to the other of the vast St Lawrence barred the newcomer's way. As the Count had foreseen, she turned out to be a belated vessel that was limping painfully towards her destination, having barely survived the many hazards of the crossing. She was listing to starboard and lay so low in the water beyond her floating line that at times the swell hid everything but her masts and their tattered sails. When higher waves struck her, she could not be seen at all and looked as if she had been overwhelmed by the waters.

She followed at a distance like a frightened animal, wounded unto death, and compelled to prowl around, being unable either to turn back or to risk being caught up in the meshes of a net that she sensed had been prepared for her by this strange fleet.

When she came in sight of the vessels that appeared to be waiting for her, she could be seen tacking pathetically in order to slow up as far as possible her pitiful approach.

Honorine put into words the peculiar feeling that moved the hearts of all the company.

'Poor, poor, ship!' she grieved, overcome with pity; 'poor boat! How can we get her to understand that we don't mean her any harm?'

She was standing on the bridge beside Joffrey de Peyrac, who, after lifting her up to his level by perching her on a gun carriage, passed his spy-glass to her from time to time.

'Are you going to sink her with all hands?' she asked eagerly.

Sometimes when she felt she was dealing with him as an equal, she adopted a familiar tone in talking to him.

'No, my little lady! She's too wretched a ship.'

Angélique was watching them both from a distance, her husband and her daughter. She was standing on the first bridge on which a number of people had assembled. She could not hear the words passing between Joffrey de Peyrac and Honorine, but, looking at them, she was amused to see how well they were getting on with one another. Joffrey de Peyrac's affection gave unexpected distinction to the red-headed mite that Quebec was waiting for too. Destiny had linked the lot of this little creature apparently condemned to obscurity and unhappiness to that of an extraordinary man, wearing the halo of a brilliant yet sombre legend. And that suited young Honorine de Peyrac down to the ground. She did not doubt that from now on she held in her hands the fate of Canada and the proud City. And that was as it should be! A moment later Joffrey and Honorine disappeared from

75

Angélique's view and she saw them a little later coming down the companion-way from the poop-deck, Joffrey giving his hand to the child. As he often did when at his post of command, he had put on his black leather mask, which made his figure appear even more impressive and emphasized the fragility of the little figure walking at his side in its full skirt.

She heard Peyrac say to Honorine: 'We shall sail on to Tadoussac and leave her to go on her way.'

'And at Tadoussac?'

'Then we'll go aboard and enquire whether there are any dangerous people travelling on her. After that we'll inspect her hold.'

'You are a pirate, Sir!' exclaimed Honorine, mimicking the intonation of Intendant Carlon.

Angélique could not help bursting out laughing. She thought that nothing would prevail against the love which united them. The night hours she had spent in Joffrey's arms had left a sensation of gladness in her heart.

Her heart was uplifted at the sight of these people so dear to her. She saw behind them their rich and dazzling lives, like a bright gorgeously coloured halo full of promise of the destiny that was to be theirs.

The dying vessel limping along in their wake seemed to symbolize the last throes of an adversary who, having failed to get the better of them, would soon sue for mercy. Was that why Joffrey was so calm about setting out upon the journey to New France under his true titles as Count of Toulouse? Was he hoping to obtain the ultimate pardon of the King of France?

In spite of appearances, she was beginning to understand that Joffrey's strength was greater at present than in the past, *because he was free.* No system of vassalage held him in its sway as it had done in days gone by when, in spite of his power as Lord of Aquitaine, he had still been a subject to be reduced to submission or to be fought. What would the King of France have to lose now by doing him justice? In what way could that distant rival cause him anxiety from now on?

Nevertheless, on the following day, the wind changed, though not the weather, for it remained drizzly although relatively mild, but Angélique's spirits relapsed into anxious-ness again as a result of something the soldier Adhémar said.

Once again they were all foregathered on the bridge. The Commanders of the vessels had come to confer earlier than usual in order to discuss the strange ship that seemed able to continue its route only with great difficulty. Should they go to its assistance? Kouassi-Bâ and the major-domo, assisted by some young helpers, passed around refreshments, but everyone's attention was concentrated upon the distant manoeuvres of the vessel in distress. They had established that it was a merchant ship from Le Havre or Honfleur and that it must belong to the Hundred Partners' Company.

Seeing the suspicious vessels that had encircled her the day before (and that she supposed to be possibly Englishmen or pirates) sailing away, the ship had resumed her laborious progress. The question was whether she would be able to hang on as far as Tadoussac. It was not clear why she had reached Canada so late in the season. Presumably she had put into port on the Gulf of St Lawrence at Shediac or even at Tidnish. But why then had she not remained there.

Spy-glasses were being passed from hand to hand, when there came the sound of Adhémar's tearful voice:

'I wonder whether by any chance that blasted ship picked up the Duchess.'

'What Duchess?' exclaimed the bystanders, turning in his direction like one man.

He refused to reply and made the sign of the cross several times, but they had all understood and, as he was something of a simpleton like the village idiots that have premonitions and dreams, dread chilled their hearts.

'What are you saying? Are you mad?' cried Angélique. 'The Duchess? But she is dead! A hundred times dead! She is dead and buried!'

'Does one ever know with such creatures?' muttered Adhémar, blessing himself more vigorously than ever.

With touching unanimity the eyes of the company looked for Count Peyrac to seek reassurance, but he had gone off, so they fell back upon Ville d'Avray.

'My friends, let us be of good heart,' urged the Marquis. 'We are still feeling the effects of events that were a terrible shock to us. But we must forget, *forget everything*. Do you hear me? We must arrive at Quebec having banished all

77

recollection of what happened on the Gulf of St Lawrence. Yes, even you, Carlon! You must forget. We have no choice, for that's the only way we can get out of the situation in which we became embroiled.'

He spoke emphatically and with a solemnity unusual in him, proving that he himself was fully aware of what lay behind the dramatic occurrences in which they had been involved – possible complications with the tribunal of the Inquisition.

'Even in the case of legitimate self-defence against ... Satan,' he went on, lowering his voice and glancing about him, 'we all know that it's an extremely delicate matter to find oneself involved with that sort of tribunal. As I say, Carlon, silence and forgetfulness, that's the best way not to get into hot water when one has to deal with over-inquisitive people.'

'And what if "she" came back?' repeated Adhémar, blessing himself.

' "She" will not come back,' said Ville d'Avray, cutting him short. 'And if you venture to make any further remarks of that kind, I shall break my cane across your back,' he added, suiting his gesture to his words. 'And I shall have you clapped in irons as soon as we get to Quebec or even hanged for desertion.'

Adhémar fled, panic-stricken.

'Monsieur de Peyrac has settled the matter in the best way possible; let's have no more talk of it,' went on the Marquis, who, beneath his free-and-easy ways, was not averse to reminding people that he was Governor of Acadia, and consequently responsible for the cure of souls. 'I should like to add that we are all arriving in Canada sound in body and mind, which, after what we've been through, is a miracle in itself, for which we should thank God.

'And, if fear of a demon spirit comes back to torment us, let us not forget that we are now in a largely Christian land thanks to the tireless labours of our missionaries, who have sanctified these pagan realms for more than fifty years with their sweat and toil and the blood of their martyrs. Canada is not Acadia, not by a long chalk, where I admit, there still are too many unbelievers living.' He cast a sidelong glance at the Defour brothers. 'But, having said that, I have always seen to it that the struggle against satanic forces should be actively pursued. It's all over now. Let us be of good cheer. Here we are safe. Furthermore, we have on our ships pious men of the Church who dispense to us the support of their ministry. We heard Mass this morning, said by Father Quentin ... Hell shall not prevail against us ...'

'Amen!' sneered Carlon. 'You should be in the pulpit.'

'You can laugh as much as you like, I've had to cope with much tougher opposition than you! ... Eighty legions of demons, at the least,' cried Ville d'Avray, brandishing his silver-topped cane. 'I know what I'm talking about! I fought side by side with Madame de Peyrac against incredible on-slaughts. You didn't come in until the end, and yet you were a pretty sorry spectacle on the beach at Tidnish when that possessed creature gave her dreadful shriek. I saw you go ashen in the face! Come, take my advice. Between our-selves, I tell you, *everything* must stay between ourselves! That's the only way we can avoid being investigated ... The wall of silence. Come on everybody, forget and smile! Life is good!'

He drew Angélique aside, putting one arm around her waist.

'Don't be alarmed.'

'But I ...'

'I know you ... I can hear your heart beating ... Ah! vulnerable Sagittarius that you are!'

He brushed his finger against her cheek.

'People do not generally recognize the deep sensitivity of this sign of Fire, which throughout life is destined to be the object of the hatred its gifts and uprightness arouse, but also to be the object of the love inspired by the flame, at once carnal and supra-terrestrial, that animates it. Because it is always bounding with life and sends its arrow flying straight into the clouds, it is thought to be indomitable and without weakness, but the fact is that it suffers because it belongs at once to the earth and the sky.'

'You're talking about my horoscope, aren't you?' asked Angélique, intrigued.

'Yes! Sagittarius.'

Ville d'Avray looked up towards the night sky as if he had seen the mythical centaur galloping across it towards the shy stars veiled in cotton-wool clouds.

'He is the messenger from this material world to the world beyond. That is why you, Angélique, have been more than other people, the victim of a demon-creature, for, to some extent' – he stooped to whisper in her ear – 'you were of the *same species* as her, don't you see? You could see through her, you could follow her fantasies ... But you also were capable of overcoming her because you belong to the terrestrial universe and cannot be duped. The Centaur has his feet firmly planted on the ground. He is not easily frightened. Don't worry any more about what has been and what will be ...'

'I feel quite ill,' said Angélique, laying a hand on her bodice. 'It's enough for me to recall that dreadful shriek she gave to feel sick. I must say, that time I really was frightened. I'm mildly superstitious ... I was telling lies when I said that she didn't frighten me. Whether they be incubi or succubi, demons scare me.'

'You succeeded in sending them packing.'

'So you are learned in the science of the stars as well, are you, Marquis?'

'I'm a learned man in almost all fields,' conceded Ville d'Avray modestly.

'And you think we haven't entirely done with our duchess yet, don't you? She was bound to the earth by too many different links. People will ask after her at Quebec and want to know what has become of her.'

'Silence, I tell you.'

'The King's Girls will talk.'

'They're much too scared. I took it upon myself to remind them that they had been in the service of a woman who was fit prey for the Inquisition and that they too might be sent to the stake. The poor creatures! I think that they will dread seeing *her* rising up one day before them until they are on their deathbeds!'

Angélique was thinking about the criminal act in which Monsieur de Varange had met his death. Silence about that too! A group of accomplices holding their tongues among other accomplices who were bound to keep quiet about another point. All these vessels were coming to carry a sort of company of conspirators bound together willy-nilly by the feeling that they had found themselves caught up in a sticky web of intrigue from which they could escape only by strength of character and the happy chance of belonging all together. Henceforth they would form a single block when the moment came to land at Quebec, carrying in the folds of their cloaks the odour of the unrevealable mysteries of Acadia.

'Do you think she's dead?' Angélique asked once again in a hushed voice.

'She is dead,' said Ville d'Avray categorically. 'And you ought above all to bear one thing in mind – dead or living, she has no further power against you. Although wounded, Sagittarius goes on his way, raising his bow on high towards victory ... As far as the science of the stars is concerned, at Quebec I'll introduce you to a priest who is a friend of mine and who is extremely well up in the art. He will tell you amazing things about your destiny and Monsieur de Peyrac's ... You'll see!'

PART THREE

Tadoussac

CHAPTER 11

'SILENCE, MEN!'

Erickson's cavernous voice hailing all ships' commanders through his megaphone rang out across the bay.

'*Silence, men!*'

Then he proceeded to run through the string of commands.

'Take in lower sails!'

'Pay out mainsail sheets ...'

The silence that had succeeded his first call gave way to a trampling of feet on the deck as the men rushed to carry out the manoeuvre.

'Clew up foot-brails and tighten leech-lines!'

'Make fast all lines ...'

The dawn was coming up, pastel-coloured, around the ships drawn up in line. On each vessel the voices of the captains repeated the same commands, echoed only by the mewing of seagulls and the croaking of cormorants wheeling above in the misty morning light in which sky and water merged imperceptibly together.

'*Lay aloft to furl!*'

As agile as monkeys the sailors sprang up into the shrouds.

'Keep your spaces on the yards and ratlines!'

'Lash back sails with furling-lines!'

Angélique was standing beside Peyrac on the fore-deck. All the passengers had gathered there while the ships furled sail and hove to. Wide-eyed, delighted and expectant, they watched the spectacle unfold before their eyes of scattered wooden cottages and big stone farmhouses set amidst orchards on the hillsides and of ploughed strips glistening beneath a thin layer of frost.

In the centre, half-way up the sloping village, stood a small church with a pointed spire, tastefully ornamented with lead openwork patterns that glittered in the diffused light.

On the left, at the tip of a promontory, stood a small wooden fort with four corner turrets and a rustic keep over which there flew a white flag bearing three golden lilies . . .

Tadoussac! France!

The rattle of anchor chains running out reverberated round the quiet bay and echoed back from the pink granite cliff's rising up on either side of the Saguenay River which joined the St Lawrence at this point.

Then peace returned and the only sound that could be heard was the clamour of sea-birds.

In the thin, clinging mist that hung over the entire landscape colours stood out muted yet vivid. Elms and maples scattered among the houses rising one above the other in a series of tiers to form the village, stood out as patches of purple and gold, while smoke rose from the chimneys in long pure-white trails, as if painted in by some artist's hand.

A haze of blue smoke hung decoratively about the palisade of a small Indian encampment that stood half-way between the fort and the nearest fir-trees at the edge of the forest.

'Everything seems quiet on first impression,' said Peyrac, his eye glued to his spy-glass. 'The inhabitants are gathered along the shore but don't look as if they have warlike intentions. And there's nothing stirring in the fort.'

'If Quebec hasn't sent anyone to reinforce the garrison, they won't have more than four or so soldiers there,' said Carlon.

'Thanks for the information, Monsieur the Intendant.'

Count Peyrac closed up his spy-glass and turned towards the Intendant of New France and the Governor of Acadia.

'Well, gentlemen, it only remains for us to go ashore. Your presence at my side will serve as final proof to these good people that my intentions are peaceful.'

'Oh, so you're showing your hand at last; you want to make your hostages walk in front of you,' said Carlon.

'Sir, it was not as hostages that you came on board my ship. Just cast your mind back a bit. You had no other choice but to remain stranded all winter in some godforsaken hole on the Saint John River, under threat from the English, or to be left to your own devices among the savages of the East Coast.

'Or perhaps you would have preferred, as a last resort, to have gone aboard the vessel that's limping along in our wake, looking as if it might well founder at any minute? ...'

All eyes turned towards the stern, but mist hung over the horizon and they could no longer see a thing.

'We'll take care of them later,' said Peyrac. 'Let's tackle Tadoussac first.'

Ville d'Avray threw a conspiratorial glance at Angélique and her customary entourage of children and girls.

'I'll come back to fetch you,' he murmured in an aside. 'I just have a couple of minor matters to settle first.'

'I want to see the Baby Jesus of Tadoussac,' demanded Honorine.

'You'll see Him, I've promised you.'

From the ship they watched the longboat pull away, escorted by a couple of larger boats packed with armed men. But apart from this precautionary measure, there was no hint of animosity on either side.

Even so everyone remained on the alert, for distant movements were difficult to discern through the mist.

'There's a bell, ringing for Mass,' said one of the King's Girls.

'No it's not, it's the tocsin ...'

Though slightly muffled, the silvery chime of the bell in the church steeple came surging intermittently across to them, bringing back familiar memories to the exiles. A French village ...

'I do hope that ...'

'Shall I see the Baby Jesus of Tadoussac?' Honorine's voice implored.

'Yes, you'll see Him.'

All remained calm. Bit by bit the tension eased. And Angélique began to understand more clearly the slant Count Peyrac was giving to this expedition to Canada. It was to be no less than a visit by one prince to another, by one governor to another. Tadoussac was just a port of call on the way. These French Canadian peasants could hardly show hostility towards Frenchmen whose behaviour to them betokened nothing but friendliness. Peyrac and his companions had always kept up the best of relations with the Canadian trappers who had sought refuge and assistance at his trading posts. He had always avoided – which was no easy matter – responding to the army's provocations by the use of force, and so far the peace had never been broken. These facts had been well known now for three years, for the men spoke of it on their return home, and even put the word about that the lord of Maine, down there in the south, stocked some excellent hardware for trading purposes.

Angélique began to realize more clearly the true nature of the anxiety that sometimes tightened round her heart.

'It isn't the people I fear but the Powers that be.'

The common people were shrewd judges. It was no easy matter to persuade them that black was white. They could only be coerced. But here in Canada the common man had fashioned with his woodman's axe, his peasant's scythe and his trapper's gun a land that was truly his own, one where he was free ... Ennobled by the idealistic feelings that had driven them to New France, these men had rubbed shoulders with the ruling classes through all the dangers and tribulations of the colonial adventure, and they had already come to be a race apart, more independent-minded and objective than their counterparts that had stayed behind in France.

The longboat returned and drew alongside the *Goulds-boro*. Count Peyrac climbed back on board and the small band of girls began to embark, while Honorine chirped like a swallow:

'Come on! Come on, Mummy, hurry up! We can go ashore now!'

Angélique hurried to meet the Count.

'All is well,' he told her. 'I have assured the town officials of my peaceful intentions. I think they would have preferred to deal with me on my own rather than have Intendant Carlon there as well. He's been reading them the riot act about an overdue shipment that should have been sent off to Europe ages ago.

'They had not expected to see him suddenly spring up like a jack-in-the-box, but, take it all in all, that's the nastiest trick they'll have to complain of from me. Our arrival has been completely overshadowed by this row, and the locals have all gone to earth in their own homes, though I wager there will be eyes behind every window pane. The moment has come. Go and bring your own weapons to bear. Ville d'Avray is waiting for you. I have not the slightest doubt that you'll have these good folk eating out of your hand in next to no time.'

He kissed her hand.

'... Off you go, my dearest! Off you go! Set your pretty foot upon French soil. And success go with you!'

'Come on then, gentlemen of Canada,' she said to herself, 'let's see what you can do.'

As the boat drew near the shore, she began to wonder whether she should not have put on more elegant clothes. She had dressed in haste that morning, in her impatience to catch the earliest possible glimpse of the village of Tadoussac, which had been announced as shortly ahead. She was wearing a drugget skirt, a loose jacket trimmed with squirrel fur, a dark woollen cloak with a deep hood, and she had hastily tied a black satin kerchief round her hair which she had brushed up into a chignon on the back of her head. Her general appearance was on the staid side, but no matter, there was no time to lose. In addition to the children, the King's Girls, Yolande and Adhémar, two of the Spanish soldiers, Luis and Carlos had also taken their place in the longboat. The sailors and oarsmen all carried, thrust into their Indian belts or hung on a cross-belt, ponderous-looking, long-barrelled, twin-shot pistols of French manufacture, such as were rarely possessed even by high-ranking officers in other fleets. For Peyrac's crews were always the best equipped.

Father Baure and Monsieur Quentin were already waiting on the quay, surrounded by a great throng of Indians and idle bystanders, while on higher ground near the church, Monsieur de Ville d'Avray stood brandishing his knobbed stick.

'Hurry up! Father Dafarel is about to open the treasure chest for us! ...'

A figure in a black soutane, the resident Jesuit in all

likelihood, could be seen standing beside him. Ville d'Avray had apparently already tackled him and reduced him to submission.

The mist was beginning to clear and the sun shone forth bright and crisp. From every point in the village, whose houses were spread out in tiers, everything that was going on could be seen. People on the shore could hail those living in the topmost houses, and even the occupants of the furthest houses could identify anyone who disembarked, while the soldiers from the fort, without so much as taking their pipes out of their mouths or pausing from digging their sloping gardens, could announce the arrival of ships or canoes by either the Saguenay River or the St Lawrence. Everyone knew who entered or left a neighbour's house, since everyone could keep an eye both on those above and below him.

As Angélique looked up at Monsieur de Ville d'Avray and the missionary, she felt the eyes of the entire population upon her. Although they had apparently resumed their daily tasks, be it in the home or in the fields, in fishing or in trading, they were not missing a single detail of what was going on down at the port, counting one by one the sailors as they disembarked from the longboat.

'Did you see the pistols those fellows have got? – The awkward gait of the soldiers wearing the black helmets and breast-plates? – Look like Spaniards, I'd say – How old would you say the girls were? ... Wherever do they come from, that lot? – The children – seem sweet, right sweet, the littl'uns, and healthy too in spite of the journey – And her, that woman, that lady over there who'se just set foot on shore and who is climbing up to the chapel holding the children's hands, how beautiful she looks! Even this far off, could it be that it's ... *Her!* ... The woman they're expecting in Canada! ...'

The pathway was as attractive as a narrow village street and Angélique found herself sooner than she expected in the church square half-way up the hillside.

From this vantage point one could look out over the St Lawrence lying spread out like a milky roadstead. The fog had rolled back as far as the opposite bank.

Finding herself suddenly almost face to face with the Jesuit, who was waiting with Ville d'Avray, Angélique went straight up to him without a moment's hesitation:

'What a pleasure it is, Father, after so long a voyage through uncivilized regions, to hear the peal of a church bell and to know that here the Presence of the Blessed Sacrament awaits us!'

Then, moving towards the threshold of the chapel, she went on:

'Before admiring the marvels Monsieur de Ville d'Avray has told us about, would you allow me to kneel with my children and these young women before Him of whom we all stand in such need, and whom your devotion and your ministry have made it possible for us to find in the furthest-flung outpost of the world. Our thanks be to you!'

Father Dafarel graciously nodded his consent. Was there perhaps the faintest twinkle of amusement in the depths of those grey eyes? But it was an expression common with Jesuits whose fifteen years of instruction in the *Spiritual Exercises* of St Ignatius accustomed them to view the world, its convulsions, and its pathetic deceits with a certain condescension. Angélique had encountered that twinkle of humour before, lurking in shrewd, alert eyes, for example in the eyes of her brother, Raymond de Sancé, the Jesuit, then in those of Louis-Paul Maraîcher de Vernon who, in the guise of an English sailor had saved her from drowning, or again in those of Father Masserat at Wapassou who brewed such excellent beer with his sleeves casually rolled up. These pillars of the Catholic Church, the Jesuits, did not unduly overawe her, for she felt a kind of kinship with them because of their independence from other members of the human race, which had some affinity with her own independence of mind.

But she did not hold out her hand to Father Dafarel as she was aware that men of the Church tended as a general rule to avoid shaking a woman's hand.

They followed the Jesuit into the tiny church consisting of a nave only, dark and heavy with the smell of incense, where a red glass oil-lamp burned to indicate the presence of the Blessed Sacrament. Angélique felt the spell of an atmosphere that brought back many memories, and found herself deeply stirred. How long had it been, how many years had gone by since she had entered a sanctuary, a place of prayer where she and the growing girls of her generation had spent so many hours! Matins at daybreak, Vespers, Benediction, daily devotions, feast days, hymns, confessions, communions, so familiar a place that they spent almost as much time there as at home.

She instinctively knelt before the tabernacle and buried her face in her hands.

'Dear France!' she murmured to herself.

And her eyes filled with tears of longing and of love, so long held back and denied, so long not even admitted to herself: love of the land in which she was born and attachment to the faith into which she had been baptized.

Thus she remained for a considerable time, plunged in the shadowy realms of meditation.

'Dear God!' she prayed in a cry from the heart, 'Dear God! You who know me! You who know who I am!'

'Bravo,' Ville d'Avray whispered to her as they made their way in a group towards the sacristy; 'that was tremendously moving; I didn't reckon on your being either so diplomatic or so pious. You act a part admirably.'

'But that was neither diplomacy nor acting,' she protested.

'Then that makes matters worse and more dangerous. I must say, I'm beginning to think we shall see some strange goings-on in Canada.'

The Infant Jesus of Tadoussac was a wax statuette that had been given to the Jesuit missionaries by Louis XIV when a child, and its silver-grey satin robes had been embroidered with mother-of-pearl beads and tags of pure silver by Anne of Austria, the Queen Mother. Honorine held out her arms towards the statuette, longing to treat it like a doll.

Chasubles, copes, illuminated missals, a pair of monstrances in silver-gilt and gold, gold chalices with lids surmounted by ruby-studded crosses and silver-gilt ciboria, went to make up this collection of precious articles, whose value and beauty seemed quite out of keeping with the poverty and roughness of the place. But the impression was not unpleasing. It was in line with the history of the colonization of Canada. *All for the glory of God.* The pure gold of passionate, mystical sentiments, juxtaposed to a starker, indeed a wretched, reality, the ruby-red blood of martyrs, shed unstintingly by men of humble origins, plebeians as in the early days of the Church, while this opulence reminded them of the vanity of wealth in such a place, since true riches lay in humble, primitive tasks, in the performance of the harsh daily round.

When they came out of the church, they found the entire village of Tadoussac assembled in the square, including the Indians from the encampments up the hill and from the Saguenay. It was rather overwhelming.

Faced with this dense crowd staring stonily at her from a few paces, Angélique at first regretted not having dressed more elegantly. She was not at all sure what these people expected of her. Perhaps they were disappointed to see her making her appearance with so little pomp and ceremony. She could see rows of calm, round faces, the women's beneath their white bonnets, the men's under their red woollen bonnets, while the Indians, of course, had gathered in the front row with their naked, grubby children pushing their way between people's legs and squabbling with the peasant children who, barefoot, were trying to do likewise.

Mothers pulled their offspring back, gave them a good shaking or even cuffed them, and in a trice all became still once more, as in a dream.

Angélique nodded her head all round to acknowledge the gathering, but her greeting went unanswered. People just stood and stared.

Among them were trappers, their legs encased in their leggings and moccasins, ploughmen in wooden clogs or heavy buckled shoes. Some of the women wore bonnets, while others had added a large shawl which they draped around head and shoulders like a blanket in the Indian manner.

Tight lipped, or pipe between the teeth, they watched her. It could have gone on like this until nightfall.

Angélique glanced round and noted that neither the Jesuit nor the Marquis, perhaps because they themselves were disconcerted and taken aback, seemed prepared to take matters in hand. Then, she caught sight of an old man sitting on one of the stone benches to the right of the church door. In spite of his great age, he seemed an alert and lively old fellow. His read woollen bonnet had grown threadbare and had faded to a shade of pink through long exposure to the weather. It was bedecked with medals and feathers and matched to perfection his face, which was brown and as wrinkled as a medlar.

She dropped him a little curtsey and said in a friendly voice, speaking very loud:

'I'll wager, Monsieur, that you are the oldest inhabitant of Tadoussac. No one could be better fitted than you to introduce me to these good people who have so kindly come here to welcome me, and whom I would like to thank for their courtesy.'

Without waiting for a response, she seated herself beside him and went on:

'I am Countess Peyrac and I have just come ashore from the ship you see lying at anchor out there in the harbour.'

She was not telling anyone anything new, but she felt that it would be helpful to spell things out.

She did, however, see no trace of hostility among the Canadians. They were merely examining her, and she felt that she should help them to form some opinion of her.

In days gone by, the Poitou peasantry she had led into battle would, given the same circumstances calling for prudence and reflection, have adopted the same attitude. These Tadoussac folk had been told of a woman who ... a woman that ... They'd have to see for themselves! ...

The old man had made no reply, but he showed he was neither deaf nor infirm. He had moved along to make room for her, and there was the trace of a smile in the sharply incised lines of his face as he eyed Honorine and Chérubin who were obviously fascinated by his woollen hat.

The Marquis de Ville d'Avray possessed a sense of atmosphere and a flair for the theatrical. He rather enjoyed a situation in which events enabled him to occupy something like the centre of the stage. On such occasions he would steep himself in the general tension of the moment, sense the atmosphere, then join in and decide what role to play. He allowed the silence to continue for a few seconds more in order to raise expectations a degree more then he winked to the Jesuit father, who appeared to be dissociating himself from the proceedings, and spoke:

'My dear Angélique, you could hardly have made a better choice than this old man to introduce you. His name is Carillon. He landed here a very long time ago with our gallant Champlain. It was he that our renowned explorer left with the Algonquins in exchange for one of their tribesmen whom Champlain took back to France to present as a specimen of the Indian race to the King. When he was still under seventeen, our friend here lived alone among the savages for nearly two years, and by the time that Champlain returned with his Indian, Carillon had mastered several of the local dialects and was living according to the customs of the tribes.

'Monsieur, I am greatly honoured to make your acquaintance,' Angélique exclaimed, turning to her neighbour.

The old man had accepted Ville d'Avray's introduction while appearing not to be really listening. His wily gaze ranged over the assembled company. He thrust forward a crooked finger, beckoning to someone to step forward. There was a commotion in the crowd, especially among the peasant women, who seemed to become agitated and to be arguing among themselves until they eventually urged a good-looking, sturdily built girl to step forward, in spite of her evident reluctance. There she stood as if under duress, while the old man went on beckoning her peremptorily to come forward. His nimble index finger was particularly eloquent, and he must have been in the habit of managing those about him in this way – whether in order to husband his strength or because he judged it pointless to be everlastingly repeating the same words to obtain the same results after some ninety-four years.

Nevertheless, the girl obstinately stood her ground.

'But it's Mariette,' exclaimed Ville d'Avray jovially, greeting her with open arms. 'How pretty she is and how she's grown! But of course, she was married last year.'

There was a further commotion among the women, and some of their faces darkened. Ville d'Avray hastened over to them, offering to mediate in the smouldering disagreement. He had the gift of winning the confidence of women-folk and it was not long before two tall women draped in shawls were volubly explaining the situation to him.

He came back to Angélique.

'This is the situation. The lass is Carillon's great grand-daughter,' he explained, stooping to whisper into her ear; 'she's having some trouble nursing her baby and the old man has got it into his head that you might be able to help since, along with all the other stories that are told about you, your reputation as a healer has reached here. They've been arguing the toss ever since it was reported that you were heading for Quebec. As for him, he's as stubborn as a mule . . .'

'And she doesn't want to have anything to do with it.'

'These country girls are stupid and superstitious.'

'No, what she's frightened of is that I'll cast a spell over her baby,' said Angélique. 'They've been indoctrinated here too. Old Carillon doesn't look to me like a man who'd believe such tales. He could be on our side, I'm sure of it.'

She turned to the old man who was working himself up into a frenzy and casting furious glances at the womenfolk.

'Monsieur Carillon, I am perfectly prepared to help anyone who wants to be helped. But do not imagine that I possess any magical powers, either for good or for evil. You may indeed be more skilled than I in the science of herbs, for you have lived in the woodlands and had many contacts with the Indians. Nevertheless I shall send someone to fetch my medicine chest, and, when we have got to know one another better, I may be able to persuade the young woman to show me her child.'

The old man appeared furious, but it was impossible to tell whether he was enraged at Angélique's words or at his great grand-daughter's insubordination, for she, in spite of her great grandfather's anger, was not budging an inch. She belonged to a generation that had grown up on the skirts of the woodlands from which at any moment the Iroquois might leap out, with hatchet raised. Such experiences make for toughness of character, and the young people were no longer as docile as in earlier times. Gone was the old Europe submissive to the will of the older generations! All that nonesense was over! It was readily conceded that young Canadians now did very much as they pleased.

The old man was working up to an apoplectic fit. He spat out a long jet of tobacco-brown saliva to a distance commensurate with his rage. Then he launched out on a whole series

96

of cabalistic signs that resulted in a barefooted boy with a shock of blond hair rushing towards him with a red stone Indian pipe, a tobacco pouch and a glowing ember.

Having lighted his pipe, Carillon deigned to calm down.

Nevertheless, the incident had put an end to the silence and immobility of the crowd, which was now in a state of great agitation, including the savages. People were shouting angrily to one another and a musket could be seen being passed from hand to hand, roughly seized by this one and that. The atmosphere was beginning to degenerate, and Angélique glanced towards the Spanish soldiers to whose care she had been entrusted. They remained utterly impassive, trained as they were to face every kind of crowd, from Indians of the Amazon to Tortugan pirates to black slaves in revolt and, more recently, the foul rabble that made up the Duchess's crew. They had had to deal with Iroquois and Abenakis, with whale fishers from the Basque country and Saint Malo ... Having to cope with a mob of true-blue Canadians after that motley array of humanity was not going to upset them any. It was as if, in serving Count Peyrac, they had acquired a sixth sense that told them when things were getting out of hand and when the time had come to make ready to fire.

The weapon the Canadians had been wrangling over ended up in the hands of a tall savage as yellow as lemon-tree wood, whom Angélique had the impression she had seen before. At one and the same time, everyone burst out laughing and the worthy folk turned towards Angélique, with expressions on their faces like children planning some practical joke.

Angélique smiled back at their beaming countenances. She felt rather as if she were back in the village square of her childhood, sitting beneath the elm tree, as she used to do with her parents, Baron and Baroness de Sancé, ever patient and indulgent spectators of peasant frolics. And the old folk, there too, used to sit with them as well. Like them, she clasped Chérubin and Honorine to her, as lovingly as her own mother had once clasped her.

The argument was now continuing in a native dialect similar to the Iroquois tongue. Angélique was unable to catch enough to understand all that was said, but the Jesuit explained briefly to the Marquis what had transpired and his face lighted up.

'Ah! so that's the gist of it! Listen, Madame, they want to know whether what is said about your being an exceptional shot is true. This savage claims he was wounded by you somewhere or other a year ago.'

'Anashtaha!' exclaimed Angélique. 'It's Anashtaha, the leader of the Hurons, now I remember. It happened at Sakoos ford, near Katarunk.'

The Huron was delighted that she had recognized him while Angélique secretly gave thanks to heaven for endowing her with a good memory for names, even Indian ones.

The Indian and his friends burst out laughing and the ice was broken. They began to dance about while the children leapt and somersaulted and the Canadians all applauded.

'But I wasn't the one that wounded him ...' she wanted to add.

But as everyone seemed pleased at the notion that she had done it, including the victim himself, she let the matter rest there.

Anashtaha, emboldened, stepped up to her and laid the musket across her knees.

'What does he want?'

'Wants you to shoot, of course! ... They want a demonstration of the skill they've been hearing about.'

Angélique hesitated. Of course she would gladly have agreed to satisfy the curiosity of these delightful people, to entertain them with a few little novelties that would make a change from the dourness of the daily round, and that they could talk about later on. All that seemed harmless enough – but was there not behind these suggestions the intention to set a trap for her? Were they not trying to establish proof that her skill was due to magical powers or to witchcraft?

'It can't be helped,' she decided. 'I'll have to go through with it.'

CHAPTER 12

SHE ASKED to whom the gun belonged and a young man wearing a fringed leather jerkin stepped forward from the crowd and came towards her with a slightly rolling gait. He also seemed vaguely familiar to her. He looked like the various Laubignières, Maudreuils and company she had encountered at fort Katarunk or in Wapassou.

After some hesitation, he pulled off his woollen bonnet but quickly donned it again. He had not, however, been scalped like old Macollet; indeed he had a very fine head of hair, but that particular item of dress, his red Canadian 'touque', seemed to form so integral a part of his person that he must have been in the habit of removing it only in church or at a pinch for the Governor – and doubtless also for the King, if the latter ever took it into his head to visit Canada.

Now he had added to his list a further occasion for baring his head, namely when faced with a lady of high rank, especially if that lady looked at you in a way that was at once overawing and friendly, giving you a meaningful half-smile that made you wonder whether she might not already know a bit too much about you.

'What is your name, Monsieur?' Angélique asked amiably.

'Martin du Lougre, nicknamed Sharp-Eye, at your service, M'Lady.'

'Well now, Monsieur du Lougre, you have a handsome Dutch firearm there.'

Her smile broadened, seeming to add: 'and you must have acquired it by trading in your furs at some post on the borders of New England or New Netherland.' But so as not to embarrass him, she paused for an instant then went on without pressing the point:

'It isn't as good as the French-made guns we have with us, but no doubt you do not find it easy to get them here. Well then, Monsieur, let us see how we measure up to one another! What matter ... I concede you the advantage of the choice of arms, as you will be shooting with your own gun. You will shoot first, and since they call you Sharp-Eye, which implies you are a good shot, I am by no means sure that I shall be able to surprise these people after you. All I can hope for, since I shall be using your gun for the first time, is to equal you.'

She rose as she spoke and held out his gun, which he took.

He shook his head and grinned. He had not reckoned with having to shoot, either, but he could not get out of it. The crowd exchanged glances and Angélique congratulated herself on having adopted these tactics. By competing against a crack shot, she could prove her competence in handling arms without being obliged to give them a demonstration of skill that savoured of magic powers.

The young man had the target brought closer. The distance he chose seemed perfectly acceptable to Angélique, and she knew she could pass the test with credit.

She watched him as he ram-loaded his gun and made it ready.

The circle of bystanders had opened to make room for the contestants. Angélique's calm demeanour and easy good manners removed any sense of aggressiveness from the match. Suddenly, all that mattered was the wager.

At the behest of old Carillon, whose instructions were conveyed by imperative beckonings with his long, bony fingers, Sharp-Eye explained that he would – if agreeable – begin by aiming at the centre of the stretched skin target then shoot one of the feathers off its edge.

He fired. The hole in the target was not dead centre but from that distance it was quite a performance. Then, after reloading and taking very careful aim, he hit the feather as he had said he would.

Angélique then asked him to help her while she in turn loaded the musket. She felt the young trapper examining her curiously, for he had never before had the occasion to assist a lady with such beautiful hands to load a heavy musket like this one. Angélique's dexterity as she cleaned the barrel, poured in the gunpowder and clicked down the pan, brought a nod of approval from him. She asked him about some points concerning the priming mechanism with which she was no longer familiar, but he could see that she knew what she was doing.

You could have heard a pin drop among the spectators and even the every day sounds of village life grew fainter. In fact the crowd had become deaf to any sound not connected with the fascinating spectacle they were watching. Even the Indian children were quiet.

A thrill of excitement ran through the crowd as she nimbly lifted the gun to her shoulder in spite of its weight. They were watching her every movement, which seemed self-confident and calm yet rapid. Without admitting as much, some of the bystanders were impressed by the graceful way she inclined her head against the butt in order to take more careful aim. It was as if the gun were becoming a friend and ally and she were talking softly to it: 'Let us work together, my friend! Let us achieve our objective!'

Ville d'Avray was lyrical:

'Isn't she exquisite!' he whispered to Father Dafarel, who remained unmoved.

At this point, Angélique lowered the musket and asked old Carillon whether he would prefer her to aim at the centre of the target or at the hole Sharp-Eye had made in it.

He rocked with mirth and his mouth spread in a toothless grin; he made a gesture of approval: the second suggestion, to hit Sharp-Eye's mark, would be a more subtle procedure. Angélique raised the gun to her shoulder once more, then, after carefully considering the line of fire, lowered it again and asked – 'if it please you, cousins' – for the target to be set back some six feet. A score of people leapt forward while others exclaimed that this was indeed a bold stroke! She was keeping them all on tenterhooks! When people had said that she was no ordinary woman, they were certainly right. If she could hit the mark at that distance, then perhaps there was magic in it!

The crowd was all agog but loving every moment of it.

At last Angélique, sensing that her audience was ready, made up her mind to fire. These various preparations had enabled her to get the feel of the gun, which she whipped up to her shoulder and fired so swiftly that the audience scarcely had time to realize what was going on and thought they must have been dreaming.

There was a general rush to the target where it was found that there was still only one hole, but that it had been slightly tattered on one side by the passage of a second shot. Furthermore, the musket was still smoking and Angélique, assisted by Sharp-Eye, was busy reloading. The spectators moved aside, she raised the gun to her shoulder, took aim, sent the feather flying, then casually handed the gun back to the young trapper.

'There,' she said, addressing the circle about her. 'I have fired, and I think I have proved that Anashtaha was not misleading you when he extolled my skill as a shot. I can shoot, at any rate as well as Monsieur du Lougre, but that does not make me a witch. Kindly note the fact.'

Her frankness took everyone so much by surprise that they were quite enchanted. There was some laughter. Then general pandemonium broke loose. Enthusiasm and delight mingled with a sense of relief had to find expression and the shooting display was discussed with many a thump on the back. Angélique noticed a man in a cloth coat and waistcoat, of middle-class appearance, counting out coins into the hand of one of the trappers. She had not been far wrong in supposing that bets were running even before their arrival at Tadoussac.

At that moment the sound of French voices shouting came to their ears:

'We're coming! ... Stand fast!'

A similar call came from the direction of the fort:

'Charge! Don't give in!' shouted the three soldiers from the garrison.

They had hastily donned their blue uniforms and were rushing in the direction of the church with their rifles at the ready, while a contingent of seamen from the *Gouldsboro* led by Yann le Couennec, all likewise armed, were charging up the slope from the beach.

A longboat bristling with cannons and muskets had pulled away from the *Gouldsboro* and was being rowed furiously towards the shore. Erickson was standing in the bows, with drawn cutlass.

In the face of this double assault there was an instant of stupefied silence.

'What's going on?' cried Angélique to Yann as he arrived puffing and blowing and halted in bewilderment on seeing her peacefully seated beside old Carillon.

'What's going on?' repeated the Canadians, who after some rushing hither and thither had regained control of themselves.

'That's what we're asking you ...' growled one of the soldiers from the fort.

The two 'armies' in confrontation gazed at one another in bewilderment, then turned to the assembled crowd to seek an explanation.

'Why was there firing? We thought you were in danger, Madame,' said Yann.

'We heard shots,' said the King's sergeant, as if he were adding something.

Erickson arrived in his turn. Monsieur de Peyrac, who had gone off to meet the ship that had been following them, had given him strict orders to stay on the alert all day. The Countess was on shore, and perhaps all would go well, perhaps not! ... Hearing shots, Erickson had jumped like a grasshopper and ordered the longboat to be launched.

With his enormous cutlass in his huge fist, he gazed all about him looking for somebody to cut in two.

The misunderstanding was cleared up. There was no need for any such turn out of the artillery. Nothing more was involved than a village shooting match.

Nevertheless, the peasants' shrewd eyes had rapidly taken stock of the forces available to defend the Countess Peyrac, if the people at Tadoussac had chosen to make trouble for her. Their three soldiers were a pitiful spectacle in comparison, in spite of their obvious courage.

These newcomers, who folks did say were pirates or privateers from French Bay, were armed to the teeth. And what fine, brand-new, up-to-date weapons they had too!

After all that, there was no more gainsaying the fact that it was indeed *She*, the Lady of the Silver Lake, whom certain people from Quebec, who had never clapped eyes on her and tried to make a bogy-woman of, while others – Indians and trappers – who had seen her spoken of as if she were an apparition from heaven.

At first they had doubted it. She had climbed up the slope

so sedately holding her children by the hand.

What were they expecting exactly? Someone overawing, although it was said of her that she was very beautiful, but one of those beauties that kill, that make people ill. Consequently, the first reaction of the population had been surprise, even disappointment.

They were looking for traces in her of powers that had a whiff of brimstone about them. They had been ready to make the sign of the cross as soon as she laid eyes upon them, but things had worked out very differently, and she was, after all, not so astonishingly beautiful as all that with her simple cape, her white collar and her kerchief tied over her hair. She almost looked like a Canadian like themselves.

But suddenly she had smiled. Suddenly she had fired and, turning towards them, had said:

'You see! I am not a witch ...'

It was *She* then ...

'Mummy! It's hot and I'm thirsty,' Honorine cried suddenly, who was bored now that there was no more talk of shooting or of warfare.

It was true that the sun was scorching. In spite of the approach of winter, it had an intensity that is found only in the regions lying nearest to the pole. It was as if the sun was concentrating itself against the earth, casting blacker shadows and making colours stand out more vividly. The twilight would bring a sudden chill night. The daylight hours could be scorching, parched and crackling, and it was a recognized fact that people suffered torments from thirst.

A woman stepped out from the crowd.

'Would you like some beer, Madame?' she asked Angélique.

'Thank you, I would prefer milk. It's so long since we've drunk any.'

'Come to my place all of you,' invited Ville d'Avray. 'Our good friend Catherine-Gertrude will bring us refreshments there.'

He took Angélique's arm.

'What, have you got a residence at Tadoussac too?' she asked.

'No, just a warehouse ... for my merchandise. An employee of the Company looks after it in my absence. He has the key. It's not far from the port.'

The warehouse was a large plain building made of planks and set on a stone base. There was a long table of the kind on which traders lay out their furs and a pair of scales to weigh ironware, and there was provision for a fire in one corner on a large stone hearth.

Ville d'Avray's warehouse appeared to be well equipped. The man in the cloth jacket who had been settling a lost bet with a trapper shortly before turned out to be the caretaker. He must have been making a good percentage for Ville d'Avray on his dealings, for the Marquis gave him a congratulatory and conspiratorial wink while explaining to Angélique in an undertone:

'When I come back from Acadia, I like to leave part of my merchandise here and then bring it in quietly to Quebec. You understand ... Nowadays you're taxed up hill and down dale, no matter who you are or what's involved. It wouldn't be worth my while to cash my dues from Acadia – and you know what dangers they have cost to me – if the lot were simply to be swallowed up in some ridiculous budget or another.'

'Does Monsieur Carlon know about it?'

'Probably, but those are details that he has scarcely the time to bother himself with. This gentleman, who is an employee of the Northern Company, works in with me and lends me his name, and his direct superior, Monsieur Ducrest, who likes to think himself king of Tadoussac, has never had the slightest inkling of what's going on.

'It's a nice view we have from here, isn't it? But at Quebec from my little house in which I shall put you up the view is even more beautiful ... Ah! I see several sails in the distance. No doubt it is Monsieur de Peyrac's fleet manoeuvring.'

The Marquis's warehouse had been opened up as soon as he had arrived. He had been counting on entertaining Angélique there, and when they went in they found the cat installed on the table and looking very much at home.

'Yes he came ashore this morning with me,' said Ville d'Avray highly pleased with himself. 'He's very attached to me.'

A fire had been lighted on the flat stones of the hearth.

The people who had followed them were jostling one another to get in, the children and the Indian dogs in the lead.

'Come, come, let's have no pushing,' said the Marquis very pleased with his popularity. 'You've quite won them over,' he added in an undertone to Angélique.

The woman who had offered beer, came back with a glazed earthenware pitcher full of warm creamy milk, and she was followed by her daughters and daughters-in-law bearing eggs and bread. Angélique and the children sat down on a bench near the fire. The cat was holding its own against some dogs that had just discovered it.

'It's Madame de Peyrac's cat,' cried Ville d'Avray melodramatically: 'Don't hurt it.'

The dogs were cuffed and thrown out, and the women present offered to beat up an egg in milk for Madame de Peyrac's children. They were considered very beautiful. There were exclamations of admiration at Chérubin's chubby cheeks, and Honorine's beautiful hair, and the eyes of the men began to turn with interest in the direction of the young women escorting Angélique. There was a rumour that they were King's Girls. Where did they come from? From Paris? From the Providences? Who had arranged the trip for them? Had they come to Canada to find husbands?

'Alas! If they knew that we have no dowries,' sighed Henriette in Jeanne Michaud's ear.

Of all that they had endured this was what distressed them the most: the loss of their royal glory-box. Without a dowry who would want them in Canada? They would have to find employment as servants and save up for years before they would be in a position either to establish themselves decently or return to France. But this was not the time for gloomy thoughts, for cider as well as beer had been brought and a few flaggons of stronger drinks, some of them more limpid than diamond and more amber-tinted than topaz.

'Yes, no doubt about it ... We've got good drinks here!' observed the Company employee in response to the congratulations of the *Gouldsboro* crew who had partaken of generous potations and were displaying an enthusiasm which went up by a degree every time a fresh round was poured out into the little earthenware cups which had come straight from Normandy or the Perche. 'Our parish priest is a keen one on distilling. That's why you haven't seen him.'

A large round wheat-loaf had also been brought in and pats of butter and various varieties of jam.

'The people are charming, aren't they?' said Ville d'Avray, moved by this display of generosity. 'Didn't I tell you?'

'Charming' was not perhaps the precise word to apply to these earthy Canadians. Hardships, the harsh rough life, the struggle against the Iroquois and the winter had fashioned a sturdy race, solidly built, laconic and exuberant in turns, but they were, in a sense, peaceful folk, readily disposed to offer open and abundant hospitality.

In fact the prevailing atmosphere of the place, in spite of French lilies on the flag, was that of a free port, somewhat reminiscent of the free manors of Acadia. The jurisdiction might be French but the officials were more often at Quebec, where they settled with their families in preference to re-siding in this township of fishers and peasants.

They were somewhat despised and had no great power. The true masters were the representatives of the trading companies, especially those engaged in the fur trade.

Angélique recalled her doubts, her fears and anxieties of the day before and was astonished to see how readily events had turned to their advantage.

'So now you feel reassured? What did I tell you?' said Ville d'Avray. 'Well! believe you me, it will be the same at Quebec. Do you know why? Because the French like nothing better than having something to gawp at. And when it comes to *seeing you*! who'd forego such a spectacle? The truth is that people are delighted that you have come ...'

As he spoke these words, they heard a cannon shot.

CHAPTER 13

THIS TIME it really was a cannon shot.

'It's nothing! It's nothing!' cried the Marquis de Ville d'Avray rushing outside.

He brandished his lorgnette and clapped it to his eyes.

'It's only Monsieur de Peyrac who's going to the assistance of the ship in distress that was following us.'

'In that case, why are they firing off guns?'

All had now gathered on the open space in front of the warehouse and were scanning the misty horizon. It was difficult to see much even for the practised eyes of sailors. Only Ville d'Avray was in a position to comment on what was going on yonder.

At intervals the whiteness of the sails could be described moving with the apparent slowness of manoeuvres that are taking place in the distance.

There was a second flash and then the dull boom of an explosion.

'Things are beginning to look nasty!'

'That's odd, it's the ship in distress that's firing,' reported Ville d'Avray.

'What a peculiar thing!'

With their hands capped over their eyes to sharpen their sight, everyone was concentrating, endeavouring to sort out the puzzle presented by the crowding together of vessels in the distance.

Everything was very hazy, and it would be a long time before they could find out what had happened, for there's nothing goes so slowly as engagements at sea. All the watchers had to go on with for the moment were the manoeuvres of the crowded white patches which grew small in the distance or sprang up and grew steadily larger, then disappeared again.

At last someone shouted: 'They're coming this way! ...'

The spreading sails of the ships were indeed now clearly visible and it was possible to count them. It was an indication that they were making course for port.

Subsequently, everything went very quickly. The white, heaving flock grew visibly larger, and towards midday, when the sun was at its zenith, Count Peyrac's fleet – except the *Gouldsboro*, which had remained out in the roadstead – escorting the French vessel, which was limping along and listing so heavily that it appeared to be on the point of going over on its side from one moment to the other, entered the port of Tadoussac.

The little yacht, the *Rochelais* commanded by Cantor was acting as pilot to the captive ship, leading it along on the end of a line.

Angélique endeavoured to pick out Joffrey's figure on the deck of one of the vessels, but she could make out nothing, and in spite of herself she was anxious. The people around here were also silent. Had there been an act of war, and if so on whose part against whom?

Then there came the rattle of chains running out into the clear water. Already there was a rush of small craft and rowing boats pulling rapidly from the ships towards the shore, while Indian canoes from the beach proceeding in the opposite direction were seen clinging like ticks to the sides of the French vessel to offer furs for sale and to demand alcohol.

Angélique, scrutinizing the stranded vessel at a few cables' length with the flotillas of small craft darting all about it, wondered whether Joffrey had 'helped' or captured the French ship.

Adhémar's words came back to her memory: supposing the Duchess was on board? In spite of herself, she realized that she had paled ...

Around her, the Canadians of Tadoussac were beginning to stir once again. It was clear from the remarks they exchanged that they were anxious not to take sides.

The good discipline of the ships that had appeared off Tadoussac at sunrise had made a favourable impression upon the population. On the other hand, popular suspicion had been aroused by the damaged French vessel that Count Peyrac had brought in to Tadoussac, and suddenly someone cried:

'But it's the *Saint John the Baptist*, the old hulk belonging to that rogue René Dugast of Rouen.'

'How comes it that it is so late in arriving ... It won't be able to make the return trip ...'

'It's a wonder it didn't sink completely!'

'It never brings us anything but a pack of rascals.'

'And a chance for his nibs Gonfarel of Quebec to make even more money.'

'Is Dugast still skipper? No wonder he fired his guns! He'd rather have gone down with his cargo than to have anyone ferreting around in it ... With all the kind of things that *he* trades in ...'

They went down to the port, and Angélique arrived just in time to see Count d'Urville coming ashore with a new contingent of seamen. Cheerful as usual, d'Urville did not seem so much anxious as busy. He gave Angélique a knowing wave.

'What's going on?' she asked as she came up with him. 'Why was the cannon fired?'

'Someone in that blasted ship lost his head. We were surrounding her and were about to hail her offering assistance when she fired a broadside at our liveworks that we only just succeeded in dodging. So our first contact was rougher than expected. Whether they thought our approach was ill-intentioned, or whether, in spite of the fact that his vessel was at risk, the captain preferred to sink rather than be arrested, I don't know. He's either a drunken brute or sick, but we haven't been able to get anything out of him. The 'tween-decks passengers, immigrants, are in a deplorable state. A third of those that embarked died during the crossing ...'

'Why did this ship arrive at such an unfavourable season?'

'It was among the last to leave Europe. With luck it might have made the journey both ways. But it didn't have any luck. Storms, dead calms, damage ... According to what some of the seamen told us ... They're not at all easy to approach.'

Ville d'Avray came up.

'Apparently she has barrels of French wine in her hold, best-quality Burgundy.'

'You are already well-informed, Monsieur le Marquis,' said d'Urville with a smile.

'I hope that Monsieur de Peyrac has seized it?'

'Good heavens, no! Monsieur de Peyrac wished to inspect the vessel before allowing it to continue on its way to Quebec, in order to check its armaments, so that he runs no risk of finding himself confronted by a hostile ship beneath the city walls. But he has no wish to lend colour to the reputation that people have all too readily thrust upon him, of being a pirate.'

'I disagree with him,' Ville d'Avray retorted. 'If I were in his shoes I would not hesitate. Burgundy, and from the Beaune region, too, so it appears ... It's criminal ...'

He assumed a meditative air.

Angélique wished to return on board the *Gouldsboro* to see Joffrey de Peyrac and talk over their first morning, which had been somewhat full of incident but seemed to have been off to not too bad a start.

She took her leave of those who had welcomed her so charmingly, in particular of the Canadian woman Catherine-Gertrude Ganvin, who seemed to be the leading spirit of the village, and she promised to return that afternoon.

Back on board her husband confirmed what Count d'Urville had already told her. In spite of its precarious condition, the ship from Rouen, which sailed under the pious name of *Saint John the Baptist*, had proved decidedly hostile, which was not altogether to be wondered at since it had found itself surrounded by a foreign fleet obliging it to heave to and identify itself. But Joffrey had the impression that the ship's arrival might well be damaging to them at Tadoussac, and he had used their hostile attitude as a pretext for taking a firm line.

'I've confined the crew to their ship with strict orders not to go ashore on any pretext whatsoever. They could do us much harm in the eyes of the people of Tadoussac, and since we have made such good friends, it would be foolish to allow the situation to be spoiled. I shall, however, this afternoon authorize a party to go ashore to fetch water under strict guard, and possibly some of the sick women and children among the passengers, for they are in a pitiful state. Furthermore I have left carpenters and workmen aboard to help them repair the damage, but they are well armed and have orders to keep an eye on the crew of the *Saint John the Baptist* meanwhile; I warned the captain that our guns would remain trained on him.'

'Why did he fire at you?'

'He hasn't the faintest idea himself. He's completely besotted with alcohol. The order may not even have come from him.'

Angélique sensed that there was something she was not being told. She gave Peyrac a long, searching look. He nodded and seemed hesitant.

'It's only a rumour,' he said, making up his mind to speak, 'but it would seem that there is a representative of the King on board who has been entrusted with an official, secret mission, someone very high-ranking, sent over straight from the Court. It could be he who gave the order to fire.'

'And who is this man? What's his name? ...' Angélique asked quickly.

She shared Peyrac's unspoken opinion that this special messenger from the Court might well be the bearer of orders concerning them. And if that were the case it might be politic to forestall him and prevent his reaching Quebec before they did.

But Joffrey calmed her imagination ...

'Perhaps he doesn't really exist at all? It is only heresay, rumours that reached me when I was trying to get hold of a list of passengers in order to know exactly who was on board. I got neither names nor details. At first the men were hostile. If such an envoy from the King really exists, he must have paid them not to reveal his presence on board.'

'He must be frightened you will capture him and demand a ransom.'

'That was the impression I got too.'

'But you should have searched the ship from stem to stern, broken down the cabin doors, forced him into the open ...'

Joffrey de Peyrac smiled.

'Easy there! You are like our hot-headed Marquis who

sees the rule of law everywhere and yet would never hesitate to behave like an out-and-out filibuster. But I have no intention of passing for such in this country, and I want to do all in my power to set people's minds at rest, not to frighten them, or to incur criticism for apparently unjustified extortions.

'So for the time being, if it is true that there is an envoy from Versailles on board the *Saint John the Baptist*, I shall allow him to remain *incognito*. He can do nothing to harm us, particularly if he refuses to show himself. It will give us all the greater freedom of movement during our stay here.'

'How long do you think we shall be staying at Tadoussac?'

Count Peyrac gave an evasive answer, and once again she had the impression that she was not being told everything.

That afternoon she went ashore again with the children.

CHAPTER 14

SHE REACHED the shore just as Monsieur d'Urville was lining up a double row of armed men on the beach.

'Why are you mounting guard?'

'The *Saint John the Baptist* is sending a watering party ashore and my orders are to keep a close eye on them.'

A boat drew in bringing seamen from the damaged vessel. They looked a villainous lot, either because they really were ruffians, or because the tribulations of the crossing had made exhausted wild animals of them. They were horrifyingly skinny and haggard, and their clothes were in rags. They swore hoarsely as they began to unload their buckets and empty barrels, glancing aggressively about them and obviously looking for trouble. The *Gouldsboro*'s crew hustled them along, and they grudgingly consented to move a few yards up the beach to where the spring flowed out into a pool hollowed out of the rock. For their part, the inhabitants of Tadoussac, who had gathered round out of curiosity,

113

gave them no welcome, for their ship was known to be one that brought all kinds of trouble, caused disturbances on shore and did not pay up. D'Urville's men escorted them up to the spring in order to avoid incidents.

Meanwhile, a woman had also disembarked after the sailors. She was wearing very plain black clothes and seemed elderly though sturdy and obviously accustomed to fending for herself come what may for she did not bother to ask one of the men to carry her to dry land but gathered up her skirts in one hand, and carrying a small child on the other arm, slipped into the water.

With her clumsy shoes slung by their knotted laces round her neck she waded to the beach, where she sat down on the sand and patiently donned her shoes again.

She had put the child down beside her, where it lay very still. The scene reminded Angélique of the Benefactress disembarking with little Pierre in her arms, but this was a grey, shabby imitation of the earlier landing, having none of its ostentation, its showmanship or self-advertisement.

The woman's complexion was ashen. Her eyes were red rimmed, probably as a result of an irritation caused by the salt air. Wisps of grey hair strayed from under her black faille headscarf, which she wore tightly tied over a grubby white linen coif. Before standing up again, she made an effort to tidy her hair. Then she got briskly to her feet and Angélique saw that she was not as old as she had at first appeared. She picked up the child again and began to climb up the strand.

D'Urville intervened:

'Madame!' he said, addressing the lady courteously; 'who are you and what are you doing here? My orders are to allow none of the passengers on the *Saint John the Baptist* ashore until Monsieur de Peyrac has given express orders to that effect.'

The woman looked up at him calmly. It was impossible to tell the colour of her eyes, so washed out were they by anaemia.

'Monsieur de Peyrac, did you say? Are you referring to the pirate who boarded us this morning? If that is the case, I can assure you that it was he himself who gave me permission to come ashore in order to care for this dying child. We have nothing that's needed on board ...'

Her voice was clear, pleasant and indeed strong, and younger than her exhausted appearance would have led one to expect.

One of the seamen from the *Gouldsboro*, who had accompanied the group, confirmed that what the passenger said was correct and handed Monsieur d'Urville a note which the latter recognized as being in the Count's handwriting and signed by him. When he had read it, he nodded:

'Everything is in order. You are free to proceed, Madame, and seek what relief you will.'

The woman thanked him; but the interruption seemed to have taken the edge off her rally of determination, and she sighed, then, after hesitating for a moment, went on her way with heavier tread.

It happened that by this time the crowd had dispersed, some being reluctant to have any contact with the sailors from the *Saint John the Baptist*, while others had followed them to find out why it was that a French ship had come so late to the St Lawrence and what was the nature of her cargo.

Angélique alone remained at the water's edge, accompanied by the children and a few of the King's Girls.

She felt sorry for the woman, arriving thus alone in a strange land after several months of travel that had left its mark on her hollow, ashen face. She thought of the state she and her companions had been in on arrival at Gouldsboro, and how thin and pitiful the little children had been, although Joffrey had looked after them all and had kept them supplied with everything they needed. She went up to the woman.

'Can I help you at all, Madame?'

The woman looked at her keenly as if not sure what to make of her; she appeared to hesitate, then once again acquiesced.

'I would not say no to some assistance, thank you, Madame. Especially for this poor little mite, who is at death's door. He needs milk or broth. But for weeks now all we've had to eat has been ship's biscuits soaked in sea water, with tainted cider to drink.'

'Follow me,' said Angélique.

They climbed up the path to Ville d'Avray's warehouse.

He himself was in the offing and hastened towards Angélique when he caught sight of her, but came to an abrupt halt, screwed up his eyes and said nothing when he caught sight of the woman accompanying her. Then he beat a hasty retreat practically on tiptoe.

The woman had not noticed him. She entered the warehouse and sat down with a sigh of relief by the fire.

'Oh, how good it is to be back home again!'

'You aren't from Tadoussac, are you?' Angélique exclaimed in astonishment.

'No, from Ville-Marie ... But this is Canada here at long last, and no sooner do I set foot on this blessed soil than I find that words fail me to thank God adequately, and I feel myself come alive again.'

Angélique hastened to put a pan of milk to warm over the glowing embers.

'Is he your grandson?' she asked, indicating the child whom the woman had begun to unwrap from his wet, salt-caked blanket so as to warm his skinny little limbs by the glowing fire.

The newcomer shook her head.

'No ... he's the child of an immigrant family that sailed with us, who all died, except for this little creature. He was given up for dead and nobody wanted him. I heard that the crew were talking of throwing him overboard, and I took pity on him. So I asked for him, contrary to the general view of our party, every one of whom was sick, exhausted and close to death also. We did incidentally lose two of our recruits.'

Angélique handed her a wooden bowl into which she had poured some warm milk, and the woman proceeded cautiously to get the child to drink some. After a few mouthfuls he seemed better and gulped the milk down eagerly.

'They say you had a terrible crossing,' said Angélique.

'It would be hard to imagine one worse. We suffered every conceivable calamity save shipwreck. The thing is that the vessel had served as a hospital ship, and no sooner had we sailed from Rouen than plague broke out. There were several deaths. Fortunately we had Monsieur Bichard, a Sulpician father, on board to bury them ... The captain is totally unscrupulous ...'

116

As the woman was speaking, Angélique fetched a small jar from her medicine chest containing some balm which both helped wounds to heal over and had a general tonic effect. This she proceeded to rub into the child's trunk and limbs, then took her own woollen shawl and helped the woman to wrap him up warmly in it.

'Now we must wait. He has taken a little nourishment, which is a good sign, and the medicine I have rubbed him with will warm and strengthen him. There is nothing more we can do for the moment.'

She settled the child by the hearth on a pile of blankets intended for barter that she took down from Ville d'Avray's shelves, then, turning to Delphine and Henriette, she asked them to go and ask Catherine-Gertrude for the ingredients for a good pan of broth.

The woman watched her and seemed to be impressed by the rapidity and deftness of her movements.

'Now it's your turn!' said Angélique with a smile. 'You may not realize it, but the looks of you would melt a heart of stone.'

'I must say we were very uncomfortably housed, and the hostility of the captain only made matters worse. When we embarked in Rouen, Monsieur Quampois the quartermaster, who is not an altogether bad man, had several more barrels of water put on board than he would normally have taken on, for the sake of my sisters and me, because we do not drink wine. But once the ship was out of sight of the harbour, they refused to let us have the water, and we had to drink whatever the sailors drank. So what with sickness as well, my sisters and I are in a dreadful state.'

Angélique handed her the cup of milk, which she had reheated and into which she had crumbled a little bread.

'Drink it up quickly! I'll wager you have not eaten or drunk anything hot for weeks.'

'That doesn't matter! God has brought us safely home.'

'But it would appear without particularly spoiling you, to put it mildly.'

'Never mind! All we asked Him was that He should get us safely to Canada,' the woman replied, a lively smile revealing her bleeding gums.

'A little longer and the poor woman would have succumbed

to scurvy,' thought Angélique.

On returning ashore that afternoon she had had her medicine chest brought with her in case it might prove useful. It was standing on the table, and she began to look in it for herbs.

'I'm going to make you a cup of herbal tea that will do you the world of good.'

'How kind you are!' the woman murmured gently. 'But who are you? I don't know you. Did you come over to Canada during my absence? I have in fact been away for almost two years ...'

'Drink up!' Angélique urged her. 'We'll have time for introductions afterwards ...'

The woman did as she was bidden with a smile. She drank the concoction in a kind of absent-minded, thorough way, making a proper job of it, which one guessed was how she set about every task. In spite of the pleasure she must have experienced in drinking the comforting beverage, one sensed that her mind was elsewhere. And yet she continued to scrutinize Angélique. Her eyes, grown pale through malnutrition, still had a special light in them, and as she gathered strength, her features grew more relaxed and one became increasingly aware that here was a person of considerable distinction and great finesse.

There came a moment when her eyes lighted with gentle affection on Chérubin's and Honorine's little faces.

She set her cup down on her knees, looking thoughtful. She had not yet finished the tea:

'Are those your children?'

'Yes and no. This is my daughter Honorine, and that's Chérubin, a little lad I have been asked to look after.'

The twinkle in the woman's eyes grew brighter, and she narrowed her gaze slightly as she examined the boy. Angélique sensed that she had immediately noticed a likeness between him and someone she knew.

'Was that not Monsieur de Ville d'Avray I glimpsed earlier on?' she asked. 'I had the impression he was avoiding me.'

No doubt about it, very little escaped her notice.

Then, changing the subject, she went on:

'Is that magnificent medicine chest on the table yours?'

'Yes, I've got a lot of things there that come in handy in case of emergency. I always take it with me wherever I go.'

She went on to explain that she was also going to prepare dressings for the sores caused by the damp, salty air on shipboard, from which she could see that the child was suffering as also was this woman. The skin of her hands was raw looking, and on her neck, at the point where her kerchief tucked in, a nasty, red, suppurating patch was visible.

'You must be in great pain!'

'Oh, it's nothing. What is a thing like this compared to the wounds Our Lord Jesus suffered!'

She held out her bowl in a simple, friendly way, and, as Angélique took it, she laid her hand on her wrist.

'Now it's your turn, Madame. I have done as you bade me; now you owe me an answer. Who are you?'

CHAPTER 15

ANGÉLIQUE HAD a feeling that the answer she gave would decide her fate in Canada. It would come about in a world where neither force of arms, nor power of wealth carried any weight, or could affect the outcome. She had to summon up all her courage.

'I am the wife of the "pirate",' she replied. 'Yes, of the man you call a pirate.'

'In other words, you are Countess Peyrac.'

Angélique nodded.

The woman's eyes never left Angélique and her expression never changed. She seemed to have got some of her strength back, had straightened up and now sat very erect as she examined Angélique who found herself doing likewise. At first she had taken her for a poor woman, one of the destitute immigrants, a peasant woman or an artisan's wife, disembarking for the first time in the New World. But when she realized that the woman was known in the country, sensing her air of authority and self-assurance, Angélique had concluded that she must at least be something approaching a native Canadian. In fact she was more than that, for in spite of the simplicity of her dress and the lamentable state of her clothes, the woman's personality suddenly struck her as being quite exceptional. They had, as it were, exchanged impressions, and she had the feeling that they had spent a long time observing one another, without a thought for what was going on around them.

The newcomer's glance alighted on the open lid of the medicine chest, which was adorned with paintings of Saint Como and Saint Damian, the patron saints of apothecaries.

'Do you revere holy pictures?' she asked in a voice in which there was a hint of surprise.

'And why should I not revere them? Is there anything about me that would lead you to believe that I lack respect and affection for the saints that protect us? ... You have been prejudiced against me, haven't you? I feel sure you have! And from as far away as Paris too. Where do you come from, and who are you?'

The woman made no reply.

She rose to her feet, then, after bending over the child and seeing that he was sleeping peacefully, went over to the table and began to help Angélique spread out pieces of lint with which to make dressings.

At that moment the sturdy peasant woman, Catherine-Gertrude, entered carrying a baby in her arms.

She gave an exclamation:

'Oh, I didn't know you were here, Mother ...'

She broke off as the woman quickly signalled to her to keep quiet.

'So you are a pioneer, the founder of an order,' Angélique went on, seeking to solve the mystery.

'You are getting very hot,' the mysterious woman replied and burst into a peal of gay, youthful laughter. But still she said nothing, delighting in Angélique's curiosity.

Then someone else came in who recognized the new arrival.

'God be praised!' he cried. 'Here you are back in Canada again, Mother Bourgeoys, what a blessing!'

'So you are Marguerite Bourgeoys?'

Then, as the children were brought in for her to treat –

for her prowess as a sharpshooter appeared to have persuaded the mothers of Tadoussac to trust her – Angélique
reflected what an extraordinary stroke of luck it had been
that had brought her into contact at the very outset with one
of the most remarkable women in the whole of New France.
It was at Katarunk the previous year that she had first heard
her name mentioned. Rough trappers and hardened soldiers
from the nobility had spoken with devotion of the woman
who had come to Canada as a young girl with one of
Monsieur de Maisonneuve's first bands of recruits in
the days when, on a tiny island in the St Lawrence, he had
founded the city of Montreal, at first called Ville-Marie
since it was dedicated to the Queen of Heaven. Marguerite
Bourgeoys had come alone, fearlessly, for the love of God,
to bring up and educate children and to baptize the savages.
She had worked in the fields, founded schools and cared
for the wounded in the fighting with the Iroquois.

Was it not she who had saved Eloi Macollet's life when
he was scalped?

'You appear to have heard things about me too, so I see,'
said Marguerite Bourgeoys.

'But not the same sort,' retorted Angélique. 'I am accused
of every possible turpitude, while you are a veritable angel of
light.'

Mademoiselle Bourgeoys's retort came swift and sharp:

'I will not listen to such talk!' she exclaimed. 'Both are
equally false. It is a sin to listen to them and I beg you not
to lend weight to such ideas in future by repeating them.'

Then her face immediately softened again and in an unexpected gesture she brushed Angélique's cheek with her
finger.

'I see what it is,' she remarked indulgently. 'You are an
impulsive child.'

Thereafter they were both caught up in the bustle of
attending to the thousand-and-one demands of the inhabitants who thronged round them to ask for advice and
medicine.

It was as if the entire population of Tadoussac, which had
been brimming over with health the day before, had suddenly been smitten with every imaginable ailment.

Marguerite Bourgeoys's experience coupled with that of

Angélique and the extensive resources of her portable dispensary offered everyone an unexpected opportunity to seek treatment, an opportunity that would be unlikely to recur for some considerable time.

The open affection the newcomer had shown her had a wonderfully stimulating effect upon Angélique, and the fact that this woman, beloved by one and all, was there beside her as she made her entry into Canada, seemed to her a lucky omen. She felt utterly at home, as if she had always dwelt among these Canadians, although only the day before she had feared them. And people were treating her as if they had always known her.

They saw that she knew how to calm frightened children and rapidly began to feel the benefit of her hands that were so deft at dressing wounds and, by resting upon an aching forehead or a stiffened limb, could divine the cause of the trouble and bring relief.

There was talk of arranging a further visit on the morrow to deal with teeth extractions and lancing of abcesses ... Then Honorine and Chérubin began to get up to mischief.

CHAPTER 16

IT WAS when Angélique was rummaging through her medicine chest to find an indispensable bag of mixed berries for treating coughs. Mother Bourgeoys noticed just in time that Honorine had made off with them and was busy trying to hide them in Chérubin's breeches, and, before Angélique had time to step in, she used the skill and experience she had acquired as a teacher to extricate her ill-gotten gains from the child.

'But they're for Mister Willoughby,' the little girl protested.

'Who's Mister Willoughby, my sweetheart?' asked Marguerite Bourgeoys with the patient good humour that schoolteachers develop.

'He's a bear, a bear who's a friend of mine. And he loves myrtle berries.'

'I don't doubt he does. But wouldn't it be better to pick him some fresh berries rather than to give him dried ones? I know a place in Tadoussac where we could still find some to pick. I've often picked them round here myself.'

'Have you got a bear?' Honorine asked while Mother Bourgeoys deftly relieved her of the medicinal berries.

'No, darling, and I wish I had, because I'm convinced that a bear can be a splendid pet. There was one on board the *Saint John the Baptist* and I came to be very fond of him; he was well behaved and a perfect gentleman.'

Honorine burst out laughing.

Meanwhile the general hubbub had died down and from the direction of the door there could be heard the sound of argument and whisperings, and someone they could not see exclaimed in irritation:

'But good heavens ... isn't anyone here frightened? What if she were dangerous? I'd never have thought ...'

The caretaker's reply was inaudible but its tone was apologetic. Then the bossy voice began again:

'Never mind ... So she's here, is she? And it appears you have allowed her to treat your children ... You really are utterly reckless ...'

Intrigued and guessing that she was the person they were talking about, Angélique went to the door holding Chérubin, who was all covered with jam, by the hand.

'Were you asking for me, Sir,' she asked a gentlemen in a waistcoat and long coat, with a plumed hat on his head, some royal official no doubt, who was angrily haranguing the caretaker. He was accompanied by a colourless woman, apparently his wife to judge by her middle-class dress, and by an ageing man who looked as if he was probably a clerk.

The personage cast an indifferent, scowling glance at Angélique.

'Where are *you* from? ... The *Saint John the Baptist*, I'll be bound! And a pretty state she's in too, that ship. No compliments from me to the gentlemen of the Company in Rouen. Where's it been wandering about all this time to arrive here as late as this, that's what I'd like to know. And even so it managed to get boarded by pirates ... right in

Tadoussac harbour ... The time has come to put a firm foot down ... And we had been warned too ...'

He pushed the caretaker aside after no less peremptorily thrusting his wife back as she tried to follow him. 'Stay outside, my dear, you never know ...' he said as he entered the warehouse, puffing out his chest.

'Where is she? ...'

He seemed to be prepared to confront all the thunderbolts of Hell and, after all, Angélique told herself, perhaps he was right. When word gets around that a she-devil is in the offing, it's no laughing matter. You lose nothing by marshalling your strength. Such situations are not easy to cope with as she could testify, for she had in fact encountered a she-devil. She recalled the arrival of Ambroisine on the beach at Gouldsboro, Ambroisine collapsing at her feet like a dying bird, and she shuddered. The worthy man was right to be frightened. Had he been there at the time, Ambroisine in her yellow dress, her peacock-blue coat, her red bodice and her feline sweetness, would have had him eating from her hand in no time. It is not so simple a matter to thwart the evil designs of demons. Did she not herself appear to these anxious people equally disarmingly harmless? She congratulated herself on having dressed simply and welcomed the calm manner in which the population of Tadoussac, small as it was, were taking events. The arrival of this new man appeared to be a matter of utter indifference to these peasants and the newcomer began to lose his temper, then calmed down a little on catching sight of Marguerite Bourgeoys.

'Ah! So you're there too, Mother Bourgeoys ...' He relaxed a little. 'Welcome, dear Mother. What's going on here? I was told ...'

He looked about him, saw the medicine chest standing open and the women with their babies undressed on their knees.

'But for heaven's sake, it's madness ... It's crazy!'

He tried to pick out a face, to discover among all these women's faces the unfamiliar and dreaded one that glowed with the marks of Lucifer: Countess Peyrac ...

'Where is she? ... Has she gone up in smoke? Mother Bourgeoys, I beseech you, you are a sensible woman ... Point her out to me!'

'But whom do you mean?' asked Mademoiselle Bourgeoys, who could not follow.

'The woman who calls herself Countess Peyrac and who was here, so I was told, just a moment ago.'

'And I am still here,' Angélique reiterated, walking straight up to him.

This time he looked at her more carefully, but only to burst out once more in imprecations:

'Enough of this! ... You are trying to make a fool of me.'

'What do you mean?'

'You are all making fun of me. It's intolerable! What is going on? ... Is everyone going mad? People are insulting me, defying me, taking no heed of my advice, my warnings ...'

Striking a theatrical pose he shouted to the company at large:

'I wish to see Countess Peyrac! ...'

'Well then look at her,' shouted Angélique in her turn: 'I am she!'

And she added, seeing his look of amazement:

'... I am Countess Peyrac, may it please you, Sir. Take a good look at me and then be so kind as to tell me what it is you want.'

The man went all the colours of the rainbow. Never was anyone more disconcerted. His face registered every shade of surprise, doubt, consternation and terror, only to return once more to doubt and consternation.

Angélique finished him off by adding haughtily:

'... And furthermore, who are you, Sir? Here you are clamouring for me, and yet you have not even been introduced to me.'

The man gave a start, and not knowing which way to turn, began to berate the caretaker, grabbing hold of his collar and shaking him as he spoke:

'You idiot! Couldn't you have warned me sooner instead of allowing me to make a fool of myself ...'

'Don't talk to my employee like that,' cried Ville d'Avray rushing forward. 'What right have you to molest him?'

'Oh, so you're involved in all this, too, Monsieur the Governor of Acadia! Well I'm not surprised that unseemly and riotous behaviour is getting the upper hand here!'

'Unseemly and riotous behaviour! Just you say that again!'

Suddenly Angélique caught sight of Joffrey on the threshold.

He was wearing his mask.

He had suddenly materialized as he so often did, without anyone hearing him coming, at the very moment he was least looked for, people's thoughts being distracted from him by some unexpected incident. He had the art of the sudden appearance and always managed things in such a way as to make a startling impression. There would be stifled exclamations, a confused notion that he had popped up out of the earth, and in that first moment of disarray, the details of his carefully chosen costume monopolized attention and captured every gaze. A single detail sufficed to distract the assembled company and prevented them from recovering their wits, thus giving the master of the *Gouldsboro* time to get a firm grip on the situation.

On this occasion it was his mask that caught attention, and, as far as his accoutrement was concerned, a diamond star of incomparable beauty that hung round his neck on a broad white silk ribbon, and sparkled on his midnight-blue taffeta doublet with its delicate silver filigree embroidery. An equally large diamond adorned the handle of his sword. With these exceptions, there was a simplicity in his attire that was more in line with the English fashion, a fact that did not fail to arouse vague feelings of disquiet among the local people who, a generation earlier, had experienced several years of enemy occupation when the English held Tadoussac.

On the other hand, he could hardly have been mistaken for a French nobleman, bedizened with plumes and lace, buckled shoes and embroidered waistcoats. He answered perfectly, in fact, to the predictable image of the stranger, the corsair, owing allegiance to no overlord, to no laws, whose fabulous wealth, originating in the Caribbean now extended to North America.

Appearing thus before them, he brought a glamorous image to remote, sub-polar Canada – a land built on the obscure sacrifices of peasant folk, a land of forests lacking the mineral wealth that had been the essential attribute of the Eldorado of the *conquistadores* – and the image he brought into this land of chill mists, to these rugged shores, was of one of those swashbuckling filibusters whose exploits figured in the stories told by much-travelled sailors or by Acadians, who had closer contact with them. The tales that went the rounds in the long evenings gave a highly-coloured picture of their feats of arms, their wealth, their crimes; but no one imagined he would ever set eyes upon a real-life specimen in this very place – and one of the most celebrated of them all at that!

And suddenly there he was at the door, with his followers, having reached it without anyone hearing a single sound because of all the shouting that was going on inside. And of course he gallantly ushered in the royal official's pale, retiring wife whom he must have found left to her own devices outside the door. To judge by his charming smile, he must have been saying all manner of delightful things to her, and it was quite likely that she had never heard so many compliments in all her life before, for she looked up at him like a frightened ewe-sheep and then over at her husband who was still going at it hammer and tongs with Ville d'Avray.

'If you weren't so pigheaded as to insist on living over the other side of the Saguenay, you could have been here when these so-called pirates came ashore this morning – and I was one of them, I'll have you know, Sir – and you would have been properly introduced to Madame de Peyrac,' said Ville d'Avray.

'You know that the air over at High Steeple farm is better for my wife's health.'

'Then you mustn't complain of always getting here late whenever something occurs within your area of jurisdiction.'

The Marquis turned towards Angélique:

'Dear lady, allow me to introduce his Worship Ducrest de Lamotte.'

Then, catching sight of Joffrey, he added:

'... And this is her husband, Monsieur de Peyrac, whose fleet is lying at anchor before Tadoussac.'

Seeing his wife standing close beside the dark figure of this masked *condottiere*, his Worship Ducrest de Lamotte suffered his second shock of the day. His distraught gaze travelled from Angélique's modest apparel to this newcomer so openly proclaiming himself the swashbuckling conqueror, and to his formidable armed escort. The combined effort was to lend the breastplates and helmets of the Count's personal Spanish guard a particularly menacing glint in his eyes.

What finally demoralized him was to see his unfortunate wife being escorted into the room by Joffrey de Peyrac, and to hear him saying to her:

'I won't have you waiting outside like that, Madame. Since everyone is inside, do please come inside and sit with us.'

In a flash Ducrest de Lamotte saw the unfortunate woman, whose state of health was already precarious, being held as hostage or used as a shield by a cruel barbarian of Morgan or Olonais's ilk, those ill-famed buccaneers of tropical waters.

He cried out:

'I beg you, Sir, do not harm her. I surrender, here is my sword ...'

CHAPTER 17

PEYRAC IGNORED the proffered sword.

'Sir, you misunderstand the situation. I have no use for your worthy sword. Put it back in its scabbard, and long may it remain there, that is my most sincere wish. Please understand that I have put in at Tadoussac as a friend, for I am the guest of Monsieur de Frontenac, your Governor. Furthermore, here is Monsieur Carlon, who is my guest on board the *Gouldsboro* and will testify to the honourable nature of my intentions.'

'Monsieur the Intendant ...' stammered Ducrest, raising his hat to Carlon as the latter entered the warehouse.

Carlon was in a furious temper, but for quite another reason than finding himself represented from the outset as an ally of Count Peyrac's. It was the matter of the consignment left for shipment that had infuriated him.

'I have just seen my consignment of timber, masts, barrels of wheat, and seal oil and salted eels still lying on the dockside ... What's the meaning of it? You know very well they were due for shipment to France ...'

'The ships didn't want to load the stuff ...'

'What you mean is that you were the devil knows where when they put in here.'

'Neither were you here yourself, Monsieur the Intendant,' Ducrest retorted; 'and you promised you would be here on the spot from the beginning of October to see to the loading of the freight ...'

'I know I did, but I was held up in Acadia ... no end of complications ... So I arrive here and find all these goods piled up to lie there all winter under the snow ...'

'But don't despair, Monsieur. There are still ships that have not yet sailed for Europe.'

'They must be crazy! Do they want to have the bottoms ripped out of them by the ice?'

'The *Maribelle* has been held up. There were reports, there were fears ... a pirate fleet ... And she's one of the King's ships carrying thirty guns.'

The Intendant slumped down on a bench with a gesture that indicated that all these details were the merest trifles compared with the problems he himself had to face.

'Nonsense!' he repeated. 'That ship will be sacrificed for nothing; Monsieur de Peyrac is sailing to Quebec with five vessels that count far more than thirty guns between them.'

'I thought you were vouching for his good intentions,' whispered the official in alarm.

'But what else can I do?'

'Come now,' Peyrac exclaimed cheerfully, 'come now, my good friend, don't disown me. As I have said, I am willing to buy your cargo from you. I can use it to keep my men and my crews supplied, for all I want to ask of New France is the hospitality that comes from the heart.'

'That did not prevent you from boarding a French merchant vessel this morning without the slightest scruple.'

'The *Saint John the Baptist*? I'm glad you brought her up,' said Ville d'Avray, breaking into the conversation. 'You know as well as I do that René Dugast is as slippery a customer as a man is ever likely to have to cope with, and that when you count in Boniface Gonfarel in Quebec as well, you'd never have had an inkling of half of what he had under his hatches. You ought to thank Monsieur de Peyrac for giving you a chance of searching the ship. I feel sure you made the most of the opportunity to take a close look, and that you'll be able to nab him before all his treasures, his Paris perfumes and precious liqueurs are sold under the counter in defiance of you by that sly old fox Boniface Gonfarel and his wife Janine. Monsieur the Intendant, if you manage to collect your customs dues this year, believe me, it will be thanks to . . .'

And he pointed vigorously a number of times in the direction of Peyrac, then went on in an undertone:

'. . . I believe they've got several barrels of Beaune and Dijon wine on board the *Saint John the Baptist*. The best of the reds, as you know. You, Monsieur de Peyrac, who complain that you have no good wine to offer your guests, should take advantage of this windfall.'

'Just listen to you egging him on. As if it was not enough that he's taken it upon himself to confine the crew and passengers on board, among whom I hear there is a very high-ranking official whose name is being kept secret and who has been sent over on a personal mission by the King. Supposing he were to complain . . .'

'To whom?' retorted Ville d'Avray heatedly. 'We are among ourselves here. What have we to do with a high-ranking official at this time? We are all quite "high-ranking" enough if it comes to that, and this gentleman from Versailles has no business to come poking his nose into our affairs. It will be a big enough bore having to put up with his presence all winter in Quebec, so let us be glad that Monsieur de Peyrac has assumed responsibility for depriving us of his company today.'

During this exchange, Angélique had introduced herself to Madame Ducrest de Lamotte and had prevailed on her to sit down in their circle. On discovering the presence of Mademoiselle Bourgeoys, Madame de Lamotte cheered up somewhat. News was exchanged. Angélique drew Catherine-Gertrude aside to ask her what refreshments could be provided for the company, but Yann signalled to her and she saw that their own major-domo had already arrived with several assistants, bringing kegs of spirits, flasks of rum and pastries. She was astonished.

Living with Joffrey was a source of perpetual enchantment. He was so sure of himself. He moved among men, never intimidated by the fact that they were strangers to him, carefully seeking to make friends of them or to circumvent them if they turned out to be hostile. Was it from some unique quality inherent in his native province, the Languedoc, that he had acquired this gift that was part science, partly an instinctive understanding of human personality? In his presence, danger acquired a certain savour.

Joffrey's eyes smiled at Angélique from behind his mask. He moved towards her.

'You seem to have captivated your Canadians already, as far as I can see.'

'But this is only Tadoussac, and Tadoussac isn't Quebec.'

'It's a step on the way, though.'

'And what do you think? I've had the good fortune to meet the famous Mademoiselle Bourgeoys of Montreal ...'

'And you'll have luck on other occasions too ...'

The many goblets drunk and the warmth emanating from the hearth and from the crowd, and the groups that formed, drawn together by what they had in common or by some topic of discussion, had brought the gathering to that stage when people dissociate themselves from one another and give themselves up to enjoyment, having, amid the anonymity of the crowd, eyes only for those individuals of either sex whose company they find congenial or entertaining, and when everything seems to be going on in a kind of isolation that prevents one from being seen while in fact one is exposed to everyone's gaze – which is the great charm of such social gatherings and the explanation of their success.

The excitement that follows upon a feeling of relief once danger is past gave rise to a general conviction that all problems could be solved provided that good will was shown.

Joffrey de Peyrac found himself beside Angélique. He had eyes for her alone, she alone existed for him. She motioned to the flagons on the table.

'What would you care to drink, my Lord Rescator?'

'Nothing ... I just want to look at you.'

She remembered the surprise gift he had given her that morning, the watch with the fleur-de-lys engraved on it that hung about her neck.

'Why did you give me this watch?' she asked.

'Why not?'

She swung round and looked deep into his eyes through the slits in his mask. Then, in an unselfconscious, familiar, friendly gesture, she placed a finger on his cheek where the trace of a scar could be seen.

'Oh, you,' she said, '*you*!'

She wanted to say: 'How full of surprises you are! What impulses of heart, of soul ... how like you and you alone they are, and how they enrapture my life! How does one ever free oneself from such a spell?' And again: 'I understand you in spite of your air of mystery ... I can decypher you. You are not a complete stranger to me ... You have always known how to make play with my heart and my innermost thoughts ... It's true ... And I am helpless in your power.'

Heedless of the hubbub all around them, he bent down, and taking her face in his hands, softly kissed her on the forehead as one would a child, then on the mouth, and she felt the edge of his leather mask against her cheek as his lips lingered on hers.

A few of those present noticed, including Marguerite Bourgeoys and the Jesuit father. A few of the peasants shook their heads. A few of the peasant girls felt a furtive fluttering of the heart.

That night, there was to be a great party down on the waterfront.

No one knew what was what any more.

CHAPTER 18

THE EVENING was made memorable by an incident which, while serving to throw Angélique's personality into sharper relief, was for a long time to come to furnish material for the legends which everywhere sprang up about her. It was almost natural, at any rate comprehensible to those who knew her and were used to living in close contact with her, whereas to others the incident appeared to border on the inexplicable, though it was so much in tune with the way the Canadians thought and felt, sensitive and intuitive folk that they were, that her recognition in Tadoussac was confirmed without further ado.

The evening's festivities were at their height with songs and dances following one upon another when an idea flashed through her mind. Suddenly preoccupied, she abandoned the gathering, standing in the forefront of which she had just raised her glass to the health of New France and the people of Tadoussac.

Yet everything seemed to be going splendidly. Huge braziers warmed the night air enabling groups to gather at various points to eat, drink and dance. A roasting ox was turning on a spit in the church square. Peyrac had had large quantities of wines, spirits, sweetmeats and religious medals distributed. The latter, which came straight from France and represented all the saints in paradise, were a personal gift from the Count to the people of Tadoussac and gave his arrival in Canada a semi-religious character, conferring so to speak Heaven's blessing upon it, so that one and all, even Monsieur Ducrest, gave themselves up without compunction to the pleasures of the evening. The parish priest emerged from his cellars with several flasks of elderberry brandy distilled by himself and agreed to bless the medals brought over by the Lord of Gouldsboro's fleet. A bottle of holy water was placed in his hands and those

133

containing the precious nectar disappeared into thin air.

Everyone had a nip and Joffrey congratulated the priest on the wonderful results from his home-made still.

All Joffrey's crews were there, along with the soldiers from the fort, the traders, peasants, trappers and, of course, the Indians from the neighbouring encampments, with their chieftains decked in feathers and appropriately painted.

The only people to be confined on board their vessel were the passengers and crew of the *Saint John the Baptist*, including its captain. Count Peyrac had taken an absolutely firm line in ostracizing them that could at a pinch be justified by the fact that they had fired two poorly-aimed cannon shots at him.

Angélique set off anxiously in search of Marguerite Bourgeoys who, on compassionate grounds, had been allowed to remain on shore with the child she was caring for. Angélique had seen her stop and speak to Joffrey and, soon after, baskets of victuals had been sent off under close guard, presumably for the nun's companions and the most needy of the passengers.

Thereafter Mother Bourgeoys had taken some small part in the festivities, going from group to group, welcomed everywhere with affection and respect. Then she had withdrawn, old Carillon's daughter, Catherine-Gertrude, having offered to put her up in her house.

Angélique asked her way to the house, which was a large farmhouse built of solid stone with a still larger barn adjoining the main building. When she arrived, evening prayers were being said, so Angélique slipped inside and knelt behind the family until the devotions were over.

That evening, in honour of Mademoiselle Bourgeoys, they were saying the Litany as well.

Angélique was bubbling over with impatience, tormented by a sudden anxious thought that had come to her a little earlier at the height of the jollifications – a stupid, far-fetched notion. She had been standing beside her husband, clapping as the young men and girls finished a dance. Then suddenly there had been this flash, this thought that there was something she must see to *or else it would be too late*. Scarcely waiting to hand her wine-cup to her nearest neighbour, she had slipped away through the crowd of spectators.

'Have you seen Mademoiselle Bourgeoys?' she enquired. 'Do you know where Mademoiselle Bourgeoys is?'

Having found her, she now had to wait, and every minute that passed was agony to her. Then at last the pious company rose to its feet and Angélique went up to the woman she had been seeking.

'Mademoiselle Bourgeoys, might I have a word with you?'

Catherine-Gertrude's family, her sons, daughters-in-law, children, grandchildren, uncles, aunts, cousins, serving-men and maids were all utterly delighted to find her there among them, but she had no time to greet them all. She drew Mademoiselle Bourgeoys aside.

'Do forgive me. You must be longing to get some rest.'

'I will not deny the fact. Although in the services of Our Lord we have to mortify the flesh and I normally make do with little sleep, I must admit that the idea of sleeping in a comfortable bed, back home here in Canada, gladdens my heart.'

She shook her head:

'Poor Saint John the Baptist! I had a special devotion for that holy man of the desert who baptized Our Lord Jesus Christ, but I must confess that it will be a long while before I am able to invoke his aid without recalling the appalling ship that bore his name. Discomfort is nothing, but such harshness, such malice! None of our exhortations had the slightest effect. It is as if the blacker the souls of a captain and his crew, the more anxious they are to give their ship a pious name . . .'

'I've noticed that with pirates too,' Angélique concurred. 'The Caribbean is full of ships called the *Virgin Mary* . . . But listen, the fact is that I'm worried about something you said to me this afternoon . . . I did not pay much attention at the time, then it suddenly came back to me and it's been worrying me nearly frantic . . .'

'Well, do tell me then.'

'You won't laugh at me, will you?'

'No, please tell me,' Marguerite repeated indulgently. 'What is it?'

'It's an insignificant detail and yet it worries me, especially on account of your crew's dreadful reputation ... I thought I heard you say, when my Honorine was telling you about the bear called Mister Willoughby, that there was a bear on board the *Saint John the Baptist* too.'

'That's right!'

'So there is a bear! That's not at all a common occurrence. Tame, I imagine? That's not a thing you see any day of the week. You don't think it could be the same bear, do you? ... Mister Willoughby that we are all so fond of?'

'That's what I am beginning to wonder,' Mademoiselle Bourgeoys admitted frankly. 'I didn't know the name of the bear we had on board, but since Honorine mentioned him, I have been wondering too.'

'How did the bear come to be on board the *Saint John the Baptist*?'

'When we were in the Gulf of St Lawrence, the captain quite unscrupulously captured a small craft and its occupants. And, strange as it may sound, the bear was among them.'

'And had they a poor little Moorish boy with them, too?'

'Yes, as a matter of fact they did.'

'It's them: the bear is Mister Willoughby and the little black boy is Timothy! ... No doubt about it, they are our friends. Do tell me what has become of them.'

'The captain regarded the capture as a stroke of luck; he hoped to hold them up to ransom or sell them in Quebec, for they had an Englishman from New England with them too. He was the owner of the bear.'

'Elias Kempton!'

'The poor folk were very roughly treated, especially the Englishman, and although he is a heretic, I felt obliged to intercede for him in the name of Christian charity that forbids us to ill-use any human being without grave cause. Vicious as the sailors were, they did take some notice of what I said. I know the kind of men these seafaring folk are, and I was able to persuade them that their interest lay in taking their captives to Quebec as a prize of war rather than in killing them.'

'And what about the bear? ...'

'They hoisted him on board the *Saint John the Baptist* in order to have his fur after cutting him up and smoking the meat.'

'Oh, how dreadful! My poor Willoughby! So what happened to him?'

'I managed to convince them, I don't remember how, that it was wanton slaughter, and in fact the bear was not easy to come at. His master succeeded in calming him down and then made him do a few tricks that amused everyone. So they were left alone and camped up on deck.'

'If you have saved Mister Willoughby's life, my dear Marguerite, I shall be eternally grateful to you, and so will Honorine ... But how was it that my husband and his men did not see them? From what you say, they must still be on board the *Saint John the Baptist*.'

'Most certainly they are! Although I have not seen them on deck since yesterday. Perhaps the captain decided to hide them away as we approached Tadoussac.'

'Perhaps he has killed them! Oh, heavens, Mademoiselle Bourgeoys! Now I realize why I suddenly felt so anxious about them. There's not a moment to lose.'

She hastened towards the door, where Marguerite Bourgeoys joined her.

'Look! I remember that one of the people from the small craft, a coarse fellow, I must admit, although that was no justification for the hammering they gave him, especially as he claimed to be seriously wounded ...'

'Slit-belly! I know who you mean.'

'Maybe! Anyway I remember his referring to the fact that they were under Count Peyrac's protection, that they were even part of his household, and his saying that the Count would avenge the wrong done them. It could be that, when Captain Dugast saw Count Peyrac himself bearing down on him, he took fright and hid his captives away somewhere after gagging them, for instance.'

'That's quite likely. Oh, the poor unfortunates!'

'Now I come to think of it,' the nun went on, catching up with Angélique once more, 'who knows but maybe, finding himself in the hands of the Count and fearing reprisals for having seized the men, he will try to do away with them.

137

That man is capable of anything. I've seen him in action.'

'Good heavens!' Angélique repeated; 'let's hope we are not too late ...'

She reproached herself bitterly as she ran. Back in Tidnish she had fallen down badly in her duty. She had allowed Aristide Beaumarchand's boat to sail without ascertaining its destination and without thanking him and his companions for their help. And indeed it was true that, like it or not, he was among those to whom they owed protection.

She lightly touched Joffrey's doublet sleeve. He turned round and was surprised to find her panting as if she had been running, which was indeed the case.

She put him rapidly in the picture about what she had just learned.

'Did you leave any men on board the *Saint John the Baptist* for the night?' she asked.

'No. Since no one could leave the ship there were no grounds for so doing, nor any necessity either.'

'In that case, they will take this opportunity to ...'

Joffrey was already working out a plan. He signalled to d'Urville, who was dancing with the young women.

'I'm leaving you to keep the festivities going,' Joffrey whispered to him. 'Set the fireworks off to distract attention, so that our absence isn't noticed. I need Barssempuy and his men for a job on board the *Saint John the Baptist*.'

He and Angélique went down to the port, accompanied by the Spanish guard. Barssempuy had been stationed near the jetty with a small contingent of armed men. Count Peyrac requisitioned four of them to row over to where the ship lay at anchor, its shape, keeling over to one side, just visible through the damp night air.

As the longboat began to pull away from the shore, the first of the fireworks, set off by the *Gouldsboro*'s artificers, began to light up the night sky to the accompaniment of cries of wonder from the crowd.

'The people on the ship will be distracted by the display as well,' Joffrey said softly. 'They'll all be looking this way. So we'll approach them from the far side in order to take them by surprise.'

There may be neither rhyme nor reason in this, Angélique

told herself as she sat close to Joffrey clasping his arm. But never mind. She wanted to be quite sure. And he understood how she felt. It was so comforting to have as husband an all-powerful man who was ready to place troops, his weapons, his cannons and his ships at her disposal, and who never made fun of her.

With all lights doused, the boarding party rowed round the hulk in order to come up to her on the far side, away from the shore lights, and indeed they had the impression that the sailors on watch had all gone over to the port rails to have a better view of the brilliantly illuminated sky and all its wonders. As one of Barssempuy's men rose to his feet, holding a gaff to cushion the impact of the longboat against the ship's hull, a woman's voice raised in a piercing shriek was heard, sounding strangely out of place in this apparently peaceful night, whose calm had been broken only by the distant explosions of fireworks.

'Help! Help! They're tryin' to do me in ...'

'That's Julienne's voice,' exclaimed Angélique, rising so suddenly to her feet that she nearly overbalanced into the water.

So her presentiment had been right. At that very moment her friends were in danger.

'Help! Help!' cried the voice. 'If there's a Christian soul on this bloody ship, come and help me! They're out to get me ...'

Then there was a pounding of feet on deck. There were lively goings on up there in the unsavoury darkness.

Joffrey had the boat-lamp lighted, a grappling-iron was thrown over the listing side of the ship, and dug firmly into the ship's rail. With a dexterity that spoke of many a boarding, the men from the boat found themselves on the deck of the *Saint John the Baptist* in a matter of seconds. The Count had been the first to leap on board. Angélique had to wait until a rope ladder was thrown down to her. As she clambered up, the spectacle that met her eyes in the light of the lanterns made her flesh creep: Joffrey, his pistols in his hands, was holding a group of extremely surprised seamen at bay, in the midst of whom a woman, her bodice torn open, was struggling to get free. It was Julienne. A little further off lay flat on the deck an inert, indistinct figure, elaborately bound and gagged, with a stone cannonball already roped round its neck.

'Weren't taking any chances, were you?' commented one of the men from the *Gouldsboro*, looking at the size of the cannonball.

Once released from his bonds, the unfortunate Aristide Beaumarchand reacted with the same incredulity and horror to the size of the stone that had been about to drag him down to the bottom of the St Lawrence.

So it was true that they had been about to drown him like a dog.

'It was the Captain what gave the order,' the sailors bawled as they were roughly hustled into a corner.

They were tied up after being relieved of their knives.

Julienne threw herself into Peyrac's arms then, after sobbing noisily over the diamond star, she threw herself into Angélique's embrace.

'I *knew* you would come and save us. I said to Aristide you would. I said: "They'll come ..."'

'You see how they've treated us, and decent folk, we are too,' said Aristide. 'It's proper shameful, that's what it is.'

'And what about the Englishman, the pedlar?' Angélique asked anxiously. 'Have they already thrown him overboard?'

'No, he and his bear are still in the goat-pen. They clapped him in irons.'

As they crossed the battery deck where the passengers were huddled, they caught a glimpse of this startled face or that. Disturbed by the commotion on deck and the distant sounds of festivities on land, most of them were awake. After enduring the innumerable torments of a crossing that had lasted almost four months, with its dead calms, its epidemic and its storms, they had at last reached Canada only to find themselves involved in an outbreak of piracy.

There were pale, resigned women's faces, the impassive forms of members of religious orders, men with bowed shoulders, while through one of the open portholes the distant, sporadic, multicoloured glow of the fireworks fitfully lit up a dismal scene reminiscent of Dante's descriptions of the damned. Yet there were children among them, alarmingly thin, who were gazing entranced at the distant rockets.

Down in the hold the air was still more unbreatheable and

foul, and they found Kempton in chains lying on a bed of rotten straw.

'Ah, dear Lady, what good fortune brings you here?' cried the pedlar from Connecticut, lifting to Heaven his hands laden with chains. 'I was really beginning to despair ... Especially on account of your shoes which I have finished. Beauties. But I didn't know how to get them to you ... And now they've stolen all my goods.'

'These bandits have taken everything from us,' Aristide whimpered. 'His goods and chattels, my rum, particularly good rum, pure Jamaican produce ...'

'Where's Mister Willoughby?' Angélique asked as they were fetching the keeper of the keys in order to set the prisoner free.

'There!' replied Kempton, pointing to the heap of straw beside him.

'What's the matter with him? He's not moving. Is he dead?'

'No, he's asleep!'

'But why? Is he ill?'

'No, he's asleep. What do you expect, Madame, it's in his nature ... You can do anything you like with that bear, Madame, except prevent him falling asleep at the onset of winter ... Had this ship not taken us prisoner, I had been going to take him to one of his favourite lairs. After that, Aristide and I were going to put in at Newfoundland where I have several customers waiting for me. Then we would have sailed on to Nova Scotia ... Come the spring, I'd have gone back to fetch Willoughby and we'd have all been off together to New York. I'm used to these to-ings and fro-ings ... But there you are! Fate decided otherwise, and we were brought to New France as prisoners. Those are the ups and downs you have to expect when you sail the seas ...'

While they talked together in English, one of the seamen arrived and reluctantly unfastened the pedlar's chains. He stood up, stretched, massaged his wrists and ankles, then, after carefully brushing his puritan-style sugar-loaf hat, put it back on his head again.

'What are we going to do?' asked Angélique, glancing anxiously at the pile of straw beneath which she could just make out the huge form of the sleeping bear. How were they going to move him? Besides, it might well be dangerous or bad for him to interrupt his hibernation.

'No, we must not disturb him,' said Kempton anxiously. 'If you waken a bear, he can't go to sleep again and becomes irritable and dangerous.'

'But you must come ashore for a good meal.'

'No! No!' the Englishman replied vehemently. 'I must stay here to look after my friend. I wouldn't put it past these French bandits to come and slaughter him in his sleep to make smoked meat of him. On one occasion already I only just managed to save his life, and that was thanks to the intervention of a most kindly lady, who, although a nun and a notorious papist, took sides with me and managed to make them see sense because she had some influence over the brutes.'

'We shall send you some food, then.'

'All right. And let me have a weapon, too. I'll feel easier about Mister Willoughby that way. If they try to approach him to kill him in his sleep, I'll be able to defend him.'

'And where is Timothy?' cried Angélique, who still had further friends to muster.

Once again they set off across the battery deck in search of the piccaninny.

On the way, Joffrey de Peyrac exchanged a few words with the clerics and assured them that the vessel would soon be able to continue on its way towards Quebec, which they would in all likelihood reach before he did. Once again he assured them of his peaceful intentions. The *Saint John the Baptist*, he said, needed to be repaired, and its captain needed to be taught a lesson. They all agreed about that. There was even a Jesuit father among them who made no secret of the fact that he had just about reached the end of his tether.

'I've crossed to Canada six times, Monsieur. Everyone knows that even at the best these trips are sheer unbroken torture to both body and soul. But I have never experienced one that has given me so many white hairs as this one . . .'

The horrors of this particular crossing seemed to have caused him to abandon the reserve peculiar to his order. He was a good-looking man with an open, alert expression. Some of the passengers were, like him, fairly excited and voluble, their eyes dilated with fever in their emaciated faces, while others were apathetic, waxen-faced, haggard or puffy, all in a sorry state.

The piccaninny was discovered in the captain's cabin, busy cleaning a pair of boots as tall as himself. Dugast was one of those seamen, half-merchant, half-corsair, who, when hailed at sea, would hoist the flag of the firm that had freighted them, call out 'From St Malo' and go on their way, shielded by their own impudence.

At this particular juncture he appeared to be in as sorry a state as his wretched shipload of sailors and passengers. He was fat enough, but seemed swollen and his eyes were glazed. He looked up at Peyrac almost as if he were a dying man, and he was so weak that, when he attempted to rise from his bunk across which he lay half-sprawled, he slumped back heavily. The reason for his being in this condition became obvious when they noticed lying at his side a long-necked black glass flask from which there rose a stench of alcohol powerful enough to stun the very flies.

'Rum!' said Barssempuy, after sniffing the neck of the bottle. 'But what rum! The most ghastly hooch I've ever encountered in all my life as a filibuster, and rot me ... I've tasted just about every form and manner of rum under the sun!'

Angélique went straight to the true explanation.

'It must be Aristide's rum.'

It appeared that the Captain had wanted to sample the booty he had found on board the captured boat and had paid dearly for it. What with the bear that had very nearly eaten him, this poisonous rum, its concocter who had won his last crowns off him at dice, and the woman who had destroyed what last semblance of order still prevailed among his crew, it looked as if the business had worked out very much to his disadvantage. And now here at Tadoussac was a pirate holding him at his beck and call and wanting to bring him to book for having attempted to drown these scum.

They left him to sleep off his rum and his grievances and removed Timothy, who was chilled to the bone. The poor little black boy was a pitiful sight to see. Angélique wrapped him in her coat, then, after they had once more assured

143

Kempton that they would send him food and would take care of his servant, the newly-freed prisoners were rowed ashore.

The fireworks lent their return a triumphal air.

'It was a close shave, all the same!' said Aristide by way of comment. 'I'd got that stone round my neck already, you know.'

A stone round his neck! A stone round his neck! The banks of that river must have had a good few secrets to tell, in spite of their brief history. The sound of oars gently striking the dark waters could be heard as the boat conveyed its occupants back towards life and light.

'If it hadn't been for Julienne, we'd have had it. She's a treasure, that lass! She saved our lives.'

'How was that?'

'Well, you see, she's such a buxom wench that that dirty scum wanted to have a crack at her before chucking her into the briny. So they untied her and took the gag out. Then all hell was let loose, as you heard! She's not one to let herself be messed about like that, not our Julienne. And it gave you time to get there. The Lord is on our side; that's what I've always said.'

'I knew you'd come, Madame,' said Julienne, kissing Angélique's hands. 'I kept on praying to the Blessed Virgin for you to come.'

The poor creatures still did not know just how narrow an escape they had had.

Once on shore they were given a place by the fire, and brought venison stew, sagamite, cheese and some excellent cider. People gathered round to have a good look at them, being somewhat under the influence of the evening's potations and the priest's elderberry brandy. As the story passed from mouth to mouth it was embellished with many a detail in which the Blessed Virgin figured for Julienne kept on repeating between each mouthful of food: 'Lucky thing I prayed to the Blessed Virgin,' which greatly moved the assembled company. There were so many references to the bear that Intendant Carlon asked:

'Was that the bear that killed Father de Vernon?'

'I've already told you he wasn't killed by a bear,' Ville d'Avray retorted.

'Well who did kill him then?'

'It's of no importance. I'll tell you about it some other time. But get this straight: all he did with the bear was fight him.'

'Fought? With a bear?'

'Yes! I was there. I saw the fight. It was tremendous, and he won.'

'Who did?'

'The Jesuit.'

'What?'

'But they let the bear think he had, so as not to upset him. He's a very sensitive bear, dear Willoughby is!'

'You're spinning me a lot of yarns!'

'No, I'm not. I was there. It happened at Gouldsboro. A marvellous spot.'

'And meanwhile Father de Vernon is dead and ...'

'Some other time,' Ville d'Avray cut him short. 'Come and have a drink! We must wash down these trappers' victuals ... They're a bit on the greasy side ... The food was better at Gouldsboro. And there isn't enough wine here. When I think that on board that battered hulk of a *Saint John the Baptist* they've got some Burgundies that stand a good chance of getting spoiled by sea water before they reach Quebec! And just so that those two rogues, Dugast and Boniface can make a fortune on the quiet ... I think Monsieur de Peyrac is being excessively scrupulous about impounding them, don't you?'

CHAPTER 19

THE STORY of the bear was all round the village by the following day. Of course, strictly speaking, it was obviously open to anyone to chew over a phrase that they had heard and to come to the conclusion that friends, believed to be far across the sea were in fact in danger a mere stone's throw away, but, between ourselves such things don't happen to

145

every Tom, Dick and Harry ...

So the episode was related. The story told how Madame de Peyrac had suddenly begun to feel anxious about these people at the very moment when a band of wretches were planning to kill them on board the *Saint John the Baptist* and how she had spared no effort to rush to their assistance.

Then, with lowered voices, they recalled the phenomenon of the 'call' which, on Christmas Eve a year back in her fort in the Upper Kennebec, had caused her to rise from the table, saying she could hear someone knocking at the door, whereas there was no one there, and how, thanks to her, four of the best-known citizens of New France had been saved: Baron d'Arreboust, Count Loménie-Chambord, Cavelier de la Salle and Father Massérat, who were all dying in the snow not far from Wapassou.[1]

So there was some truth in what people said about her special powers ...

But in spite of all the talk, Angélique's reputation emerged further enhanced from the adventure.

A feeling of respect tinged with wonder was added to the affection she had already inspired, and the fact that Mother Bourgeoys was involved in what had happened conferred upon her that aura of the miraculous that Canada so liberally dispensed, and which proved to the people of Tadoussac, who were not particularly spoilt in other respects, that they were sometimes singled out for special attention from on high by the Lord Jesus.

Thus it was that the following day was spent in a state of high good spirits. It had been decided that they should stay at least four or five days at Tadoussac, if not a week. There seemed little risk of winter weather and ice suddenly setting in, for great flights of wild geese could still be seen crossing the sky, a sign that the frosts would come late.

Angélique looked forward to the break with pleasure. After emerging triumphant from her first encounter with the Canadians, she felt a need for a breathing space to consolidate her position. Furthermore, the local people were entertaining and interesting. She liked the atmosphere, which was less oppressive than Quebec would be, with all the social and official contacts it would entail. And lastly, she was de-

[1] See *The Countess Angélique*.

lighted at the prospect of establishing a firmer friendship with Mademoiselle Bourgeoys.

The previous day's rescue operation had also gladdened her heart and convinced her, as it had the Canadians, that fate was on her side.

She knew that in fact the reason for prolonging their stay in Tadoussac was that a ship of the French royal navy, the *Maribelle*, had been kept back in Quebec, apparently to await their arrival.

In any case, the vessel would be forced to put to sea at any moment and obliged to pass beneath their guns in order to set out on its journey to Europe.

And a mere glance at the roadstead where the decrepit *Saint John the Baptist*, in which an envoy from the King was possibly concealed, lay carefully hemmed in by the *Rochelais* and the *Mont-Désert*, while Barssempuy's and Vanneau's ships guarded both the mouth of the Saguenay river and the cape that controlled the way out into the St Lawrence estuary, sufficed to make it obvious that, for the time being, Joffrey de Peyrac was the undisputed master of Tadoussac.

Nevertheless she questioned him:

'Doesn't the fact that Monsieur de Frontenac has sought to hold a ship back to ... welcome us, prove that he is less of an ally than we thought?'

'I think he has to keep on good terms with the fanatics who surround him, Castel-Morgeat among others, who is utterly devoted to Father d'Orgeval and who is the Military Governor, which is quite a post.'

'But let us take our time. A lot of issues will settle themselves provided we're prepared to wait.'

The longboat was bringing them both ashore. Their attention was caught by the sight of Aristide Beaumarchand and Julienne, who appeared to be waiting for them on the quay. Barssempuy had taken them on board his ship for the night, while Timothy had been entrusted to the kindly Yolande.

Having no doubt recovered from their ordeal, this somewhat peculiar-looking couple were awaiting the arrival of their benefactors, while a few paces behind them, a circle of idlers were watching, agog with curiosity.

'I wonder why we went to so much trouble to select our crews and our escorts?' Angélique asked with a laugh. 'Here we are now landed with these two, along with an English Puritan from Connecticut and his hibernating bear. Whatever are we going to do with them? I'm afraid they are perfect examples of the "undesirables" New France is trying so hard to keep out. Just look at them! ...'

As they drew closer they could see even more clearly the lubberly bearing of Aristide, the failed pirate, nick-named Slit-Belly since Angélique had 'sewn up his paunch' as he put it[1] and Julienne's come-hither manner that made her appear to be permanently flaunting her charms when in fact she was simply waiting for the longboat beside her husband.

As soon as the boat carrying Count and Countess Peyrac was clearly visible, Aristide and Julienne began to gesticulate wildly by way of welcome, to which Angélique replied by waving her hand.

Joffrey de Peyrac glanced down at her where she sat beside him. Her face was three-quarters turned away from him and he could just glimpse the outline of her cheek, pink from the cold morning air, but he guessed she could not help smiling at the demonstrations of friendship from 'those two', and that she was delighted to have come across them again.

'You're fond of them ...' he said, 'fond of the unfortunate, the wretched and the outcasts! Where did you acquire this talent for attaching them to you, for calming their hidden resentments like an animal tamer who manages by his mere presence to make a wild creature forget its anger and its fear?'

'I understand them,' she replied, 'I've ...'

She was about to say, 'I've lived as one of them,' but she refrained. That was still a part of her life she had never discussed with him: her life in the Court of Miracles. Had she done so, he would have been able to understand the origins of the bond that linked her to someone like Julienne, who reminded her of Polack, the woman who had been her friend in the Paris underworld, or to Aristide, who revived memories of every species of rogue she had ever encountered, but belonging to that particular type who, while

[1] See *The Countess Angélique*.

148

capable of committing the most appalling crimes, nevertheless have something in them that can suddenly make decent men of them.

'They're "your lot",' said Peyrac; 'but you must admit, my dear, that they are more disreputable than "my lot".'

'Yes, but more colourful too!'

They were laughing conspiratorially as they reached the shore, and the couple they had rescued from the *Saint John the Baptist* threw themselves at their feet. Aristide and Julienne were like a pair of children. Now that they had met up with the Lord of Gouldsboro and Dame Angélique again, they had ceased to give their own future a thought. Since everyone was going to Quebec, well then, they would go too.

'It's a pretty spot here,' said Julienne, surveying the countryside contentedly. 'It reminds me of the village I was born in, not far from Chevreuse.'

Joffrey took his leave of them and joined Intendant Carlon who was waiting for him a little higher up the beach beside his cargo left uncollected.

Angélique decided to introduce Aristide and Julienne to Mademoiselle Bourgeoys, who had been partly responsible for saving their lives. They had seen her speak up in their defence on board the *Saint John the Baptist*, but circumstances had not been conducive to more friendly relations.

Angélique climbed the hill followed by her usual escort of King's Girls, children, two of the Spanish soldiers and a group of men who were helping the young women to carry their baskets of washing and various utensils such as wooden pails, bowls and small open baskets containing soap jelly, for they had decided to do a big wash on shore that morning. The cat was there too, darting playfully around them as they went.

When they reached the lowest terrace of the village itself they encountered Catherine-Gertrude Ganvin on her way back from the morning's milking, with a wooden yoke across her shoulders from which hung two metal-banded wooden pails.

'Come and have a bowl of milk,' she said to Angélique; 'I know you like it.'

'Yes, I do. It's delicious.'

149

There would be milk in Quebec, and butter and eggs, the kinds of fresh foodstuffs they had sorely missed during their winter in Wapassou. It was a treat, almost a luxury to be able to eat such things every day, and most families in the Canadian villages were self-sufficient in that respect.

On the way up to Ville d'Avray's warehouse, Catherine-Gertrude told them how her husband had been bitten to death two years earlier by an Iroquois Indian.

As he was on his way home from the high country, laden with furs, the godless wretch had dropped on him from the top of a rock like a wild beast, clung to his back and sunk his terrible white teeth into the nape of his neck.

Her husband had with great difficulty succeeded in dislodging the Indian and had eventually killed him. But the wound had become infected and, being so near the brain, he had become delirious and died. Catherine told Angélique all about it as they walked up the hill.

'An Iroquois bite is like a mad dog's; it poisons your blood.'

Now Catherine was keeping up the farm. But as she had always managed it, since her husband was a trapper, his death had not made much difference to her situation. Now her sons and sons-in-law kept her supplied with venison and furs, as also did one of her neighbours, who was courting her and hoped to marry her. A widow found it easy enough to remarry in these regions, but she preferred to wait. She had enough people clinging to her skirts as it was: children, grandchildren, cousins. After all, what was a husband? Just another child ...

The hour was still early.

At last they reached Ville d'Avray's store where the Marquis delighted in extending the most generous hospitality to all and sundry, and Angélique found Marguerite Bourgeoys there, already busy sorting through a pile of dried peas with three or four dreadfully pale young girls, clearly recognizable as passengers from the *Saint John the Baptist*, probably travelling companions for whom the nun had managed to obtain permission to come ashore too.

'Monsieur de Peyrac authorized it,' Mademoiselle Bourgeoys hastened to tell Angélique. 'It appears he went on board the *Saint John the Baptist* this morning and assured everybody that the repairs were well in hand and that, if the crew behaved themselves, we would soon be able to continue our journey. Then he told my sisters to collect up their things and had them brought here so that they could at least get some rest and refreshment. This as a mark of appreciation shown by the passengers.'

Angélique could see that Joffrey's precision of mind and his minute attention to detail had won the heart of Mademoiselle Bourgeoys, herself a born administrator.

Angélique explained to her what had happened the previous evening and how, thanks to the information she had supplied, they had, at the eleventh hour, saved the lives of Captain Dugast's prisoners.

'You have every right to be proud, Monsieur, of having such kind and powerful friends,' Marguerite Bourgeoys said, addressing Aristide. 'I shall never forget the promptitude with which Madame de Peyrac went to your rescue and how worried she was about you. You must be a good man indeed to inspire such regard,' she concluded, her shrewd glance scanning Aristide Beaumarchand's face with its rheumy eyes, a face that, in spite of his recent reform, still bore the indelible marks of all the crimes and villainies that had been an integral part of his life before he fell in with the *Gouldsboro* folk.

Angélique said:

'Don't be misled, Mother, he's a dreadful bandit. Our first encounter nearly ended in mutual murder, but as you can see, we eventually managed to find a basis of understanding.'

'I got hurt, and she sewed up me belly,' said Aristide, beginning to loosen the laces of his breeches. 'Want to see her handiwork, Sister? . . .'

Mademoiselle Bourgeoys assented. She inspected the scar approvingly.

'That's admirable. Well, Monsieur Beaumarchand, I can only repeat what I said before, that you are a very lucky man to have encountered a nurse like this to save your life when you had been so horribly wounded. Who was it inflicted the wound? A wild beast?'

Aristide seemed surprised. He had forgotten. He looked at Angélique, and his memories seemed to have grown dim and uncertain.

'The war!' he replied in a fatalistic voice.

'And from what I observe it seems to have made a better-conducted man of you. I trust that you occasionally remember to thank the Good Lord for all the benefits you have received, Aristide. A little bird tells me you don't say your prayers all that often.'

'You're right there. But Julienne prays for both of us.'

'I got into the habit of it with the Duchess, you see,' Julienne explained; 'I just can't help it. Although I keep on telling myself that with the Duchess I said enough prayers to last me all my life and don't really need to go on doing it.'

At this point the Marquis de Ville d'Avray came up and laid a hand on Angélique's elbow.

'Everything's turning out absolutely splendidly,' he declared in high delight. 'You remember no doubt that I greatly envied you your Moorish page. Well, now we have a little piccaninny who's turned up very providentially! He'll look delightful in crimson satin. He can carry my bag, my cards and my candy box. It'll be one in the eye for them at Quebec.'

'But he belongs to Elias Kempton the pedlar,' Angélique exclaimed.

'What, to that Englishman! A heretic! Who cares?' Ville d'Avray retorted. 'Don't worry about that! I'll see he's thrown into prison as soon as we reach Quebec, or have him sold to some pious family in Ville-Marie who will gain indulgences by getting him baptized a Catholic.'

'Baptized a Catholic? Elias Kempton?' Angélique repeated. 'You must be crazy! He's a true son of Connecticut who, as a child, with his family, followed the Reverend Thomas Hooker across the Apalachians to found the town of Madford. What an idea!'

'It's a very good idea. I'm working on behalf of the Kingdom of Heaven and I'd like to see anyone try to stop me! I'll have that little Moor.'

He seemed to be adamant about it and Angélique knew that once he had set his heart on something he wanted, in this case the piccaninny, he was capable of anything. She lost her temper.

'No, you won't. I'll make sure you don't, and if you do I

shall never speak to you again in all my life ... You'll have a long wait for those evenings round your tiled stove, eating toffee-apples ...'

The Marquis saw that she really meant it. Taken aback, he let the matter drop and went outside to sulk.

Mademoiselle Bourgeoys had been following this altercation with interest.

'You see,' she said to Angélique, 'you are not so completely in accord with Our Lord Jesus Christ and His Church as not to become indignant that someone should try to save a soul from error and bring it to the true faith, as in the case of this English prisoner, whether he be from Connecticut or elsewhere. Do you not care about saving the souls of these misguided heretics? Especially when the person involved is someone you know and care about, I fail to understand you. Do you care so little about eternal life? ...'

Angélique made no reply, but sat down slowly and began likewise to sort the peas. When she did answer, she chose her words carefully.

'Yes, of course eternal life is very important, but do we not first have to live this life here on earth to the best of our ability, in harmony with our fellow men?'

'That does not mean that we should be culpably indulgent towards those whose beliefs lead them into error. So it's true, after all, is it, what they say? That you side with the English and protect heretics?'

What reply could she make to what seemed like an accusation? How could she get Mademoiselle Bourgeoys to understand the generous reality that lay behind what the French nun considered as acts of rebellion against God and hostility towards the King?

She saw in her mind's eye the figure of Abigail holding her baby Elizabeth in her arms, and standing on the forlorn coasts of Gouldsboro, and she so wanted to talk to Mademoiselle Bourgeoys about this dear friend of hers, and about little Elizabeth, such a lovely baby, as good as gold, to stand up for them and to ask: 'Have they not the right to live?'

But she restrained her impulse and confined herself to a few prudent remarks.

'Are you not perhaps exaggerating the warlike intentions of these New England protestants? ... Along the coasts of

Acadia we saw them at close quarters, and they seem to be peaceful hard-working folk who just want to be left in peace to till their fields ...'

Mademoiselle Bourgeoys pulled a wry face.

'That's not what we hear of them in these parts. Father d'Orgeval writes about the terrible extortions these rogues practice upon the Abenakis and how they're working the Iroquois up to make war upon us again.'

'It was he, rather than they, who rekindled the flames of war,' cried Angélique.

Her blood boiled when she remembered what she had witnessed at Brunswick Falls.

'How could he so distort the truth? Believe me, he is not a reliable informant. I saw with my own eyes ... lots of things,' she concluded, holding herself in once more.

She lowered her head in an effort to calm down.

'... I am disappointed,' she went on. 'I knew that this Jesuit dominated Quebec, but I did not expect you to belong to his camp. Did you not say yourself that Montreal was not Quebec?'

'As far as Father d'Orgeval is concerned, it is! The fact is that Father d'Orgeval is the true spiritual father of New France.'

'He's a sectarian, granted! If you only knew the way he has plotted against us! ...'

Marguerite Bourgeoys retorted somewhat sharply:

'Whatever he does is for the Good. He watches over his children.'

She was a spirited woman.

Angélique made a further effort to control herself.

'Do you mean by that that he intends to protect you, his children, from us, the enemy? But please tell me what grounds he has for considering us your enemies?'

'Are you not a threat to the establishment of New France by settling on land that belongs to the Kingdom of France?'

Angélique felt like retorting sharply that it was a well-known fact that the Treaty of Breda, signed by Monsieur de Tracy himself, had ceded this particular territory to the English of Massachussets, but there would have been no point. As in all sharp disagreements about ownership or possessions that matter to people, the opposite camp always seemed to have a monopoly of bad faith. Mademoiselle Bourgeoys was an intelligent, warm-hearted woman who knew what she was talking about. Fifteen years lived under constant threat of danger had convinced her that the battle she was waging was in a just cause.

'There are two hundred thousand Englishmen, Madame,' she went on, determined to make her point, 'and about as many Iroquois again in their pay. And, there are a bare six thousand of us Canadians. If we don't defend ourselves tooth and nail, they will invade our lands and destroy us. They will exterminate our poor Indians, who have cost us so much effort to baptize, and the others, that we have not yet been able to reach, will for ever lose the chance of seeing the light of the true faith which it has been our mission to bring to Canada. How can we, through negligence, take such a risk? ...'

She spoke calmly but with authority, while going on busily sorting her peas.

Angélique was far from feeling the same serenity. It seemed to her that she had never before felt so cruelly just how words, actions and their interpretation cut her off from her fellow men, from the world into which she had been born, and from those very people from whom she would have wished to seek succour and affection.

She stood up and began to pace up and down in a state of great agitation. She had thought for a while that all would be easy but now she saw the turn things were beginning to take. Arguments and attempts to prove that other people had a right to live their own lives would lead to nothing when the mentality of the people with whom one was dealing was such that they were either ignorant of the treaties confirming those rights, or considered as valid only those that were to the advantage of the Kingdom of France and its church.

Angélique saw that she must pursue a different course, however unpalatable to her spirited nature.

Concord must be first established at the emotional level. Mutual concern, understanding and an atmosphere of humanity were needed to provide reassurance and remove the threats and dangers the fear of which underlay these uncompromising attitudes.

She raised her head and smiled at the woman seated by

the fireside, who was looking at her with interest and no trace of animosity. The vitality and openness of the woman's nature commanded liking and trust.

'Mademoiselle Bourgeoys, let us leave matters there. Life, I feel sure, will consolidate the spontaneous affection I felt for you from the very first. We shall, I trust, get to know one another better, and will discover, behind and beyond what separates us, what it is that draws us together.'

The Mother Superior of the little religious community nodded her assent. She was not so much put out as preoccupied, and she remained a long while deep in thought.

'You absolutely must meet Father d'Orgeval,' she suddenly burst out emphatically. 'The more I reflect and the better I get to know you, the more I am convinced that the conflict between us stems from a misunderstanding, and that when you thrash things out with him, everything will sort itself out. Your natures are such that you are bound to get on well together.'

'I doubt it,' retorted Angélique, her face darkening.

She had sat down again.

'And I will even go so far as to admit that I am terrified of meeting him, Mother.'

'Is that perhaps because you are frightened that his shrewdness might detect your qualms of conscience?'

Angélique made no reply. With dextrous fingers she went on sorting the peas, unconscious of the fact that in the very manner in which her hands ran lightly over the brightly-coloured pods, as if stroking them, recognizing them – for had she not partaken with just such relish of the soup the Iroquois had sent them from the valley reigned over by the three gods, the marrow, the maize and the bean, that had saved them from starvation? – there was inherent a subtle sensuality, which was also evident in the poise of her head slightly tilted to one side, in the straight set of her shoulders, always drawn slightly back, giving her bearing a regal quality, and in her entire person, even when she was going about the humblest tasks. This was quite obvious to Mademoiselle Bourgeoys, accustomed as she was to observing people and to forming quick and accurate opinions of them. Since the previous day Angélique had been setting her a great many posers.

'You are in a state of spiritual uncertainty,' she suddenly decreed.

Angélique gave her a disarming smile.

'Maybe I am ... But isn't that something that happens to us all at times? Even to you yourself, I feel sure.'

Something was taking definite shape within her, something both cruel to discover and reassuring, as is everything that becomes clear and precise.

Her eyes lighted too on the nun's hands as they worked busily away, and it seemed strange to think that no man's lips had ever planted passionate kisses upon those feminine hands, or upon that bonny face which, behind its careworn lines, still showed traces of the attractiveness it must have possessed when she was twenty. She had a sudden vision of herself in Joffrey's arms, swooning with pleasure beneath his kisses, and the very thought made her heart beat faster and brought a pink glow to her cheeks.

The people she needs must confront and win over were dreadfully alien to her – even more so than Outtaké the Iroquois and Piksarett the Abenaki – or rather it was she who was the alien among them, a being of a different species, a different race, burdened with all that air of unfamiliarity she brought with her by the mere fact of her presence, and quite without willing it.

In their eyes the Demon, even unmasked, would have been less frightening, for they were accustomed to moving among spirits of Good and Evil. They had been taught how to repulse them or defend themselves against them. Whereas Angélique, who both attracted and frightened them while remaining indefinable, realized that they would see in her a harbinger of storms.

She broke off her work and lowered her head towards Marguerite Bourgeoys:

'Tell me straight, do you regard me as a dangerous person?'

'It's what you live by that is dangerous,' came the nun's reply.

It was as if she had been following Angélique's line of thought.

'Such a view of life on earth is a diversion from the path of eternal salvation,' she went on decisively; 'and all the more so because the fascination you exert over people might lead weaker souls to believe ... that you might possibly be right.'

Angélique felt her heart thumping within her as if Mademoiselle Bourgeoy's words were determining her defeat in advance.

'So you think I'm a witch, an enchantress, do you?'

'No ... But one thing is certain. *You do possess the power of enchantment.*'

She spoke without acrimony, even with a trace of nostalgia in her voice, as if she were moved by the grace of such a gift.

Once again Angélique experienced such acute stress that she was obliged to get up and begin her pacing once more. So tight-clasped were her hands that the knuckles stood out white. She looked at the women seated near her without seeing them. But her discomposure lasted only an instant. As swiftly as her agitation had arisen, her calm returned. 'It's what you live by that is dangerous,' the nun said. She had thought she had almost seen those lips framing the accusing words: 'What you live by: the delights of the senses, love of happiness, of creatures, of creation itself!' Was this not the ultimate source of a strength that could overcome everything?

And it struck her that in their devotion to a mystical cause, these ardent, righteous virgins were not so very different from herself. She would, therefore, be able to find points of contact with them. Had not she herself, Angélique de Sancé de Monteloup, been brought up by the Ursuline nuns in Poitiers? Although she no longer understood a world from which life had cut her off, she still retained some knowledge of it, odd snatches, memories, a pervasive influence ... Even in those days she had rebelled, protested, argued. From the leafy top of the convent wall where she used to go when she needed to get away, she had witnessed the appearance on the scene of one of her first admirers, a page of the Queen. Quite unexpectedly, this recollection suddenly made her laugh, and the assembled company, who were watching her, relaxed. For those who had witnessed the argument had sensed just how serious it was, just how much tension and seriousness lay behind the carefully measured words uttered by the two women.

'So you are not cross with me for having been so out-spoken?' Marguerite Bourgeoys asked.

'How could I be? Be assured that nothing coming from you, dear Marguerite, will ever hurt me. You saved Willoughby's life ... I shall always love you for that ...'

CHAPTER 20

'THEY BEHAVE as if they thought they were princes!' Carlon expostulated. 'Just because they've been given hunting and fishing rights, they regard themselves as lords! ... But where are their peasants to till the soil? How can one hope to colonize properly with these Canadians? They're here today and gone tomorrow. Only one thing matters to them, fur trading! We've even passed laws to get them to settle down. Every young man on reaching eighteen must marry within six months or be subject to a fine, payable by himself or his father. We aren't short of girls any more; we brought them over at considerable expense from France. But these fine gentlemen run off to the woods, and prefer to "light the match"[1] with young Indian girls.'

Intendant Carlon sawed the air as he talked to Peyrac, keeping one eye, from the small elevation on which the two men stood, on the goods he had left to be shipped to Europe before he had set off for Acadia early that summer, as they were loaded aboard the *Gouldsboro* and the other vessels.

Count Peyrac had bought part of the neglected cargo from him. There were planks, beams and ships' masts; dried and smoked fish, barrels of salted eels and salmon, and porpoise and seal-oil; barrels of flour, beer, and sacks of dried peas and beans, which were beginning to replace the popular broad bean in the Old World.

'We've proclaimed interdicts, refused licences,' the Intendant went on. 'We even went as far as excommunicating men

[1] An Indian custom. At night the suitor would creep up to his beloved's bedside, holding a small burning brand, or match. If the girl blew out the match, it meant she was willing. Hence the expression.

for taking alcohol to the savages ... But nothing doing! They don't care a damn for the laws. They've always got the forest to turn to. The slightest bit of bother, a tax to pay, or a conviction brought in against them, and they're up and off to the woods! I've had enough of these Canadians. They've got their backsides in boiling water! ...'

Having summed matters up thus, Jean Carlon walked down to the port.

'We'll leave a few barrels of seal-oil and some of the masts and timber for the *Maribelle*,' he directed. 'Let it not be said that she had to sail with shingle in her holds for lack of cargo, while I am left with goods on my hands. What an incredible mess! What bungling! The top people back home will never understand what I have to put up with here.'

Peyrac let him get it off his chest. He liked the man, appreciated his clear thinking, his enterprise and his openness of mind about economic matters.

Among the English, with his initiative and enterprise, and his shrewdness in commercial matters, he would already have been at the head of a prosperous colony. But here everything seemed to work a different way.

The poor fellow was doomed to fail in his efforts to give a new direction to a cumbersome piece of machinery that had for centuries past been travelling along entirely different paths – the paths of religious fanaticism, of conquests for the sake of glory rather than advantage, and of the irresistible appeal of the forestlands to these sons of peasants who, in the Old World, had been unable to as much as trap a hare or gaff an eel without running the risk of being hanged for it.

And if somewhere, a very long way off, there was a certain minister of the King by the name of Colbert, who had grasped the fact that the greatness of a kingdom can only be maintained by industry and commerce, he was fighting a losing battle in trying to impose such ideas, since he was bound to run up against the basic nature of the Frenchman, the quintessence of which was embodied in this new little nation, the French Canadians.

There were, in fact, few men in Tadoussac. Apart from the soldiers, a few of the farmers whose wives had fallen ill or whose herds were suffering from some epidemic disease, thus obliging them to remain at home after the harvest, apart from clerks and officials, artisans, blacksmiths, moulders and wheelwrights – for their apprentices or children often deputized for them – the entire male population of Tadoussac between the ages of sixteen and forty had vanished into the wilds, when the harvest was barely in the barns. Judging from the sounds coming from that direction, not much energy was being expended in threshing. Nor was much being done to protect the foundations of the houses from frost, by the customary procedure of piling up bales of straw against them, although by now every morning the landscape was tinged blue with hoarfrost, and the hard ground rang crisply beneath the footsteps of passers-by.

'The women can't be expected to do everything,' Carlon went on. 'And in any case they've been bitten by the fur bug too. Just look at them all running over there,' he said, pointing towards the Saguenay River, 'because it's been announced that a flotilla of canoes is about to arrive from the high country. Now you can perhaps begin to understand why my consignments of goods get left behind on the wharf and why famine is always rife at the end of the winter. People sell, they barter, and who cares what happens after that ...'

From the dip behind the river bank there rose a cheerful hubbub, and people could be seen hastening back and forth from house to shore carrying flasks of brandy, loaves of bread and various other objects.

Joffrey de Peyrac looked at the hamlet, with its plain, squat homesteads, at its elegant chapel enshrining its treasures, and at the sudden hustle and bustle, the fairground atmosphere called into being by the fact that round the cliffs of the Saguenay a flotilla. was about to arrive from the wilderness, Lake St John and Hudson Bay, bringing furs. The heady excitement generated by the hope of quick and substantial profits had the relish of boundless enjoyment since it held the promise of other pleasures – not always specifically identified – but at any rate the pleasure of possession, and, for a brief spell, of security, of certitude and of dreaming dreams that might come true.

These people were intensely alive and it was perhaps in

the singlemindedness with which they tackled life, with all its hardships and joys, that lay the secret of their charm.

Seeing Peyrac smile, Carlon's mood took a sardonic turn:

'I can guess what you are thinking ...' he said. 'That's what I feel too. No one is ever going to change "them", are they? I shall end up the loser, while you will turn the situation to your advantage and have the whole of New France in the bag.'

CHAPTER 21

ANGÉLIQUE HAD introduced the King's Girls to Mademoiselle Bourgeoys, in the hope that she might be prevailed upon to do something for them.

'They are a group of girls recruited by direction of Monsieur Colbert to help populate Canada. They were shipwrecked and have suffered many disasters. I wondered whether you might be able to do something to help them.'

Angélique briefly related how a ship had chanced to drift on to the rocks on their part of the Maine coastline, and had sunk opposite their settlement, and how since then the people of Gouldsboro had been obliged to care for the survivors. The present journey had provided an opportunity to escort the unfortunate young women to their original destination, Quebec.

Mademoiselle Bourgeoys shook her head sadly.

'You see, it's very difficult ...' she said. 'From what you tell me, their benefactress, who was accompanying them, perished when the ship went down. So they no longer have anyone to support them. What can be done with them in Quebec? Who will assume responsibility for their maintenance?'

'Could not their husbands provide for them?'

'In order to marry, they need a dowry, and you told me they lost their royal purse.'

In her eyes, in spite of her charitable and generous nature, that was an end to it.

She explained just how difficult it would be for the colony with its modest budget to take over the support of these girls whose dowry should have been provided by the French Kingdom. Furthermore, as they were arriving so late in the season, it would not be feasible to send them back on a ship sailing for Europe, with a promissory note to the captain enabling him to reclaim the cost of their return passage from the Treasury, or from the heads of the firm or charitable organization that had sponsored their departure.

'We had a very handsome dowry,' said Henriette, with tears in her eyes. 'An income of nearly a hundred pounds a year each given us by our benefactress, and by way of clothes we had three kerchiefs, a taffeta coif, a winter coat, two dresses ...'

Mademoiselle Bourgeoys interrupted the inventory.

'Yes, I understand. But, my poor child, your dowry is at the bottom of the sea, so what can we do? Who will guarantee your keep in Quebec?'

'Could they not find work in one of the many religious communities that I understand exist there?' Angélique pleaded.

'Work could certainly be found for them, but food is another matter. The amount of food and garden produce is carefully calculated in the summer in accordance with the numbers in each community. There's no margin as it is. And if the winter is a harsh one, there is no certainty that there will be enough to go round. And we can hardly expect help from any French source before the spring. If only they had the backing of letters of patronage that might persuade the Governor or the Intendant to release a few sacks of flour and peas from the general reserve, in the knowledge that they would be subsequently supported in approaching Monsieur Colbert for funds for additional purchases when the colony's annual budget was drawn up. But the guarantee would have to come from someone of the highest rank to convince those gentlemen that they would not be simply eating unjustifiably into stocks vital to the survival of New France.'

'And what about you, Mother, at Ville-Marie? Might you not be able to find room for some of them? You complain about the lack of recruits ...'

'That's true, but unfortunately I am also in the same financial straits.'

She explained just how slender were their reserves, and how rarely charitable donations came their way.

As she listened, Angélique began to understand how vital it was for these distant missions to have sound, stable backing, reliable support, devoted sponsors who, in exchange for prayers and indulgences for their eternal salvation, were prepared to finance the conversion of the New World Indians and the survival of the stalwart souls who had taken on the work in the field. A vast traffic in novenas, in graces obtained, even in miracles in return for hard cash was conducted between these remote regions and the *salons* or private oratories of the capital and other major cities of the French Kingdom. Great religious fervour could go hand in hand with the direst moral turpitude, the one redeeming the other.

Angélique, accustomed as she was to living with a powerful aristocrat, Count Peyrac, whose sole means of support was his own enterprises and activities, but who was both independent and able to live on a lavish scale, had forgotten that most people lived restricted lives that were constantly dependent upon the will of outsiders. People were everywhere dependent on a cumbersome, complicated system, but particularly so in a colony that had heavy military commitments and limited production. She remembered what Joffrey had said to her about Monsieur Quentin, the Sulpician who had also lacked a sponsor and had been only too pleased to find work as chaplain on board the *Gouldsboro*. Joffrey, with his knowledge of people and his skill in analysing in a flash the economic situation of nations and individuals alike, had quickly grasped that the most important thing in Canada for each and every little grouping that went to make up the nation, be they religious, administrative or simply family communities, was *not to have an extra mouth to feed*.

Life was tough, like in a prison. You had to defend yourself by paying tribute to various allegiances; as in a fortress, one had to be on one's guard against indulging in ill-considered acts of charity that could prove detrimental to the entire community.

*

164

'We might be able to help you,' suggested Angélique. 'I assure you it's not the devil's money.'

'I am sure of it, but that's not the point.'

'Are you afraid people will think ill of you if they hear you have accepted gifts from the independent Lord of Dawn East of ill renown?'

'No, it's not that. I just don't want to have to reorganize my community's plans and arrangements for this winter. I have only just got enough room for the three girls I'm bringing with me ... and only just enough patience to hearten and train them in their difficult vocation,' she added with a touch of humour. 'So you see, to take on these girls of yours whom I did not even recruit myself could well prove too much for me.'

Her reasoning was sound and Angélique agreed with her.

'... And as for you,' Mademoiselle Bourgeoys went on, 'I ought to warn you, too. You have been involved in considerable expense in assisting these young women who were no concern of yours ... It was an admirable thing to do, but I am not at all sure you will ever see your money again ...'

'It won't be our first investment in New France,' Angélique replied with a laugh.

'Incidentally,' Marguerite Bourgeoys went on, her mind still turning the question over, 'didn't you tell me that their Benefactress had chartered the ship with her own money and the backing of friends at court? Perhaps she was in partnership with someone in Quebec?'

'I've no idea.'

'We'll give it some thought,' Mademoiselle Bourgeoys said rising to her feet. 'Let's go and do the washing.'

On the banks of the Saguenay the tide, thick with seaweed and swarming with birds, was lapping the shore, while fur traders and Indians, who had disembarked from their canoes, were busy throwing into the eager arms of the local inhabitants, a harvest of multicoloured skins – autumn tinted, black as night, white as snow, and twilight grey. There were beaver furs of all shades of brown, otter skins, sable, marten, weasels whose fur had just turned white, thus increasing their value tenfold, and mink of many subtle hues. The Indians and trappers from the north had hastened down to Tadoussac in the hope that there might still be some ships sailing for Europe aboard which they could smuggle their wares at inflated prices.

One of the trappers who had just disembarked was climbing the slope, and although the light was behind him, the hint of a smile on his face seemed to be familiar. When he was within a few paces, Marguerite Bourgeoys and Angélique recognized him simultaneously.

'Elias!' one of them exclaimed.

'Macollet!' cried the other.

'Oh, what a pleasure to be welcomed by such attractive ladies!' he exclaimed in delight.

It was indeed old Macollet, looking as brown as a dried apple through exposure to the sun and wind of the forests. He looked like an Indian beneath his fur cap, with his burnished leather-like face and his laughing eyes that were, however, as light coloured and sparkling as fresh spring-water. Erect, slender and swift moving, in his costume of skins sewn together Indian fashion, the long trek which had taken him from the Upper Kennebec regions, which he had left in the spring, to Tadoussac by the autumn, seemed not to have greatly tired him.

Honorine made a great fuss of him.

As if forewarned by some invisible antennae, the village population began to surge towards them.

Angélique told how Elias Macollet had spent the winter with them in their fort in the Upper Kennebec, and how invaluable his industrious and cheerful presence had been to them.

'We went through a thing or two that winter,' Macollet commented tersely. 'Just consider my friends, we all had the smallpox, and lived to tell the tale. It was a real miracle!'

Angélique feared lest laying claim to too many miracles might turn people against them, and she attempted to explain the truth of the situation, which was that in the end it had turned out not to have been smallpox, that is invariably a killer, but purple fever or some similar ailment. But the other version of the story was the one people preferred.

'And what a Christmas we had![1] Couldn't have been a posher do in the Governor's place, the Chateau Saint-Louis. Gold, there was; gold on the table!'

[1] See *The Countess Angélique.*

166

'And didn't you look smart, Macollet, in your flowered waistcoat and your wig,' said Honorine.

'Your daughter-in-law would have enjoyed seeing you in such finery,' Mademoiselle Bourgeoys remarked approvingly.

'What have you brought me, young feller?' asked old Carillon; 'what have you brought me back from the high country?'

'A bear, granddad, a huge great grey bear I killed only yesterday near Lake Saint Paul with my own cutlass.

'It's down there on the river bank and my Montagnais Indians are cutting it up. You'll be able to have a good boil-up and eat some nice, fat kidneys like in the old days. Carillon's the only one who still calls me "young feller".' he explained, turning to Angélique. 'Well now! I wasn't no higher nor that when he used to take me off with him on expeditions right up the valley of the Iroquois. He had whiskers on him even then. And even when I began to make my own way in the world, he was still the same. I'm still a young feller to him, although by now you'd hardly tell the difference between us. He looks younger than he is, and I look older. Jest think of it. I'm only jest turned sixty. You see, I've been scalped and I've no front teeth left. The Iroquois pulled them out to make an amulet. But I'm not all that old. And if you don't believe me, ask the ladies ... ask the girls.'

People had begun to move down to the Saguenay to admire the bear Macollet had killed and the goods he had brought back. Voices called to one another.

'Have you seen old Elias's hardware? What spoil! Where ever did he find the money to kit himself up like that, the old rascal? It's not surprising he's brought back the best skins ...'

'And the bishop won't find a thing he can hold agin me,' Macollet added proudly. 'I didn't even barter a single drop of alcohol with the Indians. Those that wanted it had to look for it from others than me. But I had first-class goods to offer them, English knives and lots of other things.'

He had obtained his supplies from Joffrey de Peyrac's warehouses on the Kennebec.

'Does he still go after the Indian girls?' Marguerite

Bourgeoys asked Angélique.

'More than ever. I see you know him well. Our contingent of rogues and ne'er-do-wells, who were frozen cold and exhausted from lack of food had long since thrown up the sponge while our Macollet as fresh as paint was still going off to try his luck with the Indians girls in the neighbouring encampment.'

'You rogue!' Mother Bourgeoys said to him indulgently. 'What a pity your boy doesn't take after his father ... Sidonie is eating her heart out. They're an ill-matched pair.'

'Don't talk to me about them,' growled Macollet. 'It fair depresses me.'

'All the same you'll have to go and say hello to your children. I bet you haven't given them a thought since I went off almost two years ago.'

'Yes, you're right ... But what do you expect, she's a regular shrew.'

'She's not as bad as all that. She feels bitter. And she's unhappy.'

'What about? I ask you. The present generation of young women expect too much. All they want is their comfort. In the old days the Iroquois never gave us time to get bitter about anything. You lived with your gun at your shoulder. Every day you set out to work in the fields you never knew whether you'd come home of an evening. You remember how it was, Mother Bourgeoys, you and I remember these things ... And there's me daughter-in-law with everything: peace, a farm, her fields, her herd, and still she has to grumble.'

'She's in love ...'

'Well, it don't seem much like it. Should hear her, how she jumps down that man's throat.'

'That's not what I meant,' Mother Bourgeoys replied, with an air of concern.

And she gave a sigh.

CHAPTER 22

ONE MORNING the Marquis of Ville d'Avray approached Angélique wearing his most seductive smile and drew her aside. She thought he was going to talk to her about furs or perhaps about the barrels of Burgundy that were still on his mind, but he said to her point-blank:

'What happened to Count Varange?'

Her heart missed a beat.

Luckily for her, since they had been at Tadoussac the obscure crime that had marked their entry into Canada had been so completely wiped from her memory that it took her a fraction of a second to recall the incident, and this enabled her, however fleetingly, to react with the necessary expression of astonishment.

'What are you talking about? Varange?'

Ville d'Avray eyed her keenly. She had regained her composure and seemed honestly not to understand him.

'Yes ... you mentioned him some time back ... What reason did you have for concerning yourself about him?'

Angélique puckered her brow as if trying to remember.

'I believe I told you I had heard his name mentioned.'

'By whom?'

'Possibly the Duchess; or Fallières ... I don't remember. I just wanted to know something about him. I need to have some idea in advance of those with whom I may have to deal in Quebec.'

'Well, you won't have him to deal with!'

'Why not?'

'Because he's disappeared.'

'Oh!'

'He came prowling about Tadoussac some time ago,' he whispered, bending closer. 'He had sailed down from Quebec in his big boat with his valet. He said he had come to check up on the making of brandy and on the Basque whalers who

169

sometimes poach in these waters, but he tacked back and forth so much along the river that people wondered what he was looking for ... or waiting for. I thought perhaps you might have known.'

'Me? You must be crazy.'

He was beginning to make her feel hot under the collar with his far too intuitive curiosity and his inquisitorial stare. But she bore his scrutiny with sufficient indifference to dispel his suspicions.

He released her arm and gazed about him, muttering:

'What ever was he doing round here, I wonder?'

'You'll no doubt find that out when you reach Quebec.'

'But will I find him there?' the obstinate Marquis asked, darting so piercing a glance at her that she almost lost countenance.

'And why not?'

'Because he has disappeared, I tell you ... along with his valet.'

'He's probably gone back to Quebec with his boat ... and his valet.'

'No, he hasn't ... because the boat has been found ... empty.'

And he pointed to a spot on the horizon, over on the opposite bank of the St Lawrence.

'Over there ... near Cri-aux-Oies point. But not a trace of them.'

Angélique made an evasive gesture.

'In any event, it doesn't worry me. You warned me he was one of our enemies. Just as well if we don't find him in Quebec ... And now, dear Marquis, what are you doing on this beautiful morning? I have to go to the presbytery to see the parish priest.'

'And what are you after from the dear man and his still? ...'

'I want to help Aristide to improve his rum. The priest has a supply of wild cherry leaves and some small cherries picked before they ripened. It's a well-known way of giving a better taste to that kind of home brew and it also reduces the toxic effect of an excessive concentration of still residues. We intend to try a few experiments. As you see, we seem to be settling in here at Tadoussac. And yet there's a smell of departure in the air. What are we waiting for? For the *Maribelle*, the King's ship, to arrive with her thirty guns? Or for the King's envoy who's hiding on board the *Saint John the Baptist* to be kind enough to put in an appearance?'

'That King's envoy is a coward.'

'Unless perhaps he doesn't exist at all ... Well, Marquis, are you going to accompany me to the presbytery? or what ... ?'

Ville d'Avray hesitated. He caught sight of Joffrey, who was about to go back on board the *Gouldsboro*, and decided to join him. He was always busy being taken from one place to another. Furthermore, he had just had an idea and this seemed the perfect moment to put it into action.

So he took his leave of Angélique and ran down to catch the longboat.

He tackled Count Peyrac straight away.

'My dear chap, for some days now I've had something on my mind. I feel sure that Mademoiselle d'Hourdanne's mail is on board the *Saint John the Baptist*.'

CHAPTER 23

JOFFREY DE PEYRAC was looking back towards Tadoussac.

The village spread out before their eyes like a picture, a tapestry gradually unrolled to its full length, for them to admire it in its extensive beauty, from the promontory rising over the Saguenay to the far end where the forest came down to the very water's edge. They had a general view of the arrangement of the houses and huts and could note the sensible positioning of the fort on the left with the fleur-de-lys flag flying over it, the church in the middle, the dock warehouses at the bottom, the last grey-stone farm right at the top on the edge of the fields that led up the slope to the woods.

That was where Angélique was making her way. Joffrey could see her, striding briskly along in the company of Mademoiselle Bourgeoys and Julienne. Then came Kouassi-

Bâ, who had not been allowed ashore at first for fear of frightening the local population, but who had made a great hit especially after being introduced all round by his chum from the harsh days of the previous winter, old Macollet.

The King's Girls were strung out in single file behind them together with Mother Bourgeoy's novices.

Today Cantor and his wolverine could also be seen – which was not a frequent occurrence. After shying off at first, the village had come to be intrigued by and accept the playful creature. He could see him from afar, a great shining ball of fur, bounding along, racing down the slopes, at first pretending to frighten the children then to be frightened by them. Thin cries, bursts of laughter and the echo of female voices came across through the crystal-clear air. And Aristide went lolloping along behind, talking to Elias Macollet.

'It's like this,' Ville d'Avray went on. 'Mademoiselle d'Hourdanne is a neighbour of mine in Quebec, in the upper town. She will be yours too, since I am letting you have my house.

'She's a charming lady, the widow of a well-considered officer who came over with Carignan-Salières's regiment ten years ago. He was killed during the Marquis de Tracy's campaign against the Iroquois.

'Now, she's like me. She likes it in Quebec. Or perhaps she can't bear the idea of crossing the Atlantic again. There are a lot of people like that out here, who prefer to run the risk of being scalped by the Iroquois, or to die of hunger, or cold, and never see their families again, rather than to find themselves on a ship on the high seas again. I can quite understand them ... Are you following me, my dear Count?'

'Most attentively.'

'No, you are not. You are looking at *her* over there ... Ah, now *she* has disappeared round a bend in the path. So now I can continue. As I was saying, Mademoiselle d'Hourdanne stayed on in Canada. By now she has become fairly much of an invalid and spends most of her time in bed, but she writes a lot. Her main correspondent is the widow of the King of Poland, Casimir V. No, I don't mean Louise-Marie de Gonzague, his first wife. She died, as you know, ten years ago, and he was so grief-stricken that he abdicated his crown and became a monk in Saint-Germain-des-Prés, where he is the abbot. The woman I'm talking about, Mademoiselle d'Hourdanne's friend, is his second wife. He was allowed to marry her although in religion. She is known as "the Fair Herbseller", because apparently she used to sell herbs in Grenoble when she was a girl. Herbs and other things no doubt. She managed to get herself married to a whole succession of important people, all very old and very wealthy, and the chain of widowhoods eventually brought her into Court circles, where she married the King of Poland, who likewise left her a widow, but this time at the acme of distinction. Her story will serve to convince you that she is no fool, and that is why Mademoiselle d'Hourdanne, who is no fool either, and who knew her at Court, likes to correspond with her.

'So that is how it has come about that they write to one another every week, sometimes every day. During the winter, their letters pile up in caskets which they choose with great care so that they can either exchange them, retain them as keepsakes or send them back again full of further missives.

'Her widowed Majesty sends her first consignment by the first ship to sail for America. She sends another towards the end of the summer with the last vessel to set sail. It's incredible what pains she goes to, sending emissaries to every port, or to the Chamber of Commerce, or even to the Admiralty, to find out which is the last ship setting out to Canada. Some of them are delayed, while others decide to sail at the last moment, counting on luck and the winds to give them time to make the round trip before winter sets in, like the *Saint John the Baptist*, for example.

'To sum up, she entrusts the second casket, the one containing replies to the letters Mademoiselle d'Hourdanne wrote her during the summer, to the last ship to cross. That's the way of it, as you see. It's one of the ways women keep themselves amused, as I said; they seem to show more imagination when it comes to brightening their day-to-day lives than we men do. And it's also why I'm telling you that, in view of the *date* the *Saint John the Baptist* left Rouen, I'll wager that the casket addressed to Mademoiselle d'Hourdanne is on board. It won't be the first time Dugast has had it entrusted to him.

'I'm anxious about this, because our captain is a regular rogue, and, if the casket is a nice one, with inlay work or encrusted with gems, for instance, he might well simply appropriate it after getting rid of the letters.

'We know how keen he is on throwing things overboard. And Cleo will be so delighted to have me bring her her precious letters in person. So much nicer than that boor who always wants to be paid for his services ... So if you enjoyed my story, and if you see no objection ...'

The longboat came alongside the *Gouldsboro* and Joffrey de Peyrac climbed on board, casting a slightly ironical glance back at the Marquis who was standing up, amid the tossing of the waves, waiting for an answer, wearing the smile of an impatient, happy child.

'If I understand you rightly, you would like me to lend you the longboat so that you can go over to the *Saint John the Baptist* and claim the casket you spoke of, if it is indeed there?'

'Precisely! And these beefy chaps escorting us are an impressive lot; can I call on them for assistance, in case of need? ...'

'Of course!'

From the top of the gangway Peyrac gave his orders to the seamen, who pulled away from the ship's side and began to row towards the *Saint John the Baptist*. Peyrac laughed as the boat drew away with the Marquis of Ville d'Avray whose baby-face was radiant with anticipated pleasure.

'Agreed, then? You're giving me a free hand?' he shouted once more.

'Yes, my dear Marquis. But no bloodshed, please.'

Peyrac went on looking out towards the shore. He had taken out his spyglass.

When the weather was mild, as at present, and he had finished his general inspection of the different ships, he liked to take a few moments off. And he thought about her, as one returns to a shady spring after hours in the blazing sun, about her, his refuge of love. These times had become, in his secret life, an occasion to explore so to speak a new domain hitherto to some extent avoided, hitherto slightly feared.

'We must get to know one another better, my love ...

'Time makes demands, life passes by, and among the responsibilities, among the treasures vouchsafed to me there you stand, you emerge, and your face passes back and forth in the turmoil of my life of adventure, like a dream vibrant with pleasure and pain ... My love! ...'

There was pleasure to him in keeping a watchful eye on the big house on the hill into which Angélique and her band of followers had disappeared. And he looked forward boyishly to seeing her reappear in the distance, her lively, rapid movements expressing her grace and vitality.

'Even at a distance, she's got what it takes to drive men wild ... What on earth can she be after with that hooch-brewing priest? Improving Aristide's brew! You're very sure of yourself, my darling!'

And he had a private laugh to himself.

'Even so, anything is possible ... Light of my life, you belong to me ...'

Time was passing.

Ville d'Avray must by now have accomplished what he had set out to do, whether avowed or not.

Count Peyrac heard the Marquis's voice hailing him again.

The *Gouldsboro*'s longboat was back.

'I've got it,' cried the Marquis, holding out a small casket at arm's length. 'You see how well I know people's little ways! Cleo will be delighted.'

Peyrac leaned forward a little and caught sight of four barrels lying amidships in the bottom of the longboat. To tell the truth, he had half expected as much.

'And what is that?' he asked, pointing to the barrels.

'That? ... But, my good friend, did you not give me a free hand? And when, *purely by chance*, I happened on this Burgundy, I could hardly leave such nectar in the hands of those ruffians! It's Beaune, you know, as auctioned for the Hospital ... The best from the region, if not from the whole of France. Unfortunately I was unable to take it all,' he added regretfully.

He paused for a moment.

'... In any case, my dear Count, so many accusations are levelled against you, that one little thing more or less isn't going to make that much difference, is it? ... And meanwhile we can give our palates a treat. What shall I do with the barrels?'

'Well, let's have one of them up on board here, so that we can broach it one of these evenings and have a drink with our friends. Have the rest taken over to "your" ship since you organized the boarding party.'

'My dear Count, you are the most trusty and the most astonishing friend I have ever encountered. Thank you a thousand times. Incidentally, I found Dugast in a deplorable state. I don't know what's the matter with him, but he's a mere shadow of his former self. It's as if he'd been poisoned. You know, you ought not to be so hard on the unfortunate creature, especially as I think I glimpsed a rather fine nobleman trying to hide from me. If he is the King's representative, would it not be politic to give him a little rope? Allow him and his retinue ashore before the *Saint John the Baptist* sets sail again for Quebec and brings an advance report on us, which may be either good or bad. Tomorrow is Sunday ...'

PART FOUR

The King's Envoy

CHAPTER 24

ANGÉLIQUE SAW her husband, Count Peyrac, cross the deck with unaccustomed haste, dash up the first companion-way to the poop-steps two at a time, and race along the balcony of the starboard poop-deck, from which he trained his spy-glass on the *Saint John the Baptist*. Count d'Urville, Captain Vanneau, several other officers – and Ville d'Avray – raced after him.

'What's going on?' asked Angélique.

'Honorine is on board,' came Ville d'Avray's reply.

'Which ship?'

'The *Saint John the Baptist*.'

In her turn, Angélique sped up the companion-way and joined the group clustered around Joffrey de Peyrac.

Peyrac lowered his spyglass.

'That's it right enough. She's on board! Look!'

Within the circle of the lens, Angélique succeeded in isolating one part of the ship – rails in a sad state of disrepair, a corner of the deck untidy and neglected like the rest of the ship and, contrasting with this somewhat sordid spectacle, the silhouettes of a number of gentlemen wearing plumed hats and elegant clothes, who were, presumably, officers belonging to the escort of the King's envoy. And in the midst of them, beyond a shadow of doubt ...

'It's Honorine! ... I recognize her green bonnet. I put it on her this morning for the procession.'

Her arms dropped and she felt like collapsing.

'Honorine. On board the *Saint John the Baptist*. But what's she doing there? ...'

'She's been kidnapped,' said someone.

It was Sunday.

That morning, all the crews of Peyrac's ships had attended Mass, and the passengers from the *Saint John the Baptist* had been invited as a body.

Not a sign had there been of any envoy of the King, although some passengers with their high coat collars turned up, as seemed reasonable enough in view of the intense cold, and with their plumed hats pulled down over their eyes, might very well have fitted the bill. But they seemed not at all anxious to have any contact with the local people, although they had not been able to resist coming ashore to hear Mass after the severe ordeal to which they had been subjected. Taken all together, the Indians, the villagers, the trappers freshly arrived from the high country, made up an enormous crowd which overflowed the chapel, whose bell rang out bravely in the pure cold air.

The procession had taken place at the beginning of the afternoon. Honorine had consented to wear her embroidered green bonnet to do honour to the new forces brought in by Monsieur de Peyrac on this the day of the Lord.

Subsequently, Angélique had left the children in the charge of those usually responsible for their care. There was a great deal going on on land.

The bartering craze had infected everybody particularly strongly because, in honour of the Saint of the day, who was probably a virgin to judge by the white vestments, Joffrey de Peyrac had distributed twists of Virginia Tobacco and several bushels of 'trash' to the local inhabitants. The trash in question consisted of cheap little beads, much sought after by the Indians to decorate the costumes they wore on festive occasions.

Angélique had gone back on board the *Gouldsboro* to change her clothes and take a brief rest. There was a constant to-ing and fro-ing of light craft of all sorts – small sailboats, rowing boats and kayaks taking people from ship to shore and back again.

Just as she was about to go back on shore, she had become aware of a flurry of activity on the deck, and Ville d'Avray had cried to her: 'Honorine is on board ...'

Honorine on board the *Saint John the Baptist*! Seized by that criminal crew!

Count Peyrac took up his spyglass again and scanned the view with great care.

'I can see Yolande too,' he said; 'she's just appeared.'

The tall Acadian girl could be made out with the naked eye, and nearby a faded blue spot representing Adhémar's uniform. Chérubin was also probably in the offing but invisible because of his short stature, which prevented his red bonnet from appearing over the edge of the rail.

'My son has fallen into the hands of the bandits!' exclaimed Ville d'Avray melodramatically. 'Alas! We are lost. Why did you plunder them, Count, yesterday evening when you took that Burgundy from them? Now they'll wreak appalling vengeance.'

Intendant Carlon, who had joined them, broke in:

'My dear fellow, I would remind you that, from all I hear, you were the person responsible for that theft. In spite of all my advice too ...'

'That's no doubt the case! But they shouldn't have been allowed to go ashore.'

'Come, come! Marquis! I heard you with my own ears saying that it would be the wise course to give them a bit of rope in case an envoy of the King actually was on board.'

'Monsieur de Peyrac shouldn't have listened to me.'

'What's the point of arguing?' interrupted the latter. 'The damage has been done. Now we must think what is the best course of action. Monsieur Carlon, as Intendant of New France, you can be very valuable to me.'

'I am at your disposal,' stated the royal official. He seemed to be genuinely concerned and, on this occasion, less because of the complications that were bound to result than because he feared for the safety of the children – a fact that touched Angélique. She felt she could do with goodwill at this moment, no matter from what quarter.

'They should never have been allowed to go ashore,' moaned Ville d'Avray. 'They took the opportunity to seize hostages. And what hostages! Our poor little ones! They'll demand a ruinous ransom. I know that Dugast. He's capable of anything. Oh how I hope, how I hope ... Good God, where are they? They're no longer to be seen!'

Angélique took back the spyglass that the Marquis had snatched, and someone ran off to fetch some more at Peyrac's behest. Fretfully Angélique adjusted the instrument.

She saw that the group, which had been glimpsed a few moments before, had disappeared. The bridge of the *Saint*

John the Baptist was now deserted.

'They've thrown them overboard!' screeched Ville d'Avray. He began to take off his frock-coat preparatory to jumping into the sea in his breeches and waistcoat, but was restrained.

'Calm yourself,' said the Count. 'We'll launch a longboat and row over. We'll get there more quickly than by swimming. I beg you Marquis, do not lose your head.'

He clapped his spyglass shut and, followed by the entire party, strode down to the main deck and made for the longboat, which the seamen were already beginning to clear for launching. Fortunately, there was still one such craft on board, all the others having been requisitioned for the festivities and being at that moment on shore. Angélique thanked heaven that Joffrey regularly saw to it that their link with the shore was never broken. It was a point on which he absolutely insisted. A particularly festive atmosphere had prevailed that day, and suspicions had been lulled to the point that even on the *Gouldsboro* there had been some slackening of discipline.

It was obvious that certain persons on the *Saint John the Baptist* had taken advantage of the situation to carry out this base act of aggression. It was Joffrey, as Angélique was later to learn, who had been the first to notice that there was something untoward going on on the *Saint John the Baptist*.

Ville d'Avray was speaking his thoughts aloud as he began to go down the rope ladder to the longboat.

'I'll have them sent to the galleys, I'll have them shot by arquebuse fire ... Attack my son! They'll demand my entire fortune from me ... Too bad, I'll pay ... But let them look out! They won't take it with them to paradise ...'

Angélique tried not to lose her head. The *Saint John the Baptist* was surrounded by a substantial, well-armed fleet. It would be quite easy to overpower her. But the trump card held by their enemies was the fact that they were masters on board their ill-famed ship of innocent and valued lives.

How had it been done? What wiles had been used to entice the two children, in spite of the wariness which had been inculcated in them and the fierce protectiveness of Yolande and Adhémar? And, come to that, how had it been possible to capture Yolande and Adhémar as well? Had violence been used? With Yolande that did not seem likely. It would have taken more than that starveling crew to get her into a boat against her will. What then was the answer? . . .

And what did it all matter? There would be time to analyse reasons when everybody had been recovered safe and sound. Angélique saw that Peyrac was taking his Spanish guard armed with fork-muskets with him in the boat. All the seamen accompanying him were also equipped for action as a boarding party.

He turned towards her: 'I'll go off first . . .'

'I could come with you.'

'Be patient! There would be no point on the worst supposition, of all of us falling at one stroke into the power of those rogues. Come after me in a moment.

'I've signalled to the shore for two longboats to come back to the *Gouldsboro*. You come in one with d'Urville and his men. Arm yourselves with pistols. Ville d'Avray will take the other boat. Furthermore, a state of alert has been decreed on shore. Anyone from the *Saint John the Baptist* who is still there can be regarded as cut off and rendered harmless and prevented from returning on board his ship . . .'

'Perhaps that has been foreseen, and they're all on the ship and ready to set sail,' said Ville d'Avray who had once again snatched Count d'Urville's spyglass to see whatever was going on on the *Saint John the Baptist*. It looks as if they're up to something on the forecastle . . . Look!'

'That old hulk can't just slip away like that . . . Marquis, I beg you, don't give up while there's still hope. Let us concert our efforts.'

Joffrey de Peyrac spoke calmly. 'But he's always calm when things are at their worst,' Angélique told herself, remembering Joffrey's serenity as he stood before the fort at Katarunk when it was surrounded with howling Iroquois Indians.

She realized she must be very pale.

He laid a reassuring hand on her wrist, pressing it in such a comforting way that she felt better.

'Patience, darling!' he repeated. 'Follow close upon me, and we'll do our utmost to show these ruffians that their antics won't get them very far. But we mustn't make them feel too vulnerable either.'

She smiled weakly.

'I understand. I'm ready.'

'Courage!' he repeated; 'I need you and your coolness. You won't have less to show, will you, when it's your daughter's life at stake than you did the other evening when it was your husband you were worried about?'

'No!' she stammered; 'but ... she is ... she is so little.'

She saw a spasm pass over Joffrey's face and realized that he also was fearful for the beloved child. He turned away brusquely, and, with drawn brows, began to go down the ladder.

'Hang on!' came a voice from outside their group. 'Hang on! It looks as if there's something moving over yonder ...'

All activity was suspended, and the spyglasses rose in unison to eye level.

A small craft had come into view from round the bow of the *Saint John the Baptist* and was making for the shore.

And now it was possible to make out clearly among its occupants the patches of colour of the children's bonnets, Yolande's white coif, and the person of Adhémar. They were lost sight of as they touched land, the shore being so far off, but shortly after a longboat belonging to the *Gouldsboro* pulled out bringing the entire group back to the ship.

'The bodies are being brought back to us!' moaned Ville d'Avray.

'No! I can see them clearly now, and they look very much alive,' said Angélique, who was following the progress of the longboat attentively.

The vice which had tightened round her heart was beginning to slacken.

Nevertheless, it was all very odd. As far as could be made out at this distance, the passengers in the boat were not behaving like prisoners who had just escaped some serious danger, but, very much in their customary way, like carefree sightseers returning home after an enjoyable outing.

Honorine and Chérubin could even be seen trailing their hands in the water, in spite of the danger of falling in, which was a lark they often indulged in although strictly forbidden to do so.

And Yolande and Adhémar were apparently gassing away nineteen to the dozen with the crew, in their usual way.

'Fifteen strokes of the lash for those sluggards of rowers!' burst out Ville d'Avray, his patience exhausted. 'They're pulling on their oars as if they were rowing across an ornamental pond. Don't they realize that we're dying with anxiety here?'

Nevertheless, he had climbed back up on deck. Anxiety was now a thing of the past, and, when the little company drew alongside, worry had given way in the hearts of the parents to righteous indignation.

As soon as Honorine and Chérubin set foot on deck, hoisted up by anxious arms, they realized from the expressions on the faces of the upper echelons assembled to meet them that there was trouble brewing.

Honorine noted the fact without appearing particularly perturbed, and such was the authority of this little person that it was from her that the assembled dignitaries first demanded an account of her stewardship rather than from Yolande and Adhémar, who now emerged in their turn, and who, realizing that they must have dropped a considerable brick, exchanged anxious glances.

'Where have you been, Miss?' was the question with which Joffrey de Peyrac greeted Honorine.

She looked at him a trifle condescendingly. She considered the question pointless since Joffrey de Peyrac must certainly know that she had been on the *Saint John the Baptist*, for had they not all been watching the arrival of the small party with their spyglasses? But she was well aware of the fact that grown-ups like to labour the obvious, and that no one on board, not even she, Honorine, had the right to stand up to the undisputed master, Lord Peyrac, so she deigned to motion nonchalantly in the direction of the *Saint John the Baptist*.

'On the *Saint John the Baptist*!' repeated Peyrac. 'And would you be so good, Miss, as to tell us why you were so scatter-brained as to go on board that ship without our authorization?'

'Because I was invited to tea.'

'Really? And by whom?'

'By a friend of mine,' retorted Honorine haughtily.

As she said it she looked so incredibly funny with her

offended expression, which also conveyed sharp disapproval of such unseemly cross-questioning that the Count found it too much for him.

He just could not help smiling. Then, starting forward, he picked the little girl up in his arms and hugged her to his heart.

'You little sweetheart!' he said gruffly. 'But what a scatter-brained thing to do! Before accepting such an invitation, you should have remembered that we have enemies on that ship who might have tried to get their own back on me through you and who might have endangered your life. You made your mother and me dreadfully anxious.'

Honorine looked at him in astonishment.

'So it's true!' she exclaimed delightedly; 'it's true you were worried about me?'

'Yes, indeed I was, young lady. And please never do such a thing again! Because if anything ever happened to you, it would break my heart.'

No other words could have so utterly delighted Honorine. She gazed deep into Joffrey de Peyrac's eyes to assure herself that he meant what he said, then, squeezing him in her tiny arms and laying her chubby cheek against his scarred face, she said:

'Forgive me, father, please forgive me.'

Chérubin, seeing that Honorine was being welcomed with open arms, decided that everything must be all right and rushed over to Angélique, who could hardly refuse to take the little chap in her arms and kiss him to show that he was forgiven too.

'Go and tell your father you're sorry,' she said, handing him over to Ville d'Avray, who was weeping like a child, his feelings and retrospective anxiety having got the better of him.

Never had he realized till this day just how precious the little creature was to him.

Chérubin was only too delighted to go the rounds kissing everybody. He did not quite understand what all the fuss was about but enjoyed it in his affectionate way. It was certainly better than being scolded.

'Monsieur de Ville d'Avray was just going to swim out to fetch you back,' Angélique told Honorine.

'Was he really?' the young lady replied, even more highly delighted.

And she slipped from Peyrac's arms into Ville d'Avray's to kiss him, then went the rounds of the assembled company gauging the extent of her popularity from the warmth of her reception, while everyone repeated over and over again that she had given them – hardened filibusters and gentlemen of fortune that they were – the *biggest fright* of their lives.

Angélique turned to Peyrac:

'Will she really take it in what a scatter-brained thing she did if everyone makes such a fuss of her? ...'

But she laughed to see the expression on Peyrac's face.

'You're even fonder of her than I am.'

'She's so feminine,' he said shaking his head. 'She delights my heart and my eyes.'

He raised one of Angélique's hands to his lips and kissed it warmly.

'You have given me a delightful treasure in that little girl. And now, dear heart, calm yourself ...'

'Yes, I'm getting over it,' she murmured.

At last she was beginning to feel the blood flowing through her veins again. She began to recover her composure.

'And now I've a question to ask this fine pair,' she said, bearing down menacingly upon Yolande and Adhémar. 'Have you both taken leave of your senses? Did the fur bartering and the tippling that goes with it dim your wits so utterly that you went on board the *Saint John the Baptist* without the least regard for the consequences? Are you not aware that the captain is no friend of ours? It's less than three days since he nearly drowned Julienne and Aristide, yet today you accept an invitation to tea on his ship!'

'Yes, Madame, you are right,' Yolande sobbed into her apron. 'Beat me, I richly deserve it.'

'Yes, Madame la Comtesse, smack it,' Adhémar added, pointing to his cheek. 'I am an idiot. We let ourselves be taken in; we didn't think. The gentleman seemed such a decent feller.'

'Which gentleman?'

'Don't scold my friend Yolande,' Honorine cried, intervening on behalf of her favourites. 'I was the one who wanted to go.'

'Is that any excuse?' protested Angélique, with mounting anger. 'If you two silly chumps are going to let yourselves be led by the nose by a couple of five-year-olds, instead of stopping them doing stupid things, we are heading for disaster. Where is Niels Abbial?' she asked anxiously, suddenly noticing that the little Swedish boy who normally followed the children wherever they went, was not with them now. Had he been detained on board the *Saint John the Baptist*?

'No!' said Honorine. 'He didn't want to come with us. He's an ass!'

'No, he isn't, he's very sensible! Let me tell you, young lady, that I wish you had been as cautious. I'll wager he tried to persuade you not to accept this preposterous invitation and that you refused to listen to his advice. I intend to reward him for his pains, and you will be punished.'

Honorine bowed her head.

She had never been in much doubt about the outcome of the escapade, and on the whole, things had not turned out too badly. She also knew that Angélique was not as easy to get round as Joffrey de Peyrac. She gave a sigh and began to rummage in her skirt pockets while Angélique went on, turning back to Yolande and Adhémar:

'Give an account of yourselves. I want to know exactly what happened and how you managed to let yourselves be taken in so foolishly.'

Yolande, kneeling on the deck as a mark of contrition, and Adhémar, who after a while did likewise as a gesture of solidarity, launched out upon a complicated account of what had occurred, from which it emerged that, after both had become absorbed in bartering for beaver skins and a parcel of mink – Yolande had parted with her coralline earrings that Marceline, who had inherited them from her grandmother from the Nivernais, had given her to make an impression in Quebec, while Adhémar had parted with his powder horn that went with his uniform – and after eventually closing a deal with those 'sharks of savages', they had suddenly realized that Honorine had disappeared, had rushed off in panic to look for her, and had found her deep in conversation with a gentleman who had come ashore that day with the passengers from the *Saint John the Baptist*.

'We should have been on our guard,' Angélique said reproachfully; 'Tadoussac has been full of riff-raff today.'

'My friend isn't one,' Honorine corrected her.

'You are too young to judge.'

'It's true, what she says, the gentleman did look a decent sort of man,' Yolande argued.

'And so he turned out to be, since you are all here unharmed. But who was he? ... A passenger killing time? But why our children? ... What is it Honorine? What's this?'

Honorine, having finally succeeded in extricating the object she had been rummaging after in her pockets, had apparently lost interest in the discussion. Standing very erect and gazing absently into the distance, she held out a stiff little arm to her mother, her tiny dimpled fingers clasping a missive sealed with red wax.

'What's that?' Angélique asked.

'It's for you,' replied Honorine with an air of utter indifference.

Angélique seized the thick, white velum envelope. The seals in the middle and at the four corners bore the impress of some heraldic device representing an indistinct crest and a motto that was no doubt in Latin. The ribbon was long and wide and made of silk.

It was all quite impressive.

Angélique turned the envelope over, but it bore no name. She looked suspiciously at Honorine who went on standing there, as dignified as ever.

'Where did you get this from? Who gave it to you?'

'My friend, the nice gentleman.'

'He gave you this envelope?'

'Yes.'

'Who for? For me?'

'Yes, Mother,' Honorine repeated with a sigh.

Then, after a slight pause, she added:

'He saw you this morning in the procession.'

Angélique decided she had better draw the ribbon of this mysterious missive, thus breaking the seals.

The wax was thin and crumbling, as if it had been put on in a hurry.

She unfolded the sheet of paper. The writing was large and elegant, though hasty and smudged and blotted here and there. The scrawl traced by the badly cut goose-quill pen revealed the writer's haste and it was evident that he had scarcely taken time to sand the page. She began to read aloud:

'Oh, thou fairest of women ...'

She broke off.

'That's a promising start,' commented Ville d'Avray, drawing closer, his curiosity aroused.

'And rather loose too,' observed Carlon. 'It smacks of impiety to me.'

'Oh, do stop being so uncivil,' Ville d'Avray rebuked him. Meanwhile he leaned over Angélique's shoulder, attempting to decipher what followed, and in fact assisting her in her efforts as the letter was proving almost illegible.

But he had good eyesight and began to read aloud:

The memory of your ... of your exquisite lips and of their heady kisses, of your divine body, of your charms beyond compare, has never ceased to haunt me through all these weary years. In the dark there was the glow of your emerald eyes, unique, unforgettable in shade ...

Ville d'Avray was licking his lips.

'There's no doubt about it, my dear. The letter is undoubtedly addressed to you.'

The rest of the company were trying to keep a straight face and exchanging knowing glances.

Madame de Peyrac's beauty seemed destined to create conflicts, to cause tragedies, to unleash passions.

They were beginning to get used to the idea and even to feel somewhat proud of it. Experience had taught them that in whatever clime she appeared she brought with her a touch of the unknown, and that one could never be sure what turn events would take. It was like in the theatre.

Angélique looked at Joffrey de Peyrac, disconcerted.

'I simply don't understand it. This letter must have been written to someone else. It's all a mistake.'

'Emerald eyes ...' Ville d'Avray insisted. 'Do you really think it's such a common colour?'

She gave a shrug.

'Since you say the gentleman saw me in the procession ...

It's not all that difficult to turn compliments ... He must be out of his mind.'

'I would think he's more likely to be one of your former admirers,' Peyrac suggested, clearly viewing the incident with equanimity. 'He recognized you when he saw you at Mass. We must be prepared for little surprises of this sort now we are in New France.'

He drew Angélique to one side, and, taking the letter from her, examined the seals and both sides of the ribbon.

'It would not surprise me if he turned out to be the mysterious King's envoy. Good work! You've managed to get him to emerge from his den.'

Angélique moved to the signature in an attempt to decipher it, but it was even more illegible than the rest, being obscured by an inked seal stamped right across the name itself. What looked as if it might be a sprawling *N* could be vaguely made out at the beginning.

After struggling in vain, she gave up.

'I simply haven't the faintest notion who it could be.'

'Really? No idea at all?'

'None! As I said before, the man has mistaken me for someone else.'

'No! Ville d'Avray is right, it's the emerald eyes that prove it's you. I'll wager that at Court your eyes were famous and that there were no others to match them.'

Angélique made a tremendous effort to remember those past days. She could visualize the hustle and bustle, the Hall of Mirrors, the handsome, attentive men, with their smiles, their caressing hands that had to be brought under control with a smart tap of your fan, and their flirtatious glances whose message you had to pretend not to understand.

'And those unforgettable kisses?' Peyrac insisted.

There was a sparkle of irony in his eyes, but he seemed more amused than anything else.

'No, I can't think ...'

'Is the choice as wide as that?' he asked with a laugh. 'And what about those ... er ... favours, apparently extensive enough for him to refer to your divine body?' he insisted somewhat caustically.

'He's bragging.'

Feeling decidedly put out, she resumed her reading. Whoever this erstwhile admirer was, his writing was appalling. And the emotion under which he appeared to be labouring had done nothing to improve it. His agitated state of mind was obvious not only from the scrawl but from the high-flown language he employed:

My joy is boundless now I know you to be so near. I trust you may prove less cruel than in the past and that you will deign to remember me. If you are able to give your master the slip, I shall be waiting for you behind the isolated warehouse on the headland running out beyond the Indian village. Do not let me wait in vain. Come, so that I can at last really believe in this dream, so wonderful, so unexpected, so unhoped-for, to have found you again. I kiss your hands.

'Now he wants an assignation,' Count Peyrac remarked. 'Well, you must go.'

'No! Supposing it were a trap!'

'We'll outwit him. For a start, you will be armed ... And we shall position ourselves nearby under cover of darkness, ready to step in at the slightest hint of trouble.'

He beckoned to Yolande and Adhémar, who came forward nervously.

'Did you hear this gentleman's name mentioned? What did he look like?'

'Well, he's a handsome figure of a man,' Yolande replied. 'He's a great lord, that's for sure. But he didn't tell us his name and we didn't think to ask. He invited us very charmingly to accompany him, so we went.'

Angélique tried to find out more from Honorine.

'Did he tell you who he was when he spoke to you? And what did he say when he gave you the letter for me?'

But Honorine was sulking. She pretended not to hear, went and picked up her treasure box she had noticed lying in a corner, sat down on the deck, leaning against a partition, and began to count over her favourite treasures as if nothing else mattered in the whole wide world. Every now and then she would hold one of them out towards Angélique with an innocent babyish smile, as if to say: 'Look, Mummy, look how pretty it is!'

'She's having me on,' said Angélique. 'Because I scolded her instead of congratulating her on her prank. Now she's got me. She's acting the baby so as to be left alone. It will be ages before we can get anything out of her.'

'Never mind! In any case you're the only one who can sort things out by coming face to face with this person. The more I think about it, the more convinced I feel that the man who penned this passionate declaration of love, and the King's representative are one and the same. The important thing is for us to know *whom* you recognize him to be.'

Angélique glanced down again at the letter, the luxurious paper crackling between her fingers.

'Your kisses ...'

What kisses? What lips at Court had kissed hers?

She could remember only the King's lips in the darkness of the shrubbery.

Or Philippe's lovemaking – Philippe her second husband. But he was dead.

So who else had there been? Had she given so many kisses without now being conscious of it?

She looked at the very different setting in which she now found herself. As her eyes dwelt thoughtfully on the landscape around her, it seemed almost incredible that against the background of these shores with their plumes of smoke rising from Indian encampments, these solitudes closing in around humble dwellings, these silent, inscrutable mountains, this endless sky stretching out over the forest-clad wilderness, her glamorous past could rise up and confront her, bringing back a whiff of the hectic, exhilarating life she had lived at Versailles.

'Look, Mummy,' cried Honorine, shaking her gold rattle. 'Look! Look how pretty it is.'

CHAPTER 25

ANGÉLIQUE LEFT the village and made her way towards the large building referred to in the message. It was log built and stood beside the river, a short distance on the near side of the Indian encampment. According to Ville d'Avray, the building belonged to some high official in Montreal.

Carlon, on the other hand, claimed that it was a Jesuit warehouse. However that might be, the spot seemed well chosen since it was situated somewhat apart from the rest of Tadoussac, where the fur bartering was still in full swing.

Angélique slipped out of the village without attracting attention. Night was falling, and Tadoussac was shrouded in mist and smoke that lay in swathes along each rise in the ground – the mists rising from the river, the smoke from the village chimneys and the Huron encampment. In addition, fires had been lighted here and there in the open for the purpose of roasting moose whole, these creatures, akin to the European elk, being the largest and tastiest of the game animals in the area, or of grilling fish or roasting sweet potatoes in the embers, or perhaps hanging a cauldron of maize over the flames to regale the Indian tribesmen from the 'High Country'.

Turning her back on the last of those patches of light, Angélique plunged into darkness. In this direction, night had already fulfilled its task. The forest or the nearby river could no longer be distinguished from the sky, rendered still more opaque by the evening mist. In order to escape notice, Angélique had drawn her hair up under a coif, wrapped herself in her heavy woollen cloak, whose dark colours shaded into the mist, and pulled the full hood up over her coif. Too bad if her enthusiastic former admirer was mildly disappointed at encountering her thus roughly dressed. As she paced rapidly along, she continued to sort through her memories. A few names had come to the surface of handsome lords in the King's entourage: Brienne,

Cavois, Saint-Aignan ... Could it have been that one of those had been in love with her without her being aware of it? Anything was possible. At Versailles there had been so little time to devote to romance!

She had not far to go. She felt no trace of anxiety. She had armed herself as Joffrey had advised, and she knew that at the slightest hint of danger help would be forthcoming. But she felt that these precautions would be unnecessary, and in fact, as she walked on, curiosity began to get the upper hand along with a desire to meet someone who had known her as she had once been at the Court of the King of France.

She had been a different woman from the one she was today. On several occasions already, on the voyage to Quebec, she had felt the need to re-establish contact with her vanished self – Madame du Plessis-Bellière. She had found it difficult to recall having been that much-courted woman, loved by Philippe, desired by the King, who had dominated the festivities at Versailles. That glamorous ghost had vanished on that terrible night of carnage at the Chateau du Plessis, behind a screen of flames and shadows.[1]

And yet it was not so very long since it had all happened. A mere six years separated her from the time when the King used to write to her: *Little treasure, my unforgettable little treasure, do not be cruel* ...

What now set her heart pounding was less the thought that she was about to come face to face with a witness of her past than fear of stirring up sorrows and joys that had become alien to her.

As she strode on she forgot she was in Canada.

Hearkening to the memories that rose up within her, she realized that she was heading less for a meeting with a stranger than for an encounter with herself, for a confrontation she felt would oblige her to renew her links with certain buried aspects of her soul.

When the dark shape of the building loomed up down in the hollow, she had to halt.

The heavy tang of the forest made her catch her breath and she laid her hand on her breast as if to stifle the thudding of her heart.

Then, summoning up all her courage, she began to run,

[1] See *Angélique in Revolt*.

and without pausing for breath, came round the corner of the building.

A man was standing there, only just visible in the pale moonlight.

She gave a start: 'It's Philippe,' she thought, at the same time knowing that this was impossible since Philippe was dead, 'his head blown off by a cannon ball.' And yet there was something about the outline of the man standing a few paces from her on a rock that reminded her irresistibly of her second husband, the Marquis de Plessis-Bellière. She could not have said what, possibly his rather theatrical attitude ... The way he wore his cloak, the way he arched his leg ...

The dim glow from the fires along the distant shore gave enough light for her to make out the glitter of embroidery on his clothes. He was wearing a high-collared cloak similarly embroidered over and fastened by toggles of gold thread, casually thrown back over his shoulders. The buckles on his very high-heeled fine leather shoes sparkled too.

In a sweeping gesture he raised his hand to his plumed hat and made a low bow after the fashion of the Court.

As he straightened up, she saw his pleasant, gentle features, which did indeed seem not altogether unfamiliar. He was not wearing a wig, having thick auburn hair. She thought he was handsome, in the full bloom of his manhood. He smiled.

'So it really is you!' he exclaimed in a voice trembling with emotion. 'Angélique, passion of my life! Here you are, appearing just like an elf, with your sprightly tread ... still the same, fascinating! ...'

'But, Monsieur, where did you know me before?'

'What? Doesn't even seeing me revive your memories?'

'No, I must confess, it does not.'

'Oh, you're just as cruel as ever! ... Oh, what a blow ... Just like you!' he repeated apparently downcast. 'As indifferent as ever to my torments, plunging a dagger, almost offhandedly, into my heart ... Well then, take a closer look at me. Come on now, look at me!'

He drew closer, trying to position himself where the light was strongest. Without being unduly tall, he was taller than she was. He was elegant, a man of the world, with a playfulness in his manner that was belied by the melancholy expression in his clear eyes.

He shook his head:

'What a disappointment! So that's the only trace I have left in your memory, is it? ... Of course I knew I could not expect much, but all the same! That's what passion is. So deep was mine for you that over these past years I tried to persuade myself that you had, even if only fleetingly, understood and shared my love ... That thought alone enabled me to endure the torment of your absence ... I would call to mind words you had spoken to me, expressions I had seen on your face, I delved into my mind, trying to guess the meaning of your rare smiles, and finally persuaded myself that in spite of your reserve, I had not left you unmoved and that you had ... — how can I put it? — felt something for me all the same, although fear and modesty forbade you to reveal it. Well, now I must sing another tune, once again see my fondest illusions shattered ... The cruel truth is that you never loved me.'

'I am very sorry indeed, Monsieur.'

'No! No! Please. It is not your fault. One cannot, alas! force one's feelings.'

He gave a sigh.

'So even my name meant nothing to you? ...'

'But I don't know your name.'

'How can that be? ... What about the letter I wrote you?'

'I could not decipher your signature,' exclaimed Angélique. 'With due respect, Sir, your handwriting is appalling ...'

'Oh, so that was it! ... That's rather better. You cheer me greatly ...'

He straightened up, delighted, took her hand and lifted it to his lips.

'... Forgive me. The slightest thing you say or do revives me or plunges me into deepest despair ... I am overcome by the sheer joy of this moment. You are here, actually here ... It is like a dream ...'

Once again he kissed her hand passionately.

She felt more and more sure that she knew him, even knew him well, but was totally unable to put a name to his attractive face.

'Where was it that we met?' she asked. 'Could it have been at Court? In the circle close to the King?'

The man made a kind of strangled noise and reeled back a pace.

'At Court?' he repeated, his eyes wide in astonishment. 'Could I have met *you* at Court?'

Then suddenly as she saw the expression on his face, it came to her in a flash. She saw him again. She fancied she could hear the sound of his voice ... But where? Where had it been?

He saw that she was on the point of recognizing him and his face lit up.

'Yes? Yes?' he stammered impatiently, his hands held out towards her as he scanned her face.

'Help me,' she begged. 'Where was it? When was it? Was it a long time ago? I feel it was not so very long ago.'

'Two years!'

Two years ago! Then it could not have been at Versailles that she had known him ... Two years ago? She had been in La Rochelle!

'Monsieur de Bardagne!' she cried, as she at last recognized the King's Lieutenant-General, who had been Governor of the city at that time. As the man in charge of that stronghold of Huguenots, his primary responsibility had been their conversion to Catholicism.

'Phew! That was hard work!' he said in a tone of mock relief.

La Rochelle! That put a very different complexion on everything. Here was no admirer who had known her in the days of her splendour. On the contrary. It was better this way ...

'Monsieur de Bardagne,' she repeated, delightedly. 'Oh, how glad I am to see you again; I have such happy memories of you.'

'One would never have guessed! ...'

'It's partly your fault, too,' she said reproachfully. 'You seem so serious, so solemn, whereas, with respect, I remember you, Sir, as a cheerful, bantering man.'

'The pain I suffered on losing you may have something to do with the change.'

'I can't believe that ... And didn't you used to wear a small moustache?'

'I shaved it off. It wasn't fashionable any more.'

She scrutinized him with growing pleasure. No, he had not changed. La Rochelle! All her memories came flooding back: Monsieur de Bardagne in his coach, eager to drive her home in spite of her humble servant's apparel. Monsieur de Bardagne masked and enveloped in a dun-coloured cloak, waiting for her on her way back from the public wash-place with her big basket of washing.

'That was why Honorine said you were a friend of hers.'

'*She* recognized me immediately, adorable child that she is! When I caught sight of her this afternoon on the shore among the little Canadian children, I was bowled over with surprise and delight. I went over to her, hardly able to believe my eyes, but straight away she made a great fuss of me, as if we had only parted company yesterday.'

'Now I understand why she kept on waving her gold rattle at me, the little minx. It was you who gave it to her!'

'Yes, indeed I did! And you didn't want to accept it, do you remember?'

'It was too grand for someone in my social position.'

'You never would accept anything from me, my dearest!'

He looked at her with an expression of overwhelming tenderness.

In a spontaneous gesture, they clasped hands, seeking in one another's eyes a reflection of days gone by.

'I am so happy, sincerely happy to see you again,' she assured him. 'So give me a smile, my dear Monsieur de Bardagne, to remind me of the way you looked.'

'Yes, indeed, my beautiful servant girl.'

They smiled at one another. Then in a sudden impulsive gesture that drew them together, Monsieur de Bardagne's lips met Angélique's and pressed them fervently. Yet the embrace was friendly rather than sensual, and Angélique responded affectionately. The kiss sealed a reunion which she would never have thought could have given her so much pleasure.

During the two intervening years, she had totally forgotten Monsieur de Bardagne. But seeing him now brought back the tone of their previous relationship, its flirtatiousness, the exchange of at times rather daring gallantries that had a particular zest in the tense atmosphere of La Rochelle which was then undergoing persecution. He had been the King's Lieutenant, the Governor, the most powerful man in the city, while she was an unfortunate at the very bottom of the social ladder, who, furthermore, had a price on her head.[1] But that he had not known. She had caught his attention. He had been crazy about her. He had courted her frantically, quite unable to face the fact that this humble servant girl was not dazzled by the homage of a Governor of the King. In spite of his high position in society, he had finally laid at her feet his name, his titles and his fortune, so intolerably strong was his desire for her. He claimed that the mere sight of her sent him into paroxysms of erotic frenzy such as he had never before experienced with anyone else.

And naturally Angélique's coldness and lack of response had only served to add fuel to his passion.

And now it was all beginning again.

'Ah!' he sighed, holding her at arm's length as he looked at her; 'it really is you! I recognize your lovely face, those tremendous eyes, and the shape of your lips I have dreamed of so much. But were I to doubt the reality of your presence, I would be convinced by the langour that steals over me at the sight of you, the sweet thrill that you and you alone arouse in my heart, and the frenzy that accompanies them and makes me a slave in your presence. And yet I thought I was cured. But you have not changed.'

'And neither have you, Monsieur de Bardagne, it would appear!'

'But what is the secret of your bewitching charm?' he went on. 'At the very sound of your voice my passion re-awakens and brings me under your spell. Should I complain? How can I tell? A love like this is a gift, a heart-rending gift at times, but one that I would not have wanted never to have known, although it has already cost me dear. So come and sit beside me, my dear. There is a bench under the lee of this shack . . .'

They sat down. The eaves of the building cast a dense, black shadow across them, hiding them from sight, had there

[1] See *Angélique in Revolt*.

been eyes watching them from the bushes.

A night bird gave a soft, muffled call.

Nicolas de Bardagne slipped one arm caressingly round Angélique's shoulders. The folds of his cloak enveloped her in a delicate scent of powder, for he used a discreet touch of lilac perfume. One could not but admire how well turned out he was considering the lack of amenities on the ship in which he was quartered and the hardships he had endured during the voyage aboard the *Saint John the Baptist*. But he was one of those fashionable men-about-town in whose eyes an impeccable turn-out was at all times and in all circumstances, especially as a tribute to the ladies, an almost sacred duty.

'And yet I should hate you,' he went on after a moment's silence, as if following his own line of thought. 'For you made fun of me, you base little creature, you lied brazenly to me, you made a fool of me, worse, in fact, you betrayed me. But what can I do about it? You drive me wild, and now, this evening, I am very willing to forgive you. I can feel you close to me, with my hand on your slender, firm waist ... Can it be true? But this time I shall have my say,' he went on with mounting excitement. 'I shall not fear to speak my heart, I shall make you pay ...'

'Shh!' she broke in, 'don't talk so loud ...'

She looked about her in some concern then suddenly, as if just realizing where she was, she said:

'I must go.'

'What? Already? No, it's out of the question. Never ... never shall I let you go again. Tell me, are you still with your master?'

'My master?' asked Angélique in astonishment – she had already wondered at the term used in the letter.

'Yes, that obstinate, arrogant merchant Berne who guarded you so jealously in his house and made it impossible for me to see anything of you. Did you follow him all the way to Canada?'

'To Canada?' she exclaimed. 'A Huguenot? Whatever gave you that idea? You must be out of your mind, and you the King's Lieutenant! Who would have thought you had been in charge of matters concerning the so-called Reformed

Church? Just think for a moment! We are in New France, Sir. This is an Ultra-Catholic country where the power of the police extends every bit as far as in La Rochelle. This would be no refuge for a notorious Huguenot escaping from the King's Dragoons.'

'But of course! What am I thinking of? ... You make me say the most ridiculous things. You see what happens to me when you are there. I can think of one thing only, and that is you, so delighted am I to see you. And yet, as I said, I should spurn you, revile you, punish you for what you did to me!

'Was there ever a more crafty, more cunning inventor of lies than you, you wretched little hypocrite, that told me the flattest lies with a look on you like an angel? You've mentioned Master Berne. Well what about him? ... A notorious Huguenot, you say ... and *you were helping him* ... Now you admit it, you were helping him to escape ... And all the time you were busy telling me that you had been found a position in his house by the ladies of the Company of the Blessed Sacrament to bring about his and his family's conversion, as a penance for your errors as an all too lovely sinner ... And I, *I believed you*, I trusted you, and neglected to look into the case of that dreadful heretic and find a thousand and one reasons for sending him to prison as a traitor to his country and his sovereign ... Out of indulgence for you, I neglected all the duties entrusted to me, I, the King's Lieutenant, Governor of La Rochelle, official in charge of Religious Affairs, whose responsibility it was to report the conversion of the entire city to the King in under two years! Ah, you were a fine help! A pretty bit of work that was!'

Trembling with indignation, he took her by the chin in order to force her to look him full in the face.

'Now just you dare ... just you dare tell me to my face *that it isn't true*, that you were not lying to me as shamelessly as a fairground barker who promises to draw teeth painlessly, that you did not make an utter fool of me as if I had been a schoolboy, that you did not just manipulate me, with never a care for my feelings, to help those wretched Protestants to escape?'

He was trembling with anger and retrospective mortification, and Angélique, who understood his wrath and knew all too well how justified it was, chose to remain silent.

Then he began to calm down. He gazed tensely through the soft light at the pale oval of this woman's face up-turned towards him. He gave a deep sigh, then letting go her chin, he threw himself back.

'But what can I do? I am weak where you are concerned,' he moaned, 'even though I am more than aware of your wiles. I used to curse you, to want to hold you up to public obloquy, but it did nothing to ease my pain, and I only have to have you before me for a single moment to find myself spell-bound once more, weakly forgiving you, forgetting the shame ... and all the misery you brought me, my career ruined, my prestige destroyed, my entire life in ruins through your fault ...'

'Whatever do you mean, through my fault? ...'

'You've forgotten, of course. I had left for Paris, pleased to think that I could put in a very promising report to those in charge of conversions, both my direct superiors in the Company of the Blessed Sacrament and the Ministers of Religious Affairs, who were gathering information about the progress of conversions in the Kingdom, province by province.

'I was able to tell them of the remarkable progress achieved in La Rochelle, where the handful of diehards who refused to abjure their faith no longer had any influence over their erstwhile co-religionists. I was busy preparing my report, with the intention of stressing the fact that the city was completely calm, these exceptionally good results having been achieved without the slightest outbreak of disorder.

'I tried, as you know, to *persuade* rather than to *compel*, and never shrank from engaging in long theological arguments, as Monsieur Fénelon had advocated, in order to talk those narrow-minded Protestants round and induce them to make free, voluntary, unconstrained recantation, trying always to reconcile the often harsh dictates of the law with the very understandable feelings of families – you remember how I managed to smooth things over when old Uncle Lazarus died and his body should have been dragged through the streets on a hurdle ... I spared him that and had hoped that the Berne family would have been grateful to me and been more cooperative ... All the same, I had positive results to report and was, as I say, pretty pleased at the way things were going. But when I reached Paris, I was astonished to find myself given a cool reception. And it was only when I got back to La Rochelle that I realized why.

'For there I was met by a recital of infamies and disasters long enough to make one's hair stand on end.

'My most valuable prize had escaped. A whole Company of crack dragoons had been reduced to pulp at the foot of a cliff, a warship had been sunk, there had been scores of arrests and a corresponding number of complaints to deal with. I had Admiralty Headquarters from the Isle de Ré down on me.'

'But why? For what reasons?'

'Because of the ship that was sunk ... and also because Madame Demuris had been arrested ... Yes, you must remember the Catholic lady under whose care the Conversions Office had placed the Berne children.'

'Oh, you mean Master Berne's sister ... and she was arrested?'

'But of course! She had allowed them to escape ... and who with? ... With you, of course. Absolutely disregarding the undertakings she had given as a convert, she had handed them over to you. What lie you told her I don't know but you certainly had no difficulty in finding one ... as the outcome proved! She found herself in an extremely awkward situation. Her husband, who was an officer in the French Royal Navy, held a good position and was moreover a firm favourite with the Admiral, who had taken a fancy to him. So the wretched woman's arrest caused a great stir. As for me, I found that the lovely city to which I had become accustomed, in which I had some excellent friends, and where my life, in spite of, or perhaps because of, the Huguenots, was full of interest, where I felt I was doing a useful, worthwhile job, I found that the place had turned into a wasteland. And worse still, I found myself banished, guilty, condemned. Baumier ... do you remember Baumier?'

'Yes, a dreadful, unsavoury little Inquisitor.'

'That's him ... Well, Baumier had laid a devastating trap for me, with you as the cruel lever, or rather, the murderous chopper ...'

'What, me again!'

'Yes, you, you little hypocrite, you and your friends of the so-called Reformed Church, all the diehards of La Rochelle, who were not only the pillars of Huguenot resistance, but also of the commercial life of the city, *you had all taken flight, gone off to America*, cocking a snook at the police network I myself had deployed there, through which no one, I mean no one, could slip, as I had solemnly guaranteed to the King, and all those rogues, whose submission would have once and for all brought the proud city to its knees, had escaped the King's Justice ...

'But that was nothing compared with the blow I suffered. You had vanished, had escaped with them! ... Oh, what grief! ...'

He fell silent, breathing hard, and said no more for quite a while. Then he finished his tale in a flat voice.

'I was arrested. I was very nearly sent to the galleys – I, the King's Lieutenant, sent to the galleys! That's what it very nearly came to. I was branded an accomplice, a perjurer, a renegade ... Baumier even went so far as to say I was myself only a convert to Catholicism ... I, the descendant of an old Catholic family from Berry.'

'But this is terrible! I ... I am dreadfully sorry to hear all this. How did you manage to get out of that appalling mess?'

'I had on my side one of the assistants to Monsieur de la Reynie, the French Chief of Police, his right-hand man, in fact. He was at La Rochelle when I got back, and he used his influence to save me from being driven round the town in a coach with bars and thrown into solitary confinement.'

And noting a reaction on Angélique's part, he went on:

'... Yes, you've guessed whom I'm talking about. He's no stranger to you, this particular police officer, is he? And if he were to appear out of the blue, I wager you'd not be long in recognizing *him*. Now tell me who it was ...'

'François Desgrez,' she replied, quick as a flash.

'None other!'

Nicolas de Bardagne took a deep breath in an attempt to control his temper, but found it impossible and burst out:

'François Desgrez, yes, that's right! And kindly tell me what there was between you and that shifty lout, because he seemed to know you all too well.'

'Come, come, your Excellency, don't get jealous again, please.'

'How can I help being jealous when I remember that fellow's sardonic smile, and the cocksureness of the man who has lost count of his conquests. He spoke of you with such familiarity, such insolence! – As if you belonged to him, as if he was the only person in the world to love you, console you, understand you, the only one who knew you intimately – what agonies he made me endure!'

'But you said he did you a favour.'

'Yes, he did, and I admit that had it not been for him I would have been finished. Baumier had condemned me without mercy. Desgrez spared me the galleys, and possibly even the hangman's noose, that I cannot deny. The hidden power of these wretched policemen seems to be limitless these days! The King allows the police far too much scope. Yes, I know he wants Paris to be cleaned up, to root out the criminal elements. But he will see just what it costs him to have these men ferreting about all over the place. Nothing stops that man Desgrez, no name, however illustrious.

'Last year he succeeded in arresting a lady of very high rank, on the grounds that she had poisoned her father, her brother, in other words members of her own family ... Admittedly it's not a nice sort of thing to do, but if family connections are no longer to keep one safe from the clutches of the law what is the point of being born a duke or a prince? Desgrez boasted that he had been on her trail for many a long year, waiting for the right moment to pounce, and that he would have a whole lot more arrested too, no matter how high their rank. What insolence! The fellow cares for neither God nor King.'

'Was his poisoner condemned to death?'

'Yes, indeed she was! The King would not let the fact that she was the daughter of a Councillor of State make any difference. He wants it to be known that we are all equal before the criminal law. She was nevertheless spared the stake, though she had her head cut off. That was a victory for your Desgrez. But he'd better be careful, or he may go too far.'

Once again he endeavoured to regain his composure, struggling to hold back the diatribe he was bursting to unleash.

'... Mind you, I could have made things awkward for him

too ... It was obvious that he had deliberately allowed you to escape. He barely disguised the fact. Baumier was perfectly well aware of it too and looked at him with eyes like a rat's suffering from rabies. But Desgrez was so sure of himself that he could not have cared less. He laughed in my face when I said something about his weakness for you. He knew I was far too seriously involved myself ever to try to play that particular card. But I could have done so ... and he realized it. I said: "Tit for tat, I'll keep my mouth shut, but you get me out of this bloody mess ..." Oh, what a dreadful interview that was! You were there like a rankling wound between us, the cause of everything discreditable and unworthy we had done, of our failure to fulfil our duty and carry out the tasks assigned to us.

'I tried to explain to him the power you had over me and how my passion for you had blinded me to the true state of affairs in the city. He laughed and said: "Do you imagine you are the first man *she* had driven mad, the first man she has brought to the gallows? ..." Never shall I forget the degrading atmosphere of those conversations, and the torments I endured in that dark little office in the Palace of Justice in La Rochelle, face to face with that sneering bully whom I could not even bear to hear mention your name. I had put you on a pedestal, I used to watch you passing by looking so lovely, so serene and so demure, holding your little girl by the hand, you so dignified, and here he was revealing you to me in a different light that aroused my sensuality more strongly than ever, and it was then that appalling truth dawned on me: that you had belonged to him, to that insolent fellow, and that he, common police official that he was, was taking a pleasure in mocking me. It was dreadful! I thought of *him* holding you in his arms and I looked with hatred at his vulgar mouth that had kissed your lips.'

'Desgrez hasn't got a vulgar mouth,' Angélique protested.

This interruption plunged Nicolas de Bardagne into the very depths of gloom. It was the final blow. He uttered not a word.

After a time, he went on:

'All right, then, since you defend him, I won't say any more. May I just add, that the wretch made me pay dear for his assistance. The fact was that he wanted to get his own back for the smiles you had bestowed on me – oh, so few they were! – but he taught me a great deal. And I know he was right. You are one of those women that men can never forget, no matter how humble the favour granted, a mere glance, or a smile ... You are ... the soul of mystery on earth ... made manifest ... incarnate ... the expectation of Happiness ... Woman herself ...'

Once again he leaned back against the wall of the log building.

'... Am I dreaming?' he murmured, his voice seeming to come from a great distance. 'Where are we? At the world's end. And here you are beside me – though I never thought to see you again – emerging from the heart of this fearsome, desperate landscape, where, since our arrival, we have been within an ace of death at least a score of times ... Perhaps it's all a dream ... Perhaps I am really dead ...'

Angélique had found the strain of listening to Bardagne, his passionate declarations and his incoherent, bluntly-phrased narrative almost too much for her, and she felt very much as if she were intoxicated from it all.

She had been so captivated too by all these reminiscences that she now felt she had stood all she could bear. He had bombarded her with images from a past that, although still recent, seemed to belong to a world that was dead and gone – intense, painful images that were set against a background whose keynote was ink, dusty files and dim lighting, and which brought back to her too, memories of anguish and distress experienced in a tiny office in the Palace of Justice at La Rochelle, while the wind and the sea outside spoke to her of freedom and before her sat François Desgrez, the police official, with his fiery glances and that nasty little smile at the corner of his lips – a smile that had nevertheless turned to gentleness as far as she was concerned.

She felt sorry for Nicolas de Bardagne. It must have been a severe blow to him to fall so disastrously from favour when he had always worked so hard and conscientiously to achieve promotion.

'Calm yourself!' she said aloud, 'my poor friend! All that is past and gone now. Even so, I beg you to forgive me, from the bottom of my heart. And I am pleased to see that you have managed to fall on your feet again. You seem to have found a good position now.'

'Yes, I was lucky! Of course, I would never have actually chosen to come to Canada in order to pursue my career, but the opportunity arose of undertaking a special mission for which my good name might prove useful, so I took it on.'

'More religious affairs?'

'Yes and no ... It isn't exactly concerned with religious matters, but it nevertheless called for someone who had some experience of the conflicts to which religion may give rise, and who was used to dealing with representatives of the Church, and with Protestants when occasion arose; and that applied to me. So, because of these various qualifications, I was chosen and accepted this high office. The task I am called upon to play in Quebec is going to be a delicate one, but I have been given a free hand to do as I think best.'

'Are you, by any chance ... the high-ranking Royal Official brought over on the *Saint John the Baptist* who was said to be seriously ill?'

'What a lot of idle curiosity there is in these out-of-the-way villages!' he said with a laugh. 'Yes, I am, but not a word mind!' he added, looking about him: 'It's better that people should not suspect how important my assignment is.'

'Why ever is that?'

'Because of that pirate from the South Seas who boarded us off Tadoussac.'

Angélique surpressed a start.

'Do you mean .. the corsair who is anchored off Tadoussac at the moment, Count Peyrac?'

'Count Peyrac, indeed! Pooh! You speak of him with too much reverence. In my eyes, he's merely a pirate. It is true that people in the colonies aren't too particular about those who drop anchor in their waters, provided they come with their hands full of gold. I was warned about that. But it would be utterly disastrous if this man, whether he be pirate or gentleman, becomes too interested in me, because, and I am telling you this in confidence, and to you alone ...'

He leaned closer to whisper into her ear:

'... The mission with which I have been entrusted concerns him ...'

CHAPTER 26

AT THIS revelation, Angélique's heart began to pound violently.

Fortunately the King's envoy could not see the expression on her face or how pale she had suddenly become.

'Just note,' he went on, 'how chance has thrown him in my path as far back as the mouth of the St Lawrence. In a way, that will enable me to bring my mission to a satisfactory conclusion more quickly. I wasn't at all expecting it. I knew that he was in the south, in Acadia, where he was bent on conquering our settlements bit by bit, and I was going to Quebec initially in order to work out a plan of campaign with the Government of New France. But, lo and behold! here he is already among us, if not at our beck and call. I must admit that I felt somewhat perturbed on discovering that the unidentified ships cruising within sight of our vessel on the St Lawrence, apparently cutting us off from Quebec, belonged to none other but him. I thought that he had had wind of my coming and was waiting to take me prisoner. But not at all, and in any case, he couldn't have heard of my prospective arrival, except by magic because the arrangements were made in great haste and secrecy.

'He had no inkling that I had already heard of him. So, before our capture at Tadoussac, I took care to distribute largesse in order to ensure that the captain and sailors would not mention my name or disclose any details whatsoever about me. Fortunately, like the pirate he is, he was only interested in the holds of the *Saint John the Baptist*. Just imagine – he even had the impudence to take off four barrels of Burgundy I was bringing as a present to Governor Frontenac ... Anyway! There's nothing we can do about it for the moment. We're in his clutches and he's there in force with a fleet of five ships. The main thing is that he should think us harmless and let us carry on to Quebec without let or hindrance.'

Angélique could see that Bardagne had no inkling of her true identity. He imagined she was living in Tadoussac, like so many others, subject to the orders of the man he called 'the pirate', otherwise he would not have addressed her so openly.

'But ... but why are those in high places so interested in him!' she asked, 'even to the extent of appointing an emissary to carry out an investigation? The colony can manage its own affairs.'

'It's a very involved story, and it explains the importance of the orders I've received. To be sure, we're not dealing with a mere common sea-rover, and his French aristocratic origins make it reasonable to treat him with more respect than if he were some freebooter or other. But it would appear that he has taken possession of certain territories belonging to the French Crown. Furthermore – and it is this matter among others that I am instructed to clear up – he is also suspected of being the Rescator, a notorious renegade of the Mediterranean who wrought havoc among His Majesty's galleys, which would, obviously, make things more serious for him.'

Angélique found herself unable to control her breathing.

Seen in this way 'from the other side', Joffrey's actions could turn him into an enemy not only of New France but of the whole Kingdom and its sovereign. They branded him a renegade, which was the worst of crimes, with which no alliance could be contemplated. This view of him seemed firmly rooted in Paris, based as it was on accounts of his behaviour sent from America over the last two years or so, and also on his past record unearthed from the police archives. *They* suspected with far from common insight that it was in the past of this mysterious conqueror of North America, who threatened French Acadia, that arms should be sought to strike him down. Or at the least to expose him to public opprobrium as an implacable enemy.

Had there not already been that plot hatched in the realms of high finance to destroy him on his home ground, namely by the despatch of a corsair, Gold-Beard, instructed to take

211

his possessions back from him, a plot that had been linked with the more subtle trap of the Demon?

And now, to make an end of it, a special messenger was being sent to take, officially and politically, the necessary measures, if it turned out that the other more underhand and devious methods had failed.

The hostility showed no sign of relenting. But who was hatching these plots? Orgeval, the Jesuit? Colbert? The Merchant Companies? The Company of the Blessed Sacrament? Perhaps they were all involved.

'Who commissioned you to carry out such an investigation?' she asked after a moment's silence, in as casual a manner as possible.

'The King.'

'The King?' she gasped, opening her eyes wide. 'Do you mean to say that you've seen the King about this? . . .'

'Indeed yes, my dear child. What's so extraordinary in that? Believe it or not, I'm important enough to be given audience by His Majesty, who on this particular occasion, had orders and special instructions to give me. His Majesty attaches great importance to this mission. I remained with him for an hour discussing this man. I could see that His Majesty had studied Count Peyrac's dossier with the greatest care. Make no mistake. We have a sovereign who does everything with exemplary care and patience.'

Angélique nodded vaguely. She wanted to try and agree – 'Yes, yes, I know,' – but her lips could not form the words. She was profoundly disturbed. She pictured to herself the King, his talents, his boldness, his sense of glory and his jealously maintained conception of a role he fully assumed, which had succeeded in elevating him in a matter of years to the rank of greatest monarch in the world.

Whatever concessions had been acquired on American soil, their fate still rested in those terrible royal hands, which held the sceptre, ready to crush anyone who thwarted his ambitions or opposed his authoritarian and omnipresent will.

And now she was learning that far across the ocean the King had not forgotten them. Louis XIV had pored over the secret file in which Count Peyrac's name was written in letters of fire. Behind those pages of condemnation, those police reports and those more recent documents referring to his conquests, again bringing to the forefront the name of Peyrac in far-off America, behind that moving story of a ghost he believed for ever laid, had the King suspected a woman's presence? The woman who, one stormy evening, at Trianon, had turned to him exclaiming:

'No, you will never have me, me, his wife, the wife of Joffrey de Peyrac, whom you had burned alive on the Place de Grève.'

Count Bardagne sensed her agitation, without fully understanding the reason for it, imagining that he had frightened her, but he was charmed by the bewildered expression on her face at that moment, which made her more accessible and touching and he leaned towards her. He had kept his arm round her shoulders and, fearing she might get cold, he wrapped her more closely in the folds of his cape. At the same time he covered her temple with small burning kisses, unable to resist the temptation of the satiny flesh so close to him. She was so absorbed that she scarcely noticed. She was aware only of the strength of the embrace which at once warmed and reassured her, amidst the storm of anxiety and anguish which, once more, was rising within her. She snuggled against his shoulder. Weariness made her weak. She felt utterly broken by the bludgeoning of the unending struggle. Would they never be left to live in peace?

She was cold, but her brow burned. She felt the need of a man's strength to sustain her and, this man being a potential enemy, the need to appeal to his male strength and to cling to it was even more acute. The greater his power to destroy her life the more completely she put herself at his mercy. It was at that moment a deep-seated reflex, almost physical in nature.

She felt that her surrender aroused his protectiveness more than if she had resisted him and made herself inaccessible. She had already had the same feeling at La Rochelle. The impression that, in spite of his good nature, this kindly, tolerant man had, by virtue of his position, the power to destroy with a single word, a frown, the precarious peace she enjoyed with the Bernes, to demolish the insecure haven where she was recovering her strength together with her bastard daughter. Thus, cleverly, she had tried to placate him, and in fact he had protected her from the worst.

He was to be feared only in so far as he was the instrument of merciless power, but, because he loved her with infinite passion, she had been able through him to foil the stratagems of tyranny. She again felt the ebb and flow of the double emotion which had tormented her: the impulse to be wary of him and, at the same time, to confide in him.

'Why didn't you agree to go away with me to Berry?' he whispered. 'I would have set you up in my manor house. There you would have awaited, with your child, the coming of better days. In the midst of woods and fields, you would have eaten your fill of the produce of my vegetable garden and orchards. I have fine estates, comfort and ease, a great stock of wood for the winter, beautiful furniture, fine books, devoted servants ... Berry is a secluded province, easy going, out of the tide of events. You would have waited for me there ... Forgetting the cruelty of men and the world, you would have recovered from the wrong that has been done to you. I would have made no demands on you ... until you came to me of your own free will ...'

She no longer remembered this offer to take her away and conceal her in Berry ... It was possible! ...

'.. And now what is your lot in these wild regions? You've told me nothing.'

He hesitated. He found it a painful subject to broach. He would have preferred to know nothing about her, to hold her in his arms, only, as if she belonged to him. He made an effort to go on:

'.. If you're no longer in service with Master Berne, with whom are you placed? Or ... Who are you living with? For alas! I've no illusions,' he said half bitterly, half with a smile. 'Desgrez has told me all about you. You are not the strait-laced penitent I thought, and in my innermost heart I've come to terms with my jealousy. You are too beautiful – alone in the world and abandoned to a pitiless destiny – not to have thrown in your lot with another man, am I not right?'

She guessed that despite his debonair manner, he was hoping wildly, against all logic and common sense, that she was going to tell him that she was free, living chastely, still cut off from the pleasures of love by a sense of aversion that made her prefer a solitary life of toil and the upbringing of her daughter to subjection to a man. She couldn't bring herself to lie to him. And what she had to tell him was certainly very awkward. He expected at the most that she had married a Canadian trapper or a tradesman recently arrived from France. Yet she could not leave him in ignorance. She took her courage in both hands.

'You've guessed correctly,' she said, imitating Bardagne's rather artificial brightness. 'I don't live alone.' He could not suppress a quick smile.

'I've found a protector. Listen, I'll be frank with you.'

'That makes a change!'

'I imagine that my choice will come rather as a surprise to you, but ...'

'What are you leading up to?' asked Bardagne, suspiciously; 'please go on. What is it? Or, rather, who is it?'

'It's ... Well, it's that pirate you were talking to me about a moment ago ...'

She was going on to add: 'I'm his wife', but the diplomat forestalled her. His whole attitude signified total and utter repulsion.

'You don't mean to say that you've fallen into the hands of that pirate!'

'Er well, yes ... Something like that.'

'But it's crazy! It's madness! Wretched woman!' he cried. 'But don't you know that he's a very dangerous man? A totally unscrupulous adventurer? If you knew, my poor child, everything I know about him and what the King has intimated to me! That man had dealings with the Devil and was for that reason deprived of his rank and banished from the Kingdom, since when he has been knocking about the world. How insolent and case-hardened he is is shown by the fact he has shamelessly persisted in bearing his family name, without concern for the fact that it is stained by a conviction for witchcraft ...'

'Perhaps he wishes to make it clear in this way that the conviction was unjust ...'

'People are not condemned to the ignominy of the stake without good grounds. The Church is careful and the Inquisition more cautious nowadays than it used to be.'

'Don't be so hypocritical!' cried Angélique, beside herself with anger. 'You know as well as I do the farce that lies behind those inquisitional courts.'

Surprised by her sudden opposition, Count Bardagne gave her a suspicious look.

'You're surely not anxious about the fate of that wretch, are you? you don't mean you're attached to him! I don't believe it. You, Angélique, sunk so low! Wallowing in degradation! Please, don't add to the disillusionment you've already caused me by forcing me to see you in such a base light ... Must I lose for ever the image of you which captivated me – and in which the signs of genuine goodness were not the least of your charms? ... It's true that at that very time I behaved very naïvely and that you took advantage of it ...

'Oh well! That's the way it is,' he said, his anger subsiding; 'I know your faults, but I adore you despite them. I understood that you behaved in that way because you were a poor hunted creature. When one is a wanderer ... without shelter, without assistance ...

'Why didn't you come with me to Berry? ... I would have been willing to help you to prise apart the bars of the cage. Let's put this unfortunate business behind us. It's not too late, I'll save you. There's still time. Leave that man! Leave him, come with me. I have the power. And even a lawless and faithless pirate cannot act without due consideration towards one of the King of France's ambassadors. I will intervene and drag you from his clutches.'

'That, sir, is impossible! I am married.'

'To *him*? ...'

Bardagne's first reaction was one of fear for himself.

'And *I've* been telling you about the mission entrusted to me concerning him! Are you going to betray me?'

'Of course not. And in fact I'm very pleased that you have spoken to me so openly because I'll be able to help you to clear up certain misunderstandings.

'I can give an immediate filling to your mission by informing you that he is indeed the gentleman Rescator you have been told about. You would find out sooner or later. He became famous in the Mediterranean for his exploits though they did not include piracy. On the contrary, he promoted order and economic stability. He did occasionally clash with His Majesty's galleys. But here in Canada you can meet him without any anxiety. He holds the King of France and his emissaries in the highest regard ...'

'And what if he strings me up on a yard-arm? ...'

'He stands to gain nothing from stringing you up on a yard-arm ... He's going to Quebec to make his peace. Monsieur de Frontenac himself will confirm that he had long desired this goodwill visit.'

'With five racers! ... But I'm prepared to believe you or at least to hope that you're not deluding yourself. It's quite true that this brings my mission on much further than I expected. Fate is undoubtedly on my side ...'

Angélique was already congratulating herself on the fact that the volatile Nicolas de Bardagne seemed to have taken it so well. But this calm was only the result of the numbness of shock. After a moment's reflection on his part, there came the reawakening.

'No! No!' he cried wildly. 'Married! You! Married to that pirate! That doesn't count, it's sacrilege! You may be his mistress but you're not *his wife*. Why do you lie so? You have a need to make things up, to deceive, that is unbearable! In any case he can't marry you. He's a count and bears one of France's most illustrious names ... And you, what are you? A serving wench! It's true, Desgrez told me that you were well born, that you received a good education. I suppose you turned that on in order to get him to marry you ... No I can't believe it. You're lying again. It doesn't matter, I love you and this fated passion means that in a way you belong to me. I've languished after you too long, suffered too much from your absence ... Oh! you will always be flighty, foolishly giving yourself to men without principles but with sufficient impudence to beguile you. That rake Desgrez! That heretic Berne! Do you think I was taken in at La Rochelle ... Master and servant! Fiddlesticks! You were living under his roof. He took you into his bed, that fellow Berne!'

'Sir, that is quite enough,' Angélique interrupted him. She tried to get up. 'You bore me with your old rubbish and insult me into the bargain. I will not stand it ... I'm going ...'

Count Bardagne seized her by the wrist and forced her to sit down again.

'Forgive me, forgive me,' he said hastily. 'I'm behaving dreadfully, I can see that ... But you've so shattered me that at times I can no longer distinguish what is *You*, the delightful and fascinating creature who has bewitched me, from what is common to all women: trickery, lies ... But what does it matter? You will always make me suffer ... And I will always bless you for existing. There is no one in the whole world who possesses your charm; you are enchanting when you react so spiritedly, so fiercely, so magically ...'

Again he enfolded her in his arms with an irresistible movement, crushing her against him, and stooping over her, sought her lips, this time with fierce greed. He opened his lips and his possessive tongue demanded a like response, seeking her life in her. He kissed her like a thirsting man unable to wait any longer, maddened by the prospect of seeing the long-sought spring recede, and incapable of withdrawing from it before assuaging his most acute torment and finding certainty.

It was a long time before he felt that it was *she* whom he was savouring, *she* whom he held at his mercy, and that it was her mouth that trembled under his own and whose soft warm throbbing he was beginning to relish.

Then he drew away, very slowly, as if in a dream:

'Thank God,' he said in a toneless voice. 'How marvellous your lips taste! God be praised!'

'Do you really think God ought to be brought into all this?' asked Angélique recovering her breath with difficulty.

'Yes! because I'm beginning to understand that He is sending me my reward. I have been humiliated, flouted, I have suffered in the name of Justice ... and Love. I believed I had given everything, lost everything ... that I was forsaken of God and men ... like Job, without hope, and now you have been restored to me ... Isn't it an unbelievable miracle, a sign from Heaven? ...'

Through the misty night with its thinning clouds a faint, muted light filtered under the eaves and enabled Angélique to meet Count Bardagne's gaze. It was filled with a grave, unfamiliar gentleness which she would never have thought to see in those once frivolous eyes of the King's flighty Lieutenant-General in La Rochelle.

They were unusually pale. The light falling from the firmament, where the stars and an almond-shaped half-moon had suddenly broken through the fog, gave to those grey eyes a silvery glint as of the night sky.

'I had not noticed that his eyes were so attractive,' thought Angélique.

This feeble glow from the heavens, like a haze of iridescent dust, gave a silvery sheen to the man's close lips, half-open and panting, making their brightness irresistibly alluring, and she felt rising within herself the greedy impulse to meet them and to respond to so much desire. They embraced. This kiss was deep and endless. They abandoned themselves to it in a state of oblivion, detached from the world.

To her extreme amazement, Angélique felt the surge of an intoxicating sensation of resurrection, which sent new blood coursing through her veins. 'This time the Demon is defeated,' she said to herself. And with comic delight she saw her in her mind's eye fleeing across the night sky on a broomstick ...

He held her neck in the crook of his arm with a firm hold. His fingers had taken her chin to tilt her head gently backwards, and under the pressure of that nameless male mouth it was her turn to slake her raging thirst. Bardagne's passion infused into her an elixir to which she could not put a name, but which revitalized her body and soul, dispelled the shadows which the Demon's hatred had cast over her and which had shaken her confidence in life, her faith in herself and in her destiny, and at times, even her faith in the Other.

In him, she tasted all the mouths of the men who had worshipped her, the King, Desgrez, the Poet ... These men she had held in subjugation, declaring that they loved her, maintaining that they would always love her, that she would never die, convincing her by their passion that once more she would conquer, and, like a mighty wind, breathing into her renewed courage, the drive to struggle and win.

Down to the depths of her being she felt the exhilaration of the power she wielded: the power to gratify and enchant.

'You fill me with rapture,' murmured Bardagne. 'Oh!

What is to become of me now that I've found you?'

'Yes, I know ... I'm wondering myself,' said Angélique who was wavering.

She got up, staggering. He tried to support her, but she refused with fumbling gestures.

'No, I beg you ... I'll see you again, my darling. But for this evening, goodbye ...'

He watched her make good her escape, heard her stumbling over the stones until she turned to call back:

'Don't forget ... for the pirate ...'

Then she began to run.

PART FIVE

The Wine

CHAPTER 27

HE WAS the first obstacle she met in her path.

And how long had he been there, keeping watch? How much had he seen? Heard?

The edge of the wood was in deep shadow. They could not see one another. Joffrey de Peyrac's arms enfolded her and she threw hers round him, burying her face in the folds of his doublet on an impulse of almost childish panic. She would have been utterly incapable of explaining its cause.

'But you're burning hot,' he said in his calm slightly muffled voice. 'You're trembling, you're in a state of nerves! What's happened?'

'Oh! nothing to worry about. But it's a long story! He turns out not to be a gentleman of the King's suite, and it wasn't at Court that I met him ... And yet Versailles is mixed up in it ... And the King ... And it does involve you.'

He listened to her, leaning over her, focusing his attention on her in the darkness. She could feel that he was on the alert and noting her nervousness, the uncontrollable tremble in her voice. She was aware that her face was on fire, and her hands felt frozen.

'You're cold!'

Cold! Hot! she no longer knew. What exactly had happened? She had come down to earth again in Canada.

She was breathless.

'It was the past,' she stammered, 'the past, you understand.'

'Of course, I understand. Don't work yourself up like that, my love.'

The steady, familiar tone of Peyrac's voice reassured her and her breathing became easier. She recovered her balance, took a firm grip on herself, told herself she was a fool and, straightening up, began to walk along by his side, explaining to him who Bardagne was and what she had learned from him relating to themselves. It was much as they had feared. Matters had been taken to the King himself, and the King was on their track.

'The one thing that really intrigues me,' he commented, 'is the fact that by some stroke of fate this Bardagne, who knew you at La Rochelle and had no suspicion of your connections with the Court, should turn out to be precisely the person chosen by the King for a mission concerned with me. I'm quite prepared to believe in coincidence, but in this case there seems to be something too contrived, too organized about it. You'd think that some humorous devil was pulling the strings behind the scenes.'

'Don't speak of the devil!' she begged.

They were nearing the village where the scattered fires were still burning and people were dancing the *bourrée* round them.

She found that surprising. An age seemed to have passed since she had kept the assignation with the King's envoy.

She ran her hand across her forehead.

'Oh! I'm worn out, exhausted! Is the night over?'

'No, I should think not,' he said, laughing. 'The night is still young. Have you forgotten that we broached one of those celebrated casks of Burgundy that Ville d'Avray had his eye on, and our entire company is waiting for us on the *Gouldsboro* for the party. Come on, Madame, shake off your weariness. Thank God! the dawn is a long way off!'

He tightened his embrace jealously, and drew her along more quickly.

'As a matter of fact, we could have invited that gentleman to join in our celebrations . . .'

'No, no,' she said hastily. He would think it was a trap to capture him. 'He's very prejudiced against you.'

'I'll go along tomorrow to introduce myself and put his mind at rest. Meanwhile, let's enjoy ourselves!' he said eagerly. Things are looking up. We're going to drink to your reunion with an old flame, to the success of our plans and his, and hope that the two won't be too incompatible.'

She heard him laugh as if at the prospect of one of fate's more delicious little jokes.

'La Rochelle! So, it was La Rochelle! How exactly like you!'

He paused to kiss her passionately and continued to hurry her along. She was aware of the irresistible strength of his arm as it supported her. His energy had flowed into her. A moment before she had been listless and bewildered, now she felt herself borne along by his dynamism and high spirits.

The beach came into view, lighted by the torches carried by the men, with the longboat waiting at the water's edge.

'Why do you say that? La Rochelle! It isn't my fault. It was chance that brought me into contact with this Count Bardagne again.'

'Long live chance, every trick of chance, and let's say no more about it . . . till tomorrow.'

He picked her up in his arms to carry her to the boat, so that she would not have to go into the water.

'This evening we are princes of the world,' he cried with a laugh, and his teeth sparkled in his strongly-lined face. 'We are the masters of Tadoussac, of Canada and of the Kingdom of France. We own ourselves subjects only of the divine cluster of the sumptuous vine, in short, of *wine*, father of men. Don't let's spoil this sublime moment when we shall be raising our glasses to the glory of Burgundy.

'Come and drink, my beauty! Drink and revel! Here's to the health of our loves, to the health of our victories! The health of our friends, and our enemies! The health of the King of France!'

CHAPTER 28

HE DID not give her time to catch her breath.

In the *Gouldsboro*'s cabin she found, thanks to the attentiveness of Yolande and Delphine du Rosoy, a dress, the fan and the dress coat ready and waiting.

But it was he who, as she sat down, slipped off her stockings to reveal her bare legs. He seemed to be in an excellent mood as he sang to himself.

'It's not before time ... before time ... to put these fine stockings ... on these divine legs ...'

They were made of gold thread with stitching of scarlet silk. The shoes were covered with gilt satin. He slipped them on her feet like the prince kneeling before Cinderella.

'... My roving countess!'

He kissed her fingers lightly, then handed her over to Delphine, who came in with a small charcoal pan and curling tongs.

With the girl's help she was soon ready. She hurried out, her fan in her hand. The table had been laid in the chart room.

On the bank in the distance the local people were being regaled with another firework display.

'What a lot of junketings!' she said to Ville d'Avray as she bumped into him at the door of the banquet hall. 'If it's like this at Tadoussac, what will it be like at Quebec?'

'Like Versailles,' he replied, 'and even better, and *even worse*! ... My dear,' he went on as he drew aside to let her enter, 'let me tell you that at Carnival time in Quebec we end up by collapsing with exhaustion from too much dancing, eating, drinking, praying, processing, gossiping, twirling on skates, playing and losing at cards, not to mention all the amorous adventures that accompany these diversions. And you consider yourselves lucky if you don't have the further diversion of going to war with the Iroquois or starving to death when the spring comes round ... Oh! Quebec!'

On the table and in the hall candles had been lighted in large silver candlestick-holders. The heat and perfume emanating from the tall virgin-wax candles mingled with the warmth and smell of the dishes which the servants were beginning to carry in.

And to begin with an enormous silver soup tureen.

'I was arguing a minute ago with your butler about the best way to bring out the flavour of game soup; I maintain that pheasant and woodcock ought to be hung for six days and he claims that four is enough.'

'This particular bird was an osprey which has tenderer flesh,' the butler protested, overhearing him; 'four is enough.'

The company sat down to table. It was only a small intimate gathering comprising the usual members of the Rescator's flotilla, superior officers and their more or less obligatory guests. This company had come into being from the very beginning of the journey and it formed a homogenous group despite appearances because it was made up of individuals who had undergone in this brief period the same adventures and shared, in the nature of things, the same preoccupations and the same joys. But, in honour of the wine, the table had been set more luxuriously, and before each guest had been placed goblets of Bohemian glass.

Finally, the wine itself was served in the old-fashioned way, not from a decanter or a pitcher, but from a nef – a vessel of silver and silver-gilt, in itself a unique specimen of the silversmith's craft. The wine was drawn off through the figurehead on the prow representing a dolphin with open mouth, while every detail of a ship was faithfully reproduced, even down to tiny silver people keeping watch or climbing ladders and rigging made of twisted gold or silver threads.

The young sailor who had been promoted for the evening to the rank of cup-bearer, was greatly impressed when he lifted the wonderful vessel from its silver stand, which represented three dolphins leaping up from the waves, their eyes consisting of tiny diamonds.

The Marquis de Ville d'Avray was speechless with admiration.

It was likewise the first time that Angélique had ever seen such a fine piece. The Rescator would always be a princely figure. While being capable of putting up with the most severe hardships in order to establish his position, and of living very frugally, he was nevertheless a great accumulator of treasures.

He had caches of them scattered throughout the world, and faithful men to guard and watch over these patiently acquired masterpieces.

Angélique did not know everything about the man who was her husband.

'They no longer produce such fine work these days,' said Ville d'Avray with a sigh.

This particular piece was two hundred years old. It was the creation of Swiss silversmiths who, like the Germans, had for a long time specialized in making these boat-shaped vessels for serving wine.

The diners took their places round the table.

There were no spectators, no guests, no outsiders. It was a kind of family gathering, and it was possible to talk freely. Indeed the conversation was already well launched, and the tone was decidedly outspoken. Angélique heard Carlon say to Peyrac, continuing a conversation they had begun while standing waiting for her:

'... I'm not being huffy about it, but I do object to Monsieur de Ville d'Avray's offhanded approach to this affair. He seems to be unaware, or pretends to be, unaware that in Quebec you are regarded as enemies of the King of France, and that furthermore, you yourself were sentenced to death in your absence.'

'But we've heard all this over and over again,' protested Ville d'Avray, opening wide his damask napkin and peering alternately into the silver soup tureen and the silver-gilt nef from which rose the heady bouquet of 'his' Burgundy. 'We know all that; you're repeating yourself, my dear fellow.'

'It can't be repeated too often, when what we need to do is to clear decks for action and work out how best to tackle an apparently insoluble problem. It so happens that Monsieur de Peyrac was preceded by his ill repute as a pirate in the Caribbean, and that his reputation has suffered still further by the fact that he has conquered French Acadia right up to the source of the Kennebec. If an addition further reports of the same kind have been conveyed by some of the ships that have sailed up to Quebec this summer, it will be no surprise if feeling is running high we are greeted with cannon fire on our arrival.'

Joffrey de Peyrac noted the 'we' which the Intendant had inadvertently slipped into using, and he smiled. Carlon went on:

'... Madame de Peyrac will also have to defend herself against gossip. Her influence over the Indians, for instance, is suspect: how can it be explained? And how was it that you managed to beat off an Iroquois attack, after their own chiefs had been murdered under your very roof. That was an unforgivable crime, as anyone familiar with the Indian mentality knows ... You have been thought dead a hundred times over and yet you keep on reappearing, still alive. It all smacks of magic.'

'And what else do they say about me in Quebec?' asked Angélique.

He grew red with irritation.

'That you are *very, very, beautiful!*...'

She was amused by his reply.

'Between ourselves, my dear sir, you wouldn't rather I wept about that, would you?'

'You ought to.'

'But what nonsense! Since when have the French become so puritanical?'

'It is not puritanism. It's fear.'

'And since when have the French been frightened of beauty? ...'

As a gesture of defiance she shook her pale gold hair, held back by a double string of pearls.

'If they are expecting me to be beautiful, I'd better do my best not to disappoint them.'

They had just been served, as first course, a good rich broth to warm them up, and less with the intention of sharpening their appetites than of preventing the first taste of the wine being spoilt by drinking it on an empty stomach. They all felt the better for it, and inclined to take an indulgent view of life, even the Intendant.

So they listened patiently and politely as he listed all the 'unfortunate rumours' which he was sure they would have to face up to, and which had had time to ferment in the little colonial town.

But this did not in any way stop him from gulping down large spoonfuls of Madeira-flavoured broth.

'... I wager you will be asked to account for the death of Monsieur d'Arpentigny ... and for Pont-Briand, and for Saint-Castine's change of attitude ... But most serious of all is the death of Father de Vernon whom they will accuse you of murdering in your domains by some means still to be explained. They say he was thrown to a bear.'

'No! no! you've still got it all wrong,' wailed Ville d'Avray. 'It was he who almost killed the bear in a boxing match, the poor creature! And he even killed the minister who killed him in turn.'

229

'Were you there yourself? ...'

'Of course I was there,' replied the Marquis with aplomb.

'You'll never get me to swallow a tale like that. I knew Father de Vernon; he was a very distinguished, very level-headed priest, perhaps a trifle cold, but in fact a very gentle, urbane man.'

'That means you did not really know him. You never saw him as he really was. You should have seen him at Gouldsboro. He was a Hercules, that man. You only knew him in Quebec. Ah, but Gouldsboro, that was a delightful place! Count, promise me you'll invite us all there again one day? ... You will, won't you, Angélique?'

'Let's get to Quebec first,' growled Carlon.

Having emptied his plate, he wiped his mouth and turned towards Peyrac.

'Are we your hostages?'

'That depends upon the kind of welcome we are given when we arrive.'

'Ho, ho! So now we see you in your true colours!' Carlon replied with sombre satisfaction.

Angélique felt as though she was suffering from a split personality.

Earlier in the evening she had found herself carried back to the La Rochelle days. And suddenly here she was again in Canada trying to cope with the endless worries of arriving in Quebec with such a mixed company of people. Whichever way one looked at it the situation seemed like something out of a crazy dream.

It would have been better to have invited Bardagne to join them as Peyrac had suggested.

But that was how things would be in Quebec. There would be festivities, social events and plotting in the shadows. There would be high-flown talk, banter would be exchanged, while laughter cloaked schemes plotted with guile and determination. Death, love and happiness lay at the end of every plot. 'What are we going to do with the King's Envoy now?' she asked herself. 'And what am I to do with him? Where is his place on the chessboard, in the game we are about to play? ...' That morose specimen Carlon was still unaware of this added complication, even if he did have some inkling that something was going on. Let him exult in advance, fuel was being added to the fire of his prophesies of doom.

'His wife can't find him much fun,' Angélique murmured leaning towards the Marquis sitting beside her, and tilting her chin in Carlon's direction.

'And yet she is a charming woman.'

He smote his forehead.

'But what an ass I am! He's a bachelor.'

'Then who were you thinking of?'

'Of Mademoiselle d'Hourdanne. They are so close that people have come to think of her as having claims upon him.'

'Is she his mistress?'

'No, not even that! It's a platonic relationship. Poor Mademoiselle d'Hourdanne doesn't go out into society very much. She will only go out if I agree to accompany her. On the other hand, Carlon is her preoccupation. She's worried about his soul, his preferment, his success; she supports him in all his undertakings and talks of them to anyone who will listen, so that people have come to treat them as if they were married although they don't realize it themselves . . .

D'Urville and Carlon were arguing the rival merits of the Quebec arsenal and the *Gouldsboro*'s cannon, specifically whether the latter could be brought to bear on the ramparts of Fort Saint-Louis, and Angélique was racking her brains to find some other less contentious topic for general conversation. But she could not string two consecutive ideas together. She would have welcomed a moment of solitude in which to gather her thoughts together, rather than have to preside over and charm so sophisticated a gathering.

Her encounter with Bardagne was becoming swamped by all this hustle and bustle and she had to make an effort to convince herself that it had in fact taken place.

She looked across to Joffrey de Peyrac and found that he was looking thoughtfully at her, leaving his guests to argue among themselves without interference on his part. He too must be thinking of other things. When their eyes met, he gave a fleeting smile.

Then, concentrating his attention once again on what was going on, he said:

'But why anticipate things, gentlemen? We have not yet reached Quebec, and there is no question of firing our cannon. We are coming in response to an invitation from Monsieur de Frontenac, with whom I have always been on the best of terms.'

'But of course, Monsieur de Frontenac is like you, from Aquitaine, a rebellious province, with a taste for heresy.'

'Man of the North!' Peyrac muttered. 'But never fear! For love of Canada, I shall forget about Montfort!'[1]

There was no doubt about it: the festivities were off to a bad start. If they once got back to the Albigensian Crusade, there really would be trouble. Angélique signalled to the major-domo. It was time to serve the wine.

Then the wine began to sparkle in the glasses, its red glow comparable only to the gleam of rubies.

'Now this is an admirably treated wine,' said Ville d'Avray after sniffing it, breathing it in, then sipping it. 'Do you know exactly what it all involves? Well, I'll tell you, because I know, having spent a long time in Burgundy. Treating the wine is the process by which the red grape is made into red wine. It is commonly supposed that all that is needed is to tread the grapes and that there is nothing more to it. But that is not so, for the juice would run white. So the red grapes are not trodden straight away, but are stripped off their stalks and put into vats where, slowly, over several days, the red colouring from the skins leaches out into the fermenting juice. It is stirred about with a stick, then the red juice, blood-red, deep, almost black from certain growths is drawn off, and only after this are the remaining grapes crushed and their juice mixed with the purple essence. What pains are taken to achieve these admirable subtleties, the play of sunbeams, the savour particular to each hillside.'

He took a sip and ran the wine round his palate with closed eyes.

'... A Tillez, this is; I can just see the place, a sunny slope,

[1] A reference to Simon de Montfort, who came from Montfort-L'Amaury, and who, in 1208 put the province of Languedoc to fire and the sword in order to eradicate the Catharist heresy.

a modest little steeple and wave beyond wave of vine-covered blue ridges as far as the eye can see; that's Burgundy. And when I think that that idiot Cartier tried to persuade us that wine could be made in Canada ... Because he happened on a handful of wild vines! He saw everything everywhere he went: wine, diamonds, heaven knows what else! He had to find some justification for coming and plunging into this inhuman snare where there is *nothing, nothing*, I tell you, nothing but cold, darkness and savages, where some evil fate has led us today, far from the lovely regions of our homeland.

'But I seem to be the only one to be talking ...' he suddenly broke off anxiously, looking all round him. 'Say something, you others. It's always I who takes the lead ...'

'That's because we are delighted to listen to you, Marquis,' Peyrac replied with a smile, raising his glass to Ville d'Avray. 'What could be more pleasant than to drink a good wine while listening to you!'

'You flatter me! ... But I admit that wherever I go, I seem to be popular. At Court, after a while, I was the cynosure of all eyes and all ears. But what am I do do? I love life and its pleasures. It has brought me much that is good but also much harm, especially at Court. The King's brother was terribly jealous of me. I am better off in Canada, Cartier's briny man-trap. Just consider how well you can live here if you make a little effort, use a bit of imagination. This wine! You must admit it would have been a crime to leave it for others to drink ... For whom was it intended? A lot of ignorant, unthinking vandals.'

'It was meant for the Bishop and the Governor of New France,' Angélique announced. 'And it was not from Martin Dugast that you pillaged it, Marquis, may I tell you, but from the King of France's own representative, who had brought it over as a personal gift at the charge of those highly important people.'

'*From the King of France's Representative,*' cried Ville d'Avray, pausing, his glass held aloft, with an expression of delight on his face. 'And have you seen him? Have you met him? Do you know him? Is he the man who's in love with you? Ha, ha! So it was perfectly true that there was someone on board the *Saint John the Baptist.*'

His sparkling eyes flashed from Angélique to Peyrac, seeking an answer to his questions.

'What a marvellous story! You must tell me all about it.'

He signalled to the servants to fill his glass again and drank it down delightedly.

'Heavenly!'

'Well may you laugh, Marquis,' Angélique protested, although she too was laughing, 'but I hope you realize that it is of course my husband that he blames for this unfriendly act.'

'Oh, that *is* funny!'

'Not as funny as all that. He is a special envoy from the King. He has been entrusted with a mission. What is he bringing? Letters? Orders? And you take his wine. You will put him in a bad humour.'

'So much the worse for him, then! He should have shown himself, stood up for himself. We can't even find out his name ... Do you know it?' he asked Angélique.

Angélique tossed her head in a way that said neither yes nor no.

'You know everything!' he exclaimed. 'And you're going to tell it all to me, *all*. That's settled. In any case, this wine business is of no importance. With everything else we have on our conscience, that could get us strappadoed, hanged or burned at the stake, four barrels of wine, however good, are a mere trifle.'

'Whatever do you mean?' asked Carlon in great agitation.

Ville d'Avray gave him a baleful look.

'And to cap it all, there was the Duchess of Maudribourg's death.'

'Stop!' said Carlon, glancing in the direction of the servants. But the Marquis brushed his objection aside.

'They are in it with us, they saw everything, took part in everything that went on, what is there to hide from them? The truth is that what we are on board this ship is neither more nor less than *a band of brigands bound together by a terrible secret ...*'

He was in excellent spirits and drank a further draught of wine.

'... I just adore this! I feel I really am living. Wine, my friend!' he called, holding out his glass to the cup-bearer, who had positioned himself behind Ville d'Avray's chair in order not to have to keep running hither and thither. 'Yes, it's an utterly exhilarating sensation. Ending up on the side of the outcasts and scapegraces, who are right, because they are against the laws ... What! Do you really imagine there's going to be no fuss about the Duchess's murder? Has it not occurred to you that all the leading figures in the Church will have been informed of her impending arrival, given that she was a benefactress of vast wealth, and Father d'Orgeval first and foremost – they say she's related to him – will want to know what has become of her.'

'Oh, how dreadful!' Carlon lamented. 'You are twisting the knife in the wound.'

'No, you are over-dramatizing!'

'What do you mean, over-dramatizing? The death of a beautiful young woman, so attractive, a woman of noble birth and a *protégée* of the Court ... and of Father d'Orgeval, and dying so horribly too ...'

'You stood by and did nothing, as far as I know. There sits the only person who acted humanely to the woman,' he said, pointing to Angélique.

'My dear fellow, didn't we agree to forget all that ...'

'It's not so easy as all that ...'

The two Canadian noblemen, Grand-bois and Vauvenart, who had been trying for some time to break into the conversation, at last managed to make themselves heard.

'What on earth are you both going on about? Murder! ... she was not murdered, for heaven's sake! We were there. Remember ... She ran away into the forest and was eaten by wolves ... But Madame de Peyrac saved her life on the beach.'

'Incidentally, why did you rescue her?' asked Vauvenart, turning to Angélique. 'I've never understood that.'

'Nor do I,' Angélique replied.

She seemed to hear Ambroisine's heart-rending shrieks as the infuriated men tore at her. She drank a large glass of wine to recover her good spirits.

'I don't know why I did it ... Perhaps because we were the only women on the beach. But please let us talk about something else.'

'Ah, women!' cried Ville d'Avray. 'What would the world

be without them: without their gentleness, their kindness, their charm, their tenderness, their unpredictability and the sudden, inconsequential right-about-turns which they go in for ...'

'Etienne, I adore you,' said Angélique, embracing him.

'This wine goes to one's head,' Carlon commented, raising his glass to the light and peering suspiciously at it. 'I have an idea we are beginning to get tipsy.'

'And then the truth will become visible to you at the bottom of your glass,' said Ville d'Avray.

'Yes,' Carlon replied, still in sombre mood. 'The fact is that we *did* kill the Duchess and that is why our consciences are troubling us. You are right, Ville d'Avray, in saying that in spite of myself I am involved in a crime.'

'In two!' the Marquis cried.

'Two?' Carlon exclaimed with a start.

'Yes! First, the one you have on your conscience, the Duchess of Maudribourg's murder. And second, the fact that you are drinking with us this evening wine intended for the Governor and the Bishop.'

'But I did not know where it came from when I sat down at the table.'

'But that has not prevented you drinking it, and indeed, appreciating it.'

CHAPTER 29

FOR SEVERAL seconds Intendant Carlon appeared to be utterly discomfited. It was evident that he was trying to run back in his mind over the sequence of events that had led him into such a delicate and irreversible situation.

There had been the trap laid by the English in the Saint John River, Peyrac's intervention that had saved them from being taken prisoner in New England, then Tidnish, where he had been called upon to act as official witness at the trial on the beach and had been obliged to listen to the Duchess being arraigned for a catalogue of appalling crimes, with witnesses seeming to spring up out of the ground to tell their devastating stories, and urge him to pronounce his verdict. It had been a preposterous adventure. He still wondered what aberration of mind had led him to become involved in it all. He would never set foot in Acadia again ...

'Oh, why did I ever make that trip to Acadia?' he moaned.

'Yes, why indeed?' Ville d'Avray sneered. 'I'll tell you why: you wanted to poke your nose into my affairs, to prevent me drawing my dividends. You imagined that you could set off on a tour of Acadia as you would on a tour of the provinces back home in France to extort money from the peasants. But Acadia is something quite different. You can't treat Acadia like that. It serves you right. Acadia has crushed you. You're finished ...'

'No, things aren't as bad as that,' Angélique protested, springing to the poor fellow's rescue. 'Etienne, you are most unkind. Don't listen to him, Intendant. We've all had too much to drink. Tomorrow you will feel your old self again and will take a more positive view.'

'But you won't forget what has been said,' Ville d'Avray persisted vindictively. 'Forget! Forget Acadia! And if you forget to forget it, *I'll* see to it you are reminded!'

'You are very hard on him, Etienne.'

'Angélique, he's a hard man too, as you would see if you knew him as he is in Quebec. He's a veritable rod of iron, that man. So I'm not going to miss such a superb opportunity to get my revenge. You don't know me. I am, I can be, very, *very spiteful* ...'

Angélique's thoughts were wandering ...

Bardagne! La Rochelle! A dream, a life that had ceased to exist! But today life was beginning again. Everything was different. She was safe from all possible harm. She lived under the protection of a man who was frightened of nothing, and who surrounded her with his love. Drawn to him as by some magnetic force, she looked towards him at the far end of the table and felt a sense of quiet confidence on seeing him and knowing him there. The wheel had come full circle. Her happiness had been restored to her.

And he was slowly raising his glass to her in homage,

seeming to repeat from afar: 'Let us drink! Let us drink to the health of the King of France ...'

She raised her glass to her lips. Joy and a sense of triumph flowed through her with this nectar of the gods. She went on drinking. She was thirsty and the wine was good.

It flowed down her throat, so smooth and warming, that the sensation in the back of her throat was somewhat akin to an endless, voluptuous kiss. It quenched her thirst wonderfully but seemed to make her even more thirsty.

'Why that kiss?' she wondered.

It seemed an aberration, and yet she could not bring herself to regret it. It had given her infinite pleasure of a very special kind. Vision of La Rochelle, of sorrows and of joys that were peculiar to the place ... In those lips that called up the emotions of the past, it was as if she had embraced a ghost, a lost sister, wounded and hunted down, her own self finally absolved ...

Beside her, Ville d'Avray continued his soliloquy.

'On the other hand, there is Castel-Morgeat, who is far more dangerous than Carlon. He's Military Governor. One of your worst enemies.'

'And yet he is a Gascon too, like Frontenac and my husband.'

'Yes, but of the dour, sectarian variety. He has thrown in his lot with Father d'Orgeval as his ancestors did with the Reformation. He believes in him. He is a naturally intolerant man.'

'He isn't a Protestant, surely? In such high office!'

'No, but he's the son of a convert, and that's worse. As for her, Sabine de Castel-Morgeat, that's another story. She rules the roost in the city because she controls all the charities. She's pious in moderation, with an equally pronounced taste for good works, for luxury and for society. Intrigue and charity come naturally to her. Some consider her plain and vindictive, but I don't agree. I love her like a sister.

'But we did quarrel over her son Anne-François, whom Orgeval sent off, when he was only a very young lad, to be a fur trapper in the High Country. I protested, but she is completely under Sebastian d'Orgeval's heel. They say she is his mistress.'

'But he's a Jesuit,' Angélique said, shocked.

'Oh, you know, the Jesuits . . .'

'Hold your tongue! You've had too much to drink. You are talking scandal.'

She took another drink. The wine had a satisfying heaviness that did not, however, contribute to sobriety. On the contrary, as it flowed through her mouth and over her tongue, it began to rouse an even more essential and demanding appetite deep down inside her. It was a need that the wine both stimulated and gratified, and that prompted one to hold out one's glass for yet more. It was like a hitherto unknown craving in the blood itself, and if the desire to mingle with its red stream the purple substance of the grape made it possible for the ardour of the crimson wine to communicate to the blood the strength of the earthy sap, thus renewing its vital drive and the blissful sensation of being alive.

A wave of heat coursed through her like a fire suddenly communicating its heat to her entire body.

She had to go outside, where the fresh air, while making her feel somewhat better, still further intoxicated her, since in the darkness, the rocking of the ship made her feel even giddier.

From the braziers with their live coals glowing red and gold through the darkness, like a glint of the wine itself, rose the smell of roasting meat.

There was laughter from the battery-deck where Cantor and Vanneau had undertaken to entertain the King's Girls, while from the bridge-deck came the sound of sailors singing. Every man, including those on watch, had been given a half-pint of Burgundy in his pewter mug.

She walked a few paces through the darkness and the patches of light and, in spite of all the activity on board, she found herself alone in the marvellous company provided by intoxication: her double, suddenly captivated and full of good will. 'Who can prevail against you?' asked her vainglorious shadow. 'What is this fellow Carlon talking about? The future is yours. You have Love, you have Beauty . . . you are still young . . . You have vigour, a taste for life, a taste for all the delights to be enjoyed and the protection of an unbeatable man who adores you . . . You will merely have to appear, and Quebec will be at your feet ...'

An arm like an iron band went round her waist, drew her close, bent her backwards, while a hand tilted her face.

'They are completely drunk already,' said Peyrac's voice. 'My love! My love!'

Through the mists, through her giddiness, she felt his hands straying over her, intoxicating her even more, caressing her.

'My love! My love!'

He was kissing her again, as if he could never tire of her lips. 'Shaitan! Shaitan!' he repeated, but with a kind of tender, amused indulgence. And it reminded her of the Persian prince ... who also used to say: 'Shaitan ... little devil!'

'Come, my dear heart, the major-domo is bringing on a pheasant complete with all its feathers ... and patés ...'

He drew her away with him:

'And you'll enjoy the delicacies that are served with them, which will help you over your giddiness, and you will be able to charm us with your presence. The light goes out when you are no longer there, and we are just a bunch of rough men, cast up on the furthermost shores of the world.'

CHAPTER 30

THIS TIME the Intendant was seeing double ... And what he saw was two great dispensers of Justice watching him from the end of the table where Peyrac had resumed his seat.

'You have too much influence over us,' he said thickly. 'I understand that the King should have swept you out of his path. I know only one man who has as much power over others as you: Sebastian d'Orgeval. But unlike you he doesn't have the gold to ensure him triumph.'

'He has the heavenly hosts and even, when required, the legions of demons.'

The Intendant remained impassive and went on staring at

Joffrey de Peyrac, who must have appeared to him through a more or less Mephistophelian mist.

'You know too much about me, about us all.'

'No, you're wrong there, Monsieur the Intendant,' said Peyrac suddenly rousing himself. 'To me you are an unknown quantity, because I only know about you what you choose to reveal. A tiny fragment of yourself. We are all like that, shrouded in mystery, only showing, only displaying to the outside world an over-simplified little flag, proclaiming allegiance to a single monarch, a single idea, a single choice. And yet, admit it, Monsieur the Intendant, wouldn't it occasionally be a good thing to shatter the image that others have of us? We are condemned, stifled, shackled by these images.

'I propose we play a game this evening. Let's stand the image on its head. Let's lay another card on the table, the one we have hidden up our sleeve, the card that we value most because we know it will never be played. And yet it's the one that is our highest trump, the truth, the essence of ourselves. In this way we will feel among friends again ... and not enemies, and look one another in the face without evasiveness. You are in my province. On this ship.

'Elsewhere it's dark. You are *elsewhere*. The world is deserted. It has disappeared. The night promotes insight, predisposes to confidences. Let us look into ourselves and discover ourselves ... without shame, without embellishment or concealment ... What would you have liked to be, Monsieur Carlon, if you had not made your career in the Civil Service?'

'No, not that! ...' cried Carlon, as if he were about to be skinned alive. And he drew the lapels of his frock coat across in front of him like a frightened girl.

The game Peyrac had launched had suddenly changed the whole atmosphere of the room; faces were raised, and eyes gazed through the curls of tobacco smoke as if seeking some glimpse of forgotten dreams.

'Monsieur the Intendant, your turn,' Joffrey de Peyrac prompted.

'No! Never, I tell you,' cried Carlon. And in his stubborn drunkenness he pounded the table with his fist. 'I'm not playing ... I throw in my hand. I'm going.'

But he couldn't manage it and sank back in his chair.

'Good! Well, I'll set an example,' said Peyrac. 'Here goes.'

In the golden light of the candles, he threw back his face, which was deeply lined, but whose finely moulded lips possessed a marked and attractive sensuality. That mouth somehow softened the rest of his face, whose expression was more often than not, either unconsciously or deliberately, rather forbidding. It was a frightening face, people said. Perhaps because of its scars? Perhaps because of the sharp and penetrating gaze of the very dark eyes. His skin was so tanned as to give the impression that he had Moorish blood in his veins, and the scars with which it was seamed did nothing to make it less daunting. Yet there was this lively sensitive mouth, whose ironical curl made one long to see it break into a smile, revealing the pure white teeth. To Angélique, all the bliss in the world was embodied in this smile and to see it appear, to see it turned upon her, caused her a sense of joy so intense as to be almost unbearable.

He too seemed to be scrutinizing the beams of the ceiling in search of the materialization of a vision, seeking to project himself into the incarnation of a 'self' exactly corresponding to the aspirations of his being.

'Rather than being a mere wanderer over the face of the earth,' he began, 'gambling on the thousand-and-one chances that life or the world offers to build or lose fortunes, storm positions, take and defend lands – a way of life that, I don't deny it, exactly suits a certain side of my adventurous nature, impatient of monotony, but that nevertheless leaves me with a feeling of unfulfilment, of having turned aside through compulsion, from a destiny for which I was intended ... Rather even than regain my princedom – for I was once lord over a province through my lineage, with all the responsibilities that that entails, the honour, the glory, the life of service – I would have liked to be a man living in obscurity, left to himself and his scientific intuitions, in the privacy of a laboratory. Outside, a generous patron would furnish my den with the finest apparatus, instruments, retorts and stills, that can be found, without my having to worry about finding and, above all, buying them, for these are tasks that often prove irksome to a man of learning whose mind is often like a bird with clipped wings. He wants to take off.

He sees. He knows. *But he is powerless*. He has not the resources. The time, the peace of mind ... He is hounded, pursued, an exile on the face of the earth. Oh! To shut oneself away, as if in a cell, and to investigate these invisible, unknown, infinitely teeming worlds. To be oblivious to day and night. To witness the miracles of an ever-renewed and endless creation. To know that one has the power, the force to go further, ever further. To push back the frontiers of human knowledge.'

'I don't believe you,' said Ville d'Avray. 'You're too much of an epicurean and a fighter to content yourself with such an existence. What about glory? Fame?'

'They are of little consequence.'

'And women, my dear fellow? Would you manage so easily without them?'

'I never said that a scholar who had the opportunity to work unremittingly at absorbing tasks should as a result deprive himself of the pleasures of life.'

'Living surrounded by retorts, isn't that a bit dull?' said Grand-bois.

'Their attraction is of the type that cannot be explained and which the uninitiated cannot understand. That is true of many spheres. Moulay Ismael, a Moroccan Sultan, a bloodthirsty sovereign, voluptuous and lusty to the point of lewdness, told me once that one of his greatest pleasures was prayer. But for anyone who is not inclined to mysticism the pleasure is far from self-evident. It's quite possible that if Moulay Ismael had not been born King of Morocco, he would have made a great hermit of the desert.'

'Do you mean to say that science also has its secret raptures?'

'Yes!'

And the smile that Angélique loved spread across the Rescator's lips.

'It is about this unslaked thirst, peculiar to each individual, that I have in mind when I say: what would you have liked to be if? ... Barssempuy, ready? ... Over to you.'

Gold-Beard's erstwhile second-in-command blushed. He was still a very young man, handsome, agreeable, nobody's fool, equipped with a sound education in duelling and horsemanship, a rather fine specimen of those younger sons who see no other way except through the Army, the Church or freebooting, to keep up the extravagant way of life befitting their rank. He had chosen freebooting. To his mind there was little difference between fighting on board a corsair and fighting on board a ship of the King's fleet. Just a better chance of making a fortune. At least, that is how it seemed at first. More recently the death of his fiancée Marie-la-Douce had cast a gloom over his spirits and given him an embittered expression.[1] He contended that all that rubbish did not matter and that he really had nothing to say, then changed his mind.

'I would have liked to be my elder brother,' he said, 'less for the honours and riches due to his heritage than for the estate on which we lived. I would have lived to improve it and hold magnificent entertainments. Like Fouquet at Vaux-le-Vicomte. I would have held a little court with men of letters, artists; I've studied the humanities, and I had a penchant for intellectual matters. But my brother lives at Court, extorts money from the peasants in order to keep up his position, and the estate's going to the dogs. I try not to think about it. This is a card which can't even be played. One's position in the family is a matter of luck.'

'Where did you come in the family after your elder brother?' someone asked.

'I was his twin brother,' answered Barssempuy simply.

Such a blow of fate stirred the emotions of the assembled company, already disposed to be emotional by the number of glasses drunk.

'Why didn't you kill him?' asked Ville d'Avray bluntly.

'It was to avoid that temptation that I ran away.'

'Who knows, young fellow, perhaps the day isn't so far off when he'll make way for you?' suggested Grandfontaine.

'He has sons.'

'Don't pine after it, Monseiur Barssempuy,' Angélique interjected. 'These days, it is no longer possible to reside on one's estate let alone live there like a prince. The King does not tolerate it. You would lose his favours and largesse. Holding the candlestick or the nightshirt at the King's *coucher* at Versailles is the way to get on and earn one's keep and make enough to repair the roof of your country house.'

[1] See *Angélique and the Demon.*

Erickson then took everyone aback by declaring that what he would have liked was to have been King of Poland.

'Why Poland?' asked Ville d'Avray.

'No particular reason.'

'Just a dream, eh! given the power.'

'But he's abdicated and gone into a monastery.'

'Not that one, the other.'

No one was very well up in the history of Poland. So a beginners' course on the Polish monarchy was put off till later as likely to be heavy going, especially as Erickson was involved.

Fallière had for a long time fancied himself as one of the King's musketeers, but to start with he was not a Gascon and did not have the financial means to make his way in that exclusive brotherhood. Furthermore, his skill at swordplay left something to be desired. After a good education he had had to content himself with following in his father's footsteps and had then gone on to the position of head of the municipal survey department.

Comments flew back and forth, the wine went round and the food was forgotten in the excitement of hearing so many unexpected revelations. One said that he had never had any dreams or regrets and that he was quite happy as he was, looking no further than the end of his nose and living from day to day. Another scratched the back of his neck, assured the company that it would all come back to him, that there was in fact something that would have suited him better only he could no longer think what.

Most of them could. Grand-bois confessed that he had ever had but one dream: to be very rich, to wear a wig, to keep a carriage, have maids and footmen and never leave home – Grand-bois who was in fact always on the move, canoeing up and down the rivers of Acadia or sailing about in Frenchman Bay! But, unfortunately, his money always burned a hole in his pocket. Not a penny stayed in it. So goodbye to manor house, carriage and the quiet life!

'But what would you have found to do all day long in your stately home?' asked Angélique.

'I would have played cards, struck my servants, nursed my gout, pruned my roses and, every evening, I would have found a woman in my bed . . .'

'A different one?'

'No, always the same, young, not so young, no matter, but my own wife, you know. A woman for me alone, always there, without having to go to look for her, without having to put myself out. That's what I've always missed. I don't like to sleep alone, I feel cold, and sometimes I get frightened like I did when a child ... The life we lead on the Saint John river doesn't give me much chance. Indian women! Bah! ... Oh! forgive me, Madame, my tongue's running away with me ... I'm rich, that's a fact ... Never sufficiently so to go back to the Kingdom of France ...'

'Try mending the holes in your pockets, Grand-bois,' cried Vauvenart laughing uproariously. He was slapping his stomach with mirth.

'You talk when your turn comes, you blackguard,' rumbled Grand-bois; 'you won't laugh so loud then.'

Vauvenart fell silent and became thoughtful.

'I saw myself as a priest,' he said at last, 'a Jesuit in fact.'

This declaration out of the blue, coming so seriously from this portly Acadian squire, whose distinguishing characteristics were jovial heartiness, initiative and reckless courage in war, with never a hint of the ecclesiastical, produced an unexpected reaction in his audience, who were convulsed with laughter. He took it in good part and waited for the storm to subside.

'Yes, I wanted to be a Jesuit,' he repeated. 'I wanted to dominate.'

'It is one particular kind of power,' said Peyrac.

'Yes, indeed! And I could have got there too. I'm well enough born, and I was doing well in my studies. I even spent a year in a seminary.'

'You don't say!' ejaculated Grand-bois, highly diverted.

'And what happened?' asked someone else.

'I lost my nerve. I felt ... Well, you had to have one foot in the Other World. I was succeeding only too well. Breaking off your attachments to the earth is a tremendous sensation, but you have to keep your nerve. Orgeval manages it as easy as breathing. I once saw him praying at least a foot off the ground. Like Saint Ignatius. But it scared me. They told me: "You have the gift, you have a sense of the mystical." It's probably true. But I left. Now, when I see the Indians conjuring up their devils and speaking with their spirits, I tell myself that it's not really so frightening as all that, and that I could have got used to it. Sometimes I think I've missed my vocation . . .'

'You wouldn't have been hitting the bottle too hard by any chance, would you,' asked Grand-bois, 'and be trying to have us on?'

'You're surprised are you? But that sort of thing really does happen at times. When Cavelier de la Salle, who at the moment is knocking around somewhere on the Mississippi looking for the China Sea, gets back, you ask him. He's been a Jesuit too.'

'You depress me,' said Grand-bois. 'We'll have plenty of time to find out all about that sort of thing when we're dead. I told you I'm afraid of the dark . . . Is the barrel empty? Wine, steward!'

'Well! Now *I'm* going to surprise you,' said Ville d'Avray with disarming directness, 'but I would have liked to be a woman. I used to envy the gaiety which seemed to be the prerogative of the beauteous creatures and the fact that all they had to do was to get married in order to live as they wished, to spend money, to dress elegantly and to flit hither and thither without having to bother about obtaining a post or performing dreary duties. But I managed tolerably well with what I inherited and, seeing all the advantages of my status as a male, I stopped regretting my sex.'

'Monsieur the Intendant, your turn now.'

'I have nothing to divulge.'

'Tell it to me,' pleaded Angélique, taking his hand across the table.

This appeal overcame Jean Carlon's resistance.

'Oh very well, then. When I was eighteen I met someone.'

'Was she beautiful?'

'No.'

'What was the point, then?'

'It was not a woman!'

'Oh!'

'And who was it?' asked Angélique gently.

'Molière,' said Carlon so softly as to be almost inaudible. Then he roused himself again.

'He was called Poquelin in those days at Orleans where he

and I were law students together. Jean-Baptiste and I spent most of our time writing tragedies and putting on plays. Under his influence I decided to go in for a career in the theatre. But my father waved the big stick. He told me I would be damned, buried like a dog, without rites, in unconsecrated ground. He had a more respectable career in mind for me. It's understandable. I've followed the lines he laid down for me.'

'And you've succeeded too,' Angélique remarked. 'So has Molière in his way! But if you take my advice, Monsieur Carlon, you won't grieve over what you may have missed. An actor's life is sheer folly, and your former fellow student knows the price he is paying for making the Court laugh today. It's better to be in the stalls than on the stage.'

'So we're all happy with our respective lots,' concluded Peyrac as he raised his glass. 'Monsieur Carlon, you will not be damned. For my part, I am well content with the roundabout way I have come since it has resulted in my celebrating so joyfully with you this evening in Canada. Let's drink to our lives! To our successes! To our dreams! To Molière,' he added, turning to Carlon.

'To Molière,' repeated the latter in a low voice and his eyes grew misty.

And as all the glasses were raised, red and sparkling, there could be heard in the distance the music of Cantor's guitar and the flutes and harps accompanying him while clear voices sang: *'Alouette! gentille alouette! Alouette, je te plumerai . . .'*

'Youth does not know what we know,' said Ville d'Avray. 'These youngsters don't know that they have up their sleeves the card that will never be played. They look before them and see all roads open. Let's drink to their hopes! . . .'

They drank deep and long. At the bottom of the glasses was the sparkle of sunlight, hillsides, the dark depths of cellars, the glint of old presses, the poetry of the grape harvest, an image of the bare bodies of men treading down the bubbling fruits of the vine in huge white oak vats.

'To Burgundy! To French wine! To the King of France!' cried Ville d'Avray in a crescendo of lyricism.

He began to weep, saying that the Kingdom of France was far away, that they were being forgotten in barren lands.

There were those who would like to see them dead, scalped, sacrificed on the altar of the Nation, elder daughter of the Church: France. The exaltation of sacrifice and the sorrows of exile made his heart overflow, and it was impossible to tell whether his tears were or bitterness or emotionality.

Carlon too was weeping, thinking of Molière.

Things were degenerating.

Angélique got up, none too steady on her feet. The gentlemen were going to smoke, and she intended to collapse thankfully into bed and sleep the sleep of the just.

'Madame, you have not spoken,' protested a voice.

'Oh! You're right! Gentlemen, what can I say to follow on after all these impressive confessions? For a long time I wanted to go off to America.'

'Just fancy!'

'But I was a child. Later, amidst all the trials and tribulations of life, I saw the haven which suited my heart as an elegant, comfortable house, with a man living in it whom I loved and who loved me, and I imagined myself making cakes for grandchildren as they sat round the table watching me.'

'A modest dream in fact ... Like Grand-bois's. Have you never, like all women, dreamt of greater honours, Versailles, the Court ... to please the King?'

'I could have pleased the King, Gentlemen, but it pleased me to displease him.'

'What madness!' they exclaimed.

'You don't expect us to believe that you turned your back on the Court ... a paradise where the great and distinguished foregather ...'

She had begun to move away.

Suddenly, turning back to them, she said:

'What about the poisoners?'

And, as had happened to Vauvenart shortly before, her remark, so obviously against all common sense, aroused an enormous burst of laughter. Like Vauvenart, she let the storm blow over without losing her temper. Everyone was happy and it was all very funny: poisoners! At Versailles!

Then she finished:

'... That's why I'm here.'

249

'. . . In the hands of a pirate,' interjected Joffrey, who had lit up one of the long cigars which he particularly enjoyed.

'So it's true is it? . . . You captured her too, did you, my Lord?'

'Not exactly . . . but almost . . .'

'When was that? . . .'

Angélique slipped over to Peyrac and laid her fingers on his lips, as he seemed prepared to furnish an explanation.

'No, darling, be quiet! You'll confuse all these gentlemen! It's too long a story.'

Peyrac caught her delicate fingers as she withdrew them and kissed them passionately, regardless of the assembled company. And she ruffled his thick black hair with a light caress. The wine was loosening the chains which sometimes inhibited their displays of affection.

As she passed, Ville d'Avray caught the retreating Angélique by the dress and held her.

'You'll tell me everything, won't you? The story of your love affair with this mysterious character, Monsieur de Peyrac . . . When we're at Quebec?'

'Will we ever be there? You heard the Intendant? I'll be stoned out of the place, burned alive . . . He'll put the torch to the wood personally. I have an intuition . . .'

'Madame, what are you saying? . . . God preserve me from such a deed,' exclaimed Carlon as he staggered to his feet, quite beside himself. 'You misunderstood me . . . I was saying . . . it was simply to put you on your guard . . . your guard . . .'

'On guard, musketeer,' Grand-bois sang to himself.

'The people of Quebec are not fools . . . I'm sure, they'll fall under your spell . . . They'll fall . . . *on their knees* . . .'

'I don't expect them to go quite that far,' exclaimed Angélique laughing heartily. 'Monsieur the Intendant, *all* is forgiven, for those kind words . . . Don't forget them tomorrow when you're sober . . .'

The difficulty was to get to the door and breathe a lung-full of fresh air, before tackling the problem of crossing the deck safely and climbing the companion-ways.

CHAPTER 31

PEYRAC, LAUGHING too, had followed from a distance the dialogue between the Intendant and his wife. Everybody was completely drunk and no uncertainties remained. People's true natures were laid bare. Even Carlon, that cold, fretful bachelor, had succumbed to Angélique's charm.

The danger with that woman was that she was always herself. And even more so when wine put that fire into her cheeks, that light in her eyes and imparted that flash to her teeth as they were bared in a hearty laugh. It was a rare thing to see her laugh! And it was as incomparably delightful as it was novel. She was ... she was the personification of seductiveness. Angélique at Versailles ... Angélique laughing in that way before the King. What man could resist that, be he king, peasant or puritanical treasury official. Where was he taking her? ... The whole town would succumb ... would fall on its *knees*! ... A tiny spasm of pain, which he knew was always accompanied by happiness and pleasure, passed through Peyrac's heart. This matter of sharing was no easy one to accept! To see her so accessible to all and endowed with obvious power over men heightened his desire and his adoration for her.

He caught himself standing as if spellbound, his gaze fixed upon the door through which she had just disappeared.

Ever since Count Peyrac had snatched and kissed Angélique's fingers with undisguised passion, the Marquis de Ville d'Avray had become pensive, indeed peevish.

He suddenly burst out.

'It's not fair.'

'What isn't?'

'But she loves you,' the Marquis protested; 'she *really* loves you. You're the only one that counts ...'

'Are you so sure of that?'

'It's blatant ... a blind man could see it.'

'What makes you think that, Marquis?'

The Marquis then made a startling statement, which seemed in no way to follow logically from what had gone before. But they were all beyond caring for logic.

'*You alone have the power to make her suffer,*' he said.

'Just a minute,' said Peyrac, indicating with a gesture that his thoughts were elsewhere.

He raised his cigar to his lips, and gazed at the blue smoke issuing from his mouth, in which the absurd joy which Ville d'Avray's words had caused him seemed to blossom and take shape.

'She really loves you ... She's mad about you ...'

And again: 'You alone have the power to make her suffer ...'

It was there that the mark lay which he had hitherto not succeeded in identifying – who knows, perhaps the specific mark of all love – the power to make her suffer, to make her cry. Then, when the heart is rent, one knows ... one is in love ... A mark of preference for which there is no accounting.

But, he remembered hearing her sobbing like a child behind the door, the night he had struck her.[1] And he had been left badly shaken, unwilling to acknowledge the admission that represented.

He alone had the power to wring her heart, to plunge her into despair, to render humble and touching those magnificent emerald eyes, which, when turned upon others, could be so implacable.

Suddenly, he no longer envied his rivals, from whom she could part from with undisguised coldness, cruel directness, the insulting indifference of a woman accustomed to the homage of men, merely taking pleasure from them, and casting them aside without scruple. The King ... Moulay Ismael ... Poor fellows!

He was the only one of her lovers who could make her tears flow, the heart's blood. He had seen her on her knees before him ...

He drew again slowly on his cigar, his eyes half closed. He was reluctant to believe it, testing the sharp point of the weapon, not without feeling that sensual, voluptuous, boundless pleasure that is aroused by the awareness of possessing

[1] See *The Temptation of Angélique.*

252

such power over a being given over exclusively to one's domination.

But with Angélique ... Look out! He suspected he might be tempted to abuse that power for the exquisite pleasure of obtaining the avowal of a submissive look, of seeing her bend her slender neck, and surrender ... But with her ... Beware! He began to laugh again. He knew only too well that she was capable of returning him like for like ...

Oblivious of the effect that the words might have on the Count, Ville d'Avray went on speaking in a rueful, disgruntled voice.

'But why *you*? You alone! There's the mystery! There's the injustice! You're not handsome ... You're rather frightening to look at in fact, intimidating. True, you're rich ... But we all are ... And in any case, it's not that that binds her to you ... You live on the grand scale, it's true, but is sharing the life of a gentleman adventurer a suitable fate for such an exquisite and regal woman? Yes, that's what I said: *regal*. She ought to be at Versailles as I said a moment ago ... Oh well! too bad! Failing Versailles, *I* will make her queen of Quebec.'

He cast a quick sidewards glance at Peyrac.

'Are you jealous?'

'I can be.'

The Marquis de Ville d'Avray's face lit up.

'You're fallible, then? But that's marvellous. You are indeed the complete man. You're even capable of feeling jealous. You hold all the trump cards. I can understand that she loves you. Although I can't imagine how a relationship could have grown up between two people who are so different, so unlike.'

Peyrac leaned across the table towards the Marquis, moving his face close to the latter's as if about to confide something:

'I'll tell you ... I bought her when she was seventeen, to get a silver mine. Her father, who was a country bumpkin of a squire, would not let me have the mine unless I took his daughter into the bargain. I closed the deal. I hadn't seen the girl that was on sale.'

'And it was her.'

'That's right.'

'You've always been lucky, Peyrac.'

'Not always. It depends! It was Love, but we were separated.'

'Who took her from you?'

'The King.'

'Then the King is your rival?'

'No, it's worse than that. I am the King's rival.'

'Ah! I see! You mean that the King loves her, but you're the one she loves.'

'Yes.'

Ville d'Avray appeared to be turning the matter over in his mind.

'That's serious. Let's hope ... Perhaps the King has forgotten her?'

'Do you believe that even a king could forget her?'

Ville d'Avray shook his head. Joffrey de Peyrac's confidences, as valued as they were unexpected and unusual, consoled him for everything. He rubbed his hands together.

'Ha! Ha. The situation is becoming more and more complicated, it seems to me. It's magnificent! Life is good!'

PART SIX

Arrivals and Departures

CHAPTER 32

BARDAGNE WAS waiting ... waiting ...

Angélique saw him a long way off, pacing up and down the shore. There were several people in full cloaks and plumed felt hats standing at some little distance from him, looking in his direction, but respecting his solitary impatience which they doubtless found it impossible to comprehend. They were presumably members of his household and retinue, passengers like him on the *Saint John the Baptist*, whose demeanour gave, however, clear indication of their position with regard to him, and reflected the importance of his rank and function.

Things seen from a distance, for instance things on shore seen from the deck of a ship, often fall into a clear-cut, revealing pattern.

What one sees through the end of a telescope cannot lie, and it is rare not to discover some truth or other that is invisible from close to.

As Nicolas de Bardagne waited on the beach at Tadoussac for his lovely servant girl from La Rochelle, his whole demeanour bespoke the man in love, who has but a single thought. Would she come? Would he see her again?

It seemed incredible that he was there.

Angélique was obliged to watch him closely in order to convince herself that he really was.

After the carousals of the night that had virtually obliterated the memory of their encounter the previous evening, she now had to face the facts. He was there and waiting for her.

Yet another ghost to make its appearance along her way. Since their entry into the St Lawrence, she had sometimes had the impression that she was making her way through some nameless limbo, in which nameless shadows waited to greet her. And now one of them had risen up out of the mists: Nicolas de Bardagne. And behind him stood Desgrez the police officer, Monsieur de la Reynie the French Lieutenant-General of Police and the King himself.

The King was like a ghost, too, his muffled voice calling: 'Angélique, my unforgettable one . . .'

The previous evening, Nicolas de Bardagne, a man who had come back from a past that had ceased to exist, had held her in his arms and she had kissed, on his lips, all those forgotten faces.

The merry evening spent drinking Burgundy on board the *Gouldsboro* seemed to have opened a great gulf between that obscure moment and the new day. There was no denying that when the diners on the *Gouldsboro* rose from the table in the early hours of the morning, they had only just been capable of tumbling into their bunks, or, if such was their luck, of giving themselves up to the frenzied delights of love. Angélique had herself woken from a sleep full of glimmering lights to find herself lying up against Joffrey as he took her in his arms.

It had been a delectable, intoxicating night, from which she had woken in the morning with the impression that she had dreamed it all, even her past existence, even the tragedies and the follies . . .

A new day was dawning in Canada. The air was icy, crystal clear, while the river flowed by with dull silver gleams as the first of the drift-ice mingled with its waters. And now the time had come to remember: Bardagne was there. And with him went a vague sense of anxiety.

Why, oh why, if the King felt he must make enquiries about the strange Lord of Gouldsboro and Wapassou in the American province of Maine, who threatened, as some saw it, his overseas territories, why oh why did he have to choose this particular man?

Joffrey thought it was more than mere coincidence. And yet the King could not have known that Nicolas de Bardagne had ever met Angélique in La Rochelle, any more than it had ever occurred to the erstwhile Governor of the city that Angélique could possibly ever have set foot in Versailles, poor servant girl that she was, working for an upper-middle-class Huguenot family.

'A much-admired servant no doubt,' Joffrey de Peyrac had said, laughing. But he had given her a shrewd glance. And Angélique recalled his jealousy of Berne, and more recently the conflict that had arisen between them on account of Colin Paturel. And he had killed Lieutenant de Pont-Briand in a duel because he had dared to lust after her.

'I'm in a nice fix,' she told herself. 'That man Bardagne is impossible. He has always been impossible. He never would understand what talking meant when it came to obtaining my consent. I sent him packing in every way I could, and still he came back.'

And she had to admit that, in spite of the repugnance she felt at that time for any male advances, his faithful persistence and his stubborn, ardent desire for her had eventually resulted in her occasionally feeling a stirring of response.

'And now here he is in Canada, heading for Quebec, where he, like us, will be spending the winter. That will set the sparks flying ...'

What lay behind it all?

Having decided to go ashore to see her former suitor in the full light of day, Angélique began to hesitate.

As she watched him in the circle of the spyglass, she wondered where Joffrey was, feeling she would have preferred this second interview to have taken place in his presence. To have gone forward side by side with him to meet the King's Envoy, so as to make it abundantly clear to him that she was Joffrey's wife, bound to him, and that there could be no possible alliance between herself and Bardagne that did not include the man he called 'the pirate'.

Suddenly she caught sight of Count Peyrac walking up from a point on the shore towards Nicolas de Bardagne, followed by his Spanish guard. Her heart began to thump.

But she was foolish to be anxious. She was dealing with men who were above all determined to avoid any possible conflict. Their responsibilities were far too serious for them to allow personal considerations to get the upper hand.

She saw them greet one another courteously, bowing low to one another, their plumed hats sweeping the dust in true gentlemanly fashion.

Then they drew together and conversed for a moment, exchanging what seemed to be purely social remarks. Both seemed to have taken the shock of meeting very well.

Nicolas de Bardagne was slightly less tall than Joffrey, but neither showed any trace of arrogance or wish to dominate.

They talked as would men of high rank at some diplomatic encounter, each man possibly representing opposing interests, but none the less keen to find the common ground necessary for the success of both their undertakings.

Angélique put down her spyglass and ran over to larboard to climb down into the waiting longboat and join the two men before they parted company.

But as she drew in to the shore, she saw that Joffrey de Peyrac had taken leave of the King's representative and had gone off. Count Bardagne was once again alone on the shore awaiting her arrival.

He stood there motionless, staring intently in the direction of the *Gouldsboro*.

He was looking for her on deck and had not realized that she was in the boat that was approaching the shore. She refrained from waving to him in a friendly way as they drew in.

She went on observing him as he came more clearly into view in the morning light.

'It's a pity,' she thought to herself; 'he really has got something of Philippe about him, as I felt last night. I wonder what it is?'

Was it because his alternately grave and flippant expression of two years ago had given place to a kind of distant melancholy she had never seen in him before?

His agreeable features seemed to have grown more noble. He looked younger without his moustache. She could see that he had that naturally matt complexion often seen in people from the West of France, and this contrasted pleasantly with his blue-grey eyes.

There was no denying that he was what was known as a fine figure of a man.

He was one of those gentlemen who knew how to wear a cloak, a rarity in these days when the middle classes were so much to the fore – as that dreadful Ambroisine woman had remarked the day Joffrey had greeted her with such superb gallantry in the French manner, on the shores of Gouldsboro.

Bardagne was wearing a wig beneath a round, plumed hat of the latest fashion, and his whole person breathed an air of distinction.

There was no doubt about it, his moustache, or rather the lack of it, made him look very different. She would have been hard put to it to say precisely in what way the man she now saw was different from the one she had known two years back.

His expression was somehow clouded.

But the mildly morose expression melted away at the sight of her. He caught sight of her as she stepped ashore, and she saw the flash of his teeth as he smiled and found him quite his old self again. He came eagerly forward to meet her then halted a few paces off to bow, arching his leg as he did so.

'What goddess do I see before me!' he exclaimed. 'My dear Angélique! Now I see you in the light of day I know it was not a dream. I see you now as I guessed you to be, yesterday evening in the dark, but even more beautiful, more dazzling, if that is possible. What a miracle! I will not disguise from you that fact that I was so shaken, so anxious lest I had made some dreadful mistake, lest I had gone mad, or something, and so impatient to assure myself once again that you were real and that I had not been taken in by some fleeting illusion, by some wild imagining, that I was quite unable to rest all night ... I did not sleep a wink.'

'And we got hopelessly drunk!' thought Angélique to herself, 'and on *his* Burgundy, too! How dreadful!'

With the feeling that she must make amends, she held out her hand to him, and he kissed it rapturously.

'I saw that you met my husband,' she said.

Monsieur de Bardagne's face darkened.

'Yes! Not an easy encounter for my afflicted heart to endure. But I must admit that he introduced himself with great courtesy. As soon as I caught sight of him in the distance, surrounded by that guard of grim-faced foreigners, I guessed easily enough who he was. A Spanish guard! As if we were not at war with Spain! Just one more piece of bravado. In short, I immediately realized that the gentleman with the air of a *condottiere* was also your conqueror, alas!

261

'His face is somewhat disconcerting. But he approached me with good grace and affable words and assured me of his devotion to the King of France, which I have every reason to doubt, and of my complete freedom of movement. It seems somewhat late in the day to say that, after the way he ostracized us when we first put in at Tadoussac. But perhaps I have you to thank for this mark of indulgence? He tells me we can set sail tomorrow if we wish, as the repairs carried out to the *Saint John the Baptist* make it possible for her to continue on her way. In short, I cannot complain of his approach. But it will take a good deal more to wipe out the resentment I feel at the sight of him.'

He was silent for a moment, then went on:

'I have been thinking. If he is the Rescator, then he is the pirate with whom you fled from La Rochelle. We were not sure of his identity, but I remember there was mention of that name, well known to all seafarers – the Rescator. The way he manoeuvred beneath the walls of La Rochelle to avoid the cannon fire seemed to be very much in his style.

'Now I see it all. That was how you met him.'

'Not exactly,' Angélique tried to say.

But he was pursuing his own train of thought.

'Yes, I understand what happened. He had done you a service, and out of feminine sentimentality, which can so easily go astray, you regarded him as your saviour. You wanted to show your gratitude. But why on earth did you marry him, you poor unfortunate child? What a disaster! Why ever didn't you wait for me to arrive?'

'I could hardly have guessed you would come over to Canada.'

'No, I mean wait for me to arrive back in La Rochelle, instead of suddenly taking it into your head to run away?'

'We were all about to be arrested. Baumier had a list of our names. And in any case, he told me you would not be coming back, that you had fallen out of favour.'

Bardagne ground his teeth.

'The blackguard! How I wish I had run him through with my sword like the stinking rat he is.'

'That would not have helped.'

'Let's not talk any more about that dreadful episode,'

Monsieur de Bardagne said with a sigh. 'So now you are Madame de Peyrac.'

'Now and long since.'

On the point of explaining how she had married Joffrey de Peyrac a long time ago, and how, after fifteen years' separation from him, she had been miraculously reunited with him by chance in La Rochelle, she paused. The magnitude of the task seemed just too much for her.

He had already shown a tendency to consider her a shameless liar, and she could just see him protesting at the unlikelihood of such a tale. She could foresee that she would not be able to get half-way through her story before he began to challenge every word she uttered.

He was a man who wanted to hear only what suited him and who found it exceedingly hard to accept facts that looked like destroying his illusions and his hopes.

So what was the point of putting herself at his mercy by confiding imprudently in him? He might well divulge her secrets, thus strengthening the position of their enemies in Quebec.

What was known of Joffrey and herself in the city? What information, true or false, had already been spread abroad?

It would be time enough to find out when they got there. But it was pointless to add grist to the mill of their enemies. They were already suspected of every imaginable misdemeanour.

She was fully aware of the fact that, as the Rebel of Poitou, having taken up arms against the King of France, she was still subject to the laws of France, which had put a price on her head. Her position was even more perilous than Joffrey's, whom the King had secretly pardoned. Added to all the other dangers already awaiting her in New France, as a woman branded like a criminal with the fleur-de-lys, was the further risk of being recognized and arrested.

The net was closing round them. To tell the story of her past life would be tantamount to handing herself over, bound hand and foot, to the King's Envoy. Even though he was in love with her, would he not perhaps take a severe view of what she told him? She must never forget that here was the very man whom Louis XIV had commissioned to find out what he could about the pair of them and to discover whether the woman accompanying Count Peyrac was the Rebel of Poitou.

It was not going to be easy. When she heard him, as she now did, speak of the King, and describe how he had been seated respectfully before him – she had been held in the King's arms! – and how His Majesty, after giving him his final instructions, had escorted him to the door, and how unbelievably beautiful a place the Palace of Versailles was in the June sunshine, she felt like breaking in and saying, 'Yes, I know . . .' and asking him:

'Have they built the new Orangery yet? Is the left wing of the palace finished? What plays did Molière put on for the royal family this season?'

But she checked herself just in time and changed the subject:

'Oh, by the way,' she exclaimed out of the blue, 'I forgot to ask you . . . are you married? . . .'

'Married!' he spluttered, 'Me! What ever do you mean?'

'But why not? You might well have decided to marry during the past two years.'

'Me! Two years of hell, that's what they were! You simply have no idea what I have been through. First, my despair at losing you, and then my fall from favour! Married! You are incredible . . .'

This man, once so pleased with himself and with life, had obviously been dealt a severe blow. He took everything very seriously.

She began to wonder whether what she had done to him had not indeed affected him very deeply.

He told her that, in spite of Desgrez's protection, he had been thrown into prison, and that Monsieur de la Reynie, the Lieutenant-General of Police, had come in person to set him free. Angélique seized this opportunity to ask him a question that had been burning the tip of her tongue.

'Incidentally, how was it that after so many misfortunes, you came to be recommended to the King for so important a mission?'

'It was through Monsieur de la Reynie, in fact . . . I imagine that this is how it came about. The King was looking for someone he could trust to undertake this mission in

Canada. His usual practice is to consult his Lieutenant of Police, Monsieur de la Reynie, who has full information about almost anyone of any consequence in the Kingdom. Now Desgrez is his right-hand man and never leaves his side. So when he saw Monsieur de la Reynie keen to do his utmost to satisfy His Majesty, he mentioned my name, having promised to help me, and must have been persuasive since Monsieur de la Reynie intervened personally to obtain my release from the Bastille and arranged matters for me before submitting my name to the King. That is why I owe a certain debt of gratitude to that wretched Desgrez, in spite of all he made me suffer.'

'Yes, I understand ... Desgrez, was it? So it was Desgrez who recommended you to serve the King in Canada! It was he who sent you to find out everything you could about Monsieur de Peyrac ... Now just fancy that!'

'Incidentally, it was Desgrez that Monsieur de la Reynie appointed to accompany me to Versailles. But for once he behaved with great discretion and kept well in the background in one corner of the King's study while I was conferring with His Majesty. He seemed impressed by Versailles. He bowed very low and held doors open for me. For once in his life he seemed to understand where his rightful place was. We scarcely spoke more than a couple of words to one another and never again referred to the unfortunate occurrences in La Rochelle. I preferred it that way. So you see how it all happened!'

Yes, Angélique saw very well how it all happened.

And Joffrey had not been mistaken in suspecting the influence of some malevolent humorist at work in the background, engineering this particular appointment, and pulling strings in order to launch the unfortunate Bardagne, unbeknown to him, on the trail of the woman he had so deeply loved.

She could visualize the King, seated in all his majesty beneath the chandeliers of Versailles, saying to Nicolas de Bardagne, in a voice that he may have had difficulty in keeping steady:

'And try to find out, Monsieur, when you reach Canada, whether *the woman living with Count Peyrac* is not perhaps the same woman who once fought against us in our provinces under the name of the Rebel of Poitou. She has vanished and my police force has been searching for her for the past two years ... She and he are both dangerous characters ...'

And Desgrez, the police officer, would have been standing there, discreetly in the background, in the shadows of those long blue curtains embroidered with gold fleur-de-lys, listening to those words and, concealing behind an impassive mask a mocking smile.

Desgrez must have enjoyed himself weaving the threads of this intrigue. She could just see him, pondering, planning, with that glint in his red-flecked eyes. Might he possibly have had it in mind, under cover of this Machiavellian scheme, to search for her, the Marquise of the Angels, to find her again ...

'Desgrez, my friend, Desgrez ...' she said to herself, overcome with sudden nostalgia ...

'You are thinking about Desgrez,' Count Bardagne said bitterly. 'No, don't bother to deny it, it's obvious. I saw your eyes shine and soften. But it would ill become me to resent him too strongly. In spite of all I dislike about him, I can only admit that it is thanks to him that I am a free man here in Canada, near you, instead of rotting on a pile of damp straw in a dungeon.'

What an innocent Bardagne was!

As they conversed they had walked a few paces, oblivious of the usual crowds that thronged the port.

In front of these Canadians, this strange race of men, these fur trappers, these filibuster crews, Bardagne, conscious of being observed, assumed an air of confidentiality with her. He tried to pose as the only person who knew her well in this new land.

They alone came from Europe, from La Rochelle, and he had known her long before this motley assemblage of humanity. He consoled himself with the thought that length of acquaintance gave him priority of position in her heart, and that the two of them shared memories, almost, one might say, family memories.

'How I loved La Rochelle!' he said with a sigh.

'So did I.'

'I often dream about the place. I think it must have been the happiest period in my life. It was so lively, and the problems one had to deal with were often unusual ones. It was a town with a character all its own. That's where I met you. But even those intolerant heretics I found I liked. They had a strong family feeling that I approved of, and their women-folk were dutiful and intelligent. You talk of marriage, well there was a time when I would happily have married Monsieur Manigault's daughter, pretty Jenny. But the family were horrified when I mentioned the matter – they were Calvinists, of course, and I was the Devil incarnate! They preferred to marry her to a junior officer called Garret, who was stupid, but Huguenot.'

The mention of Jenny upset Angélique. Poor little Jenny, carried off by the savages. She had vanished into the depths of the American forestlands. It was a cruel country ...

Since Bardagne did not ask her about Jenny, she thought it better not to tell him what had happened to her.

'... What was I asking of them?' The King's Envoy went on. 'A conversion ... They made a great fuss about it. And yet, there is nothing very terrible about a conversion. If these people want to be French what they must do is obey the laws. One cannot allow a state of anarchy to develop. Have the Kingdom divided into two States with one of them disapproving of their sovereign and refusing to obey him. If people were to get rid of the King, what would they replace him with? The English beheaded theirs, and look what it's brought them to now ... They had to put another on the throne. I had many a passionate argument with those stubborn Huguenots, but there was no moving them. They preferred to abandon all their possessions rather than give in ... Pig-headed that's what they were! And to top it all they reckoned they were His Majesty's best subjects.

'I now realize that with typical feminine wrongheadedness you were on their side. Now you can see that you misjudged things. You were influenced by that man Berne, your master. A full-blooded man with healthy appetites, that was obvious ... He had his eye on you. I noticed that when you were in the room he made a point of never looking at you. I sense these things ... Did he resist the temptations such close proximity exposed him to? I very much doubt it ...'

'When ever will you leave poor Berne alone?' Angélique asked with a sigh. 'He is far away and there is not much risk of you running into him in these parts. And please will you get it straight that I am no longer his servant . . .'

'That's true! You are married to that pirate, that overbearing lord. He seduced you with his wealth. Of course I can see why. But it's quite unfair and I am not going to accept it. You should be mine, you should be my mistress. I am going to have you.'

'What, here?' asked Angélique, indicating the little village square where they had halted.

Then she burst out laughing at his look of discomfiture.

'Come now, dear Monsieur de Bardagne, curb your tongue a little, I beg you. Your words betray feelings I find flattering and touching, but you must be sensible. You have before you the wife of Count Peyrac, which means, with all due deference, that I have pledged him my faith and fidelity. Furthermore, I would not do you the insult of reminding you that men of his stamp have a very keen sense of honour. And you, alas! are not among those who are deterred by fear of a duel.

'So please will you merely regard my warning as a mark of my friendship for you and the distress I would feel were you to find yourself in trouble.'

She noticed that Bardagne was listening to her with an air of dreamy devotion, paying far more attention to the inflexions of her voice than to the meaning of the little speech she was making. He was smiling delightedly.

'There is the maternal side of you I remember so well,' he said with a sigh of rapture. 'I can still see you running that household of yours with a firm yet indulgent hand. How good you were at talking to the children! I used sometimes to feel jealous of the little Bernes when you spoke to them, and I'd began to dream of one day being in your arms with you scolding me gently in that very tone of voice, as you stroked my forehead.'

'I *am* scolding you.'

'But I am not in your arms, alas! and you are not stroking my forehead.'

But he had become less tense, and together they laughed like old friends.

Count Bardagne slipped an arm beneath Angélique's.

'Don't worry. I took in your little lecture and have noted

what you said. It's a hard pill to swallow, but' – and he kissed her hand – 'you are too lovely for me to hold it against you for very long. I'd be quite justified in feeling resentful, for you have poured poison into my veins, but you have also brought me such happiness! It would be unjustified of me to make you bear the weight of my miseries and to importune you. So I promise to behave myself in future. But don't disappear again.'

'Where ever would you have me disappear to, my dear man,' she said, laughing yet more heartily. 'Can you not see that willy nilly the current is sweeping us all on to Quebec as if caught in a net and that we shall all end up, big fish and little fish, spending the winter there?'

'So I'll see you ... I'll see you,' he murmured, as if unable to believe in such bliss. 'That's what I sensed yesterday evening; that meeting you like this was a wonderful, almost providential stroke of luck.'

Angélique did not altogether share his view of the matter, for what she saw was rather Desgrez's ironical face grinning in the background.

But when she thought about the life that awaited them in Quebec, with all the pitfalls that would undoubtedly be placed in their path, especially in her path, the unexpected presence of Bardagne was a new and on the whole favourable factor.

If he loved her to such an extent as to be utterly blinded by his passion, and ready to do anything to please her, she would continue to wield power over him and he would be useful to her as he had been before at La Rochelle.

For even Monsieur de Frontenac owed a kind of allegiance to the King's Envoy.

Because he was endowed with hidden power, due to his being for a time the King's eye in the colony, everyone would endeavour to curry favour with him, fearing lest an unfavourable report might result in a fall from grace.

While his job consisted in resolving the dilemma posed by herself and Joffrey, he would tend to lean to their side in order to avoid incurring her disfavour.

All things considered, it was, as he himself said, a stroke of luck that he had been entrusted with this mission rather than someone else.

This thought gave her such a sensation of relief that she instinctively gripped Bardagne's arm, on which she was leaning as she walked, and he, surprised by the affectionate squeeze, looked at her in happy astonishment.

At that moment Angélique's eyes were resting on the point where the river met the horizon, as if to draw calm from the spectacle of the peaceful waters and distant banks, and she descried a white speck up river which grew larger as it drew nearer: it was a sail.

People began to move down towards the port, and several small boys came bounding down from the upper terraces of the village, calling out as they passed:

'The *Maribelle*!'

CHAPTER 33

'THE *Maribelle*!' exclaimed Nicolas de Bardagne. 'Isn't that the King's ship which is to come from Quebec to my assistance?'

'Oh! you're not under attack ...' cried Angélique angrily.

She pulled away her arm which he was holding tenderly beneath his own.

'... Do stop perpetually thinking you're in danger. No one's threatening you. And hope to God that that idiot down there doesn't have it in mind to open fire on us with his guns! For then your position would become decidedly unenviable. As far as I'm concerned, get it into your head once and for all that what strikes at Count Peyrac, my husband, strikes at me too. It would be no good hoping to remain a friend of mine if you sided with his enemies.'

She left him standing there disconcerted and distressed, and ran down towards the shore, where she rejoined the children and her bodyguard.

She almost collided with Marguerite Bourgeoys who was arriving followed by her girls and a group of passengers from the *Saint John the Baptist*. The two women exchanged a rapid glance. This was their first meeting for two days.

Angélique said sharply:

'Don't entertain any hopes that the ship about to arrive will make any difference whatsoever. We haven't come for a fight . . .'

'I share your hopes,' Marguerite Bourgeoys assured her.

But there was a kind of indecision among the local people. The ripple of doubt which ran through the spectators despite themselves, quickly subsided. Groups of armed sailors were to be seen to have been quietly deployed round the village and to be slowly encircling the beach which was black with people.

Monsieur de Peyrac's men showed no particular signs of hostility, but their general aspect was a deterrent to anyone who might have tried, in the heat of the moment, to take sides before the cannon spoke.

And as she looked out to the roadstead, Angélique saw that a change had occurred in the formation of the ships.

Amid the comings and goings of the morning it had not been noticed that the ships had spread their sails and begun a manoeuvre. One of them, under the command of Barssempuy, had taken up station a short way beyond the *Gouldsboro* and, as it tacked to and fro, kept guard over the fine ship which was, itself, still riding at anchor, but its raised gun-ports revealed the black mouths of cannon. Some were trained on the *Saint John the Baptist* whose entire crew was lining the rails, the rest pointed towards the quarter from which the ship was expected.

The two small yachts and the larger vessel were heading straight for the open sea. Following the same procedure as in the recent action when they had picked up the *Saint John the Baptist* as she limped towards Tadoussac, they were forming a semi-circle, blocking the channel of the St Lawrence and cutting off any movement towards its mouth, to the north.

The new arrival, supposing that she refused to halt, had only one way open to her – to make for Tadoussac, thus plunging, willy nilly into the net spread to receive her.

Thus, while Angélique was exchanging pleasantries with the King's representative, and everyone was going unsuspectingly about his business, Joffrey de Peyrac and his crews, without any fuss, had set up a whole system of defence, which at least precluded the possibility of their being taken by surprise.

He had doubtless received advance warning, as usual, of the *Maribell*'s arrival. She was looming rapidly larger, heading straight for the port. She must have weighed up the situation and realized that concealment was out of the question.

It remained to be seen whether, for honour's sake, she would do something disastrous.

'I should hate to have to fire on one of His Majesty's ships,' murmured Peyrac.

And Angélique noticed that he was behind her, having just arrived with his guard and senior staff officers.

'Would you like to go back with me on board the *Gouldsboro*?' he asked her. 'It's possible that we may have to receive the captain of the *Maribelle* there shortly and having you there can only be an advantage in our discussions.'

He politely greeted Nicolas de Bardagne, who was standing a little way off, and handed Angélique and the children, Yolande and Adhémar, into the longboat.

Despite Peyrac's calm, Angélique was so preoccupied that it never occurred to her to look in the direction of the King's representative.

As they rowed out towards the *Gouldsboro*, the *Maribelle*, now so close that the boatswain could be heard giving orders on her bridge, began a manoeuvre.

Men could be seen swarming up the rigging and running along the yard-arms, sails being put on, others being taken in and rapidly furled, and the heavy vessel put about.

'She's going back to Quebec,' cried Adhémar.

From the longboat they all followed the activity, fascinated.

But the *Maribelle* was simply going to moor broadside on in the mouth of the Saguenay, behind the headland which protected the entrance.

'If they disembarked, couldn't they take Tadoussac from behind?' asked Angélique in an undertone.

'Both banks of the Saguenay are guarded,' Peyrac replied, 'and our men hold the port.'

All that could be seen of the *Maribelle* was her topsails, projecting above the headland, then she reappeared further off, moving further towards the far end of the estuary, having perhaps found the first mooring place chosen uninviting.

She drew away further and further, then hove to, and they heard the rattle of her anchor chain running out and echoing back from the high cliffs of the Saguenay.

'Very wise of her! I don't think these gentlemen of the French Royal Navy are over-anxious to take us on.'

They were all back on board and were following from afar the manoeuvres of the new-comer. Barssempuy's ship continued to stand by, ready to intervene, but that no longer seemed necessary.

A boat was seen pulling away from the ship's side and making for the *Gouldsboro*.

'Didn't I tell you to expect visitors?' said Peyrac.

Ville d'Avray was trying to make out who was coming.

'Those novices of the Royal Navy ... always behave as though they owned the place ... And then, take *Maribelle* ... I ask you. Is that a name to give a ship? A sexless name. Unless she takes herself for English.'

'And what name have you given your ship, Monsieur de Ville d'Avray?' asked Honorine.

'I don't know yet, my child. I'm thinking about it ...'

In the boat, alone with the rowers, was seated a powerfully built man. His coat collar was turned up, hiding his face. He was wearing a fur cap.

'It's not the captain of the *Maribelle*,' observed Ville d'Avray. 'Usually they're decked out in gold-braid and ribbons and very proud of their wigs.'

They moved towards the gangway.

The man climbed briskly up the few rungs of the hanging ladder which had been let down in his honour.

He stepped on to the deck. He was wearing heavy seal-skin boots. His lace ruff was fastened all askew, but he was wearing a sword.

'Monsieur the Baron d'Arresboust!' they cried, recognizing the President of the Council of Quebec, who had been a guest at Wapassou during the previous winter.

He stopped, turned his gaze on Peyrac, then on Angélique, and his stern countenance brightened.

He went up to them with outstretched hand, kissed Angélique's with obvious pleasure, and registered in dumb show his astonished delight at finding a great lady in place of the pioneer woman he had known in the rough setting of the fort. He paused on catching sight of Ville d'Avray and the Intendant, whom he certainly did not expect to find there as guests of Peyrac's on the *Gouldsboro*, and turned towards the latter. Standing on the deck of his ship he too appeared in a different light, master of his fleet, of a numerous and well-trained crew, and master of Tadoussac to all appearances.

'Welcome on board the *Gouldsboro*,' said the Count as he stepped forward. 'Have you been sent by the *Maribelle* bearing a message from her commander?'

'No, why?' asked Baron d'Arresboust in apparent astonishment.

He glanced across towards the *Maribelle*.

'That fellow Luppé will bestir himself when he considers it consistent with his dignity and safety to do so. It's no business of mine ...'

'But I demanded that a boat be put at my disposal because I very much wanted to come and greet you, and, above all ... warn you.'

'Of what?'

Baron d'Arresboust took a step back. An expression of terror passed across his face.

'The fiery canoes of the ghostly hunt have been seen in the sky over Quebec,' he said.

CHAPTER 34

'THE FIERY canoes of the ghostly hunt have been seen in the sky over Quebec ...'

Monsieur d'Arreboust was standing before them. In a voice that was at once tragic and solemn, he had made this statement:

'The fiery canoes of the ghostly hunt have been seen in the sky over Quebec.'

Then he fell silent.

Behind him, in the distant reaches of the St Lawrence, tinged with pink, a ship, which had loomed up out of the winter mists, presented the ghostly profile of her three masts, her sails furled.

And that was all. What could this ship, whose arrival had been promised, and which had been held back to no purpose, do, when there were five well-armed vessels lying in wait for her? There had never been any question of challenging them. She had merely dropped anchor and despatched a longboat to the *Gouldsboro* out of which had climbed a vigorous though massive man with an agreeable face, who seemed genuinely pleased to see them – which was entirely unexpected.

But Monsieur d'Arreboust was a genuine friend.

The real drama was not the arrival of the *Maribelle*, but the announcement the President of the Council of Quebec had just made.

'The ghostly hunt has passed over Quebec ...' And there had been a note of despair in his voice.

Angélique's impression was that he had been on the point of adding: 'Go back, go back whence you came, you are accursed! ...'

She looked around to see how the news was being taken by those present. As one born in the province of Poitou, *she* realized that he was talking about ill omens.

In her region, people sometimes spoke of a fiery hunter and his pack of hounds crossing the skies of Poitou en Saintonge. Death and pestilence followed in their wake.

But most of Peyrac's officers and companions had no idea what it was all about. They received the tidings with indifference. Peyrac reacted calmly and with a touch of irony, for a multiplicity of premonitory omens held no fears for him, Carlon's reaction was terror and dismay, while Ville d'Avray was amused.

'It heralds disasters, invasion, defeat,' intoned the gloomy Intendant.

'These folk legends are quite delightful, don't you think?' enthused Ville d'Avray. 'Yes, you know, my dear,' he said turning towards Angélique, 'in these parts the story is that from time to time, fiery canoes pass across the sky. It's the

275

ghostly hunt of Canada. Just as, over there, in the West of France, people see the hunter and his pack flying from Parthenay to Saint-Jean-d'Angely, here we have canoes which fly from Montreal to Gaspé ... It's only what you would expect – we're in Canada. The popular imagination cannot find enough to keep it occupied. It needs the miraculous ... It needs to know that Heaven sends it signs ... I saw one myself,' he went on. 'In 1660, at the time of the big earthquake, do you remember, d'Arreboust?'

'Of course I remember,' agreed the Baron, 'and that's why I want to warn you, Monsieur de Peyrac. The canoes of the ghostly hunt passed over Quebec, several days ago ... There are too many witnessess to doubt the authenticity of the story. Most of them say that they saw a flotilla of them in the middle distance crossing the sky in the direction of Ville Marie.

'But a man who had gone to locate bears' dens before the winter sets in claims that as he was coming back from the woods, he saw a canoe passing close in front of him, silently ...'

'And who was in it?' asked Ville d'Avray, consumed with curiosity.

'The Jesuit martyrs: Fathers Brebeuf, Lallemant and also a backwoodsman, but he's not very sure of his identity, because flames were licking round his face, but he thinks it was Nicolas Perrot.'

'Nicolas Perrot?' exclaimed Angélique, as upset as if she had just been told of the death of her good Canadian friend. 'Don't tell me that he has met with misfortune ...'

'That's enough of that rot,' Carlon interrupted impatiently. 'The whole thing, as we well know it, is the superstitious imaginings of demented peasants.'

'Steady on, my friend,' interposed Ville d'Avray. '*I* saw them with my own eyes, I tell you.'

'Oh! Trust you! You always see everything. Well! *I've* never seen them ... And besides, it's irrelevant. Whether they've been seen or not, it means that the town is in uproar. I bet you that one half the population is in the churches and the other half on the ramparts ...'

'You win your bet. The Ursuline nuns have begun a

novena to turn back Monsieur de Peyrac's ships.'

'That's not going to make your arrival any the easier, Count.'

'Have you come on behalf of the frightened population, Baron?' asked Peyrac turning towards d'Arreboust, 'in order to beseech me to retreat like Attila before the walls of Paris, at the behest of St Geneviève?'

D'Arreboust seemed taken aback by the question. His face darkened then he shook his head in a vague sort of way.

'No, no, I bear no message, quite the opposite.'

'What do you mean quite the opposite?'

The Baron bowed his head.

'I am returning to France,' he said. 'That's why I'm on board the *Maribelle*.'

He seemed prostrate with dejection.

'I've been arrested,' he said.

'Arrested, you? ...'

The same exclamation was on all lips.

'On what charge?'

It was Angélique who asked the question.

Baron d'Arreboust gazed steadily at her.

'Because of *you*.'

In the ensuing silence stupefaction was the dominant emotion. Monsieur d'Arreboust was virtually one of the founders of Canada. His ill fortune seemed incredible. And no one could make out how Angélique could have caused his fall from favour.

'When I say, you! ... forgive me, Madame. You too are responsible, Monsieur de Peyrac. In a word, I have been excessively zealous in your support.'

'See what's in store for us,' came Intendant Carlon's gloomy voice from the rear.

Without neglecting the Baron, Joffrey de Peyrac turned his attention back to the *Maribelle*.

'Do you think those gentlemen over yonder intend to regard us as enemies?'

'I don't think so. Monsieur de Luppé, the captain, who is a relative of mine, is a young man who doesn't lose much sleep over the squabbles of the Canadians. That's why, on his ship, I'm on parole. Are you willing to parley with him?'

277

'Of course.'

'Well then, have you a white scarf or some kind of pennant or flag so that I can send him a signal?'

'So you were given a mission to carry out after all!'

Ville d'Avray handed him the scarf which covered the belt from which his sword hung and Monsieur d'Arreboust waved it to and fro several times.

'I assured him of your good character, but he was wary. So many stories about you do the rounds, and with the passing of the canoes of the ghostly hunt in the sky excitement had reached fever pitch in Quebec when we weighed anchor.'

Monsieur de Luppé was a tall, well-built young officer. He affected a disdainful, haughty air. His type of courtier was fairly common; he looked like the Marquis de Vardes or Louise de Lavallière's brother. The spoilt scions of a dissolute society which flattered them for their fine bearing and sharp tongues, once away from the Court were none the less able leaders and mindful of their responsibilities.

He had brought with him an escort of six naval guards armed with muskets, but was well aware of the realities of his situation.

'Sir,' he said to Peyrac as he stepped on to the *Goldsboro*'s deck, 'do you have hostile intentions towards me?'

'I think, Sir, that that is a question *I* ought to be asking *you*,' was Peyrac's reply.

The Marquis de Luppé glanced pessimistically around him, pointing to the sailing ships which were cruising and turning in the wind.

'I'm not blind, sir, and I can count. I'm single-handed against five ships. I have received no orders from my superiors about you, you have committed no act of aggression against me, there is no state of war between France and your country, whatever it may be. Why should I have hostile intentions towards you?'

'Well then, that settles matters. You may go on your way.'

'I would like to spend two days at Tadoussac, to take on supplies of fresh water and firewood.'

'As you wish, on condition that you respect, and ensure that your men respect, your pact of non-belligerency with me.'

'And just a minute, my fine fellow,' interrupted Jean

Carlon; 'I want you to take on a consignment of timber and masts for Le Havre ...'

'But my holds are full,' cried the officer changing colour, 'my cargo is stowed, and in any case who the devil do you think you are to take that tone to me?'

'Who am I? You'll soon find out who I am, my lad,' cried the Intendent of New France, drawing himself up to his full height. 'If you think that just because you command a warship ...'

Angélique didn't wait to hear the introductions completed, for they promised to be stormy.

Seeing that all seemed to be turning out for the best, she had drawn Baron d'Arreboust towards the chartroom. She wished to have a few words with him, to find out the exact circumstances of his fall from favour and why he blamed her for it.

CHAPTER 35

'WHAT HAPPENED?' she asked him when they found themselves seated before a glass of the famous Burgundy, that panacea of all ills.

'Well may you ask,' he sighed. 'Alas! It's *your* fault, you again ... Yes, I know, Loménie and I acted like a pair of fools. When we got back from Wapassou, we kept on protesting that we were in love with the Lady of the Silver Lake ... in other words with you.'

'I cannot quite see Monsieur de Loménie coming out with such a statement,' said Angélique with a laugh. 'It's not his style. And isn't he in religion? A knight of Malta, wasn't it?'

'Yes, exactly! His attitude shocked people even more than mine. You don't know him. Monsieur de Loménie is a very open, passionate man, and where his affections are involved and I might add his beliefs too, he tends to go the whole hog ...

'Well, the fact was that we had been sent out there to

form a first-hand opinion of you and we gave it. I had naïvely imagined that, as we had been chosen because our compatriots trusted us, they would listen to our advice. It was only when it was too late that I realized that what they wanted was for us to tell them what they *wanted* to hear, in other words to denounce you as enemies that had to be fought.

'But as we had not come back with this answer, we soon found ourselves disowned and regarded as unreliable. We were accused of having allowed ourselves be outwitted, bribed or even bewitched. But we did not realize the truth even then.

'We thought that if we told the simple truth people would get things in proportion. Yes, we behaved like fools,' he repeated. 'On our return from Maine we were in a peculiar state of euphoria, as if the world had changed colour. One has to be on one's guard against the heady sense of exaltation frequently experienced in winter when the air is limpid and clear, and makes you feel mildly inebriated. But we did not, in fact, say anything but what was sensible, even when we were joking. Can one no longer joke in New France? It would seem not.'

'Have a little wine,' said Angélique, interrupting him, for she saw that he was under intolerable strain.

What had happened to the calm, level-headed man whom they had lodged last year at Wapassou?

'. . . It's Burgundy . . .'

'Yes, it's excellent. Nectar of the gods. I feel better . . .'

'Calm down. You are with us now and we shall help you . . .'

'That's impossible. I am a ruined man, beyond helping. All that awaits me in France is the Bastille.'

At this juncture, the Marquis de Ville d'Avray entered the chartroom rubbing his hands.

'Ha, ha! Excellent. This encounter with the *Maribelle* will enable me to write to Madame de Pontarville in Paris to ask her to let me have one of her little Moors as a page. By catching this mail, I gain a whole season . . .'

He sat down nearby and poured himself a glass of wine.

'. . . You were speaking about the Bastille, Baron. Don't

worry about that! Which of us has not done his little spell in the Bastille? ... I did myself, like everyone else. But *I*, let me tell you, I always took my own valet and my cook with me. Do not hesitate to demand first-class service, which they are perfectly able to provide.'

'Thanks for the advice,' d'Arreboust replied bitterly.

'I must admit I'm going to miss your company playing faro on winter evenings in Quebec.'

Baron d'Arreboust eyed the little Marquis's bland smile with undisguised resentment.

'You needn't be so cheerful about it. You may find yourself fired, too.'

'Me? Gracious! No one would dare to touch me.'

'I would have said the same a few months ago, but as you see,' he went on, turning to Angélique, 'things have turned out extremely badly, virtually without our realizing what was going on. Without suspecting it, Loménie and I were saying things that brought us into conflict with a deliberate, wilful longing for catastrophe. It was reassuring to identify enemies to attack and drag down. A mystic sense of danger reinforced their faith, making their bravery and efforts seem worth while.

'By depriving them of a reason for feeling they were favoured by Heaven, we were regarded as working on behalf of the Devil. I realized this too late, being reluctant to take seriously an obsession that had taken shape and must needs now be followed. Haven't we enough to worry about with the Iroquois?

'Men are mad! We are mad ... but be that as it may, one morning the police came and arrested me, *me*, the President of the Quebec Council.'

'The police!' cried Ville d'Avray, wide eyed. 'That's the limit. You're not going to tell me that Frontenac gave any such orders.'

'No, but he let Castel-Morgeat steal a march on him. Don't forget that he is Military Governor of the City, in fact of New France. It was he who sent the police ...'

'And what about your wife?' asked Ville d'Avray, as if suddenly struck by a new idea. 'Is she returning to France with you?'

He struck his brow.

'You don't mean to say that Lucile is on board the *Maribelle*?' Quick, get me a longboat, so that I can go and see the adorable creature.'

'No, she isn't on board,' d'Arreboust shrieked, springing to his feet and checking the mercurial Marquis in his rush for the door. 'No, she is not with me! You know very well she has been cloistered in Montreal for the past year.'

'Cloistered! Cloistered!' Ville d'Avray repeated, as if unable to understand. 'You mean cloistered, shut away ... worse than a nun or a recluse? And you let that happen ... And you're capable of going off to Europe and abandoning her? You are a monster ... Had I been you, I would have gone and smashed in the wall of her cell with a pick-axe. Lucile cloistered ... Such an incredibly beautiful woman ... A little doll ... Did I not say she had the most beautiful breasts in the world, and you disregard ...'

'Be quiet! Will you be quiet!' roared d'Arreboust, shaking him by his cravat. 'Be quiet, you wretch! You're just turning the knife in the wound, *deliberately* ...'

He was so red in the face that he seemed on the verge of apoplexy.

The two men had grappled so rapidly that Angélique had not had time to intervene, and she could not think what to do to separate them.

They realized how uncivilly they were behaving, broke off their quarrel and made their excuses.

'Forgive me, Madame,' said Baron d'Arreboust. 'It has all proved too much for me, and Monsieur de Ville d'Avray is provoking me without a care for my grief.'

Ville d'Avray straightened his clothes. He was highly displeased, but especially at the news about Lucile d'Arreboust.

'So, you're depriving me of Lucile's company and expect me to congratulate you on it! Off you go then! Let them lock you up in the Bastille ... I'm delighted.'

He left them to go and write his letter to Madame de Pontarville.

'He's right,' said Baron d'Arreboust despairingly; 'if I go, I shall never see her again, I feel sure of it. With her shut up there in Ville-Marie, and me, shut away too in the Bastille. Who will give us so much as a thought? Whatever has happened that in so short a time such a storm should have broken over our lives! ...'

'We must do something for Monsieur d'Arreboust,' cried Angélique, hastening to Joffrey de Peyrac. 'They're trying to separate him from his wife ...'

She related to her husband what the Baron had just confided in her, and how he had compromised himself through his friendship and loyalty towards them.

'If he goes off to Europe, he may never see her again. And who will concern himself with obtaining his release from the Bastille? Years will go by. I suggested to him that he should remain on board the *Gouldsboro*, but he said he had given his word as a gentleman to Luppé ...'

Joffrey de Peyrac looked in the direction of the commander of the *Maribelle* who was already going ashore to do some fur trading. He had spoken to the man about Baron d'Arreboust and realized that he wanted no kind of trouble, nor to be accused of collusion with a pirate, but that he did not particularly mind whether Monsieur d'Arreboust remained in Canada or was locked up in the Bastille. Nor was it Monsieur de Frontenac who had placed him in the role of gaoler to the Baron, a role made all the more distasteful by the fact that the d'Arreboust family we distantly related to his.

Monsieur de Frontenac had rather let things take their course.

'We might possibly find a solution,' said Peyrac.

He and his wife rejoined the Baron in the chartroom.

'Monsieur, do you wish to remain in Canada?'

'Indeed I do! A thousand times yes! This is where I have made my life, and where my heart lies. But the Grand Council has deprived me of my rights and New France has no room for me any more. Furthermore, I have given my word to Monsieur de Luppé not to attempt to escape.'

'Never mind that, Baron! You are powerless to resist a pirate's will. For once, I intend to live up to the image people have of me. You have fallen into my hands. I need hostages. So Monsieur de Luppé will have to yield to the demands of the filibusters.'

'What do you mean?'

'It's very simple, *you are my prisoner*.'

CHAPTER 36

'THAT MAN Desgrez is a scoundrel.'

The old term used by the *matterie* sprang to her lips as she thought about the story Bardagne had told her.

At the Court of Miracles the word had been used to mean a traitor, a double dealer . . . but it had a trace of indulgence and admiration about it:

'A scoundrel!'

A scoundrel was a 'cove' with ideas out of the ordinary, as they said in the Court of Miracles, ideas such as 'you didn't know where he got them from', terrible notions, a genious for cooking up dirty tricks. Crafty, unbelievable tricks, although one could not actually describe what he was doing as unfair or beyond the pale. A scoundrel was some-one who knew how to stand up for himself and who would employ every available means to do so.

Angélique was alone in the *Gouldsboro*'s stateroom. As she stood before her writing desk, she thought about Des-grez. It was evening, and a steatite seal-oil lamp burning on a console table glowed with a soft, yellow light. The Eskimo savages from the far North traded these primitive night-lights for supplies of salt and beads. They provided both light and warmth, giving off a honey-like glow, that spread wide in an intimate halo of light, in which Angélique's face had assumed a thoughtful expression.

She had not gone back on shore that day, Monsieur d'Arreboust's 'capture' having given her quite enough to do. She did not feel like seeing Bardagne again. She had got everything she could out of him. The *Saint John the Baptist* was apparently setting sail the following day.

So let them sail! There would be time enough to see her lovelorn admirer in Quebec. But behind Bardagne, the figure of Desgrez nagged at her thoughts.

Desgrez, come to life again, Desgrez watching her through

the shadows, saying: 'Here I am, Marquise of the Angels.'

She reasoned as follows: if Desgrez is involved in all this, it is a good thing since he is very efficient, but it is also very disturbing, since it proves that the situation is a dangerous one. Desgrez had always stepped in when things were going very badly for *her*.

He had not intervened simply to play a nasty trick on Bardagne. Count Bardagne knows nothing. He thinks Desgrez sent him on this mission because of his inherent merits.

But it was Angélique he was seeking through Bardagne. He had sent her a man who was not a danger to her; a man who would follow his instructions, or find himself back in gaol again.

Now it was her turn to play. Over in France and here!

The fact that d'Arreboust had been arrested, that Loménie-Chambord was more or less disgraced, and that a very real threat hung over Ville d'Avray, in spite of his brave talk, and even over Intendant Carlon, by the mere fact that they had accepted help from the Peyracs in Acadia, proved the strength of collusion between those who wanted to get rid of them.

There had been Ambroisine. She had been almost symbolic, the quintessence of people's rejection of them. She had been something like a link between the accomplices in the Old and the New World working for Angélique's and Peyrac's downfall.

She had gone. But others would spring up. It was like the hydra with a hundred heads. Why? In her place Desgrez had reappeared, taking his place once more on the merry-go-round. He had in all likelihood never left the spiralling round that was sweeping them all along . . .

She searched her memory.

Ambroisine had told her that Desgrez had been about to arrest her friend, the Marquise of Brinvilliers, the poisoner. She had said: 'I ran away because of him. He was too inquisitive, he was on my track . . .'

She gave a sudden start.

An invisible presence *was moving* somewhere close to her, as if some thing was creeping up on her and was brushing against her dress. She leapt backwards, mouth open, ready to scream with terror. She was still terribly nervy since the episode of the Demon.

'Oh, it's you ...'

'...?'

'You gave me the fright of my life!'

'...?'

'Come here, puss ...'

The cat must have followed her as was its wont ... Or had it been asleep on the bed?

Intrigued to find her standing there, motionless, it came still closer, leaping up on to the table until it was very close to her, brushing her cheek with its tiny pink satiny nose, its golden eyes looking into hers, questioning and curious. 'What's the matter with her? Is she ill or will she play with me?'

She began to laugh.

'Come here, puss ...'

She put her arm round the cat, and looked into those fearless, mysterious eyes.

'You saw her!' she thought. 'You saw the fire of Satan like a halo round her beautiful face, and you bristled and spat in fury ... Evil ... You could see it, my little puss! ...

'And the Redskin did too. Piksarett! "A woman full of devils" he used to say. And he took to his heels, calling out to me: "Say your prayers." '

Would she encounter Piksarett in Canada? Or would he leave her to the demons?

She stroked the cat. Its sleek fur was comforting. It had a long, silky coat. As a fully grown, well-fed cat with no other cares in the world than to keep itself looking beautiful, it would spend the greater part of the day washing itself vigorously. For the time being it was calm and confident about the future. It curled up beside the lamp with a view to having a long, dreamless sleep.

It was when she had discovered the cat covered in blood, that night in the village of Gouldsboro, its paws burned, tortured by some invisible devil, that she had realized that Evil was on the rampage ... Evil that attacks Innocence.

Back in Versailles, one night long ago, in one of the boudoirs, in the light of the candles she had seen a new-born baby killed with a long needle.

'Don't look in the basket,' the hideous witch had said in her raucous voice to the Palace guards, as she took away the tiny sacrificed corpse as dawn broke.

The same old sickening terror came back to her again at the stirring of these memories.

Angélique sat down at her writing desk.

The cat, with its paws tucked under as if in a muff and its eyes half closed, nevertheless watched with interest as the unaccustomed preparations were made: sheets of raw silk vellum, an inkwell, a carefully sharpened goosequill, a scraper, a penknife, sticks of sealing wax and the gold-set mother-of-pearl bowl filled with fine sand. This last object appeared to intrigue the cat, which from time to time would very gently poke out its inquisitive little nose, give a sniff, then resume its former sleepy yet vigilant pose.

Angélique felt a sudden impulse to sit down at her desk, a rare thing for her to do, and to open the writing box containing what she needed to compose a letter.

Seeing Ville d'Avray planning to despatch a final letter to Europe had given her an idea.

Outside, a foghorn sounded through the still, muffled air. Fog would delay the *Maribelle*'s departure.

Somewhere in the bowels of the *Gouldsboro*, Ville d'Avray was scribbling away furiously, unwilling to miss a chance to despatch across the ocean some well-baited missive calculated to result in the ultimate receipt of a host of coveted treasures: a Moorish page, some knick-knack or other, or some exceedingly rare liqueur. His men and women friends back in Europe could surely put themselves out a little on his behalf. After all, what else did they have to do?

Angélique hesitated, then sat down. She picked up the pen.

'With all I know I'll silence those vipers' tongues, those sarcastic courtiers, those jealous bigots who are always so ready to destroy others.'

Desgrez, my friend, I am writing to you from a far-away land. You know where. You must know or at least have some idea. You have always known everything about me . . .

It all went back a long way. To the time when he had accompanied her to Master Georges' bath-house in the Rue Saint-Nicolas, the time when he had chased her through the

287

streets of Paris with the dog Sorbonne.

'Here, I'm giving you back your knife ...'

On that bitter Paris night, a dagger had fallen at her feet. Her dagger ... And the policeman had gone away, had disappeared into the shadows. Desgrez had been after her. Appearing and disappearing wherever she went.

At La Rochelle, he had let her escape.

Desgrez, my friend, This is what I have to say to you: Six or seven years ago, you wanted to know certain secrets concerning people in high places whom you suspected of committing crimes. Today I shall reveal them to you.

Now she was writing rapidly.

I know of a little house on the corner of the Rue des Blancs-Manteaux and the Place Triquet. There lives, or lived until a short time ago, a soothsayer by the name of Deshayes-Monvoisin. She also owns a very fine house in the Faubourg Saint-Denis, along with other haunts, and it is there that she prepares her philtres and poisons. There too the throats of new-born babies are cut ...

Her pen raced over the paper with a light scratching sound, while the cat followed the trembling white feather's progress suspiciously out of the corner of its eye, as it quivered in Angélique's fingers. Every now and then, it caught at it lightly with its paw.

Her pen slipped sideways, but Angélique was unconcerned. She was entirely absorbed in her memories. Secrets which, some years back, Monsieur de la Reynie and François Desgrez had tried in vain to make her reveal,[1] she was now willing to tell.

At the time, the things she knew could have made a whole world topple, exposed the entire Court to the opprobrium of the multitude and brought some to the executioner's axe, if not to the stake by order of the Inquisition, have sent princes, at the summit of honour, into exile, wrecked fortunes and careers and even smitten the heart of the King himself. The magistrates' eyes, as they looked upon her, made no secret of their certainty that she knew. They knew that she knew and they were entreating her to tell.

'Tell us, Madame,' Monsieur de la Reynie urged. '*Who* is this enemy of yours and *who* is the witch in her pay?'

[1] See *Angélique and the King.*

She had kept silence . . . But now . . .

Now that the battle had been joined once more, or rather now that it was entering its final phase, a combat forged from obscure treachery, jealous ostracisms, underhand manoeuvres, the secrets concerning them revealed, exploited against them, dangerous calumnies that seemed destined to repulse them once again in their struggle for survival, to deal them the final blow, now that what she knew could silence her invisible enemies, now she would talk.

This Voisin woman has access to Versailles. If you can lay hands on a certain Mademoiselle Desoeillet . . .

Desgrez had been waiting a long time for this moment. He could not himself, without some denunciation, penetrate into Versailles to reach the criminals. He knew that he would always have to go higher and higher up.

This woman is the key to everything. She is the companion of a lady of the highest rank in the King's immediate circle. That is where you should be looking.

She stopped writing and called to mind Madame de Montespan, her erstwhile friend, the ever-triumphant mistress of the King, who, having come to consider her as a rival for the King's favours, had attempted to murder her.

She added: *It was this high-ranking lady who once had 'the shift' prepared for me through the good offices of the said Monvoisin . . .*

She hesitated to spell out the devastating name of Athenaïs de Montespan.

No matter! Desgrez would understand.

Either her letter would reach him, or, if it fell into the wrong hands, it would be better if people could not understand everything in it.

Monsieur d'Arreboust had said: 'My valet will continue the journey. He wanted to go back to Europe. He can take any letters you care to give him, of a strictly confidential nature, too. He will make sure they reach their destination.'

So Desgrez would at last discover the hinge upon which the door to this fortress of crime would begin to open. The fortress was well guarded. These Court folk were arrogant, amoral, secure in their privileges, proud of their vices, prepared to go to any lengths to satisfy them; and around them gravitated a multitude of accomplices: valets, servitors, confessors, tradespeople, all too keen to remain within the ambit of the mighty not to realize the importance of keeping their mouths shut.

The black claws of de la Reynie's minions of the law slid off the brilliant protective shell, without ever finding a chink in the armour-plating. Bodies with stab wounds were fished out of the Seine, there were rumours about a sudden death, or some court case that had been settled all too quickly, people were dismissed for being over-inquisitive. But in any event, even the boldest policemen never managed to grasp more than empty air.

The Duchess of Maudribourg had been an example of this prized game pursued in vain. She had nevertheless found it necessary in the end to leave the country and continue her exploits overseas. Angélique remembered that when she had arrived in Gouldsboro Ambroisine had known a great deal about her past life: that she had been at Court, that she had been called Madame du Plessis-Bellière, that Athenaïs still hated her. But in spite of it all Desgrez had managed to arrest Madame de Brinvilliers, although all things considered, this redoubtable prisoner was only small fry. She was merely a marginal character, operating within the small, closed circle of her own family, her lovers, and a few of her acquaintances, for her own pleasure and personal satisfaction. Glazer, who supplied her with arsenic, must have been a cautious sort of man, certainly less free-and-easy with his wares than the enterprising La Voisin who kept the whole of Paris supplied.

Having brought the Brinvilliers woman to the scaffold, Desgrez now risked finding himself with nothing substantial left to go on. The other bird, Ambroisine, had flown. And the really important people remained inaccessible. How could she give him some positive point of departure so that, instead of starting from the bottom and working his way up, she could enable him to start at the top, at the other end of the chain? For it was by no means certain that La Voisin would reveal anything, even under torture.

Then suddenly a detail came back to Angélique. In a burst of activity that startled the cat, whose purring had been interrupted by sleep, she grasped her pen once more and began to write.

To know all, open the letter I left with Monsieur de la Reynie at the time in question, with instructions to open it only on hearing of my death. I am not dead, but I say to you now: Break the seals at my request. In it you will find everything you need to know about the attempt made at Versailles on my life.

You will also find names that will enable you to track down and successfully denounce the wretches who, sure of their impunity, do not scruple to murder their fellow-men and to give themselves up to Satan.

She crossed out the last sentence, then recopied on to another sheet, stopping at the words; 'everything you need to know'. No further comment was necessary ... She remembered that in the letter she had left with la Reynie, in addition to the name of Mademoiselle Desoeillet, Madame de Montespan's personal maid, who on her mistress's orders brought aphrodisiac drugs into the Palace to give to the King, there also figured those of the Palace porters and guards who took bribes to let La Voisin into the Palace by night. They were all aware that in her basket she brought a new-born infant destined to be sacrificed shortly afterwards on the altar of Satan.

Once the Black Mass had been celebrated, the witch would leave again carrying the same basket containing the tiny corpse, and the Swiss guard and other watchmen all received their payment in good hard cash.

It would be very surprising if these good souls, once on the rack, did not come out with the name of Madame de Montespan ... In the end she too would make a clean breast of it, for all her ambition.

Thousands of children slaughtered in order by these wicked arts to achieve love, death, beauty, youth or fortune.

Thousands of phials of poison passed secretly from hand to hand.

Angélique took a deep breath.

They had all burst out laughing the other evening when she had said: 'What about the poisoners? ...'

Regardless of the rumours rife throughout Paris or elsewhere, people would always burst out laughing: 'No, you're joking! Poisoners at Court? You don't believe that kind of tittle-tattle, do you?'

Desgrez alone was sufficiently tough, sufficiently cruel to silence the laughter and turn it into tears and gnashing of teeth, into terror and fear of retribution ...

My friend, consider the goodwill I am showing towards you in making these revelations. Meanwhile, I beg you to be watchful in future of what is being said about US (he would guess she was referring to herself and Joffrey), *endeavour to find out who are our enemies in the Kingdom and who, to gratify their desire for power, still seek our downfall, far off as we may be. Please, in so far as you are able to exert you influence, do your best to defend our interests with the King.*

She crossed out this last sentence too. Desgrez was perfectly capable of thinking of their interests with the King without any prompting from her. For it was the King who held everyone's fate in his hands.

She merely added:

Thank you, scourge of the lawless.

Then she hesitated before signing:

Marquise of the Angels.

That was how he would remember her, a mere child still, fleeing nimbly through the streets of Paris. A putrid night, full of foul stenches. The dog on her heels.

'Sorbonne,' she murmured softly.

The dog Sorbonne must be dead by now. What terror she had felt! How was it that her heart had not burst in that chase!

Sorbonne! Sorbonne!

Thus would Desgrez remember her. When he had lifted her up in his arms, so frail and dishevelled, the Marquise of the Angels ...

'Your ticker is beating nineteen to the dozen ...'[1]

She raised her head and looked at the cat, which was looking at her.

'We are here all right, pussycat. Life is going by; here we are at the half-way point, on board a ship. But we still carry the past with us, with all its weight. That's life, you see!'

The cat purred.

'Maybe we are reaching the end of the race? The summit? Victory?'

[1] See *Angélique*.

She looked at her letter, with lines struck out here and there.

It was a message that would impinge upon Desgrez, Paris, the Court and the obscure dramas upon which their fate depended.

She sanded the letter, then added a few words at the end:

We may soon need a report on the Duchess of Maudribourg. Could you possibly gather the relevant documents for us? Let us have all the undisputed facts you know about her, and if you know someone you can trust to bring us the letter, please let us have it.

The Duchess of Maudribourg was dead, but if one day 'they' were to hold the Peyracs accountable for her disappearance, it would be desirable for them to be able to reveal, with evidence to back it, just how dangerous a person the so-called 'Benefactress' had been.

Since the battle was being waged by means of denunciations, revelations and investigations, she too would open a few drawers and bring out material that would confound a society that claimed to possess a monopoly of honour and justice. She would fight it with its own weapons. That was what ships were for and distance mattered little when it came to the brisk exchange of damaging secrets.

CHAPTER 37

JOFFREY DE PEYRAC had come in and was standing behind her looking over her shoulder. She guessed that he was surprised to find her writing. It was not a thing she did often. 'And yet I was kept busy enough book-keeping and writing letters when I was in business in Paris!'

'Have you been bitten by Ville d'Avray's bug?' he exclaimed. 'Who on earth could you be writing to in France?'

'To the police official François Desgrez.'

She rose and handed him the letter.

'Would you care to read it?'

He read it through in silence. He did not ask her why she

had decided to write the letter and send it to that distant friend from whom their departure for the New World seemed to have separated her for ever.

She was guided by a sort of instinct, sudden impulses behind which often lay long periods of thought and reflection, which had come unconsciously to maturity. Then, she would act.

He read and a shudder ran through him at such ruthless determination. This delicate white hand was about to smite the King of France to the heart.

He understood what he had already suspected, that to some people this woman could seem daunting, even relentless. That was how in the past she had defended her children when she had been alone. That was how she was now coming forward in his defence, in his defence and hers, to protect them all with astonishing artfulness and skill.

He examined her as she looked up at him, seeking his approval. Her eyes were limpid as clear spring water, with those thick, dark lashes casting a languid, slightly dreamy shadow across them.

Her beauty – even more so by the light of the oil-lamps – was quite breath-taking. Her face, so smooth and open, her aristocratic features further refined, that, with mature years, were becoming still more regal in their calm, regular perfection.

The line of her eyebrows had grown more elegant, her nose more finely chiselled, and the curve of her lips more exciting.

And always there were those huge eyes that seemed to reveal so guilelessly the depths of her soul. But here was proof that nothing was in fact so inscrutable as those clear, limpid pools.

The face of a goddess, sometimes that of a madonna, with never a trace remaining on it of all the horror, the torments endured, the humiliations and sorrow she had suffered. On the contrary, a kind of sublimation had taken place. Everything about her affirmed the toughness of the human spirit that can rise in dazzling beauty from Hell itself.

He spoke:

'The King will be smitten to the heart.'

'Did he hesitate to strike me? And is he not at this very time still hounding me? . . .'

She went on, her voice coming in short bursts, as if she were injured.

'... He has hounded me in a hundred different ways ... He forced me to make humble submission, dressed in black ... then after that sought my total surrender ... and in his bed ... He persecuted me with all his might, with all his power ... to force me to give in ...'

She broke off, then asked almost shyly:

'What do you think?'

'Of what? Of the letter? Or of your decision to write? ...'

'Both.'

'I think this letter is like a fire-ship, loaded with gunpowder and shot, set to drift down on other ships that it will sink without trace.'

'Except that it won't drift for long and will go straight to the target.'

'And that Monsieur Desgrez will be the one to light the fuse and do the blowing up.'

'Yes, Desgrez, our only ally over in France.'

She stood up and laid one hand on his doublet, instinctively smoothing the velvet at the place over his heart.

'Do you remember him? He was your lawyer.'

'I remember him. He put up a good fight at the trial.'

Angélique's hand was a shy caress whose warmth he felt through the cloth. A frail woman's hand, that possessed so much power. He trembled with love beneath its touch.

'After the trial, he was threatened with death. He vanished. It's strange, I've come to realize that you and I share a long past in common, since we have a mutual friend dating back to those days ... Desgrez. I met him again later. He had become an officer in the police, while I had become ... a hunted woman. He recognized me. And in that way our paths kept crossing from time to time ...'

'And of course, he was crazy about you.'

'Desgrez is never crazy about anyone or anything.'

'But ... surely, you were a minor exception!'

'Maybe I was. But never to the extent of losing his head.'

'Only to the extent of granting special privileges! That's quite a bit! Notorious indulgence shown, active help supplied. He helped you to escape from La Rochelle. For a high-ranking policeman, that's a great deal.'

'So you see, I owe him a good turn.'

She outlined briefly the revelations she had made in the letter she had deposited with Monsieur de la Reynie with instructions to open it if she were to die.

He listened to her, trying to imagine as she spoke what kind of a life it had been for her. That ferocious struggle, fought out in high places as well as in the Paris Underworld, made him realize why she sometimes seemed to react hurtfully to certain things, as if she feared in him some obscure desire for vengeance, or some vindictiveness peculiar to the male.

This attitude of suspicion had been inculcated into her by a life entirely taken up with protecting herself from men, their wiles, and their demands in a society entirely dominated by them and their outrageous, selfish laws. Everywhere it was men. Forbidding, demanding, taking. At the top stood a man – the King. A man whose power could destroy all solidarity among his victims, even among womenfolk themselves. In order to serve the monarch, Mademoiselle de La Vallière chose to offend God, and to affirm her power over him Madame de Montespan killed off her rivals and gave herself over to the Devil. To defend herself, Angélique had struck as many blows as she had strength to strike, and had been vanquished.

It was hardly surprising that she should have been exhausted and maimed in this terrible game.

'I've just thought of something,' she suddenly exclaimed. 'It's just occurred to me.'

'Yes? ... Go on. I want to hear about it all.'

'The fact is that ... *I did, in the end, make my submission to the King.*

'It was at Plessis, where I was kept under house arrest. I wrote my letters of submission. I told him I bowed to his wishes. That I would come to Versailles and make formal submission before the entire Court ... I promised to come and kneel before him as his liege-woman ... That's right, I remember now, I wrote that letter ... because ... I couldn't stand any more. I couldn't stand seeing my province ravaged by those pilfering soldiers, seeing the Huguenot peasants tortured by the "jackbooted missionaries" while I myself was kept under surveillance and constraint.

'And above all, there was our son Florimond. He was there with me, watching all these disasters. One day he came to me and said: "What about me, what am I to inherit?" And I had to reply: "*Nothing*, my son!"'

'Not only had he been stripped of everything because he was Count Peyrac's son, but he had only me left to defend him. And I was powerless, held prisoner in my own chateau, I whose only source of strength was the King. And I had dared to defy him! So I wrote to the King. Molines, my old steward, set off straight away to deliver the letter. But it was too late!'

And she was looking at him, he thought, as if he were a confessor whose verdict she awaited.

As he listened he took care not to make the slightest movement nor show the least reaction, be it of emotion or anger, at what she was saying. For now, at last, she was telling him about it all, and he wanted to be particularly careful not to frighten her. He felt her emotions to be precariously balanced, as if in doing her best to tell him about what had happened she was through him addressing an entity she dreaded. Man! Man the enemy! She seemed very frail.

'... Luckily Florimond managed to get away in time,' she went on. 'Beneath that scatter-brained exterior he has always had intuitions that brought him through to safety ... He had a dream in which he saw you in America with Cantor ...'

Her voice died away. She gazed into space without speaking.

'And then?' he murmured.

'Then ... You know what happened ... Don't you? Did I never tell you? ... Then? ... "They" came the very evening Molines set off on his mule to take my message to the King. "They" came and set fire to the chateau, they slit my youngest son's throat, killed my servants, they ... destroyed everything ... the most terrible carnage ... Do you understand? ...'

As he made no move, she went on rapidly:

'"They" were not under orders to do this. It was the situation that got out of hand. *But we were the victims*. I had acted too late! I had delayed too long before offering my submission. The things that happened that night, that flaring up of violence, seemed to me to be the final blow struck by the King. I felt it to be the final attempt of a tyrannical monarch to destroy me. I became the Rebel of Poitou and led my troops into battle against those of the King.'

As he still offered no comment, but went on listening calmly to what she had to say, she continued:

'But now I remember that letter in which I promised obedience. It might count for something when the King finds us crossing his path once again and comes to pass judgement on the case of the Rebel of Poitou and that of the Rescator.'

Angélique felt as if a great weight had been lifted from her. In the space of a few moments all kinds of things had grown less oppressive and clearer in her mind.

'... I shall ask Desgrez to get in touch with old Molines ... if he's still alive,' she decided.

Once again her pen sped swiftly over the paper. Angélique's hair was slightly dishevelled, for she had crossed the deck earlier when the wind had been blowing hard, and she had not bothered to tidy it. Wisps of fair hair hung in locks over her forehead and cheeks, giving her a girlish look that contrasted with her manner, which was that of a self-confident, business-like woman used to managing her affairs. He noticed that she wrote swiftly, decisively and competently, and he wondered at her boldness once she had made up her mind to join battle.

Count Peyrac's eyes met those of the cat over Angélique's head as it watched him with a wise and, it seemed to him, quizzical look.

'Yes, indeed, Mr Puss,' he thought to himself, 'what are we compared to certain women? ...'

Angélique sanded the concluding lines she had added, folded the paper, deftly melted the wax, applied it and sealed the letter. She was far away in Paris, standing beside Desgrez as he broke the seals.

Peyrac watched her affectionately.

She was afar off, but close to him. She was reliving her old battles but this time he was there and could take her in his arms and clasp her to him if she was assailed by fear.

She looked up at him.

'There, that's done. Desgrez has been told what is going

298

on. And our cause will be helped as long as he goes on fighting on our side over there.'

For a moment she was silent.

'What is hard,' she went on, 'is the fact that we have to fight against shadows.'

'Yes, that's what I feel, it is a conspiracy of shadows. Shadows from the past and shadows of the present. Those that haunt me still from France and those that await us in Quebec. We shall have to disarm them one by one. List them first, then seek them out, bring them out into the open. Put names to faces. One cannot do battle with shadows. The masks must be ripped off. That is why I am especially frightened of the Jesuit, this Father d'Orgeval, who has come to detest me without ever having met me. He too is a shadow, almost a mythical figure. I sometimes wonder whether he in fact exists. He has gathered together his forces then sent them out to do battle in many different places. Perhaps, although he does not realize it himself, since he cannot know *everything* that goes on, even were he to seek to call a halt he would no longer be able to do so. Things will have to move on to their logical conclusion.'

She spoke vivaciously and her direct gaze had something dazzling, something of the prophetic about it. He leaned towards her, examining her with the utmost attentiveness, moved to the very depths by the expression in her eyes that made her even more exciting, all the more seductive.

She suddenly said:

'You are just like Nicolas de Bardagne. He never listens to a word I say, only to the sound of my voice. Is that what you do, too?'

He took her passionately in his arms.

'Me? I am lost in the beauty of your eyes when you are afraid of something. There is nothing more fascinating.'

'Oh, you man! You exasperate me!'

But all the same he had managed to make her laugh.

He clasped her to him and gently kissed her hair.

'My darling, I am not saying your forebodings are wrong. But I see things a man's way, and I would not say this to comfort you: believe me, there are many, many people in this world who could share with us the fraternity of a wider vision of life. But they are kept, so to speak, in solitary confinement. I do nevertheless have contacts in Quebec, in particular one man who has the greatest influence and who is a true friend of mine.'

'Do you mean Frontenac?'

The Count shook his head.

'I shall not mention his name until we enter Quebec. If I were to reveal who it is, even to utter his name, his life might be in danger. But I shall tell you eventually.'

'All the same, I feel very anxious about it all.'

'I'm sure you do ... But you have given me the wrong reasons for your anxiety. I know what it really comes from, and I shall tell you.

'You are worried because you have not yet chosen the *dress* you are going to wear for our entry into Quebec. The dress you will have to put on to face the ordeal.'

'The dress?' said Angélique; 'no, come to think of it, I had not given it a thought.'

'... The dress! That's the great point! But which is it to be? There are three to choose from: one pale ice-blue, one gold-coloured, like the one you wore to the King's wedding in Biarritz, and one purple velvet. The blue one comes from Paris, the gold from England and the purple from Italy.'

Angélique was dumbfounded.

'And you thought even of that?' she exclaimed. 'But when?'

'All the time. Because I dream all the time of seeing you looking lovely, and happy, and acclaimed by the crowds ... even in the depths of the forests!'

'Oh, you are wonderful!'

She threw her arms round his neck. He was right. What he had just said had lightened her heart. She would be beautiful. She would dazzle them all ... win the hearts of the crowd, dispel all their preconceived notions. What better way to win over the idle curious than by whipping up their enthusiasm, and gratifying their insatiable appetite for the spectacular, the unusual, in a word, for beauty?

She would be faultless; she would live up to their expectations.

'You always seem to guess everything, my dear lord. I am still a child, then?'

'Yes, you are. Didn't you know?' said Peyrac gently, and he kissed her on the lips.

CHAPTER 38

ANGÉLIQUE HURRIED through the thick fog that lay over the banks of the river, followed by Delphine, the Moorish girl, and Kouassi-Bâ, who was carrying her baskets.

Dawn had scarcely broken, but she feared to arrive too late for the departure of the *Saint John the Baptist*. The *Maribelle* would be likewise setting sail towards the end of the morning, they had been told. The Marquis de Ville d'Avray had not completed his correspondence nor the captain his purchases of furs. Angélique had, however, met Monsieur d'Arreboust's valet as soon as she had risen that morning and handed over the secret letter for Desgrez. She had given him her final instructions by word of mouth. The man seemed to be an honest, loyal servant. His faithfulness to his master shown in his willingness to follow him to the Bastille spoke highly in his favour.

A purse bulging with gold louis, given to him by Count Peyrac, strengthened his determination to carry out the task entrusted to him, whose attendant risks he had in any case been prepared to face out of sheer loyalty. The extra money would enable him to enjoy a safer and more comfortable crossing, and once in Le Havre, to hire a horse in order to reach Paris more quickly than by taking the stage-coach or one of the passenger barges up the Seine. Also to buy assistance when necessary. He might, as soon as he arrived, have to allay the suspicions of the bigots, who would have been warned about Monsieur d'Arreboust. The members of the Company of the Blessed Sacrament knew how to take swift action when their interests, especially their power and influence, extending as it did throughout almost all strata of society, seemed to be at risk. They had a reputation for knowing how to get rid of troublesome people under the best of pretexts. Angélique knew something about this, having had to contend with them on a number of occasions, including having found herself shut up in a convent from which she had had considerable difficulty in getting away. So she provided for every contingency, and gave the valet a great deal of advice. He was to learn Desgrez's address by heart, along with certain names and places he was to mention to him should he by any chance be forced to destroy the document.

On no account must the letter fall into anyone else's hands.

At last the *Saint John the Baptist* was preparing to set sail. Authorization to proceed seemed to have been granted in as arbitrary a manner as it had been withheld earlier. Was Joffrey de Peyrac keen to speed the King's Envoy, on his way?

'Go on ahead of us to Quebec and announce our arrival,' he told Nicolas de Bardagne and the ship's captain, now somewhat recovered from his excesses.

Angélique, who had received the news of the departure at the eleventh hour, set off in great haste to say her goodbyes to Mademoiselle Bourgeoys, until they met again later in Quebec.

Fortunately the fog was very dense that morning, and the starting manoeuvre, which in any case promised to be a difficult one, was delayed.

When Angélique reached the landing stage, she found Mademoiselle Bourgeoys still there with her girls, accompanied by a few people from the village and, of course, Catherine-Gertrude who had had them all staying with her.

Letters and messages for people in Quebec and Montreal were handed over. The local folk were poor and had no merchandise to send to towns that were better provided than they themselves.

'I've brought you some food,' Angélique said to Mother Bourgeoys, thinking of her role as Superior of the teaching order, 'and some medical supplies too. And here is a moose bladder filled with cod liver oil which I obtained from some Breton fishermen on the East coast. It's said to be wonderful for constitutions weakened by the cold or poor food throughout the winter. It will help to strengthen the baby. Put some on your sores and scabs, too.

'In any case I imagine we shall be seeing one another again soon. Even if the *Saint John the Baptist* arrives before we do and we don't have to come to its assistance on the way, it will not be long. We shall see one another again, won't we?'

The nun seemed reticent and somewhat cool, which in any case Angélique had rather expected.

So dense was the fog that even those standing closest looked like so many ghosts. The slightest shift of position and they were alone. Angélique drew Mademoiselle Bourgeoys aside.

'Marguerite, what is the matter? Do you not want to be my friend any more?'

There was a questioning look in the Superior's eyes that reminded her of their original meeting.

'... I know what is worrying you,' she said; 'you have heard about the fiery canoes passing over Quebec, haven't you? Isn't that it?'

'Listen,' said Mademoiselle Bourgeoys, 'these omens are bound to alarm us, for we have been through dreadful times in these parts. We have stared death so often in the face, and faced imminent disaster, we have so often been within an ace of seeing our entire population exterminated by the Iroquois, the wiping out of our colony here, that when these signs of impending disaster appear, we cannot help being terrified and wondering what new danger God is trying to warn us of. Does He perhaps want to reproach us for not being vigilant enough towards the Evil One, his temptations and his lures?

'One of the last occasions we saw the fiery canoes cross the sky above Quebec was when the Iroquois attacks were so terrible that we were on the brink of total ruin. The Iroquois reached Orleans Island and massacred every inhabitant. Now a little before that occurred, there had been an earthquake in Montreal. Wailing voices were heard over the Trois-Rivières area, and the very same canoes were seen in flames, floating through the air in the neighbourhood of Quebec. Afterwards we realized the meaning of these omens: the earthquake foretold the Iroquois attack, the wailing voices were the lamentations of the unfortunate prisoners the Indians took off to the Five Nations, while the canoes represented the enemy canoes that prowled around our shores all that summer, setting fire to houses and throwing the wretched occupants into the flames, after subjecting them to the most appalling tortures.

'So what does the appearance of the canoes forebode

today? What fearsome coming? What danger is Heaven trying to warn us of, as we approach the winter months in which we are, yet again, forced to rely on our own resources? We are justified to ask ourselves: "What are you bringing us? Who is sailing towards Quebec with those well-armed ships? Is it Good or Evil?" '

'God in Heaven!' cried Angélique; 'surely we are not going to kill one another for the sake of visions! I beg you, Marguerite, you who are the soul of common sense, please remember that we are not the Iroquois. On the contrary. Everyone agrees that this year you have hardly suffered at all from enemy raids, and I can assure you that this is the direct result of our influence over the Big Chief of the Five Nations, Outtaké, which has had the effect of abating his dreams of vengeance. Our ships are indeed approaching your shores, but we have not yet, to the best of my knowledge, thrown anybody into the flames. Could it not be that the Evil we should fear resides in those who, without revealing their identity, knowingly spread alarmist rumours in order to wreck our attempts to seek peace and an alliance with you?'

'The fog's lifting,' someone said.

There was indeed now a paler, lighter glow in the air, the lines of the ship came into view, and the passengers waiting to embark went down to the water's edge.

Angélique hoped that Count Bardagne would not see her and suddenly put in an appearance in order to make his effusive goodbyes, for she was in no mood for flirtatious behaviour. The time was drawing near when they would be lying under the ramparts of Quebec, and she was above all concerned to ensure that those who preceded them were on their side.

They must avoid setting a spark to the powder-keg. If they were fired on, they would have to fire back. The unleashing of bloody massacre hung by a single thread, and in these circumstances, any voice raised in their defence that would help to avoid panic, would be valuable.

Mademoiselle Bourgeoys was greatly loved and listened to, and she could help to calm people down.

'Listen, Marguerite,' she said with a note of urgency in her voice, 'I beg you, say something on our behalf in Quebec, help to restore confidence among the frightened populace. I am not asking you to distort the truth in order to help us, but merely to tell people what you have *seen* . . .'

Marguerite Bourgeoys looked away and said something about having little influence in Quebec. Her fief was Ville-Marie, in other words, Montreal, whither she was anxious to proceed as soon as possible. She had been warned that there were sorry things going on there.

Angélique saw that poor nun's face looked grey and it occurred to her that she herself probably looked no better. They were both distressed by the same thoughts.

Angélique felt quite out of breath after so much talk and argument. She felt that Marguerite Bourgeoys was slipping from her grasp, her early good will having been eroded by the rumours she had heard since the arrival of the *Maribelle*. And, as Angélique sensed, it was not just the matter of the blazing canoes that had made her change in this way.

Swathes of fog blew back and forth across their faces, like the touch of mysterious hands.

'We're not embarking yet,' came a voice out of the mist.

'No! The fog's back again.'

'Thank God for that! Now I have time to talk to you. I cannot let you go off in such a state of mind, Marguerite. Tell me what is going on. Something has upset you, and it isn't just the apparitions. Please tell me what is is, I beg you.'

'I have just heard that my community in Montreal is on the point of being disbanded by the Bishop,' the nun confessed. 'I am returning to the wreck of all my work.'

She added that she had been replaced as Superior of the order by an Augustinian nun from Quebec. And finally, that Monsieur de Loménie-Chambord had gone out of his mind.

'Loménie-Chambord! But that's impossible,' cried Angélique.

She could not quite see the connection between the misfortunes of the teaching community of Ville-Marie and the Knight of Malta. But she was beginning to realize that these institutions were very complicated.

'But what happened?'

'He's in love with you,' Mademoiselle Bourgeoys blurted out miserably, plunging her face into her hands in despair.

'So saintly, so perfect a man! Oh! My goodness, it's terrible!'

'But it isn't true,' Angélique protested passionately. 'You know as well as I do that Monsieur de Loménie-Chambord is not at all the sort of man to be affected by that kind of passion.'

Mademoiselle Bourgeoys shook her head dejectedly.

'... Like Pont-Briand, like so many others you have lured to destruction, people who, because they have seen you, met you, are suddenly prepared to renounce their vows, their friends, and ally themselves with the enemies of God and the King ...'

'But none of this makes sense, for goodness' sake! Oh, but of course, we are in France, I was forgetting ... Whether it be to make use of it, or to attack it, Love figures everywhere. Marguerite, come to your senses, wait till you get to Quebec and see Monsieur de Loménie-Chambord again before you despair. All this is just wicked gossip. When we were in the Upper Kennebec, he came to see us twice, that's all.

'I suppose that as a reasonable man he claims that matters can be settled without resort to bloodshed, which does not please everyone, as there are some who long for bloodshed.'

In an impulsive gesture, she grasped the poor nun by the wrists and forced her to look her in the face.

'Not you, I beg you. Please don't you desert us. You have faced more difficult situations than this and I know that in your heart of hearts you sense the truth.

'Honestly, are there no other means of solving our problems than through massacres, killings, vengeance, an eye for an eye, a tooth for a tooth? Oh, Marguerite, I know the Scriptures, I know the Gospels. I was brought up by the Ursuline nuns in Poitiers. I know we were told: "Peace on Earth to Men of Good Will."

'Are we to believe that all this is just so many words to hide a secret desire for violence, a desire to crush and suppress other men, nothing more than that? That the truth consists in a desire to shed blood, as Satan himself desires to do?

'Tell me, Marguerite, are you yourself convinced that there can be no alternative for us both to warfare and cannon fire?'

'You make me begin to doubt,' said Marguerite Bourgeoys. But she seemed somewhat brighter. She bent down and began to transfer the food Angélique had brought them into their wretched knapsacks.

'Don't bother to do that,' Angélique broke in. 'Take the baskets with you ... You can return them to me in Quebec ... And think about what I said: "Peace on Earth to Men of Good Will" ... If we women don't do our utmost to sort things out, what can we expect of our menfolk, who are all too inclined to think in terms of wounds and broken pates?'

They were beginning to load the longboat and help the women and children aboard.

'Might I ask you to keep an eye on the poor English pedlar,' Angélique went on. 'He won't leave his bear, and I'm afraid that in spite of everything, he may suffer at the hands of the crew as soon as the ship has left Tadoussac.'

Marguerite Bourgeoys gave her a sidelong glance.

'Don't you know, then?'

'Know what?'

'I gathered that Monsieur de Peyrac had detailed some of his crew to accompany us as far as Quebec, or at least to Orleans Island. I don't know whether they are there to help with the handling of the ship or to guard us as prisoners of war, but in either case, as long as they are there, your Englishman isn't likely to be ill-used.'

'Oh, so that's the way of it? ... That's good news both for the Englishman and for you and your shipboard companions. So Joffrey decided to do that ... He never tells me anything ... I wouldn't have worried if I had known. I am very relieved.'

'And so am I, I must confess,' Marguerite Bourgeoys said good-humouredly.

She seemed to have regained her self-possession. The harsh turn events had taken had upset her for a while, but she had pulled herself together again, and Angélique's words had helped her to regain her composure.

'Of course we must wait and see exactly what the situation is before losing our heads.'

She gave Angélique another quizzical glance, but the latter did not lower her eyes.

The women were asked to take their places in the boat. Mademoiselle Bourgeoys sat down and she was handed the baby she was caring for.

She had made no promises, but Angélique cherished the hope that her words had made some impact.

The men were still marking time before pushing the boat out into deeper water, and Marguerite took advantage of the opportunity to beckon Angélique to come closer, as if she had just remembered something important she had been meaning to say. Angélique stepped on to the little wooden jetty and bent down towards Marguerite.

'You have reprimanded me most skilfully, Madame,' she said, 'and I thank you for doing so. Now it is my turn to give you a word of advice.'

'I am listening.'

'You may remember something you once said to me. Speaking of other people and the false image one can form of them, you said: "All too often one sees the scarecrow rather than the human being." '

'Yes, indeed.'

'Well try to remember that when you meet Father d'Orgeval.'

CHAPTER 39

ANGÉLIQUE PREFERRED not to think too much about Father d'Orgeval. But Mademoiselle Bourgeoys had hit the nail on the head.

Almost imperceptibly over the course of the past year, Angélique had allowed vague feelings of fear, resentment and even repulsion to crystalize around the invisible person of the Jesuit, from the time she had come to associate his name with Ambroisine and Zalil.

The words uttered by the Demon in her delirium had conjured up a weird image of the childhood of the man who was now the spiritual leader of Canada.

'There were three of us, three depraved, vicious children in the Dauphiné mountains: he, Zalil and I. Oh, what a wonderful childhood I had! He with his blue eyes and his hands covered in blood! He and Zalil dripping with human blood ...'

Angélique shuddered in the fog. She tried hard to put the memory of that demented voice out of her mind. She would have to be calm when she came face to face with the man who had once been the child thus described, when he appeared before her wearing the apparel of his Order, the soutane and the black cloak. She would have to look straight into those blue eyes of which everyone spoke. Then, perhaps, the human side of things would indeed come into play on the side of the Good, and ill-considered animosities would fade away.

'He's never even seen me.'

At that precise moment the thought that had half formed in her mind released a whole train of images that took a relentlessly logical shape, and she realized something that had so far escaped her.

In the uncontrollable emotion of the moment, her face went a burning red that took some time to fade, so disagreeable was the thought that had just occurred to her.

She had been told that 'someone' from Canada had glimpsed her, a year ago, bathing naked in a lake in Maine, one blazing autumn day.

That was where the legend had originated of an evil woman with a fatal power over men.

She asked herself: 'Who was it that saw me?'

Now she knew. Now she felt quite certain in her own mind who it was.

'It was *he* who saw me. He saw me bathing naked in the lake ... And that is why he hates me! ...'

It took her some time to recover her inner poise.

Then she decided that whether it were true or not, it was not of the slightest significance. So she dismissed that particular worry. There would be time to think about that when she found herself face to face with Father d'Orgeval. Or rather it would be better not to think of it at that moment.

Then suddenly she burst out laughing. All these things were really rather funny. People were a mass of contradictions, of surprises, passions, fantasies. No two were alike. People could frighten you, then suddenly you felt sorry for them or affectionate to them.

She was not alone. Joffrey would be there at her side.

CHAPTER 40

THE *Saint John the Baptist* had sailed, limping lop-sidedly upstream while the *Maribelle* spread its sails and headed downstream towards the Sea of Darkness.

Angélique did not envy it.

She at least, in company with their small fleet, was making for Quebec which was not far off now. And, God willing, once the awkward moment was over they would surely find themselves in nice warm houses, among people whose roots had been well and truly put down in this familiar, even though wild, dangerous land.

Meanwhile the *Maribelle* would be making her parlous way across the wintry ocean, facing monsters, unfathomable depths, deadly ice-floes, howling gales, black, lashing rain-storms, livid, foaming waves, high seas and tempestuous weather, and in the midst of these hostile, unbridled elements, the ship would bob up and down on the crests of the waves, or disappear into the gulfs between them – a ship as frail as a nutshell, drenched with salt and water, in which the people huddled together, would rot, bleed, die, struggle, abandon hope.

Let the planks creak, the wind whistle in the rigging. Every man goes on his way, bearing his dreams, his hopes, his own little destiny, as the only remaining light buried deep within him beneath the skinny ribs, the sallow skin, the sodden rags.

Life, existence, desires, struggles, needs, passions, dreams. All these throb within these tabernacles of wretched flesh. Hopes for the future, glory, fortune, success, victory, salvation, survival, for as long as a man continues to breathe in the depths of a hold, tossed by the waves, these bells dance on with him across the blind ocean.

'On the corner of the Rue des Blancs-Manteaux you will find a house ... That is where babies are butchered ...'

'King of France! ... Justice! Justice! ... Madame, please

310

let me have one of your little Moors as I need a page to wait on me in Canada . . .'

From one wave to the next, gradually they would approach Europe! With its teeming population, its proliferating cities, pinnacled turrets upon steeples, houses upon ramparts, chimneys on rooftops, weather-vanes, peals of bells . . . It was like a vision, a coloured picture rising tier upon tier into the sky. A distant Paris, more of a legend than a reality.

Reality, now that the messages had been sent on their way to Desgrez and the King, reality was this vast, deserted waterway in Canada, these majestic mountains rising tier upon tier through the cold mists, these islands peopled with birds, and, in the background, some days away, the lost city.

The past two days had been so crowded with happenings, that once things had begun to sort themselves out, it was possible to breathe more freely again.

Monsieur d'Arreboust's 'capture' which had had to be negotiated with Monsieur de Luppé, the temporary removal from the scene of Monsieur de Bardagne on his way to Quebec, the *Maribelle* setting sail with the letter to Desgrez on board – all these things had been intermingled or had followed one upon the other, and the place had echoed with shouted orders, the splashing of oars, the transfer of goods from vessel to vessel, oaths and lamentations, for the *Maribelle*'s holds had had to be emptied of half their shingle in order to load the Intendant's cargo.

In its turn Peyrac's fleet was preparing to sail.

There was intense activity on board all the ships.

Seeing rolls of scarlet frieze decorated with heavy gold braid brought up on deck for the sailors to sort out and examine, Angélique knew they were on the last lap of the voyage.

These long rolls of cloth were a kind of bunting stretched between rods to decorate the upper works of the ship, both the solid balustrades and the rails above them. Originally intended to provide cover for men in battle, these hangings made such a fine show that they had come to be used for festive occasions and arrivals in port.

On the last evening they went the rounds of the village to bid everyone goodbye. Then, escorted by the local inhabitants, the *Gouldsboro*'s passengers walked down to the

Saguenay to look at the river.

In the twilight glow, it looked like a still sheet of gold. The tall cliffs had not yet cast their cold shadows across the waters.

The river glittered under the full light. As the party reached the hilltop near the cross they saw the surface of the water break in a dazzling shower of spray, open up and fall back again, revealing a number of supple backs and smooth flanks which themselves looked as if they had been cast in molten gold, and a huge tail uplifted like a gigantic wing.

The children began to race down to the beach, shouting in wonder.

'Mummy! Mummy! Come and see the whales!' cried Honorine.

Whales, which had for so long been hunted in these regions, had for several decades now, deserted the local shores. But occasionally at the time of the year when they left the northern ice-floes to migrate to warmer waters, they would wander into the St Lawrence, discovering old familiar currents, distant memories.

And there they were that evening: a huge whale and three smaller ones, with a young one among them that exactly repeated every twist and turn its mother made, repeatedly diving just as she did.

There they were, those lovely ancient monsters, gambolling in the mouth of the Saguenay, dancing a kind of ballet with incredible grace.

'They've come for us! They've come for us!' the children shouted, leaping for joy.

Little Niels Abbials raised his pan-pipe to his lips and a note floated up into the air, long, pure and ardent, like an incantation. It was taken up by Cantor on his guitar, in a joyous rhythm that seemed exactly to follow the girations of the whales out in the water.

Carried away by the music, the children ran together and joined hands to form a circle.

'Be careful!' shouted Catherine-Gertrude. 'The children are dancing!'

Her grandmother, who had come over from Perigord with the 1630 immigrants, had always told her that it was a very dangerous sign when children began to dance. Perigord, with its majestic oak forests, and abounding in spicy truffles growing at the foot of the trees, was also steeped in pagan lore. In those days it was a not infrequent occurrence to see children suddenly become 'possessed' and rush off together to the forest. Then the adults would chase after them, only to find them, naked and pink, dancing like a lot of crazy goblins round a great oak tree. Children are very prone to bewitchment.

Catherine-Gertrude made a bee-line for her house to fetch some holy water.

Angélique, who had failed to grasp the reason for her upset and her rapid about-turn, continued on her way down to the shore.

The children were dancing. But they were dancing for joy and delight. Dancing to the sound of the pipe and the guitar, excited by the intoxication of the sunset and the music, they danced with the happy whales, cavorting in the golden waters of the Saguenay, and it made an unforgettable spectacle.

'We shall prevail,' Angélique told herself, overcome by the sheer beauty of the moment, offered to them as a kind of advent gift, a promise.

Night fell and the lights went out one by one, the sun, the sky and the river. The lights of the earth and of men took their place; fires were lighted along the beaches. Turning towards the upper reaches of the Saguenay river, where the shadows were beginning to thicken, Angélique saw, or rather devined the movements of an Indian flotilla making land after emerging from between the night-dark cliffs. One last golden glow from the setting sun illuminated the silhouette of Joffrey de Peyrac, standing on a narrow strip of land at the edge of the river, striding rapidly along as if he had just leapt out of one of the canoes. The sight of him there gave her a shock, since she had only shortly before left him at the other end of the village, and she had a disagreeable impression of having either to admit that he was capable of being in two places at once, or that she herself was suffering from hallucinations.

'Am I going mad, too?'

Catherine-Gertrude had rejoined them. The children had ceased their dancing and were quietly looking for shells, so the good woman was spared any worse ordeal than to have to stand with her bottle of holy water in her hand.

She too looked in the direction in which Angélique was still gazing thoughtfully.

'They say that trappers from Lake Mistassin and even further up are arriving. They should have some fine sable with them. I must go and see them. Maybe my cousin Eusèbe is with them.'

On going back on board the ship, Angélique found Count Peyrac busy with the boatswain and his mate, who, armed with the 'freight plan', were beginning to extract from the holds various crates and coffers containing the objects, presents and clothes destined for their use in Canada and in particular for their arrival at the port. There were presents for the city officials ranging from a precious clock to votive chapels for a mountain Way of the Cross, all carefully laid out and labelled. The clutter on the deck proved that the operation had been going on for some time.

'Weren't you on the banks of the Saguenay just a moment ago?' Angélique asked Joffrey.

He looked at her in astonishment and confirmed that, after finishing what he had to do at the dockside he had come straight back on board the *Gouldsboro*.

'And yet I thought I saw you beside the Saguenay.'

('I really must be going out of my mind,' she told herself.)

Some time later, Cantor came over to borrow the cat for his ship. He had rats in his holds, or at any rate mice, that were attacking his supplies. And for several days Wolverine the glutton had vanished. Cantor was not anxious about the animal, as this was by no means the first time it had decided to travel overland, following the ship at a distance, and it would suddenly turn up again when they put into port somewhere. The almost human intelligence of the wolverine made it quite capable of this feat.

'All we ask is that it should not suddenly turn up in Quebec when we are in the middle of an official procession the day we arrive there,' Cantor said. 'The Canadians and Indians already regard wolverines as animals inhabited by diabolical spirits. It is a fact that they are the craftiest animals in creation.'

The lad came on board, and by the time he had located the

cat who was doing his rounds of the ship, the night was already well advanced. Honorine had made the most of the opportunity in order not to go to bed, for she wanted to escort her pet cat and her brother as far as the gangway. It thus happened that the entire family were to be gathered together for what was to follow. Count and Countess Peyrac were there, along with Cantor, Honorine and the cat, not to mention Monsieur de Ville d'Avray.

Lights could be seen quivering on the surface of the dark waters as a birch-bark canoe came towards them, the Indians in it holding aloft resin torches to light its progress.

'Oh, look!' cried Cantor. 'But what ever is that carnival figure?'

Emerging from the shadows, they saw a hideous hairy mask, representing a wild boar or a bison, with red-painted horns, staring white stone eyes, worn on the shoulders of someone dressed in suede and fur, seated like the Indians in the narrow canoe.

'It's a medicine-man! What does he want here?'

The canoe came to a halt beside Cantor's, which he as captain of the little yacht, the *Mont-Désert*, had left alongside the *Gouldsboro* at the foot of the rope ladder. Another occupant of the canoe, whom they had at first taken for an Indian, so bedizened with feathers and leather fringes was he, stood up to reveal the full height of his slender body, and hailed them in a clear voice:

'Ahoy! men of Europe, would you care for the finest furs in the world? We have brought these from the Frozen North, from Post Rupert itself.'

At the sound of this voice, Ville d'Avray uttered an exclamation and leaned over the side.

'But it's Anne-François de Castel-Morgeat!'

'None other! Who hailed me?'

'Ville d'Avray.'

'Delighted to see you, Marquis. What happy chance brings you to Tadoussac?'

'And what about you, my handsome friend?'

'I'm on my way down from Hudson's Bay with some superb furs.'

'A fur trader stinking of alcohol, Redskins and leather,

that's what they've made of you, my handsome page! ...
What a shame!'

His remark was greeted with a gust of laughter from the
young trapper, echoed, so it seemed, beneath the bison's
mask.

'And who is that carnival animal you have with you, who
seems to be enjoying himself at our expense?'

'Someone seeking to approach this vessel without being
recognized. Guess who.'

The individual with the bison's head also stood up in the
boat and Angélique was certain that this was the figure she
had seen leaping out on the shore and had taken for Joffrey.

Honorine's positive little voice made itself heard:

'*I* know who it is ...'

Perched on a crate, she had been examining the man in the
red-horned bison's mask through the gaps in the ship's rail,
fascinated by it for several different reasons.

'*I* know who it is!' she insisted. 'I recognized him by his
hands and his knife. *It's Florimond!* ...'

CHAPTER 41

ORLEANS ISLAND was gliding by to larboard, like a huge
shark with a rough, black back, blocking the horizon and
suddenly narrowing the waterway. They tacked, wary of the
currents as if sailing down a restricted channel. Beyond the
furthermost foreland, forming the monster's nose, Quebec
would first come into view.

The sky was low and heavy, swathing the tops of the river
banks in mist. The waters were sea-green.

The winter solstice was drawing near, that distressful time
of the year when everything dies, when men and their world
seem to be plunged into icy darkness.

Night came down in the middle of the day.

On board the ships, which were occasionally swept by
flurries of fine snow, each day saw yet further preparations
for the arrival, and there was nothing more striking than the

contrast between the cheerlessness of their surroundings and the intense activity reigning aboard these vessels, tossed by the waves but driven relentlessly on by the wind towards the city.

Thought had to be given to uniforms, to dressing the ships, to finery, to rehearsing the drums and the heralds-at-arms whose trumpet blasts were to echo back off the Rock announcing Lord Peyrac's arrival.

Adhémar had to have a new uniform made for him, and Honorine and Chérubin to be taught how to curtsey and bow to Governor Frontenac.

These preparations for the festivities and pageants to come were even more of a preoccupation than the bad weather. Chests lay open in the holds or on the battery-decks ready to dispense their treasures, and the Marquis de Ville d'Avray was by no means the last to come poking his nose into them. 'Everything is permissible to the forgotten ones of this world,' he said; 'no overlord can prevent them dancing amid the inaccessible ice-floes . . .'

The arrival of Florimond and his friend Anne-François de Castel-Morgeat had brought a new liveliness to the expedition. For who could fail to be delighted by these two fine upstanding young men, more Canadian than the Canadians themselves, more French in bearing and spirit than any of those who awaited them, nobler knights-errant in speech and achievement than any hero from the *Romance of the Rose* or the *Round Table*?

The circumstances of their meeting in the Far North had been by no means made clear, Florimond being unable to recount his adventures in detail, as the management of the fleet in its advance towards Quebec occupied everyone's attention. The two young men had in fact met by chance at a trading post in the region of the Lakes, and, recognizing one another as brother Gascons by descent, they had proceeded on their way together. Neither had the slightest inkling of what was going on in New France. The fabric of their life had been the colours and smells of the forest, the delights of the wandering life, the taste of cold, of woodsmoke and of Indian sagamite. But they were delighted to exchange their deerskin clothes for Court dress and after several months of life in the wilds were making ready every bit as spiritedly to

317

dance with the young ladies of Quebec. Forming a threesome with Cantor, they could be heard singing old French airs whenever the handling of the sails on the *Mont-Désert* allowed the ship's somewhat restricted crew a little respite.

> *J'ai trois vaisseaux dessus la mer jolie*
> *L'un chargé d'or, l'autre de pierreries*
> *Malbroug s'en va-t-en guerre*
> *Mironton-Mirontaine . . .*

As for Angélique, she had been utterly delighted by Florimond's unheralded appearance. Such a coincidence lent credence to the widely-held view that Canada was no ordinary country, and that it enjoyed the special protection of the saints and angels. Since she had entered Canada, she had begun to worry about Florimond, who had vanished into the depths of the forests with Cavelier de la Salle.

In spite of the confidence she felt in her eldest son's destiny, the thought of the dangers he might be facing had haunted her from time to time.

Yann Le Couennec had returned to Wapassou almost immediately after the departure of the expedition, as he had injured himself in a fall. He had told them that it was not proving easy to get on with the leader of the expedition, and Florimond confirmed that that was why he himself had refused to go any further with him. The Mississippi expedition had been hanging fire.

As for Count Peyrac, who was also delighted to see his son again, he told himself that while one does not always have children that physically resemble oneself, it is hard to avoid having children of one's own type.

Count Peyrac could not help recognizing in Florimond's odyssey – for he had set off towards the south to discover the Mississippi and the China Sea and had returned via the north after exploring the region round Hudson Bay – a variant on the wandering life he himself had so happily led when he had knocked about the world in his youth. As to Florimond's abandonment of Cavelier de La Salle's mission on the grounds that the leader of the expedition 'didn't know what he was doing' and that he himself 'knew more than he did about cartography and lots of other things', which was in all probability true, there would be time to talk about that later. He had been just the same himself between the ages of seventeen and twenty, and had always felt that he had done the right thing, just as Florimond felt now, not being in the least downcast by his adventures since, after all, what better outcome could one have wished for than to find oneself re-united with one's family in New France, having furthermore brought back notes and maps from his explorations in the north.

CHAPTER 42

'THEY WILL discover you,' said Peyrac, 'and their eyes will be opened on a new world, the world of Beauty! ...

'Beauty that does not disown itself. Beauty that enchants and consoles for the injustices of life.'

'Am I as beautiful as all that? What *is* this legend?'

'It goes beyond you yourself,' he murmured. 'And even if you lend no colour to it, you must live up to their expectations.'

Angélique smiled. She smiled at the words he spoke. She smiled at her reflection in the mirror.

'It isn't hard to do, with such splendour.'

He had helped her to try on the dresses. They were all magnificent.

She was, at that moment, wearing the purple dress with the rich, glowing texture. The velvet folds gave greater fullness to her figure, the chief characteristic of this rather heavy but sumptuous dress being its regal quality.

Joffrey stepped behind her.

Across her bosom and over her shoulders he placed a diamond necklace. Each stone was crowned with a small ruby. It was like a breastplate of incalculable worth.

He stood there very erect, looking very dark beside the whiteness of her skin and the pale gold of her hair, and ex-amined her critically in the mirror, and she was back once again reliving that day long ago when he had clasped his first gift about her slim seventeen-year-old neck. She quivered under the caress of his masterful hands. He was still the same, the Troubadour of Languedoc, with the same passionate flame burning in his eyes.

'Have we come back again to the beginning of our life together, after all these years?' she asked herself.

Living with Joffrey de Peyrac was an adventure one could only come to know through him.

Thanks to Joffrey de Peyrac everything was blotted out: reality, the leaden river, the bitter forebodings.

Wonderful objects lay strewn about the stateroom: clothes from every capital city, a profusion of priceless gifts, lay on every piece of furniture throughout the room, with still more in the holds. And in addition to what the *Gouldsboro* had brought back from Europe at the end of the winter there were the things Joffrey had bartered for with Van Ereck on the shores of Tidnish.

It was he the singers had had in mind when they hummed the song:

> I have three ships a-sailing
> Over the sea so bold,
> And one is filled with precious stones
> Another filled with gold;
> The third is for my lady fair
> So lovely to behold ...

All those presents! Presents for the Governor, the ladies, the nuns, the orphans, the rich and the poor, saints and sinners.

She had not paid much attention to all the unpacking, for she was still feeling the effects of all the excitement and could not concentrate on trivial distractions. He, on the other hand, found no difficulty in so doing. The blood had scarcely dried on the beach at Tidnish than she had seen him with Van Ereck bending over chests full of goods, examining various curios and paintings ...

All these presents! One wondered how he managed to keep his impeccable taste for fine objects and how he found time in a life fraught with perils to go on with this hunt for the refined and delicate, with a view to making their lives more beautiful, more ethereal. She sometimes found it hard to imagine life without a savour of earth, of labour, of tears and of disasters. Then suddenly he would open his hand in which lay some dazzling jewel; or he would decide to put on some mass festivity, and would broach barrels of wine, or distribute to every immigrant woman a mirror, to help restore their morale.

His capacity for enthusiasm and pleasure had in no way been blunted by the tribulations he had been through. On the contrary: one had the impression that he attached greater value, a sort of respect and tenderness, to this world's goods, and that he would never tire of contemplating the handwork of some artisan who had put all his skill unstintingly into his creation.

The same happy admiring glow could be seen in his dark eyes as he savoured the reflection of Angélique's elegant figure in the purple dress that had transformed her into a queen fit for the Louvre.

He was aware of the extent of the power exercised by so perfect an apparition.

In Quebec at that moment, a great many people were busy drawing up plans, aligning their guns, but were talking more of defending their city than their hearts.

They did not know what was about to happen to them.

'You look like a cat that's looking forward to having a go at the cream,' she commented.

'You're not far wrong. I'm thinking about our enemies and what is in store for them.'

'Do you intend to treat them very harshly?'

'Not really. I just intend to send you forward to join battle with them.'

'Joffrey?'

'Yes, my fair commander in the field.'

'Am I strong enough to succeed in what you want of me and to help you to triumph?'

'You used to be. What is a single town to you? You managed to win over the Court, the King. You could have had every one of them at your feet if you had so wished . . .'

'It's perhaps not quite the same sort of thing today. I am a different person. Less . . . less headstrong perhaps. Love

321

weakens one. What I fear most is finding myself face to face with Father d'Orgeval.'

'I shall be there,' he said gently.

And her anxiety melted away. He would be there. He would be her bastion. A man of spirit and vigour, who loved her, his wife, more than anything else in the world.

She bent her head and laid her cheek caressingly against his hand holding her shoulder. He bent down and kissed the nape of her neck.

'I want them to surrender to you,' he murmured. 'They will all love you. I shall see the city at your feet. Him too. I want to see him, that enemy of yours defeated, whose wicked fanaticism has got so strong a grip on him that he has dared to attack you, to defame you, and to stir up dangerous enemies against you. One day he will discover the power of Love.

'One day he too will love you. *And that will be his punishment.*'

CHAPTER 43

THAT EVENING they dropped anchor almost at the extreme point of Orleans Island.

Two men came on board, of whom one turned out to be Maupertuis, and the other his half-breed son Pierre-André.

The loyalty of these excellent fellows, who had suffered from throwing in their lot with the Peyracs, was heartwarming. The last time Angélique had seen them was in the English village of Brunswick Falls, shortly before the attack by the French Canadians. Their compatriots had more or less compelled them to return home, where they had naturally enough found themselves in hot water. But everything had eventually been settled, as was always the case between relatives in Canada. Nevertheless, since the announcement of Peyrac's arrival, the town was in ferment, and Maupertuis had thought it advisable to wait for them on

Orleans Island, where he had relatives. The people of Orleans Island were not to be equated with the inhabitants of Quebec. They were a race apart, somewhat given to dabbling in magic, if popular rumour was to be believed, and the majority were survivors from the Iroquois massacre of fifteen years before, an experience which had made them sparing of speech. The rest of the population were 'independents', preferring for various reasons to set up their cottages on an island rather than live in too close contact with the authorities of the capital. One would never have thought that the island was inhabited. Its shape could hardly be made out in the thick darkness, but it seemed to be vast and its rugged backbone merged with the night sky, which was, however, free of clouds on that particular night. But there was no moon and the sky was like black velvet.

Joffrey de Peyrac asked for details about the town. Festivities were being prepared, said Maupertuis, in order to receive them with great pomp. Monsieur de Frontenac was firmly decided that it should be so, and the majority of the members of the Grand Council thought it advisable to treat their powerful visitor courteously. But the Bishop was cagey. The Jesuits? No one knew ... Monsieur de Castel-Morgeat advocated resistance. So far he had found little support, but since the canoes of the ghostly hunt had been seen in the sky, the Military Governor had a more numerous following.

'There's a great gathering of savages on the plateau behind the town,' Maupertuis reported, 'and they are highly alarmed by these visions in the sky. If Castel-Morgeat, who has great influence over them, takes them in hand, events may turn against you.'

'What about Piksarett? Where is he?' asked Angélique.

'No one knows. He may be among them, but these savages are very changeable. You musn't count on him, Madame.'

Angélique shook her head.

'No! Piksarett will not betray me ...'

Monsieur d'Arreboust, who was listening to the conversation, looked at her curiously.

'So it's true then. As well as Outtaké the Iroquois, you have tamed his sworn enemy, the Abenaki Piksarett ... In a bare few months ... How did you manage to win over creatures like these who are so hard to get through to, so difficult to pin down? It looks very much as if all you needed to do was to put in an appearance. That's what arouses misgivings. At Quebec the betting is open.

'The fact is known that you caused the failure of the summer campaign in the south against the English establishments by diverting the chief of the Patsuiketts from the path of duty.

'What did you find to say to him so as to get him out of the war? He's no easy man to deal with, I know. Only Father d'Orgeval can manage him and his tribes, but this time he escaped from his control. How did you go about it? Did you cast a spell over him?'

'Of course not! We're friends, that's all.'

'Friends? It's not as simple as that. You only have to come on the scene. Is that all? ... And you say, Maupertuis, that savages have gathered in the heights above the town? The Hurons and the Abenakis hate one another, and all we need to have a real disaster on our hands is for our baptized Indians to slaughter one another because of your arrival in Quebec, or rather the disputes resulting from it.'

Ville d'Avray drew Angélique aside:

'Show it to me,' he whispered.

'What?'

'Outtaké's wampum necklace that he gave you as a mark of friendship and alliance with you. Apparently it's one of the finest that were exchanged as tokens in that way between the Indian nations. It's worth ten victories in itself. A superb specimen!'

'I'll show it to you one day, but be sure of one thing, I shall never give it to you ... I feel that I must not part with it. I missed it very much when I left it behind on our last journey. Perhaps that's why we had so many misfortunes at Port-Royal and other places.'

Abigail had sent it back to her on the East Coast with her luggage.

The Marquis de Ville d'Avray pulled a wry face. He was insatiable when it came to collecting rare and precious objects. He could not resist getting in a dig at her.

'You can say what you like, my dear ... To have got hold of such an object ... You must after all ... be something of a witch! ...'

A name mentioned by Maupertuis caught Angélique's ear and she hastily rejoined the group.

'Did you say something about Nicolas Perrot?'

'Yes, I saw him a bare two days ago.'

'Oh! I'm so glad! I was dreadfully anxious about him.'

Since she heard the rumour that he had been recognized among the occupants of the canoes of the ghostly hunt, that had passed in flames across the Quebec sky, she had had a distressing presentiment of some disaster befalling him. She realized that she had allowed herself to be influenced by these tales about visions.

Joffrey de Peyrac gave her a wry smile.

'What a deucedly superstitious little creature you are, with your Poitou background!' he exclaimed when they found themselves alone.

'I admit that I fretted foolishly and pointlessly. I find that one comes to be scared by everything that people say in this place. These men and women are so very much at the bounds of the earth and sometimes so appallingly cut off that it is only to be expected that they should be on the look out for spirits. It reminds me of the stories my nurse used to tell that made my sisters and me shiver with fright at night-time ... The fact remains that sometimes there is a certain something that makes one think that the world is vaster and more mysterious that what our eyes can see.'

'I don't entirely deny that either,' said Peyrac. 'In particular the New World abounds in unexplained phenomena that science will elucidate one day. What I mean is that one mustn't be frightened of them. I personally saw ...'

He broke off and shook his head.

'Lights off the coast of Florida ... My men were terrified. There was no logical explanation for what we saw that day ... It just has to be accepted. We have to take the world as we find it without losing patience with its mysteries, just because we are inadequate to cope with them.

'Just think! Until recent centuries mariners who launched out on to the Sea of Darkness thought that the ocean was flat and ended in a large hole into which they would plunge. Nevertheless they set sail, fearful as they were, towards the abyss, impelled by an instinct that told them that something would be discovered.

'The earth was round. Who could have suspected it? One must be prepared to set sail if one wants to find anything out.'

Changing the subject, he asked: 'Have you and your maids decided on the dress you're going to wear for the entry into Quebec?'

'No, not yet,' sighed Angélique; 'and I haven't got a maid either.'

'That's a more serious matter than what may or may not be going on in the unseen world.'

Angélique rushed off, resolved to put an end to her delays and hesitations. She would ask Delphine du Rosoy to be her personal maid; it was the best solution. She would ask her to keep the secret of the brand of shame on her shoulder – a curse upon the King of France and this appalling custom of the branding iron! – whenever she thought of it, the fact that she could never again wear low-cut dresses was what infuriated her the most with Louis XIV. It complicated everything. She felt humiliated at having to confide in Delphine, although she felt certain that the girl would not abuse the trust placed in her.

As she passed by the door of the battery, she heard the King's Girls saying their prayers and took advantage of the delay to do a round of the deck.

She strode briskly along. The night was dark and yet she felt that the darkness was somehow vibrant with a certain brightness or phosphorescence. It was not exactly like other nights. There were unaccustomed noises, different smells. Before her she was conscious of the presence of Orleans Island rising up like a wall, and in front there was space, the endless night outstretched over the waters and forests. She had come deep into the net and felt no fear but rather a need to change her mind and soul, to become different in order to begin all over again with new strength.

All the way up the river her life had been concentrating itself about her, and now that she had arrived at her goal, she felt greater lucidity of mind, without having to wonder, as previously, where one part of her being had gone, and what fragment of her heart she had forgotten she knew not where. Everything was present. She knew who she was and why she was here and what game she was called upon to play in these parts.

The air seemed strangely still to her in the lee of the coasts of Orleans Island. The rocking of the ship was imperceptible. The swell of a river is not at all like that of the sea, she reflected, sensing something abnormal in the movement. She turned round with an uneasy feeling that there was something hovering over her. Her eyes encountered a huge, luminous, oblong-shaped patch upon the dark expanse of the sky.

Hardly had she noticed it than it began to shrink, literally to melt away at fantastic speed, as if springing out of sight, unless it was that the thing was not moving but going out like the flame of a candle blown upon by a giant's breath.

She was petrified.

'What was it? What was it? A flash of lightning? A thunderbolt? Looking towards the bridge-deck she caught sight of Joffrey who was climbing the companion-way to the poop.

She thought she caught the rattle of the anchor being hauled up and the stamping of seamen's feet as they rushed to swarm up the rigging and shake out some of the sails.

The instructions of the St Lawrence pilot could be heard one after the other in the darkness. The ship was drifting very slowly.

She made an effort to wrest herself free from her stupor and join her husband. It was only as she reached him that she felt the cold breath of the night. She threw herself against him and clasped him to her with all her strength. In broken phrases she attempted to explain to him what she had seen.

'You've just had your baptism of the great dread of seamen,' he told her when she had completed her account of what had happened.

'Many sailors have seen this phenomenon. But sailors are never believed. It's better not to mention it. Off the coast of Florida when I was searching for treasure from Spanish galleons, I saw an apparition of this sort. It took the form of lights almost as brilliant as the sun. They disappeared as if fading away. Before me Colombo the Genoese had seen them, and his terrified crew brought him back in chains to Portugal . . .'

'Why is the ship drifting, and why have we hauled up anchor in spite of the darkness?'

'As a precaution. These phenomena have been sometimes associated or have been thought to be associated with exceptionally high tides, sudden storms, driving ships without warning on to the coast. It seemed better to stand offshore. But I personally have never experienced anything of the kind. Keep calm. Nothing will happen.'

He held her by the shoulder.

In spite of his calmness, she could not help feeling a sense of unreality, and at the same time a sense of being alone with him outside time.

She looked around her to persuade herself that the world still existed, and her teeth would have chattered and she would have shivered with cold if he had not held her against him under his cloak.

'Ah! There they are again,' she cried. 'There! There!'

'No, they're not, you little silly.'

'Well what are those fixed luminous points spread out in the sky?'

'Take a closer look and you will realize. We have been drifting and now we are beneath Quebec. What you see are *the lights of the town*! . . .'

She understood. She forgot the unknown worlds. There had been no storm. The town lay before them in the darkness, rising up against the sky. From the lower to the upper town lights spangled the night. Behind every window there were people waiting – families, children that had been put to bed, women who were clearing the supper dishes from the wooden tables, old men lighting a last pipe. Were they talking about what would happen next day? About the strangers who were going to disembark?

Little by little details emerged from the thick shadows, and she thought she could make out a pale patch of roofs covered with a thin layer of snow rising tiers one above the other up the flanks of the Rock.

The red, moving spots were fires lighted on the beach, the up and down movement of riding-lights indicated the position of the port. A penetrating smell of smoke came to them.

She thought she caught the barking of dogs, dogs wandering about the streets of the town, pet dogs or dogs with no master . . . just like in every town in the world.

And that moved her more than anything else.

CHAPTER 44

AT DAWN there had been scarcely time to rest a little before it was necessary to think about proceeding with the final preparations. The night was still very dark, but activity on the ships had resumed as in full day.

Yolande knocked on the door of the stateroom where Angélique, seated at her dressing-table, was completing a light make-up. There were so many pots, unguents and powders that went with her toilet outfit that it would have been a pity not to use them.

She enjoyed outlining her eyelids, her lips and her cheeks, and this restful occupation put her in a cheerful mood. To-morrow, or rather today, would be a great day. She no longer felt any fear. After her visions of the evening before, she felt in tune with Quebec. Quebec that was awaiting her outside and that she still could not see.

Delphine would shortly come in bringing her dresses. She and Henriette would help her to do her hair. Then she would dress.

'Yolande, how beautiful you are!' She said to the young Acadian woman, who was indeed looking very smart in an orange faille dress with an attractive white collar and a stiffly starched bonnet.

'But what a pity you bartered away your coralline ear-rings! They would have gone so well with that dress!'

'It was silly, I know,' agreed the girl. 'When the fur fever gets you, you just don't know what you're doing. I'll just have to lump it.'

'What did you want me for?'

Yolande explained that they were beginning to have problems. Honorine had flatly stated on getting up that she did not want to wear a dress but to wear boy's clothes. In any case, there was no use arguing, she would not curtsey to the Governor.

'Bring her to me,' said Angélique.

She put away the objects on her dressing-table and slipped on a fur-lined housecoat, for in spite of the brazier, the temperature was rather sharp. While engaged in these various activities, she had invented enough arguments to tackle her daughter – knowing full well that Honorine would demolish them without difficulty.

Honorine came in looking very self-possessed.

She had put on back to front the little pair of breeches which were part of a musketeer's costume that Peyrac had given her, knowing that nothing could please her more.

'My little darling!' exclaimed Angélique, 'how can you prefer a dingy rough, grey pair of breeches to such a pretty dress?'

The dress prepared for Honorine was indeed very pretty, a lovely vibrant sky-blue colour, that she had already tried on. It suited her marvellously, and Yolande dutifully held it out. But Honorine looked away.

'It's because there's going to be war,' she said. 'If there's to be a battle, I want to be dressed like a soldier.'

'But if there's a party, you have to be dressed liked a princess. Just look at me, I'll be wearing a dress.'

'But you're the Demon,' retorted Honorine imperturbably. 'They're expecting you.'

She added feelingly: 'You *must* be beautiful!'

Honorine never missed a scrap of what was said round her. Angélique was dumbfounded. Thank God Honorine had not been at Gouldsboro during that dreadful summer. Ambroisine, who had not hesitated to attack the kitten out of jealousy, would have endeavoured to injure the beloved child. At the thought Angélique shuddered with retrospective fear. She took her daughter in her arms and crushed her against her heart.

'Darling! Nothing has happened to you, what a blessing!'

'So you don't mind then, if I dress like a boy?' asked Honorine in surprise.

'No, I'm sorry, I do mind, but we'll just have to put up with that. I don't want you to be unhappy ... I only think that ... perhaps Monsieur de Loménie-Chambord will be disappointed ... not to see you in all your finery on such a special day.'

This argument seemed to carry weight. Honorine had a weakness for Monsieur de Loménie-Chambord. She was wavering. Angélique had a sudden brilliant idea.

'As far as the curtsey's concerned, you can do it on your own if you want to.'

She had guessed rightly. The truth was that Honorine detested the idea of curtseying to the Governor in company with that dolt Chérubin. She knew him full well. He would be only too capable of tripping her up at the crucial moment and the whole effect would be spoilt.

She gave her little friend a proud, disdainful look as he slipped into the room after the manner of a prowling kitten. They had lots of fun together, but on serious occasions Chérubin had no sense of the responsibilities incumbent upon him.

And, in any case, since she was Monsieu de Peyrac's daughter, what was the point of pairing her off with such a little clown?

So she would step forward alone, wearing her blue dress, and Monsieur de Loménie would be delighted to see her looking so beautiful.

Taking advantage of her abstracted look, Yolande began to dress her, and Honorine offered no resistance.

Within the room a subtle change was taking place.

The brightness of the candles and lamps was paling.

Suddenly, as she looked towards the stateroom casements, Angélique saw that they had turned a scarlet, glittering, flickering hue as if behind each piece of opaque glass a sudden dormant fire had come to life.

'Good heavens! We're in for a fire this time!' She rushed over to the windows and banged them open.

She could hardly catch her breath, both because of the flood of ice-cold air into the room and because of the wonderful picture that was spread out before her eyes.

The ship remained at anchor in the same position where the previous evening she had seen at Peyrac's side the lights of the town rising up in the darkness. Now it was dawn. What she had taken for the glow of a fire was only the brilliance of the rising sun bathing Quebec in pale pink or carmine red, in rapid shimmering flashes of brightness. In the fresh, clear air of the morning, it turned it into a city of crystal. The fretted stonework of the church steeples looked as if they were made of pure silver. The snowy roofs, glimpsed the previous evening in the darkness, were the colour of sugared almonds.

Wisps of bright smoke rose peacefully from the chimneys and clothed the town in a rainbow-tinted halo through which it appeared like a fairy-tale city, soft and dreamlike.

At her feet, the river water was flaxen blue, a homely blue, as limpid as a cloudless summer sky.

Angélique had sometimes dreamed of Quebec, but she had never imagined it; it was a dream.

'Honorine!' she breathed; 'Come here, my sweet, and see the town . . .'

She took her child's hand in her own. She felt an unspeakable joy holding that plump little hand in hers, while both of them silently marvelled at the picture presented to them. The peal of bells swelled and died away, but the distance was too great to distinguish any people. The town, as if deserted, held out to them a pure and loving countenance.

At that moment Joffrey de Peyrac entered followed by the tailor and his assistants with the three dresses: the blue one, the purple one and the gold one, and by Kouassi-Bâ wearing his plumed turban and bearing on a cushion a sandalwood coffer with a row of large pearls in the middle. When opened it revealed a heap of pearl or gold necklaces, bracelets and diadems.

Joffrey de Peyrac made his familiar sweeping gesture reminiscent of a magician commanding a transformation to take place.

'Here are the dresses,' he said, 'and here are the jewels! Let the festivities commence!'